"YOU FOLLOWED ME!"

"Yes, I did. Matter of fact, on the same stagecoach." Garnet faced him unflinchingly, which only made him madder.

"Dammit, woman, I meant it when I said good-bye. Why in hell did you follow me?"

"You forgot to take back the shirt and pants you let me use."

He felt a flush of pleasure that she had followed him—he was even flattered. She sure was a lot of woman! To his surprise, his hankering for her began to outweigh his anger.

"Come on over here, Widow Scott."

His words sent a blush of expectation through her, and her legs began to tremble. "If you want me, cowboy, you come over here and get me."

"Characters who creep right into your heart . . . I'm eager for the next eposiode in the saga. FLINT can't come fast enough!"

Romantic Times

THE MACKENZIES
FLINT

ANA LEIGH

AVON BOOKS  NEW YORK

VISIT OUR WEBSITE AT
http://AvonBooks.com

THE MACKENZIES: FLINT is an original publication of Avon Books.
This work has never before appeared in book form. This work is a novel.
Any similarity to actual persons or events is purely coincidental.

AVON BOOKS
A division of
The Hearst Corporation
1350 Avenue of the Americas
New York, New York 10019

Copyright © 1996 by Ana Leigh
Published by arrangement with the author
Library of Congress Catalog Card Number: 96-96467
ISBN: 0-380-78096-8

First Avon Books Printing: December 1996

AVON TRADEMARK REG. U.S. PAT. OFF. AND IN OTHER COUNTRIES, MARCA
REGISTRADA, HECHO EN U.S.A.

Printed in the U.S.A.

RA   10 9 8 7 6 5 4 3 2 1

This book celebrates the bond of family.
I dedicate it to—or in the memory of—

Dad and Mom
Olga and Richard
Garnette and Al
Don
Mike and Dottie
Betsy and Elmer

FOR THE GOOD TIMES

Chapter 1

Texas Panhandle
1869

Flint MacKenzie smelled them even before he saw them.

The sound of a buzzing drone led him to the spot. He rode up to the four bodies and dismounted. Glutted flies swarmed over the corpses. From the condition of the bodies, he figured they'd been lying there for at least two days. The three dead Comanche had been shot and the fourth body was that of a white man, arrows protruding from his back and chest.

Since all the bodies were in the same vicinity, it appeared to Flint that the two men he'd been trailing had probably ridden up on the Indians while they were sleeping. The cold ashes of a campfire were still in place. And so was the white man's scalp—which meant none of the Indians had gotten away. Besides, Flint reasoned, if any of them had survived, they'd have come back for the bodies of their brothers.

But someone *had* ridden away. He hunched down to study the prints of two horses. One of the horses carried a heavier load than the other, leaving a much deeper impression in the dirt. Most likely a man was riding the horse while leading the dead white man's horse. The deep print had a slit in the iron on the right rear hoof. Flint recognized the flaw at once; it was the same track he'd been trailing since leaving Dos Rios

1

five days earlier, where he'd been told by the town's sheriff that the two men had boasted of riding with Charlie Walden. He checked for the tracks of the Indians' unshod ponies and found where their horses had been tethered and apparently broken loose.

Flint stood up, swinging a bitter glance toward the trail leading away from the carnage. If what the sheriff said was true, the surviving rider might even be one of the same Comancheros who had raided the Triple M five years ago—one of the same gang of ruthless cutthroats who had raped and murdered his mother and sister-in-law.

Returning to the bodies, Flint rifled through the white man's pockets. He found a few coins and an almost empty tobacco pouch, but there was nothing to identify the corpse. Tucking the packet into his shirt pocket, Flint checked out the bodies of the Indians. Their faces were streaked with black pigment.

"They're wearing war paint, Sam," he said to the dun gelding who had remained motionless in the spot where Flint had dismounted. From habit, he continued to speak to the animal. "Wonder what ruffled up their dander?" He swung himself onto the back of the horse. "Reckon we best get out of here while the getting's good."

From Flint's high vantage point on the rocky ridge, he swept his gaze to the floor of the canyon far below. Suddenly, he stiffened and leaned forward in the saddle. On the flat plain, hundreds of feet below, he saw twelve wagons, moving like canvas-topped schooners on a sea of green grass splattered with dark patches of brown earth. "Reckon them dead Comanche must have been scouting those wagons, Sam. That sure explains why they were painted for war."

He'd seen enough Indian sign in the past few days to know there'd be more Comanche waiting at the right spot to hit the wagons. He had no choice but to warn the train.

"Goddammit!" he cursed. He glanced back at the deep prints leading away from the bodies. "We're gonna lose that bastard, Sam!" Then he tightened the reins and began to descend the thread of a trail that led to the canyon valley.

In the pitch blackness of the moonless night, the glow from a half-dozen campfires drew Flint to the circle of wagons clustered near a small creek. To his disgust, he rode unchallenged into the camp, amid the low murmur of tranquil voices and the homey scent of wood smoke.

He was soon surrounded by a cluster of curious migrants. A lean, middle-aged man spoke up in greeting. "Howdy, stranger. You're welcome to climb down and have some vittles."

"Appreciate the offer," Flint said, dismounting. "You the wagon master?"

The man grinned. "Guess so. Al Masters's my name," he said, extending his hand.

"Flint MacKenzie." Flint shook his hand. "You ever been this far west before, Mr. Masters?"

"Can't say I have, Mr. MacKenzie."

Flint followed him over to one of the campfires and they sat down. "Thank you, ma'am," he said to the woman who handed him a plate heaped with stew and thick slices of sourdough bread. Silence ensued as he devoured the food. "Mighty tasty, ma'am," he said, handing her the empty plate. "Much obliged."

"Would you like some more stew, Mr. MacKenzie?" she asked.

"No thank you, ma'am. This coffee will do fine." He picked up the steaming mug.

Her eyes twinkled with warmth. "I bet a piece of apple cobbler would set fine with that coffee, young man."

"Reckon it would, ma'am." His gaze followed her as she hurried away to get the pie. She reminded him of his mother. Recalling her fate, and the peril that lay ahead on the trail for these people, his eyes darkened with sorrow.

For the first time since entering the camp, he settled back and took a good look at the small crowd around him. Most looked gaunt and tired. He didn't have to hear them speak to know they were from the south. He had fought for the Confederacy and had seen more of the same ilk—wretched souls, weary and desperate from trying to sustain homes and farms devastated by the war.

As his gaze continued to sweep the faces around him, he spied the slim figure of a woman. Although she hung back in the crowd, Flint couldn't miss the red hair streaming halfway down her back. *There's no hiding a peacock among a gaggle of geese*, he thought. He figured every Comanche scouting the train had already envisioned the red scalp lock dangling from his coup stick.

"Where you folks from, Mr. Masters?"

"Georgia, Mr. MacKenzie."

"You got someone scouting this train?"

"Yes, sir," Masters said. "Name's Moore."

"Bullwhip Moore?" Flint asked. Masters nodded.

Flint had met the scout before and had a low opinion of him. He considered Moore to be a blustering bully, a man who put his own interests ahead of the people who trusted him. He had heard a rumor that Moore had once deserted a wagon party after leading it into an ambush.

"Where's he now?" Flint asked.

"Mr. Moore rode off yesterday morning to scout ahead," Masters said. "He told us to keep the wagons pointed straight west."

"He tell you about the Indian sign around you?"

"What do you mean?" Masters asked worriedly.

"I've seen a lot of Indian sign in the last couple of days," Flint warned. "The only chance you have is to turn around now and try to make it back to Dos Rios. I'll take you there if you don't know the way."

"Mister, I don't think Indians would be dumb enough to attack a wagon train this size," one of the men remarked. A low mumble of agreement rippled through the crowd.

Grimacing with disgust, Flint eyed the challenger. "Twelve wagons ain't gonna scare off a Comanche war party." He turned to the wagon master. "Any of you have much experience fighting Indians, Mr. Masters?"

Masters shook his head. "No, Mister MacKenzie. Most of us are just Georgia farmers."

"Then what the hell are you doing out here in the Indian Nations?"

"There ain't much left back home, so we're heading to California. Hope to join up with a wagon train in Santa Fe."

" 'Sides," one of the men scoffed. "Fightin' Indians cain't be much different from fightin' Yankees. We all sure had our share of that during the war."

Flint shook his head. "It's a *lot* different. Comanche are the best light cavalry you'll ever come up against. They'll sweep through you before you even know what hit you. And they're not gonna blow any bugle charge to warn you they're coming."

"Well, we dodged enough Yankee bullets during the war to know how to take care of ourselves," the skeptic responded with a derisive snort.

"You forgetting you lost that war, soldier," Flint shot back angrily. He was trying to warn them, but the damn fools weren't willing to listen. His gaze drifted toward the redhead. Her face was indistinct in the darkness, but the fire glistening on her hair had turned it to copper. "Well, folks, since you won't listen to me, I sure wish you luck, 'cause you're gonna need it."

"Mister, sounds like you're just trying to scare our womenfolk," one of the men said indignantly. "Come along, Ma, he's gonna set the children to crying."

"Mr. Masters, I didn't ride in here just to scare you. If you're going on, keep your rifles handy at all times and I'd advise you to send out outriders during the day and post sentries at night."

Masters nodded. "I'll take your advice, Mr. MacKenzie." He slipped an arm around his wife's shoulders and they walked away. Silently, the others followed, the women clasping their children to their sides.

Once alone, Flint shook his head in despair; there wasn't one thing he could do except warn them and hope they would get through. He finished the cup of coffee, unsaddled his horse, and spread out his bedroll. Stretching out, he closed his eyes to grab a few hours sleep before moving out.

"Mr. MacKenzie, may I talk to you?"

Flint opened his eyes, leaned on his elbow, and looked up at the slender silhouette. In the shaft of moonlight, her red hair had deepened to auburn.

"Ma'am."

She knelt beside him. "I heard what you told the others, sir."

Her voice had a husky Southern softness that curled around his spine like fresh-cooked honey around a finger—all warm and tempting like. He felt a hankering to close his mouth over hers, trap that sweetness, and set his tongue to licking.

"My name is Garnet Scott. I'm a widow on my way to Santa Fe."

Her remark caused him to study her more intently. She wasn't uncomely, but she wasn't the best-looking woman he'd ever seen either. Her thin, oval face was shaped by high cheek bones and generously spattered with freckles. In the dim light, he couldn't tell if her eyes were blue or green. An appealing dimple softened her angular chin.

But that voice and red hair sure as hell wouldn't discourage him from opening his blanket to her if she had a mind to it. He shoved aside the thought; he'd been too long on the trail without a woman.

"What can I do for you, Mrs. Scott?" He shifted nervously, wishing she'd hurry up and get to the point.

"Mr. MacKenzie, I don't believe you exaggerated the danger. I want you to take me with you."

Flint avoided women like the plague. Woman was spelled "T-r-o-u-b-l-e" in his dictionary. Not to say he didn't occasionally enjoy a woman's body as much as any other normal, thirty-four-year-old man. Lord knows, he had had more than his fair share of "soiled doves."

But a *good* woman? Not on your life!

A good woman meant tying yourself down to one spot. Marriage! Babies! Not being able to saddle up and ride off to discover what was over the next mountain.

Sure, he adored his brother's wife Honey, and revered the memory of his mother and sister-in-law Sarah. But he'd rather wrestle a grizzly than get tangled up with a good woman.

And despite that red hair, which was tempting enough to make a man lust something fierce, Widow Scott looked to be a good woman.

So, crediting himself for having the strength of character not to capitulate to Lucifer's latest enticement, Flint smiled smugly. "Not a chance, Mrs. Scott."

The discussion had ended as far as he was concerned. He lay back, plopped his hat over his face, and closed his eyes. For a long moment he could feel her stare, then he heard the rustle of her gown as she turned and walked away.

Within seconds, he started feeling guilty. What in hell could he do for any of these people? From the Indian sign he had seen, it was already too late. He had even risked his hide riding in to warn them. Now the Comanche knew he was around too. They'd be on his trail tighter than a suckling shoat at a sow's teat.

Maybe he was being too pessimistic. Maybe they would get lucky and a cavalry unit would show up and escort them to safety. Or maybe it was just a small band of Comanche and those Rebel sharpshooters would be able to stop them. Ma had always told him never to lose faith. He wasn't a praying man, but he closed his eyes and said a prayer for these doomed souls.

Then he tucked his rifle to his side, drew his Colt, folded his arms across his chest, and fell asleep.

By the time the starless gray sky had begun to streak with carmine, he was back on the trail. When his empty stomach started to growl, he hankered for a cup of hot coffee to knock the sass out of it, but he sure as hell wasn't gonna stick around for one. He figured he could crest the ridge before sunset. Out in the open, he or his trail would be easy to spot, but once on the high ground, he'd have a chance of evading any pursuers. He pulled a piece of beef jerky out of his saddlebag and chewed on it as he rode.

Throughout the day, he didn't see any further Indian sign. Before it became too dark to see, he settled down for the night in a clump of ponderosa pine surrounded by a granite wall. The rock wall would prevent anyone from sneaking up on him from behind, and the pine trees concealed Sam. He made a cold camp, no fire. After taking care of Sam, he ate more of the jerky and lay down to sleep.

Flint had just begun to doze off when a soft whinny in the quiet night caused him to bolt upright. Rifle in hand, he listened alertly for a repeat of the sound. Then he heard the slow tread of a horse coming along the narrow path. He strained his ears to listen, but could not detect more than one rider. Beside him, his horse began to lightly paw the earth.

Flint stood up. "Steady, Sam, I hear it," he whispered and gently stroked the animal to calm it. He sheathed his rifle in its holster, knowing a gunshot would alert any others in the area. Drawing his bowie knife, he grasped it firmly and waited for the rider to appear.

As the thud of hoofbeats drew nearer, Flint knew the rider would round the curve on the narrow trail at any second. Preparing to leap at him from the rear, Flint crouched behind a clump of mesquite. The instant the horse appeared, he sprang out of the shadows, pulled the rider to the ground, and raised an arm to render a lethal thrust with the knife.

He froze in shock as he stared down into the terrified face of the Widow Scott.

Chapter 2

"**W**hat in hell are you doing here?"

"I . . . I foll . . . followed you," she stammered.

"You followed me!" Flint walked away in disgust. Her mare trotted over to his gelding, and he tethered the horse next to Sam.

For a long moment, Garnet Scott lay trembling. When she finally felt her legs would support her, she stood up and brushed herself off. Approaching Flint apprehensively, she said, "I know you think I had no right to follow you, Mr. MacKenzie, but I don't agree with you. I do have the right to stay alive."

Flint glared at her. "You figure riding around in the dark in these mountains is a good way of staying alive, especially with hostile Comanche hankering to get their hands on that red hair of yours?"

"Frankly, yes."

"You've got more nerve than brains, lady."

"I've never lacked for either, Mr. MacKenzie. I draw my courage from my instinct. And based on the grim picture you painted last night, my instinct told me I'd be safer with you."

"And what in hell do you expect me to do with you, now that you're here? I've got my hands full just trying to save my own scalp."

"I won't be a burden to you. I can take care of myself, sir. Four years of war have taught me how to survive. All I'm asking is that you allow me to accompany you to the nearest town."

"Well, lady, since it's too late to turn back now, I ain't got much choice, do I?" His dark blue eyes glinted with anger. "But if you hope to keep up with me," he said contemptuously, "you best get some sleep because I'm moving on before dawn."

Flint lay back down and closed his eyes. Since she had made it this far, he figured they were safe for the moment; but he knew that the Comanche would eventually discover one of their tracks.

Garnet lay down on her side and tucked her hand under her cheek. Why did men figure women were helpless or afraid of the dark just because they were born female? Even as a child, she had never been afraid of the dark! Furthermore, she could handle a rifle as well as any man. In her twenty-six years, she'd had to fight off cottonmouths, cougars, bears—and Yankees.

"Ah, you depending on that mare to carry you out of here?" he asked suddenly.

She raised herself up on an elbow and looked over at him. "Of course."

"Then I hope you can take better care of yourself than you have the mare. She's tired and thirsty, and she's been climbing all day. Needs a drink and her cinch loosened."

What an unpleasant person he is, she thought to herself as she got up and hurried over to the horse. Had he not startled her to distraction when she'd first arrived, she wouldn't have been so negligent. She'd handled stock since she was a child. She was sincere in not expecting any special treatment just because she was a woman, but considering how he had unnerved her, the man could show a little tolerance.

"Don't unsaddle her in case we have to move out in a hurry," Flint ordered gruffly.

Garnet gritted her teeth and held her tongue, but she was quickly becoming irritated with him. *Fine specimen of a man that he is*, she admitted grudgingly with a sidelong glance at him.

Despite his menacing appearance, she had been attracted to him from the first moment he had ridden into camp. He was tall, standing easily several inches over six feet, with long, muscular legs and the widest set of shoulders she had ever seen. His buckskins were dusty and sweat-stained, and his boots were shabby and run-down at the heels. His long, straight black hair was tied at the neck with a piece of rawhide. The front brim of a battered, army-issue Stetson was bent up in the favorite style of a cavalryman, worn at a cocky enough angle to discourage the more faint at heart from messing with him.

It was hard to determine his age because of the moustache and thick beard that covered most of his face, partially concealing a narrow scar on his right cheek. But the nonchalant grace of his long, loping strides led her to believe he couldn't be much older than his midthirties.

Garnet suspected she might feel threatened by him, learn to dislike him, or even abhor him—but even so, she sensed she could trust him. There was an inherent quality of strength and honesty in his compelling sapphire eyes, and a bearing of pride in the manner he held his head and firm jaw.

She returned to her blanket and lay down near his outstretched form. She fondled a locket that dangled on a chain around her neck. Even though it was too dark to see the faces on the picture inside, she stared at it for several moments. Then she closed the tiny case and tucked it under her bodice. Within minutes, she had slipped into slumber.

* * *

She woke near dawn and sat up. Disoriented, she glanced around until she recalled her whereabouts and looked for MacKenzie. Seeing no sign of him, she jumped to her feet in momentary panic, then relaxed when she saw him standing on the rim of the high canyon. "Looks like we're in for a storm," she said.

He gave her a cursory glance when she walked up beside him. "Storm?" he asked.

She nodded toward a distant red glow. "My mother always said, 'Red sky at night, sailor's delight. Red sky in the morning, sailor take warning.'"

"I'm afraid that's not the sun rising, Mrs. Scott."

"What do you mean?" she asked, confused.

"The sun doesn't rise in the west. Least it didn't the last time I looked."

"Then what . . ." Suddenly she had a terrible foreboding. "What's causing that red glow, Mr. MacKenzie?"

"That's about where that wagon train would be."

She swallowed past the lump in her throat. "You mean that's the campfires?"

"It's the wagons burning, Mrs. Scott. Let's pack up and get out of here."

When he turned to leave, she grabbed his arm. "You don't know that for sure. Maybe it's just a couple of them." She stared with desperation into the inscrutable expression in his eyes.

He put his hands on her shoulders, and for the first time since they'd met there was a gentleness in his voice and eyes. "The fire's too big. They're all burning, Mrs. Scott. The last thing they do before they ride away is torch the wagons."

She knew who he meant by "they." "Oh, God! Then everybody is . . . all the women . . . the children . . ." She broke off in sobs, burying her head against his chest.

He curled his arms around her and held her for a long time as she gave way to her tears. "We best get out of here. It'll be daylight soon and they'll be picking up our trail."

She raised her head and stepped out of his arms. "I'm sorry for my outburst, Mr. MacKenzie. Are we going to double back and return to the wagons?"

"What for? You can be sure they're all dead. The Comanche would have made certain of that. There's nothing we can do for them now." He walked over and rolled up the blankets.

"We can bury them, sir. Some of those people were from the very town where I grew up. I've known them all my life. The least we can do is give them a decent burial."

"Once a person's dead, it don't much matter whether the worms get 'em or the buzzards."

"That remark is reprehensible, Mr. MacKenzie."

"Look, lady, right now I'm alive, and I intend to stay that way." She watched in astonishment as he tightened the cinches on the saddles, then swung up on his horse. "You said earlier you wanted to stay alive, too. Well, if you've got half the brains you claim to have, Widow Scott, you'll get on that mare now."

He rode off without a backward glance. Still reeling from his callous attitude, she climbed up on her mare.

A short distance ahead, the trail narrowed to a steep and barren path barely wide enough for even two mules in passing, and continued to climb higher above the level valley below. A rocky incline formed the inside wall of the trail and a sharp drop the outer edge. From a strategic aspect, Flint figured it was impossible for anyone to lay in ambush on the trail ahead, and no one could pursue them without being observed.

When Flint heard Garnet following him, he sighed in relief but didn't turn around. He hadn't realized how worried he'd been that the damn redhead would be fool enough to go back to the train. He had his reasons for staying clear. It would have taken two days to get down from the mountains and reach the wagons. And if they were lucky enough not to lose their scalps along the way, what would they have found? Those bodies, lying two days in the hot sun, after the Comanche, predators, and buzzards had finished with them, would have been a sight she'd never forget. He was doing her a favor, though she didn't know it.

Let her think what she wanted to. He wasn't about to explain his actions to anyone. That was why he'd chosen this kind of life. Occasionally he scouted for a wagon train to keep money in his pocket, but generally he liked solitude. He needed only his own company and that of a good horse like Sam. He wanted the freedom to wander at will, to bed down under a blanket of stars, and wake to the glory of God's rising sun. Hell, he knew damn well he wasn't a religious man, but just like every Indian he'd ever known, he saw the sacredness in nature's beauty. There was no call to build them fancy cathedrals like he'd seen in the east.

But he wasn't a talking man. Had never even tried to explain these feelings to his brothers, Luke and Cleve. Only one person had ever guessed how he felt—Sarah. Remembering the shy, sweet woman who had been Luke's first wife, and recalling the way she and his mother had suffered, he knew he'd never know peace of mind till their rapes and murders were revenged. If it took the rest of his life, he'd track down and kill the man responsible—Charlie Walden.

A splatter of moisture jolted him out of his reverie. As he pulled his poncho out of his saddlebags, he glanced upward. The day had dawned to a gray and overcast sky with not a patch of blue. He suspected they were in for an all-day rain.

"Well, Sam, 'pears like we're gonna get a little luck after all. A rain this heavy is sure to wash away our tracks."

Glancing behind him, he saw Garnet Scott huddled in her saddle. " 'Pears like we're in for a steady rain. Better put on your poncho, Mrs. Scott."

"I didn't bring one with me."

"Shit!" Flint reined up Sam. "Might have known she wouldn't have even that much sense, Sam," he grumbled as he climbed down. Pulling off his own poncho, he carried it over to her. "Here, put this on. There's no place to stop and get under cover, and I've got enough to worry about without having a sick woman on my hands."

"I appreciate your chivalrous and *gracious* offer, Mr. MacKenzie, but it's not necessary. I've ridden in rain storms before. Believe me, I have a strong constitution."

She jerked the reins to get around him. As she did, the horse hit a slippery patch of granite and lost its footing. With a piteous whinny, the mare stumbled over the edge and started to slide down the side of the gorge. Garnet had managed to clear the stirrups and barely missed being crushed under the animal as it fell to the ground. The air was knocked out of Garnet, and her scream snuffed off as she slammed against the ground and rolled along in the wake of the mare. She groped helplessly, trying to check her roll. The sky and earth flashed before her eyes as jagged rocks bruised and lacerated her hands and cheeks. Frantically, she grabbed at a small clump of mesquite. The brush stung her hands, but she struggled to hold on. However, the pull was too great. The wet underbrush slipped through her fingers, and her scream tore from her throat as she slipped away. Fortunately, the mesquite had slowed her descent before she slammed into the boulder a few feet away. Her bunched up skirt helped to cushion the blow as well.

Dazed, she lay on her side, aware of having survived, but too numb to move. She closed her eyes and said a prayer of thanks.

Finally, a sound penetrated her stupor. Painfully, she raised her head. Several yards below, the mare lay on its side against a mammoth mound of granite, the animal's agonized neighing and twitching body a pitiful sign of its suffering.

Her hands and cheeks were stinging as she pulled herself up, only to fall back, wincing from the jolt of pain in her ankle.

"Don't try to move," Flint yelled down to her. He grabbed a rope off his saddle and tied his blanket roll to his waist. Then, after looping the rope firmly around a tree, he started to descend.

Oblivious to the pelting rain, she watched his descent with dazed eyes, aching too much to try to stand up again.

"Anything broken?" he asked as soon as he reached her.

She had lost her hat in the fall, and her hair was thoroughly saturated. Tiny rivulets of rain ran down her face. "Maybe my ankle. I can't put any weight on it."

"Let me see." He gingerly ran his fingers over her ankle and leg. "Nothing feels broken. You sure you're not hurting anywhere else?"

She wanted to scream there wasn't any part of her body that didn't hurt, but answered instead, "I don't think so. What about my mare?"

"I'm going down to check on her now." He removed the oilskin off his blanket and covered her head and shoulders. "Just sit still until I get back."

Garnet watched anxiously as Flint lowered himself to where the mare lay in a tangled heap. She saw the horse raise its head, look at him, then slump back down. With a sinking sensation in her stomach, she watched him draw his knife, and turned her head aside the instant before he slit the mare's throat to put the horse out of its misery.

Rain continued to pour down as she watched him brace his feet against the rock and begin to climb, pulling himself up with his powerful arms and hands. When he reached her, he knelt down to regain his breath. "If I hold the rope taut, do you think you can shimmy up it?"

"I can try," she said, showing him her skinned hands. "Wish I had a pair of gloves, though."

He startled her when he suddenly laid her down and wrapped her up like a mummy in the blanket. "What are you doing?"

"I'm gonna carry you."

"How do you expect to do that and climb too?" she protested.

He tied the rope around his waist and the loose end around hers, then picked her up and slung her over his shoulder.

"Why don't you go back up and try to rig some kind of a sling," she shouted above the sound of the rain. "You can't climb to the top holding me like this."

"Just be sure you lie still, that's all you have to worry about."

"You're a stubborn fool, Mr. MacKenzie. And you're going to get us both killed," she cried out, but he had already begun to climb.

Her view of the steep slope below caused Garnet to hold her breath and remain motionless as he scaled the steep cliff. His foot slipped and she screamed as she felt herself start to slide off his shoulder. His arm clamped around her like a vise.

For a moment, he clung to the rope with one hand while securing her firmly in the curve of his shoulder. She could feel his shoulder muscles bunch and expand as he resumed the climb.

After covering about half the distance to the top, Flint paused to catch his breath. The rest took a little strain off his arms and legs, but his muscles felt numb from the exertion, and he wished he could let go of the rope to rub his arms. He had thought she wouldn't weigh much more than a hundred pounds, but he quickly changed his mind. Her rain-soaked clothes had to weigh a good ten pounds alone. Drawing a deep breath, he started to climb again. With every inch gained, he could feel the strength waning from his arms.

With the top of the ledge in view, he was forced to stop once more. His lungs were burning and his arms felt rubbery. Drawing strength from sheer determination, hand over hand, step by step, he continued the climb toward the top, which always seemed to be just a few feet further.

Breathless, he finally reached the top and pulled himself over the rim, placing her on the ground beside him. He turned over and lay on his back with his eyes closed and his mouth open, dragging in the welcome air.

Garnet succeeded in unwinding herself from the blanket, crawled painfully over to his side, and lay in silence. For a moment she didn't know if he had passed out or fallen asleep.

Suddenly he sat up. "Let's get out of here. We've got to find cover."

As he rolled up the rope and blanket, she tested her ankle again. The injured limb still hurt too much to bear any weight. Hopping on her right foot, she managed to get herself over to his horse, but once there, she met with immediate censure.

"You trying to break a leg now?" he snapped. Angrily, he swung her up onto the saddle. Grabbing the reins, he began to lead the horse along the narrow trail.

Garnet shivered with cold. Thanks to her refusal to put on his poncho, both of them were now soaked to the skin.

"Oh, my saddlebags!" she suddenly exclaimed in distress.

"You can forget about them now," he replied gruffly. "I'm sure as hell not going to climb down there again."

"I don't expect you to, Mr. MacKenzie."

How could he think she'd expect him to endanger his life again, just to recover her saddlebags? But now . . . now she had nothing. Everything she had left in the world—every remaining link to her past—had been lost with those saddlebags: clothing, a little money, a few hygiene and grooming supplies, the pewter-framed daguerreotype of her parents on their wedding day . . . even her Bible.

Garnet almost sobbed aloud. The Bible had been in her family for generations and bore the record of the births and deaths of so many she had known and loved.

In panic she groped for her locket, sighing gratefully as her fingers closed around the tiny gold case. All had not been lost! She still had the one item she had cherished above all else. She clutched it like a drowning woman clinging to a lifeline.

Gradually, her feeling of hopelessness began to ease. Shrugging off her despair, the optimism that was so intrinsic to her nature surfaced. She may not have anything but the clothes on her back, but once again she had survived a disaster.

Survival. It sure seemed there must be some kind of purpose—a hidden design—to explain why she had survived when all those she had ever loved had perished: her brother Robert, drowned in a flood when they were youngsters; her father, killed at Gettysburg; her mother, taken during a cholera epidemic. Then—twice widowed—she had been left alone and near destitute. But she had survived the ravages of war for four years, and now, an Indian massacre.

But was it a hidden design or simply her own instinct for survival—the instinct that had given her the courage to ride away from the wagons alone, despite the many warnings from those on the wagon train?

She stared reflectively at the back of the man leading the horse. Even in the fierce downpour, he still walked tall. Whatever the good Lord's reasons, He had sent this stranger, as unpleasant an individual as he was, to deliver her from an Indian massacre; had given him the strength to carry her up that mountainside; and, beyond the shadow of doubt, would give him the wits and wherewithal to deliver her safely through these hills.

And as the heavens poured down on her, as she endured the threat of hostile Indians and the knowledge that she no longer possessed anything except the clothes on her back, Garnet Scott could only conclude that fate had led her to this bearded stranger.

Flint MacKenzie was her destiny.

Flint brushed aside the rain dripping down his face and peered ahead. Rain had fallen throughout the afternoon, and he couldn't see beyond a few yards, but he continued to scan the terrain, looking for some kind of cover in the rocks. It had been five or six hours since the accident, and the redhead needed her ankle bound and her bruises tended to. He had to find cover, get them out of their wet clothes and dried off.

He stopped, again wiping the rain off his face, and peered at a nearby rock formation. He thought he saw a narrow opening, possibly an entrance to some shelter among the rocks. "Let's take a look, Sam."

He led the horse to the wall of boulders and found his hunch had been right. "I'll be right back, Mrs. Scott," he said, handing her the reins.

The narrow passage led to a natural cave formed by the pile of mammoth boulders. In several places, the rain streamed through crevices between the rocks, but the cave still offered dry areas that were high enough to shelter even Sam. Flint checked the area for snakes or any other animal that might have been driven in by the storm. Satisfied, he went back out and lifted Garnet into his arms. "Come on, Sam."

He set her down in one of the dry areas, then went

over to Sam and dug into the saddlebags. He came back with a shirt and pair of jeans. "You best get out of your wet clothes," he said, returning to his horse.

Garnet didn't have to be asked twice. Glancing over, she saw that Flint had stepped to the other side of Sam and begun to change his clothes. The horse shielded them from each other's view. Her every movement was painful as she pulled off her clothing. Her locket felt cold against her bare skin, but she didn't remove it. She rolled up the shirtsleeves to her wrists and the pants legs to her ankles.

"You ready for me to take care of that ankle of yours now?" he asked.

"Yes. I sure could use a comb or brush though."

He stepped out from behind the horse, carrying a tin of medical supplies. She noticed he had removed his boots and was wearing moccasins. "Does it hurt?" he asked, bending down on one knee.

"Only when I try to stand on it." In truth, the ankle pained her greatly, but she wasn't going to make an issue of it. She felt foolish enough as it was. She had told him she could take care of herself and here he was having to wrap up her ankle, after she'd already caused him a lot of inconvenience.

She sucked in her breath when he grasped her calf. His heated palm sent marvelous warmth up her leg. He hadn't missed her sudden start. Glancing up at her, he asked, "Did that hurt?"

"No . . . no," she said quickly. "Your hand's cold, that's all." She was relieved when he shifted his penetrating blue eyes back to her foot. She sat silently watching his long, tapered fingers move gently over her foot and ankle.

"Sure don't feel like anything's broken." Within minutes, he had her ankle bound. "What about your hands?"

"Oh, they're fine now. They quit stinging a long time ago."

"Let me look at them." She stretched out her hands, palms up. He held her hands in his palms and silently studied them. The redness was gone, but he rubbed some unguent into them anyway. "That should keep 'em from stiffening up on you." Then he did the same to the scrape on her cheek. "Resting that ankle tonight should help it. You sure you don't hurt anywhere else?"

"No," she lied, determined not to be a further burden to him. "I'm sorry to be such a bother, Mr. MacKenzie."

He closed the tin box and stood up. "Well, it was a damn fool stunt you pulled. We lost your mount and any advantage we could have gained from the storm."

In their short acquaintance, the one thing she had learned to expect from him was his unpleasant attitude. "Advantage? The Indians are human beings too. Why wouldn't the storm slow them down as much as it did us?"

"A rainstorm's not gonna discourage Comanche when they're out for blood. That rain would have washed away our tracks, lady. Now when they spy your dead horse, they'll know they're on the right trail and we're short a mount."

"Oh," she said, somewhat abashed. She felt more guilty than ever, but even if he was right, he could attempt to be a little more chivalrous.

"Well, I've got some jerky in my saddlebags," he said. "At least we've got food and water. It'll soon be too dark to see, so you best eat now and get some sleep."

After returning the tin to the saddlebags, he gave her a piece of the smoked beef and a tin cup of water. Sam trotted over and lapped at one of the pools.

When Garnet finished eating, she lay back, curled her hand under her cheek, and watched Flint move around the cave. There was a restless energy about him that held her spellbound. After unsaddling Sam, he wiped the horse down with the wet shirt he had

discarded, then took a handful of oats from his saddlebags and fed the animal. Then, after spreading out
their wet clothes and the blanket, he dug the poncho
out of his saddlebags and carried it over to her.

"Here, put this on now. It'll keep the dampness
away."

Long shadows darkened the cave entrance when he
finally filled the tin cup and drank. Her eyes had begun
to droop by the time she saw him sit down at the
entrance, where he had a view of the outside. With his
rifle across his lap, he leaned back against the stone
wall and began to chew on a piece of jerky.

She woke up several times during the night. The
cave was in pitch darkness, the silence broken only by
the sound of dripping water. But she knew he sat in
vigilance near the entrance of the cave, prepared to
protect her from all danger.

Chapter 3

Garnet awoke to a glimmer of light shining through the boulders. Sitting up, she glanced around the cave and discovered it was empty.

Her first thought was that Flint had abandoned her. Then she saw the note tucked under his rifle on the floor next to her. Lying beside it was a comb and mirror.

She quickly read the short message telling her that he was scouting their back trail, and she was to remain there until he returned. He added a warning that she was not to fire the rifle unless it was a matter of life or death.

Garnet yawned and stretched. It was a mistake. She became infused with pain. She flexed her ankle a few times. It felt sore and stiff, but she found she was able to stand and walk around. Checking her bodice and skirt, she discovered they were still wet, so she remained in his shirt and jeans. Deciding to make good use of the time, she gathered up all the damp clothing, the rifle, the comb and mirror, and went outside.

The previous day's rain had left the air smelling fresh, and she welcomed the warmth of the hot sun on her aching bones. After spreading the clothes on rocks, she sat down, laid the rifle aside, and picked up the mirror. Just as she feared, her hair was a mass of tangles and knotted curls. Grimly, she set to the task of combing out the snarls.

The aggravating process was painful. Each time she stopped to look in the mirror, it appeared she had made little headway. After a while, she began to feel hungry and hoped Flint had more jerky in his saddle-bags.

Flint was on his way back to the cave when he saw the flashes. They could only mean that the Indians had spotted the camp and were signaling to each other. Soon there would be others converging on the area. He goaded Sam to a quicker pace as the flashes were repeated several times.

Much to his irritation, he found Garnet outside the cave with their clothes spread all over the rocks. "Let's get out of here quick," he ordered. There was no time to explain anything to her. Suddenly, drawing his Colt, he pivoted toward a nearby flash, then immediately sheathed the pistol when he saw where the glare was coming from. "What the hell!" He hurried over and snatched up the mirror. For several seconds, he stared mutely at it, then looked angrily at her. "It was you!" he said in a voice filled with disgust.

"What do you mean?"

"The flashes! They're coming from the sun reflecting off this mirror! Goddammit, lady, do you realize you've just alerted every Indian in these mountains to our whereabouts!"

"All I did was comb my hair. You're the one who gave me the mirror."

"And I told you to stay put, didn't I? That meant inside, not out here." Angrily, he strode over and began to scoop up the clothes. "You might as well have raised a red flag to make it easier for them to find us."

Reeling under the unexpected force of his attack, she mumbled a weak apology. "I guess I wasn't thinking."

"You can say that again." He hurriedly shoved the clothes into his saddlebags. "Let's get out of here before the whole Comanche Nation shows up."

He swung her up on Sam, then handed her the reins. Carrying his rifle, he jogged ahead of her.

The hours passed slowly. She had no watch, but by the position of the shifting sun, she knew it was past midday and well into the afternoon. Much to Garnet's relief, the path had widened and swung away from the treacherous rim. Now another danger existed—the possibility of hostile savages lurking behind the tall pines and cottonwoods that now lined either side of the trail.

Despite Flint's earlier demand to hurry, he set a slow pace. She didn't ask why. He hadn't spoken to her since his outburst that morning. On occasion, he spoke to his horse, but not one word to her. In fact, she observed, it seemed he had forgotten her presence entirely. She was aching, thirsty, and hungry, but she wasn't going to give him the satisfaction of knowing it. To her chagrin, her empty stomach began to growl.

She had started to doze when the sudden sound of his voice startled her so thoroughly that she almost fell off the horse. "Sam needs a rest. We'll set for a while." He led her off the trail to a nearby clump of cottonwood and swung her off the horse as if she were a feather.

Sighing, Garnet slumped down against a tree trunk. After loosening Sam's cinch, Flint came over carrying a canteen and sat down beside her.

"Here, you best eat this." He handed her a piece of jerky. Hungrily, she took several bites before she became aware that he was not eating.

"Mr. MacKenzie, why aren't you eating, too?"

"I'm not hungry."

She sensed he was lying. "I've never doubted your honesty, Mr. MacKenzie, but this is the last of the jerky, isn't it?"

"There'll be enough for tonight's meal. 'Sides, I ain't much for eating during the day," he repeated. Irritation had crept into his voice again.

"It embarrasses you to be caught doing something chivalrous, doesn't it?"

"Don't embarrass me at all. Just don't like to make a habit of it."

"I doubt there'd be much chance of that happening." She handed him the stick of jerky. "There's enough here for both of us."

He grinned, his white teeth a striking contrast against his dark, bearded face. Reaching into his pocket, he pulled out the plug of tobacco he had taken from the dead man's body. "I can offer you a chaw of tobacco if you've a mind to."

"No thank you, sir. I don't chaw tobacky and I don't smoke a corncob pipe."

Chuckling, he popped the plug back into his pocket. "What's a Georgia Cracker like you doing this far west, Widow Scott?" He took a bite of the jerky, then handed it back to her.

"I'm on my way to Santa Fe to get married."

"Do you still have kin back in Georgia?"

"No, they're all gone now. My brother Robert drowned fourteen years ago when he was thirteen. My daddy was killed at Gettysburg, and my mama died in '66 during a cholera epidemic." She tenderly fondled the locket. "I have a picture of the four of us in my locket. But it's hard to remember the sound of their voices." He saw a faint trace of tears in her eyes. "Especially Robert's."

As much of a bother as she was to him, he couldn't help but admire her fortitude. "It's good you have the picture," he said, staring into space. "I never had one of my ma. No matter how I try, I can't see her face anymore. I can remember the way she wore her hair, and her habit of rubbing the back of her neck when she was tired, but her face . . ." He broke off, suddenly aware he had been speaking his thoughts out loud.

He glanced at her, and saw the tears in her eyes. Embarrassed by how much he had revealed of himself, he took a bite of the jerky.

"Sure wish this jerky was coffee. I can get along easier without food than I can coffee. Maybe tonight we can have a fire."

He was relieved when she made no further attempt to bring up the subject of the picture. They continued to pass the stick of jerky back and forth until it was gone. Then he unscrewed the cap on the canteen and handed it to her. "At least there's no call to go thirsty. There's plenty of fresh water."

A short time later, they prepared to get underway again. "Can't we ride double?" she asked.

"No sense in tiring Sam by loading him down right now. He's gonna have to get us out of here fast if there's a need. Besides, the double weight on him would leave a sure trail."

Suddenly Flint stiffened. Before Garnet could guess what was happening, he shoved her to the ground, his hand clamped over her mouth to stifle her scream. He put a finger to his lips, cautioning her to silence. When she nodded in understanding, he removed his hand and pointed to the trail.

She could barely keep from gasping aloud when she saw the reason for his actions. Two mounted Indians had appeared on the trail. At the moment, they were studying the ground intently, but she feared that at any second they might look over and see them. Worriedly, she glanced at Sam tethered a few feet away. A mere shuffle of his hooves would attract the Indians' attention.

Garnet held her breath. She could feel the tension in Flint's stance as he knelt beside her with his rifle in hand.

In the hushed silence, the low murmurs of the Indians' voices carried to her ears. From their gestures, they appeared to be arguing. Then, to her relief, they moved on.

She looked at Flint and he shook his head in warning not to say anything. He slid his Colt out of its holster and handed her the pistol. Signaling her to stay where she was, he moved cautiously after the braves.

Garnet huddled, listening intently. The very shadows that had offered refuge only moments before suddenly took on a sinister cast as they deepened and crept across the trail. Every sound seemed to be intensified: the strident caw of a jaybird, the chatter of a squirrel, the rustle of a leaf. The pungent odor of Sam nearby suddenly smelled suffocating to her. She jerked her head as a grouse burst abruptly out of the brush and took flight. Shuddering, she wiped her perspiring palm against her pants leg and tightened her grasp on the Colt.

It's just an old grouse. Get a grip on yourself, Garnet, she scolded, but she couldn't stop trembling. She had lost track of how much time had lapsed since Flint's departure. It seemed like hours. What if the Indians had spotted him? He could be dead. She almost cried out aloud when he suddenly appeared before her.

"Let's get out of here."

"What about the Indians?"

"They took another trail, but they might double back. You're gonna have to walk though. A rider can be seen too easily."

Garnet wasn't about to argue.

They fled throughout the night, stopping only long enough for brief rests and an occasional sip of water. Their progress was slow, but as darkness slipped into daylight, he set a faster pace. Her ankle ached and at times her chest heaved from exertion, but Garnet forced herself to keep up with him.

Later in the afternoon, Flint finally stopped to rest by

a stream. As Garnet leaned over to drink, she paused to study her reflection in the water. Her hair was wildly disheveled and her face was spotted with dirt and bruises.

"I'd like to do something with this hair," she grumbled, shoving it back in disgust.

"Maybe I can help you out," he said.

She looked up hopefully and saw him reach for his bowie. "You don't mean cut it off?" she asked, alarmed.

He chuckled. "I'd never do that, Redhead. Wouldn't want to spoil the fun of those Indians." He dug out a string of rawhide from his saddlebags and lopped off a hunk of it.

"You have a twisted sense of humor, Mr. MacKenzie." She snatched the string from him and quickly tied back her hair.

The cool water felt soothing on her bruises as she returned to rinsing the dirt off her face and hands. As she bent over, her locket dangled dangerously near the water. She wiped off the case with her shirttail and sat down on the ground. When she opened it, she found that the picture had not been harmed.

"Think you looked at that long enough, Widow Scott. We've wasted enough time here." Grabbing the horse's reins, he started off again at a fast walk.

Winking at the picture, she murmured, "He's a grim taskmaster, my darlings, but I'm sure we'll all grow to love him." Then she snapped the locket shut, rose wearily to her feet, and followed him.

Garnet collapsed in relief when Flint called a halt only a few hours later. He'd chosen a spot that provided a wall of stone at their backs. A gap in the rock offered an opening to conceal a fire. He immediately gathered enough wood to start a blaze.

"If we're being followed, won't the Indians see the glow from the fire?" Garnet asked.

"It's too light right now to see the glow."

"Well, what about the smoke? Won't they see that?"

He gave her a disgruntled look and put a battered, blackened coffee pot on the fire. "Too dark to see the smoke."

She decided to shut up and just wait for the coffee. As soon as it had brewed, he put out the fire. Sharing a tin cup, they drank the coffee and ate the last of the jerky. Then he tossed her the blanket. "You'd best get some sleep."

With the setting of the sun, cool air had drifted into the range. Garnet spread out the blanket. "We can share this, Mr. MacKenzie. There's no call for you to sleep on the damp ground."

Much to her surprise, he accepted the offer. Coming over, he laid down beside her, rifle in hand.

"I can keep guard if you want me to," she said. "After all, you've hardly gotten any sleep in the past few days. I'm sure you're much sleepier than I am."

"You any good with a rifle?"

"Been hunting since I was ten. My daddy always took me and my brother with him." Instinctively, she reached for her locket. When she failed to make contact with it, she began to grope frantically at her neck. "It's gone!"

"What's gone?" he asked, sitting up.

"My locket. It's gone." In near panic, she stood up to shake out her clothing. "I know I had it when we stopped just a few miles back. Remember? The place where I tied back my hair. I must have lost it somewhere between there and here." She sat down again in despair.

"Well, we can't go back for it," he said. Lying back, he tucked an arm under his head and closed his eyes.

"I'm not asking you to."

Silence ensued as she sank into gloom. She shut her eyes to force back her tears. *He's wrong. I don't care what he said. I'll never forget what you look like*, she vowed silently.

When she finally forced herself to put aside her sadness, she glanced over at Flint and saw he was sleeping.

Awake, there was always his anger, irritable nature, or boorishness to contend with. In this rare moment, when she had caught him asleep, he looked different. Could there be any tenderness under that tough hide? She wanted to believe that there was—and that some-day he would reveal it to her.

Unable to take her eyes off him, she began to feel the rise of a new sensation. Seeing him stretched out asleep, with all his anger and harshness blanketed by slumber, she became aware of the one quality that sleep could not disguise—the pure male essence that emanated from the long, sinewy body of this man lying beside her.

The draw was magnetic. She felt the warmth of her heated blush as she fought an urge to reach out and run her hand down the long, muscled length of him. Stroking. Caressing. Feeling all the power and passion of him under her fingertips.

Her breathing quickened, and her pulse pounded in her ears. She allowed her fantasy to climb a step further, and began to imagine how she would feel lying imprisoned beneath all that muscled might—with him doing the same thing to her. A shiver shook her spine and she turned away, curling up on her side on the far edge of the blanket.

When she awoke the next morning, once again there was no sign of Flint. Seeing Sam tethered to a nearby tree, she figured Flint had gone into the trees to relieve himself. She walked over to Sam, took the comb out of the saddlebags and started to comb her hair. While pulling at a stubborn knot, she sensed she was not alone. Turning around to offer Flint a morning greet-ing, she screamed in horror. A half-naked savage, his face painted with red and black stripes, stood before her. For a few seconds she stood paralyzed, then as she turned to run, another Indian sprang at her from the bushes, knocking her off her feet. Scrambling frantically, she tried to crawl away, but he grabbed her and clamped a hand over her mouth. The odor of stale grease assailed her nostrils. With a threatening motion of his tomahawk, the Indian cautioned her to silence as his companion checked Flint's saddlebags. Her captor released her and she stood up, her eyes fixed on the two Indians, who had begun talking between themselves.

Although she could feel her heart beating rapidly, Garnet was not prone to panic: she had faced too many similar showdowns with Yankees during the war. The delay gave her time to regain her composure. As her initial shock faded, she began to formulate a plan. Flint's rifle lay less than a few yards away. Somehow, she had to distract them for a few seconds so she could reach it.

Flint had not gone more than three miles when he spied the locket lying on the path. Relieved, he picked it up, slipped it into his shirt pocket, and started back at a run. At dawn, he had changed into his moccasins and set out on foot to retrace their trail. It was probably the most damn fool thing he had ever done in his life; not only was it risky, it wasted valuable time as well. The redhead's silent grief over the loss of her locket had been harder to tolerate than a tearful outburst would have been. And Lord knows, he couldn't stand to see a woman cry!

Nearing their camp, he froze at the sound of a scream. When he heard it repeated, he knew it was Garnet and not an animal. He raced ahead, then slowed his pace and approached cautiously. The first thing he saw was Garnet standing stark naked in the clearing.

The startling sight momentarily distracted him. Her

slim body was small breasted and long-legged. In the bright sunshine, her red hair glistened like flame. Then he spied the two Comanche standing a short distance away. Jolted back to the present danger, he drew his Colt. On second thought, fearing the sound of a gunshot would draw more Indians, he sheathed his pistol and drew the bowie at his hip. The Indians were close together, but he had the element of surprise.

He crept closer, then hurled the knife at the nearest Indian. The savage grunted and for several heartbeats groped helplessly to reach the knife shaft embedded in his back. Flint sprang from the bushes, and, ducking the swing of the other Indian's tomahawk, he knocked the savage to the ground. They rolled over and over, their bodies locked together. Fighting to break the Comanche's grasp on the tomahawk, Flint felt a painful gash when the sharp blade nipped his shoulder. Straining his wounded muscles, he fought to keep the Indian from landing a blow.

Garnet had just pulled on her drawers when she saw blood on Flint's shirt. She picked up the rifle, but unable to get a clean shot, she dared not fire. Horrified, she watched the life and death struggle between the two men, but was helpless to render Flint any assistance. She cried out when the Indian rolled over, pinned Flint beneath him, and raised the tomahawk to deliver a lethal blow. Before she could aim and fire, Flint drew his Colt, pressed it against the Comanche's midsection and pulled the trigger, the Indian's own body muffling the shot.

The tomahawk slipped out of his hand. With an incredulous look, he rose to his feet, clutched a hand to his stomach, and started to stagger toward her. Staring wide-eyed, she backed away from the hideously painted apparition. His eyes were circled in black. One side of his face was red, the other side white, with a black stripe across his forehead and along his nose. Yellow paint streaked the bare parting of his hair, which had been divided by two braids. Horrified, she continued to back away until she butted up against Sam. The savage reached out to grasp her hair. Suddenly, his eyes glazed over and rolled to the top of the sockets, and he toppled to the ground at her feet. Stunned, she stared down at the dead man.

Flint sat up, the red stain on his shirt widening. He untied the bandanna from around his neck and stuffed it against the wound. Still dazed, Garnet went over and knelt beside him. "Let me help you."

"For God's sake, lady, get some clothes on," he lashed out.

The harsh retort felt like a slap to her face, snapping her out of her stupor. Abruptly, acutely conscious of her near-nudity, she hurried back to her pile of clothing. Her skirt and bodice were still in his saddlebags, so she quickly put his shirt and jeans back on.

As Flint rose shakily to his feet, Garnet watched him warily. Clutching his wounded shoulder, he moved to his horse and pulled off his bloodied shirt. After shoving it into the saddlebags, he rooted around until he found a bottle of whiskey and poured some of the liquid on the wound. Then he took a deep swallow.

Garnet strode purposely over to him. "Sit down," she ordered. Either he was shocked or too weak to refuse, because he obeyed her without an argument. As she rummaged through the saddlebags, he brought the bottle to his mouth again.

The best she could find was a clean bandanna. After folding it into a neat, square wad, she covered the wound. While she tied the compress to his shoulder, she noticed a scar on his chest and another on his back. Despite her curiosity, she thought it wouldn't be prudent to ask about them. She was more than casually aware of the dark hair on his chest, and the width of his muscular shoulders. Considering the gravity of the situation, she hurriedly censured herself. When she finished, she helped him put on the clean shirt.

"Do you want a sling on that arm?" she asked.

"What for?" he grumbled and took another deep swig of the whiskey.

She snatched the bottle out of his hand, recapped it, and returned it to the saddlebags. She did not intend to suffer the company of a drunkard.

Apparently she had misjudged his stamina. Neither the loss of blood nor the consumption of alcohol appeared to slow his pace. His step was steady and straight as he walked over, picked up his hat, and plopped it on his head. Then he yanked his bowie out of the Indian's back. After wiping off the blade on the dead man's leg, he sheathed the weapon and, to her astonishment, removed the moccasins from the men's feet.

Flint was angry as hell, but not at her. At himself. He shouldn't have barked at her the way he had. He hadn't even asked her if she'd been hurt. Maybe the Indians had ravaged her before he arrived. "Are you okay?"

"I'm fine," she snapped.

"I mean they didn't . . . ah . . . harm you, did they?"

"No, but I see no reason why you found it necessary to kill them. I had the situation in hand."

He glanced askance at her. "How do you figure that?" He picked up the rifle she had dropped. "What I saw was you standing here buck naked."

"Exactly," she said smugly. "And that's what those Indians saw too. My mother once told me that if I ever found myself in such a predicament, I should remove all my clothes."

Arching a brow, he snorted derisively. "What for, to keep them from being ripped off you?"

"She said a naked woman is a distraction to a man, and I would be able to use that time to my advantage."

"And just how long did you figure you could keep those two Indians *distracted*, Widow Scott?"

"Long enough to reach the rifle you just picked up. It was a few yards away from me. Then I would have forced them to disarm."

He threw back his head in laughter. "A tomahawk would have cleaved your skull before you even took two steps."

"I think you're wrong, sir. You saw for yourself that they were obviously arguing over me."

"They sure were. Do you speak Shoshone, Widow Scott?" he asked, clearly amused.

"No, why do you ask?"

"Because that's what they were speaking."

"Mr. MacKenzie, one doesn't have to speak their language to guess what they were discussing. I think it was pretty obvious."

"They were discussing which one would claim you as coup."

"Coup?" She frowned in confusion. "You mean which one of them would . . . use me first?"

"No, I mean which one of them would get Sam and which one would get your scalp."

She stared at him, aghast. "I'm not certain I understand your meaning."

"Well, Widow Scott, from what I heard, neither one was *distracted*. That red hair of yours was the trophy to whoever *lost* the argument. Comanche are right fond of horses."

She lifted her chin with hauteur. "I don't believe you."

"Don't much matter to me if you do or not," he said, studying the two sets of moccasins. He handed her the smaller pair. "Here, put these on."

"Put them on? Surely you don't think I'd put on a pair of shoes that you just took off the feet of a dead man!"

"Until we get out of these mountains, Mrs. Scott, you're better off wearing moccasins than boots. You can move swifter in them, they're not as slippery on the rocks, and they don't leave tracks."

"Then put them on the horse, sir, since he's doing the walking." She flung the moccasins back at him.

Grumbling under his breath, he moved over to Sam and shoved the moccasins into the saddlebags. "She's a difficult woman, Sam."

"So here are some more bodies you're going to leave lying without a proper burial." She stood with her hands on her hips, angrily tapping her bare foot on the ground.

"If you want to bury them, lady, go right ahead, but I'm riding out of here now before any others show up." He climbed on Sam. "Since you're so dadblamed worried about doing what's *proper* for those two savages who were about to lift that red hair of yours, Comanche don't take to burying 'less it's on a western slope. They figure that way their spirits can slide into the spirit world along with the setting sun. Oh, and they like to be buried sitting up. And when you're finished, you might look around to try and find where they hid their horses. I ain't got the time, or I'd do it for you."

Exasperated, Garnet grabbed her boots and hurried over to him. She wanted to punch him in the face at the sight of his smug look when he reached down and pulled her up behind him. To avoid falling off, she had no choice but to slip her arms around his waist and hang on.

Chapter 4

The day that had begun with such violence ended peacefully, Garnet reflected when they made camp that evening. Flint had discovered another cave in which to spend the night. He thought it was even safe enough to build a fire.

Fortunately, his injury was only a flesh wound, and once the bleeding stopped he appeared to regain his strength. With the horse carrying a double load, they halted frequently to rest Sam. Flint appeared more concerned about the horse than he did about her or himself.

On several of the brief stops they managed to gather a few nuts and berries, but at the moment, Garnet thought of how delicious a plate of stew would taste.

Once again, she tested her ankle. It no longer pained her, so she removed the bandage. By refolding the gauze to the reverse side, it could serve to protect Flint's wound.

While Flint built the fire, Garnet went out and set a small trap using several of the twigs and branches they had gathered for the fire. She baited the trap with a nut and some sassafras leaves.

"What are you hoping to catch in that?" he asked as she stepped back to admire her efforts.

"A rabbit or squirrel. Maybe even a mountain lion,"

she teased with a side glance in his direction. "You'll see. Just wait until tomorrow morning."

There was nothing much more to do except lie on the blanket and study him. He sat deep in thought, his profile reflected in the firelight. At times like this, she felt calm and secure just knowing he was near, and tried to keep her thoughts from traveling down last night's licentious path.

"How long do you think it will be before we reach a town?" she asked.

He turned his head and looked at her. Once again he had that faraway look, as if he were suddenly remembering her presence. "I reckon a couple more days. Comanche Wells is on the other side of this range."

"Do you live in these parts, Mr. MacKenzie?"

"No."

"But I can tell you're a Texan. During the war enough of you cowboys passed through Georgia for me to easily recognize a Texas twang when I hear it."

"Yeah, I was born and raised in Texas. My folks had a ranch near the Red."

"You said 'had.' Did they lose it, like the rest of us lost our homes?"

She could tell by his hesitation that he didn't like talking about himself. Much to her surprise, he continued. "No, Pa died at the Alamo. Ma took us back to the ranch and raised us."

"Us?"

"My brother Luke was two years old then, I was one, and Cleve was on the way."

"Did your mother ever remarry?"

"Nope. Raised us by herself."

"She must have been a remarkable woman."

"Yeah, she sure was. Ain't ever met a woman who could compare to her."

Garnet would have liked to refresh his memory about what the women in the South had endured during the war, but she didn't want to discourage him from talking. "It must have taken a lot of courage to run a ranch and raise three sons."

"Ma had more than her share of courage. She was killed when a gang of Comancheros raided the ranch while me and my brothers were off fighting for the Confederacy. Luke's wife was killed in the raid too, but his son survived."

When he fell silent, she asked, "Where are your brothers now?"

"After the war, Luke took to sheriffing for a spell in California, then he remarried and now he's back running stock on the ranch. That's where I was headed when I got sidetracked at Dos Rios."

"Mr. MacKenzie, what's the difference between Comancheros and Comanches? Are they a different tribe?"

"Comancheros are white men who ride with the Comanche." The bitterness in his voice sent a chill down her spine. "The murdering bastards prey on ranchers along the border. Stealing cattle . . . raping and murdering the womenfolk and children."

Fearful he would withdraw again into his reverie, she quickly asked, "And what about your brother Cleve?"

"Last I heard he was heading to Dallas. But I reckon he'll show up at the ranch, too. Luke'll need help with the roundup."

He stood up and tossed out the coffee grounds. It was clear he had ended any further discussion about his family.

"I wish my brother were still alive," she said wistfully.

"How long have you been a widow, Mrs. Scott?" he asked, stirring the fire with a long stick.

"Well, in truth, I've been widowed twice. I was married for the first time in '61. Bobby Joe and I were only eighteen at the time. Shortly after, he went off to war. I never saw him again."

"Where was he killed?"

"Well, he wasn't killed in a battle. He . . . ah . . . died from the effects of a disease."

"What disease?" He waited for her to continue.

"He . . . contracted a . . . ah . . . contagious disease," she said.

Puzzled by her hesitation, he asked, "What was it? Consumption?"

"Gonorrhea," she said in an undertone.

"I couldn't hear you. What did you say?"

"He contracted gonorrhea in a house of ill repute," she said hastily. She stood up quickly and turned her back to him, making a big show of fussing with her hair.

"Your husband died of the clap!" he exclaimed loudly.

She spun around on her heel. "Well, sir, why don't you just go outside and shout it from the top of the highest mountain."

"I don't think anyone heard me except Sam—and he don't carry tales."

"Furthermore, I said he died from the *effects* of the disease, not the disease itself."

"What effects?"

"While he was in the hospital being treated, due to the contagious aspects of the disease, he was denied the usage of any of the hospital . . . accommodations." Seeing his confused frown, she said, exasperated, "The bedpan, Mr. MacKenzie."

"Oh. Do continue, Widow Scott."

His obvious effort to keep from laughing only irritated her further. "Well, one night during a storm Bobby Joe went outside to the outdoor . . . facility designated for such diseases." Flint's brow arched quizzically. "The outhouse, sir!" She folded her arms across her chest and said quickly, "It was struck by lightning while he was in it."

Her glare dared him to laugh.

"So how'd you figure he died from the effects of the clap?"

"Well, isn't it obvious?" she said with disdain. "If it weren't for the disease, he never would have been in the outhouse when it was struck by lightning."

Shaking his head, Flint sat down on the blanket. "Reckon only a woman would come up with that kind of logic."

After a long silence that seemed to stretch on for an eternity, he said solemnly, "I'm curious, Widow Scott, did young Bobby Joe pass his disease on to you?"

She gasped in shock. "How dare you ask—much less think of—such an outrageous question! On our wedding night, sir, Bobby Joe Renfrew was as innocent—*and virginal*—as I was. The following morning he left to answer the call of duty, Mr. Mac-Kenzie. I never saw him again."

"Well, he sure figured out in a hurry just what that duty was all about," Flint agreed, stroking his bushy beard. "So what happened to your second husband?"

"I married Mr. Scott in '65. His death was very tragic. He had been suffering from chronic pain for several years, and one day while I was away, he went into the study, wrote a note saying he no longer wished to live with the pain, and shot himself."

"He wouldn't be the first man. During the war, I saw more than one gut-shot man put a pistol to his own head. Where was his wound?"

"In his toe."

"He was wounded in his toe?" Flint's eyes widened in surprise.

"It wasn't a wound. He had gout."

"Gout! How old was he?"

"Mr. Scott had been my schoolmaster. He was fifty-five when—"

"Only fifty-five? Sure seems strange he'd kill himself over a pain in his toe."

"I was about to say, he was fifty-five when he became my schoolmaster. I was eight years old then."

"You were eight years old and he was fifty-five?" Flint did some quick arithmetic. "That made him about sixty-nine or seventy when you married him." He stood up, tossing the stick into the fire.

"Sixty-nine," she said in a snippy tone. She watched the stick burst into flames, recognizing the similarity between the flare-up and the blaze of her anger. "Mr. MacKenzie, I didn't intend for this to become an inquisition."

"I'm sorry, go on. How long were you married to Mr. Scott?"

"For two years. He . . . died . . . in '67. And don't you dare speak disrespectfully of him. Mr. Scott was a fine gentlemen. He educated me."

"Well, did *Mr. Scott* have a first name?"

"Frederick. Frederick Scott. I guess I have always been in the habit of calling him Mr. Scott because he had—"

"Been your schoolmaster since you were eight years old."

"Please wipe that smirk off your face, sir."

"There's no call to go digging your spurs into my hide. Ain't my fault your husbands weren't the pick of the litter."

She slumped back down on the blanket. "I've never implied my husbands were exactly what romantic legends are made from, sir, but have you heard me express one disparaging word of complaint about either of them?"

"No. And I gotta say I admire your fidelity, Widow Scott."

As he plopped down beside her, she saw a dangerous gleam in his eyes. "Tell me, Redhead, was *Mr. Scott* the one who taught you that 'distracting' lesson?"

"What distracting lesson?"

"The one you performed for those Comanche."

"I told you my mama taught me that." Damn! The man was driving her to distraction. She threw up her hands in a gesture of concession. "Mr. MacKenzie, I'm willing to accept *your* explanation for not sparing the lives of those two misguided savages, if you accept *my* explanation for the drastic actions I resorted to. Please put it out of your mind."

For a moment his eyes were clear of mockery. "I wish I could, but it's a hard thing to do. You're a handsome figure of a woman, Widow Scott."

The sincerity in his voice caused her to raise her head, and their gazes locked for a long moment. "I will take that as a compliment, sir," she said, barely above a whisper.

"Have you ever known a real man, Redhead?"

The look in his eyes set her heart palpitating. "I don't know what you mean, sir."

"I think you do."

"And I think your boldness is insulting."

"Be honest with me. That thought has entered your mind, hasn't it?" The huskiness in his voice had begun to raise holy havoc with her senses.

"So what if it has?" she lashed out defensively. "Everyone fantasizes sometimes."

"Maybe you've even thought about what it would feel like to be in *my* arms—and have me kiss you."

Good Lord! On top of all his other disturbing qualities, he was a mind reader, too. Or were her feelings so obvious to him? She would have to get a grip on herself and stand up to his seductive draw. "Are you presuming I'm equating you to the man in my fantasy, Mr. MacKenzie?"

"Could be, Redhead," he said. "Could be you've been thinking about it from the first time we met."

The time had clearly come for her to take the offensive, or sure as the sun would rise in the morning, she'd wake up in the arms of Flint MacKenzie!

"Could be you're right, Mr. MacKenzie."

He grinned. "I figured as much. Time you quit calling me 'Mr. MacKenzie', too. Makes me sound like some stiff-necked banker—or schoolmaster. Name's Flint."

Smiling sweetly, she said demurely, "Thank you, Flint. Since we're being so informal, I confess I have thought about you kissing me. You see, Bobby Joe hadn't begun to shave by the time we parted, and Mr. Scott's face was bare except for a mustache; so I've always wondered what it would feel like to be kissed by a man with a beard. I've always imagined a beard would feel silky or velvety." As if pondering the question, she twitched her chin. "Then again, considering your beard, Flint, it looks to be kind of scratchy. Is that because your beard's so scruffy and unkempt?"

"You expect me to believe that cock-and-bull story?" he scoffed. "Beard or not, I'm thinking you'd like for me to kiss you right now, wouldn't you?"

"Perhaps you've misunderstood me. I said the thought once crossed my mind, but I've had second thoughts since then. I imagine I'm not the only one who ever complained about your beard. What does your wife say about it?"

"I don't have a wife. And from what you've told me about young Bobby and ole Freddy, Widow Scott, sounds like I've got a better chance of living longer without one."

"Well, don't get any false hopes about me, Flint. I must remind you that I'm spoken for."

"Reckon that'll be your next husband's problem, not mine. Hate to hear how old this one is."

"Milton Brittles is my second cousin. He's fifty-seven years old and owns an apothecary. I'm told he's a man of means—unlike you, Mr. MacKenzie. You are simply a mean man," she said pointedly.

He ignored the jibe. "So you're heading west to marry a rich man."

"Exactly. Therefore, I will warn you: it's been my experience that whenever a man remains in my company for too long, he invariably falls in love with me." The statement was so outrageous that even Garnet found it hard to believe, but she was enjoying knocking some of the cockiness out of him too much to stop.

"By 'man' are you referring to the wet-nosed boy who finally discovered his pecker was good for something other than peeing with, or the old schoolmaster with his gouty foot already in the grave?"

"Mr. MacKenzie, I have already informed you it is not proper to speak disrespectfully of the dead, and I feel further compelled to remind you that you only diminish your stature in my opinion by such crudity and vulgarity."

Lying back, he tucked his hands under his head. "My apology, Widow Scott. I'm used to talking to Sam and he don't take no offense."

"I just want you to understand that I do not invite your attentions—and I certainly will not encourage them. Nevertheless, you *will* fall in love with me," she said smugly. "I can see it's beginning to happen already and it pains me to think that, when I reject your advances, I'll appear ungrateful for everything you've done for me." Sighing deeply, she cast her eyes downward. "I can't tell you how much the thought disturbs me."

Flint had started listening with amusement, but it soon changed to incredulity. "Lady, you must have been chewin' on locoweed. You've got several problems worth fretting over right now. Like where our next meal is coming from, and whether or not we'll get out of these mountains alive, and, if you have a mind to, you could even worry about how long it will take to reach the next town. But . . . Widow Scott . . . the *one* thing you *don't* have to worry about *is that I'm gonna fall in love with you!*"

"We'll see." The corners of her mouth curved in enough of a smile to raise his hackles even more.

Scowling, he turned onto his side and closed his eyes.

Chapter 5

Lying in a somnolent stage between sleep and wakefulness, Garnet cuddled against a pleasant warmth. Slowly, through the haze of drowsiness, she became aware of an added titillation. She flickered her eyelids several times before she fully awoke. Raising her head, she discovered the source of the sensation— Flint MacKenzie. Sometime during the night, she must have curled up next to him. Gingerly, she withdrew and stood up. Knowing he would want to get under way, she considered waking him.

Then another thought crossed her mind. What if he had suffered a setback from his wound? It hadn't appeared to be deep when she put gauze on it last night, but perhaps he had developed a fever. The even rise and fall of his chest dispelled that fear; he was sleeping too peacefully to be ill. Reflecting on how little sleep he had had in the last couple of nights, she decided he was simply exhausted and she would not wake him.

Last night it had taken her a long time to get over their conversation. He had no idea how close he had come to the truth—how tempted she had been to slip into his arms. She dared not let her mind dwell on these dangerous thoughts until she had formulated a plan to keep him from leaving her. Which was what she should have been doing last night, instead of lying there thinking about his nearness.

And what to do about her plans to wed? As much as she prided herself on keeping her word, she also recognized the hand of Fate knocking at her door. Mr. Brittles would just have to find a different bride.

She intended to marry Flint MacKenzie.

Clearly, marriage was the farthest thing from his thoughts—he'd bed her, not wed her. If he ever suspected she had marriage in mind, he'd be over the next mountain before she even knew he was gone. She didn't like the idea of being a manipulating female, but Flint MacKenzie would need a lot of convincing. Somehow, she'd have to hold his interest until he admitted he loved her. It wouldn't be easy.

Garnet moved to the entrance of the cave. It was almost sunrise and the black of night had faded to a hazy gray. The birds had begun their morning chirping, and the scent of pine permeated the air. She drew a deep breath, then paused to thank God for the blessing of being alive.

The pious reflection was disrupted by a low grumbling in her belly. Remembering the animal trap she had set, she hurried over to it and squealed with pleasure at the sight of a rabbit. At last, they would have something to eat. Back home in Georgia, a rabbit or squirrel had often been her only source of meat, especially after the Yankee army had commandeered all her chickens along with the rest of the livestock. Her mouth watered at the prospect of a hot meal.

She would show Flint MacKenzie just how useful she could be. By the time he woke up, she'd have the rabbit roasting and the coffee brewed. After quickly gathering wood, she built a fire, set the coffee to boil, and prepared to skin and dress the rabbit. Then she realized she was missing one thing—a knife to do it with. Flint MacKenzie had the only knife, and that was in a sheath on his hip.

Glancing again at the sleeping man, she came to the conclusion that with some delicate maneuvering she could extract the knife without waking him. Approaching cautiously, she knelt over him and with thumb and forefinger eased the knife out of its scabbard.

Suddenly he rolled completely over on top of her, flattening her on her back. She was helpless.

"What are you doing?"

"I . . . I needed your . . ." She swallowed nervously. "Your knife."

"My knife!" His mouth curved into a smirk. "You change your thinking since last night, Widow Scott?" She couldn't miss the innuendo, especially when she saw the devilment in his eyes and one dark brow arched at a rakish angle.

"Your bowie, Mr. MacKenzie. I needed your bowie." She realized she still clutched it in one hand, held pinned to the ground above her head. She was very conscious of his chest crushing her breasts, the pressure of strong thighs holding her legs locked between them—conscious of every place where their bodies touched. As if to make her even more aware, he slowly began to move. Her stomach seemed to slam against her spine and her heart thudded in her chest. She opened her mouth, gasping for breath.

Instantly his mouth was on hers, filling it with his heated breath as his tongue plundered possessively; a single kiss fueled her with a magnitude of pleasure she had never known. The unfulfilled passion she had suppressed for years erupted in an outpouring of exquisite, fiery sensation that surged through her, clouding her brain while inflaming every nerve in her body.

When breathlessness forced an end to the kiss, she felt a burning need for another. Realizing the danger of succumbing to such a temptation, she drew away. *It's too soon. Too soon,* she cried inwardly, struggling to resist the thrill of his arousal.

For several seconds she lay quietly, regaining her breath. Pretending to be unaffected, although her mouth still burned from the touch of his lips and tongue, she raised her eyes and met his dark-eyed gaze. "Please release me, Mr. MacKenzie, or I shall drive this knife into you," she said calmly.

As if spurning the threat, he released only her hands. "I don't think you'd carry through on that threat, Widow Scott, but considering your bungling so far, you might be careless enough to do it accidently."

Flint stood up and offered his hand to assist her. Refusing his help, she jumped to her feet. "Well, my *bungling* managed to produce a rabbit."

He followed her out to the trap. With a theatrical bow, she pointed to the caged animal. "Look at that beautiful sight. What have you got to say about that, Mr. MacKenzie?"

"Do you intend to eat it or pet it?"

"That's why I need your knife."

He spread his hands in concession. "So what do you want me to do?"

"Well, sir, since your kiss was as unpleasant as I suspected it would be, I suggest you consider shaving."

"There was nothing unpleasant about that kiss, lady, and you damn well know it." He took the knife out of her hands. "I'll skin the rabbit."

An hour later, still savoring the taste of their first hot meal in five days, they were back on the trail.

"With any kind of luck, I figure we should reach Comanche Wells by tomorrow night," Flint said that evening, after another day's long and silent ride.

"Is there a chance the Indians will attack the town?" she asked.

He shook his head. "I doubt it. The town's large

enough to withstand an attack. It's in the open on all sides, so it'd be pretty hard for a large raiding party to sneak up without being sighted. I've checked our back trail and there's nobody following us. The two I killed were the same two we saw earlier. If the Indians were mounting an attack on Comanche Wells, there'd be more sign of a buildup right here in these mountains. And I haven't seen any. Figure the rest have gone back to bury their dead. The damn savages got enough coup from the wagon train massacre to show off when they ride back to their village."

"I hope you're right." She sighed. "When I think of all those poor people—"

"You'd be better off not thinking about them," he said sharply. "It's the kind of thing that can eat you alive." He walked away hurriedly.

Garnet realized the conversation had probably dredged up the tragic memory of his mother's death. She thought of her own family. They had never seemed completely lost to her as long as she wore the locket. Now, how long would it be before their images started to fade?

Perhaps she had been wrong in coming to this wild country. Instead of hoping to build a new life in the West, maybe she would have been wiser to head north to the safety and security of one of the Yankee cities like New York, Chicago, or Boston. Cities that had remained untouched by the ravages of war. But, had she done that, she would not have met Flint MacKenzie.

She smiled with woman's intuition. The decision had never been hers to make. Destiny!

Flint returned, sat beside her, and put down a handful of nuts and berries. "This is the best I can do. I don't want to risk a shot."

"I'll set a trap again tonight. What is your preference, *Monsieur* MacKenzie?" she asked theatrically. "A plump rabbit? Perhaps a tasty grouse?" She moved a short distance away and began to build another trap of sticks.

Chuckling, he folded his arms across his chest and leaned back against a tree. She had a lot of grit and a good sense of humor—that is, when she wasn't rolling down mountainsides or attracting Indians.

She glanced up, smiling. "Well, what's your preference?"

"I like most any food, but I reckon if I had my druthers I'd want that beef roast Ma used to make. If I ever met a woman who could make roast beef like Ma's, I'd probably up and marry her."

Garnet made a mental note of the importance he placed on roast beef and listened attentively as he continued his reminiscence.

"Ma'd put a slab of beef in an old iron kettle and roast it in the Dutch oven Pa had built in the fireplace. She'd cook it for hours, then she'd add a heap of potatoes and carrots . . . toss in some herbs . . . and little round onions all bubblin' in the juice. When we'd come in at sundown, the whole house would smell of it." He paused, slipping into a deep reverie.

The moment was too poignant to intrude upon, so Garnet waited in silence, hoping he'd continue. Suddenly, he snapped his head up and grinned sheepishly. Picking up a hazel nut, he cracked it with his pistol butt and handed the crushed nut to her.

Garnet studied it for a brief moment. "I wish this nut was a peach. A big, golden peach, juicy and sweet. Back home, we had a peach tree just outside my bedroom window. In the spring it was full of tiny, sweet-smelling pink blossoms. I used to lay in bed at night breathing in their fragrance. It broke my heart when we lost that tree."

"How'd you lose it? Yankees couldn't commandeer a tree."

"No, but they did the next worst thing. There'd been a skirmish nearby and one of their shells went astray.

Missed the house, but lopped off the top of the tree. It never bloomed again," she said sadly.

"Told you it's plumb loco to ponder on things that are lost," he said.

"I don't think it hurts to hold on to sweet memories—like the taste of peach juice running down my chin or the aroma of that beef roasting in the oven. It's the bitter ones we mustn't dwell on."

"Well, you can savor your sweet memories, Widow Scott. I prefer to chew on my bitter ones." He lay back and plopped his hat over his eyes.

"Don't choke on your bitterness, Flint," she whispered tenderly, for her ears alone. She curled up and went to sleep.

The first thing she did upon waking the next morning was to hurry over to the trap. A squirrel had wandered into the snare. "It's not much for the two of us, but it's better than nothing," she told herself.

Garnet started to gather sticks for the fire. Then, from the corner of her eye, she caught a movement in the nearby boulders. The flat head and lidless eyes of a reptile poked out from an opening in the rocks. The rattler dropped silently to the ground, and the yellowish-brown body with its ringed tail slithered across the ground toward the caged squirrel that had begun chattering with fright.

"Oh, no, you don't," Garnet declared, "that's our breakfast, not yours." She picked up several stones and tossed them at the reptile to divert it. Her ploy worked and the snake wriggled away.

Garnet built a fire, and had just put the coffee pot on when she caught a movement again, this time near Flint's sleeping body. The snake appeared to be sunning itself on the rocks right above Flint's head. If Flint awoke and shifted, he would be in striking range of the reptile. If she tried tossing stones again, they could roll off the rocks and hit Flint, causing him to wake and sit up. And, as usual, he had the weapons.

She grabbed a long, sturdy stick and approached cautiously. "Flint. Flint," she whispered. "Wake up, and don't move a muscle. There's a snake on the rock right above your head."

He opened his eyes. "I heard you. Just stay where you're at. I'll figure something out."

She saw it was too late. The snake reared up and coiled to strike, the ominous rattle a chilling signal. Garnet lashed out with the stick and knocked the snake aside, but winced with pain as the serpent's venomous fangs grazed her hand. Flint jumped to his feet, and before the rattler could squirm away the bowie knife pinned it to the ground. He crushed the snake's skull with a rock, then released the embedded bowie and decapitated the reptile.

He hurried back to Garnet. "Did it get you?"

"Yes."

He snatched the bandanna from around his neck and quickly tied a tourniquet around her upper arm. Then he sat her down gently. "Don't move, I'll be right back."

"I've got more sense than to move after a snakebite. Remember, I'm a Georgia Cracker. I was even bit by a cottonmouth once."

"That doesn't surprise me, since you won't take orders," he mumbled, thrusting the bowie's blade into the flames. "Goddammit, I told you not to move, didn't I? What the hell were you trying to do?"

His words angered her. After all, she was the one who had been snakebit, not him. And while trying to protect his hide!

"I think that was pretty obvious, Mr. MacKenzie. I was trying to drive away the snake. It had its mind set on the squirrel I trapped."

He came back with the bowie and sat down. Grasping her right hand, he studied the two puncture marks on the fleshy part of her palm just below the thumb. "Take a deep breath, Widow Scott. As the saying goes, this is gonna hurt you worse than it does me."

Garnet clenched her teeth to keep from crying out as he cut a crisscross between the two marks. Then he lowered his mouth to the wound and sucked out the venom. Spitting it out, he repeated the action several times.

She yelped when he poured whiskey into the wound. Releasing the bandanna, he bound it in a figure eight around her wrist and hand.

"Looks like we can forget about going anywhere today," he said, "but at least we got rid of the worst of the poison before it could circulate. Just the same, you're gonna run a little fever, so let's get you to bed."

"I don't see any reason why I can't ride," she argued. She was beginning to feel dizzy and he seemed to be weaving back and forth. "Mr. MacKenzie, will you please stand still?"

Then she pitched forward into his arms.

Flint swooped her up and carried her into the cave. He knelt down and gently placed her on the blanket. Stubborn little fool, he thought affectionately as he studied her face. She'd probably be in for a rough ride for the next couple days. Well, she had more fight in her than a cornered bull.

His hand lingered on her cheek as he brushed aside the hair clinging to her face. He lightly traced a finger along the curve of her jaw.

To think he had once thought she wasn't beautiful. A man's eyes could sure play tricks on him at times— she was one hell of a beautiful woman.

He'd never forget the vision of her standing naked in that clearing with sunshine blazing on that red hair of hers, her ivory body tall and graceful, her long, slender legs, her firm, rounded breasts—full enough to fill a man's hands.

Those damn breasts of hers! They could drive a man wild thinking about them. He could still feel the sensation of them pressed against his back as she rode behind him on Sam.

And God, the taste of her!

That kiss earlier had set a fire in his loins that would take the whole Rio Grande to put out.

He placed his hand on her brow and discovered she was feverish already. All he could do now was try to keep her as comfortable as possible until the fever passed.

As he cut up the squirrel and made a soup with it, he watched her like a hawk. She slipped in and out of delirium, mumbling incoherently and thrashing wildly. There were times when he had to hold her down to keep her still. She constantly clutched at her neck as if she couldn't breathe. Those times scared him the most because he was afraid she was choking to death.

Not once did she open her eyes but remained unconscious, writhing in stages of delirium and hallucination. In her calmer moments, he held up her head and shoulders and forced the liquid down her throat. He knew she needed the nourishment to keep up the strength to fight the fever.

Throughout the night, he continued to nurse her: wiping the perspiration off her, keeping a cool rag on her brow, and forcing the soup or water down her whenever it was safe to do so.

By the next afternoon, he could tell she was getting better. She began resting more comfortably, the delirium appeared to be passing, and her temperature had dropped.

Garnet whirled through an alternating haze of light and darkness, heat and cold. At times, she cried with joy and reached out to caress her mother's cheek, and then suddenly beneath her fingertips, the image would change to the face of a painted savage and her joy would turn to terror, her laughter to sobs. She screamed and cringed in horror as a huge serpent slithered toward her, its fanged jaw gaping open to swallow her. Then she mercifully was lulled to calmness when the voice of Flint MacKenzie cut through the nightmare. Finally she drifted through the murkiness into fluffy, placid clouds.

Awakening to the sound of the crackle and pop of a fire, she opened her eyes and saw Flint sitting nearby, forking food into his mouth.

"Oh, my, I must have fainted," she said. "I'm sorry."

He glanced up from his eating. "You feeling better now?"

"Yes," she said hastily. "I can't remember ever fainting before."

He forked a piece of meat out of a skillet. "You hungry?"

"No, but I'd appreciate a drink of water."

He knelt down and held the canteen up to her mouth. "Not too much all at once," he cautioned. "And I think you better eat something too."

"I'm not hungry." She watched him walk back and fork meat from the skillet onto a tin plate.

Returning to her side, he handed her the plate and fork. "Eat this. You haven't eaten solid food for a couple days. You need to start building up your strength." He sat down again and picked up the skillet, using his fingers to eat.

"I ate rabbit yesterday morning, remember?"

"That was the day before yesterday. You didn't faint, Redhead, you've been unconscious for the past couple days."

She stared at him, astounded. "You mean I've been—"

"Burning up with fever since that snake bit you yesterday morning. Sure glad you finally came around.

Now eat," he ordered. "I'd like to get out of here by morning if you're up to it."

Still amazed, Garnet stabbed at the food, occasionally putting a bite into her mouth. "I can't believe I've been unconscious all this time." She gave him a grateful glance. "And you were kind enough to nurse me. I don't know how I can ever thank you."

"You can begin by not pulling any more of your fool stunts. At least not till we get to Comanche Wells. That's where we part company, Widow Scott."

Don't be so sure of that, Mr. MacKenzie, she thought confidently. She leaned back and took several bites of the meat. "This sure doesn't taste like any squirrel I've ever eaten. Tastes more like chicken."

"It's not squirrel. Ate that yesterday."

Smiling pleasantly, she glanced over to him. "What is it?"

"Snake."

The fork clanged against the metal plate. "Snake!" She swallowed past the lump that had suddenly formed in her throat.

"Yep." He picked up a piece and popped it into his mouth. "Same snake that bit you."

The thought was appalling to her. She slammed down the plate with such force that the fork flew up into the air and landed at his feet. Picking it up, he looked at her, perplexed. "If you're not going to eat that, I will."

As his words penetrated the roaring din in her head, Garnet felt as if she couldn't breathe. The man she intended to marry, the man who had saved her life, was an insensitive oaf! His indifference to her ordeal was difficult enough, but to have the effrontery to eat the very snake that bit her—and to feed it to her, too— was more than she could bear. Garnet clenched her hand into a fist and shook it at him. "You mark my words, Flint MacKenzie, if I have to live to be a hundred, I'll get even with you for this," she declared in a voice hoarse with outrage.

He shoved his hat off his forehead. "What the hell are you talking about?"

"Oh, you are a despicable, loathsome excuse for a human being," she continued. "To think I trusted you, considered you worthy of my respect. Why, you're lower than a . . . than a . . . snake's belly!"

"Lady, either you're still feverish, or just plain loco like I always thought."

"I'm not the one who's loco, Mr. MacKenzie. You are! How could you eat the very snake that bit me? Don't you have a conscience, sir? Then to have the audacity to feed it to me, too! Oh, you're a completely nasty man!"

"Lady, I figure the venom you're spewing ain't any worse than the snake's. I never took to listening to a mean-mouth woman, and I ain't gonna start now."

"Mean-mouth woman, indeed! You, sir, are the most unpleasant person I've ever had the misfortune to encounter. You just don't want to hear the truth about yourself, do you?" She rolled her eyes in disdain. "Oh, you're quick to remind me of my faults or stupidity, but now that the shoe's on the other foot, you don't want to hear it."

"Lady, I sure don't see as how you figure the shoe's on the other foot. I wasn't the one dumb enough to get snakebit."

"I suppose I should have just let it bite you."

"You should've just let it have the squirrel. Anyone who risks a rattler bite to save a squirrel's gotta be plain loco."

"Don't you mean that in your eyes, anyone who puts another's welfare ahead of their own is just plain loco?"

"Squirrel was gonna end up in somebody's belly anyway. 'Pears to me you were wrestlin' that snake 'cause you figured that belly was gonna be yours. That's not nobility, Widow Scott, that's hypocrisy."

The logic of his argument only angered her more. In her frustration, Garnet forgot her weakened condition and jumped to her feet to do further battle. A wave of pain slammed against her head. Her knees buckled, and the last thing she heard was Flint MacKenzie crying out, "Goddammit, not again!"

Chapter 6

It took Garnet several seconds to realize that the rhythmic motion beneath her was Sam's steady gait. Was she dreaming?

She opened her eyes. The glare of sunshine and the warmth of the arms around her were sensations too vibrant to be part of a dream. Sitting up, she discovered she had been cushioned against Flint's body.

"So you finally came to." His voice sounded at her ear.

Now fully awake, she realized they were astride Sam, and Flint was holding her in the circle of his arms.

"What happened?" she asked, in somewhat of a stupor. "I can't believe I passed out again."

"You got your feathers ruffled over a few bites of snake meat. 'Pears to me like you're set on letting that snake kill you—one way or another!"

She shook her head to clear the cobwebs that seemed to cloud her thinking. "Well, where are we?"

"If I calculated right, I figure as soon as we top this rise, we oughta be in eyeshot of Comanche Wells."

"You mean I've been unconscious all day again?"

"You passed out last night. But since you're over the fever and you're breathing normal, it made no sense to wait around until you woke up. So I figured it was safe to move you as long as Sam was willing to carry a double load."

"Am I to believe you asked Sam if he'd mind?"

"Sam and I have been together for a stretch of time, and we've gotten to know each other pretty good by now. We kind of look out for each other. He knows I don't think he's a pack mule, and I know I can depend on him when I need him."

"It must have taken a lot of horse sense between the two of you to come to such an understanding," Garnet said sarcastically.

"Yeah, it takes some doing, but Sam and I just kind of cozied real easy like into each other's habits."

"I may be the one who was bitten by a snake, Mr. MacKenzie, but I'm afraid you've been in the sun too long." Shaking her head, Garnet relaxed and leaned back against him.

"You sure smell good, Widow Scott," he whispered in her ear. "I've been enjoying the ride. You toting around some of that fancy eastern toilet water?"

"Of course not. I used to have some Attar of Rose, but I left the bottle behind in the wagon. You know I've lost everything I had except for those few pieces of clothing stuffed in your saddlebags."

"Well, you sure didn't lose your scent. You smell part like the sweet-smelling rosemary plant Ma used to raise in her garden and part . . ."

Garnet turned her head and looked into his sapphire eyes. "Part what?" she asked, her curiosity fully whetted by his hesitation.

He dropped his gaze to her mouth. "Part woman." A shiver raced down her spine in response to his husky murmur. "I could find you blindfolded, Redhead."

For a brief second their lips hovered only inches apart, then she quickly turned her head away from the temptation. Garnet leaned back in his arms again and tried to relax. This time it was more difficult. His words echoed over and over in her ears, stimulating her passion like an aphrodisiac. He was the most exciting man she had ever met; resisting him was harder than she once believed.

Then she smiled, relieved he couldn't see her face. Attar of Rose! So she had discovered another thing he liked. And his repeated references to her red hair couldn't be ignored either.

Roast beef . . . Attar of Rose . . . red hair. For a man who claimed he didn't need a woman to clutter up his life, the list of things he liked about women was getting longer every day.

They continued the ride in silence until they crested the rise, then Flint reined up and dismounted. "We'll rest Sam for a spell." He reached up and swung her off the horse. "That's Comanche Wells down there."

With unabashed astonishment, Garnet gazed at the valley below. In the distance, the houses and structures of Comanche Wells looked like a wooden oasis set in the midst of a wasteland. Nature had provided a flat plain devoid of any hill or rock formation, and the good citizens of the town had carried the barrenness to a greater length: with the exception of telegraph poles, for a mile stretching in each direction every tree, shrub, cactus, or piece of sagebrush had been removed. The town had virtually become a natural citadel. Neither man nor beast—nor marauding Indian—could approach unobserved.

"How many people live there?" Garnet asked.

"Couple hundred, I reckon. At least there were the last time I passed through. That's not counting the neighboring ranchers. You'll be able to send a wire to Santa Fe or catch a stage there."

"How long do you intend to remain in town, Mr. MacKenzie?"

"Most likely a couple of days."

She would have to think of something quickly. Two days wasn't long to formulate and execute a plan to make him take her with him. For no matter what Flint MacKenzie had in mind, she did not intend to part company with him.

"We best get moving. I'll help you mount. Do you feel strong enough now to ride alone?"

"I'd like to walk too, if you don't mind," she said.

"Reckon Sam sure won't mind, but watch your step." Together they descended the trail leading down into the valley.

As they approached Comanche Wells, Garnet saw that what had appeared from a distance to be narrow rivulets were actually ruts made by the countless horses, wagons, and stagecoaches that had traveled to and from the town. "Where's their source of water?" she asked, studying the barren plain.

"The town's built over a natural underground spring. Some of the folks have dug their own wells, but many use the community one in the center of town. Twenty-five years ago, this same area was all woods, and a favorite drinking spot for the Comanche until the white man decided to build a town here. After the Comanche attacked them a few times, the folks got wise and cut down everything surrounding the town. With no cover, the Indians didn't have much of a chance against rifles. So they pulled out."

"You mean we just took it from them?" she asked. "That's as bad as what those Yankee carpetbaggers did to the South after the war."

"Lady, this is a big country. Plenty of land for everybody, and there's no reason to be killing each other over it. If you've got any second thoughts about that, just remember what happened to those people you knew in the wagon train." He tugged on Sam's reins and walked ahead of her.

Once within the town, Garnet saw that the newer buildings were made of stone or adobe. Most of the older, wooden structures appeared weatherbeaten and showed the effects of twenty-five years of sun and rain.

Flint halted in front of a large, wooden building painted with whitewash. A sign tacked to the front of a second-floor balcony identified it as the hotel.

He dug into his saddlebags and pulled out her bundle of clothes. "I reckon this is where we part company." He handed her the bundle and two gold eagles. "This'll get you a room, some clothes, and a ticket on the stage, Mrs. Scott."

"I can't take your money, Mr. MacKenzie."

He grinned and shoved it into her hand. "It ain't much. Wish it were more."

"You've done so much for me already. Just saying 'thank you' sounds so inadequate." She glanced around, visibly uncomfortable, and she wanted to hug him just to feel his arms around her again. Instead, she reached out and put her hand on his arm, drawing his attention back to her. "I owe you my life, Flint."

Their gazes locked and for a long moment they stared deeply into each other's eyes. "Nobody owes anyone else for their life. Life and death are destiny."

"Destiny!" She thought her eyes would pop out of her head, and had to restrain herself from jumping up and down. "Do you believe in destiny, too?"

"Yeah, I reckon so. Well, you take care of yourself, Redhead," he said gently. He turned and led Sam toward the stable.

Garnet watched Flint until he was out of sight, then took a long look at the hotel. She squared her shoulders, drew a deep breath, and stepped up on the planked walk.

The lobby was dominated by a wide, carpeted staircase leading to the floor above. The tinkle of a piano sounded from beyond a pair of swinging doors off to one side.

Two men were engaged in a heated argument behind the registration desk, so Garnet walked over and peeked through the swinging doors into a smoke-filled barroom. She turned up her nose, then walked back and sat down on one of the lobby's half-dozen red velvet chairs. As she waited impatiently for the argument to end, she couldn't help but hear the heated exchange.

"I warned you for the last time about drinking on duty, Wallace. Get out of here and don't come back," declared the shorter, heavier-set man. Puffs of smoke from the cigar clenched between his teeth punctuated each word.

"My pleasure, Mr. Closky," the other man replied. "I've taken all your cussin' I have a mind to. Good luck in findin' a desk clerk, 'cause I don't think there's another man in this town fool enough to work for a skinflint like you." He thumped across the floor and slammed the door on his way out.

Garnet walked up to the desk. "Whatta you want?" Closky grumbled without glancing up.

"A room, sir."

Hearing a feminine voice made him look up in surprise. She saw his expression change to suspicion at the sight of her dressed in Flint's shirt and trousers, her hair tied back with a piece of rawhide. "You new in town, sister?"

"Just arrived."

He shifted the cigar to the other side of his mouth. "How long you planning on staying?"

"Probably a couple of nights."

"Room's a dollar a night." He shoved the register at her. "In advance," he added pointedly.

"I have a proposition, Mr. Closky," she said.

"Not interested, sister. Town's full of whores. Even got a couple working the barroom. If you don't have a buck for the room, move on. This is a respectable hotel. Go down to the Golden Slipper, you might get lucky there. Although with that getup you're wearing, I can't promise."

The thought that this unpleasant little man believed she would prostitute herself simply for a night's lodg-

ing infuriated Garnet. She wanted to shove that cigar
down his throat. Instead, she held her tongue.

Smiling sweetly, she said, "Mr. Closky, I couldn't
help but hear your argument with your recently dis-
charged clerk. Since I expect to remain in town for a
short while, I'm willing to take the job in exchange for
a room."

He eyed her warily. "Night clerk's not a job for a
woman, sister."

"Sir, I've faced Yankees during the war and have just
survived an Indian massacre. I think I could handle
this desk for a couple nights."

"Were you with that wagon train the Comanche
wiped out east of here 'bout a week ago?"

"Yes, I was."

She saw he had enough decency to look contrite. "I
heard there were no survivors."

"You heard wrong, sir. I was fortunate enough to be
found by a Mr. MacKenzie."

"Flint MacKenzie!"

"That's right."

"You got lucky, lady. If anybody could get you
through, he could." He snorted. "MacKenzie's too
mean to die."

Garnet quickly jumped to the defense of the man she
intended to marry. "Mr. Closky, I found Mr. MacKenzie to be noble and courageous," she declared indignantly. "I will not stand here and listen to you speak ill
of him. Do I have the job, or don't I?"

He shifted the cigar to the side of his mouth and
stroked his chin. "Reckon it'll take me a couple of days
to find a new clerk. Can you read?"

"Of course."

"Not just printing, sister. I'm talking about writing
too."

"I am not your sister, sir. My name is Mrs. Scott. As
to your question, I certainly can read. Script, print—or
man."

With a part grin and part snort, Closky nodded. "You're all right, Mrs. Scott." He shoved a key at her. "Okay, but the deal don't include meals. Upstairs, number 6 at the end of the hall. Hurry back."

"I do need time to bathe and press my clothes."

He motioned toward a door near the rear of the lobby. "Go find Juanita; she's probably in the kitchen. She'll take care of it. Try to be back here in an hour. I have to get home for dinner. It's my kid's birthday."

"I shall do my best, sir." Garnet picked up the key and hurried to the kitchen. She found the Mexican maid talking to the cook.

After making arrangements with Juanita, Garnet went next door to the general store and quickly picked out underclothing, a pair of stockings, and several necessary toilet articles—a tiny bottle of Attar of Rose toilet water among them.

The hasty trip didn't take more than ten minutes, and by the time she returned, Juanita had a hot bath waiting for her. As much as Garnet would have liked to luxuriate in the steamy water, she took time only to bathe and shampoo her hair.

The bed in her room looked inviting. The thought of stretching out for a change on a mattress with sheets and pillow was tempting enough to tell Mr. Closky to find himself a different desk clerk. However, she toweled her hair and put on the new camisole and pantalets. She had just finished when Juanita tapped on the door and came in carrying her pressed clothing and polished boots.

"Oh, you're a saint, Juanita," Garnet exclaimed, pulling on the bodice and skirt. "I'm not used to being waited on."

"*Gracias, señora.*"

With time running out, all that remained was her hair. When she began to struggle with it, Juanita took the brush out of her hand. "May I help you, *señora?*"

"Oh, thank you, Juanita. I feel like I'm all thumbs."

"You have lovely hair, *señora*," Juanita said. Within minutes she had pulled back the mass of red hair and woven it into a single long plait.

An hour after she had left the lobby, Garnet reappeared at the desk. Closky's pleasure at the change in her appearance was apparent. "You sure had me fooled, sister. You look halfway decent when you're prettied up." His leer got her back up.

"I am not your sister, sir. My name is Mrs. Scott," Garnet corrected.

"So you said." He grabbed his hat and covered his bald head with it. "Well, mind what you're doing. And remember, nobody gets a room without paying first. I'll be back to relieve you in the morning."

"Yes, sir."

"If you've got a problem, call Juanita. She sleeps in a room off the kitchen. Your job is to stay awake. Sometimes saddle tramps sneak in and slip into a room. Come morning, they skedaddle with no one the wiser. So keep your eyes open."

"I certainly will, sir," Garnet said, sighing with relief as he departed.

Garnet immediately checked the register, but Flint's name was not there. She wondered where he was and what he was doing. Probably with some woman, she thought, and felt a tug at her heart. Well, she would change all that, she told herself—as soon as she figured out how.

The raised voices and laughter of people in the bar carried to her ear. Hoping to see Flint, she walked over to the swinging doors and peeked in again. She saw no sign of him.

Back at the desk, she propped her elbows on the glossy surface and rested her chin in her hands. At least somebody's having a good time, she thought glumly.

The time passed slowly and not a soul appeared in

the lobby. Before retiring, Juanita brought Garnet a sandwich and a glass of milk. She then left, warning Garnet not to mention it to Closky. Garnet found herself alone again.

She saw no reason to sit on the uncomfortable wooden chair behind the desk, so she moved to a plush velvet chair, wishing she had a book or newspaper to read. Her eyes began to feel heavy and she tried to shake off the drowsiness.

"What the hell are you doing here, Mrs. Scott?"

The sharp question awakened her. She opened her eyes to discover Flint MacKenzie scowling down at her.

"Oh, my!" she exclaimed, jumping to her feet. "Hello, Mr. MacKenzie. I must have fallen asleep."

"You damn well better believe you did! And what the hell are you doing sitting here sleeping in the lobby? I gave you money for a room."

"Well, I figured I could save room rent by—"

Flint shoved the hat off his forehead. "Lady, don't you have any brains under that head of red hair?"

"If you'd let me finish, Mr. MacKenzie, I was about to tell you that I've been hired as the night desk clerk in exchange for a free room. Quite enterprising of me, wouldn't you say?"

"I sure wouldn't. This town's pretty wild. 'Bout time you remember you're not back in your snug little town in Georgia."

"I thought you believed in destiny, Mr. MacKenzie."

"Destiny? I was referring to dying, Widow Scott. A lot can happen to a person before that, and it ain't always pleasant."

"Oh, really!" she said sarcastically. "I never would have guessed. Of course, why should I? I've only lost my family and been widowed twice. Not to mention the war." She stormed over to the desk.

He followed her. "Well, my advice to you is go back

where you belong 'cause you ain't got a snowball's chance in hell of lasting here." He stalked to the swinging doors.

"When I want your advice, I'll ask for it, Flint MacKenzie!" she shouted at his back as he entered the barroom.

Chapter 7

After stewing for several more minutes, Garnet gradually realized anger was no way to convince Flint MacKenzie he couldn't live without her. Despite his muleheadedness, nothing would be gained by acting equally stubborn.

As the evening progressed, the thought of how she had driven him away began to wear on her conscience. Only the noise from the barroom kept her spirits from sinking lower.

Finally, as the music and laughter grew louder, Garnet walked over, opened the doors, and glanced in. Hoping to catch Flint's attention, she caught instead the attention of a drunken young cowboy near the door.

"Look at that, Joey, the little lady wants to come in," he said.

Before she could guess his intent, the cowboy grabbed her arm and pulled her up against the bar. "No call to be shy. Come right in, little lady. I'm Jeb Boone and this is my brother Joey. We'll buy you a drink."

The two brothers were both blue eyed and blond haired; they looked enough alike to be twins and not a day older than eighteen. *If that*, she thought. She realized they meant no harm, but simply had had too

75

much to drink. "No thanks, gentlemen," she said good-naturedly. "I have to get back to my job."

"Sure don't sound right for you to be working while the rest of us are having a good time," Joey said. "Just have one little drink?"

"No, thank you." She glanced at the nearest table. "I'm just looking for . . ." Recognizing one of the men, she stopped and gasped in surprise. "Mr. Moore!"

One of the men at the table stood up. A dark, shaggy beard covered his chin and cheeks. Ponderous in size, he stood at least eight inches over six feet and had a flabby girth that bulged over the top of his belt. If his size wasn't intimidating enough, he had a black bullwhip wound loosely around his left shoulder.

His thick, bushy brows were knit in a frown as he looked at her. "You look kinda familiar, sister, but I can't remember where I seen you before."

"I'm sure you'd rather not remember, sir, since I was on the wagon train that you so cowardly deserted."

Moore's eyes narrowed until they looked like two black beads. "Nobody calls Bullwhip Moore a coward, sister. Man or woman," he bellowed.

Garnet thrust up her chin defiantly. "I certainly am calling you one." The room quieted. Even the piano player stopped to listen, and all attention was fixed on her. "And I think these other men will agree when they hear what I have to say."

"You best leave now, ma'am," Joey Boone said softly. Releasing her arm, he appeared to have gone cold sober in an instant. His brother Jeb looked just as solemn.

Having begun, Garnet had no intention of stopping until she finished speaking her mind. She turned her attention back to Moore. "You deserted the wagon train two days before the attack."

"I heard nobody survived that massacre."

Garnet glanced at this new speaker, who was seated

at Moore's table. "I was fortunate to be rescued," she declared. "No thanks to Mr. Moore."

"Who rescued you?" the man asked.

"A Mr. MacKenzie," she said defiantly. "Your Mr. Moore left without even warning us about the Indian signs and the danger of our situation."

"She don't know what she's talking about," Moore denied.

"You're a liar, sir. A coward and a liar."

"Them's pretty mean words to make about a man, lady. 'Specially in these parts," the seated man said.

"That doesn't make them any less true, Mr.—"

"Bodine. Nathan Bodine." In contrast to Moore's bulky frame, Bodine appeared to be half Moore's size and had a narrow face with a neatly trimmed moustache.

"Don't pay her no mind, Bodine," Moore grumbled. "She don't know what she's talking about."

"I know you were hired as our scout, Mr. Moore. That we depended upon you. And that you deserted us and left twelve wagons full of men, women, and children to be massacred."

A current of low murmurs arced around the room. "That true, Moore?" a man asked from one of the tables.

"Naw. The lyin' whore's got a grudge against me 'cause I never gave her a second look."

"You've got no cause to be callin' her names," Jeb Boone said, coming to her defense.

The huge bully turned his wrath on the cowboy. "Boy, you tellin' Bullwhip Moore what he can and can't do?"

"Don't you mean Bullshit Moore?" a new voice uttered calmly.

Garnet recognized the voice at once. Her heart leapt to her throat as she swung her glance to a far table in a darkened corner.

Flint MacKenzie stepped out of the shadows.

From the time Nathan Bodine and Bullwhip Moore had entered the barroom, Flint had sat in the corner unobserved. He couldn't help wondering what the two bastards were doing together. *Birds of a feather!* he reflected. Both men needed killing, and he despised one as much as the other. Moore was a cowardly bully, but Bodine was the more dangerous of the pair, a scheming sneak and back-stabbing murderer who usually succeeded in getting others to do his dirty work. Flint figured Bodine sure had found the right pigeon in Moore.

For as long as Flint could remember, Nathan Bodine had never been any good. They'd grown up in the same area of Texas and their paths had crossed often. He wondered what Bodine was doing out of prison since the bastard had knifed a Mexican in the back a couple of years ago. Flint knew that it was only due to his own testimony against Bodine that the sonofabitch had been sentenced to serve five years in the territory prison for the crime.

Flint downed his drink and poured another. For the next hour, he sat in silence, drinking and hoping to build up enough anger to start an argument with them.

When he had emptied the bottle, he tried to motion for another, but the bartender's attention was on a ruckus at the end of the bar. The moment Flint looked and saw the redhead, he knew there'd be trouble. What in hell was she doing in the barroom? The damn woman had a knack for sniffing out trouble like a hound dog with its nose in a skunk hole.

The two cowboys were probably harmless; nothing she couldn't handle. Then he cursed to himself when he saw that she had caught sight of Moore. Now all hell was about to break loose and she was right in the middle of it.

When Moore called her a whore, Flint shot to his

feet. It was plain to see that the young cowpokes didn't like it either, and now, more than likely, one or both of the well-meaning young fools were about to get killed. And that damn little redhead could get caught in the cross fire.

"Don't you mean Bullshit Moore?"

The words slipped past his lips before he even knew it.

"Who the hell said that?" Moore growled. He spun around and Flint saw his surprise when the bully recognized him. "Well, I'll be damned! So, you're the MacKenzie this gal's been talking about."

"That's right, Moore. And I'm inclined to agree with that cowpoke there. You owe the lady an apology. We don't take kindly to calling women names. And I can vouch that she's telling the truth. You deserted that train."

"You ready to back up that talk, MacKenzie?" With a flick of his shoulder, he slid the whip down his arm and into his hand.

Flint didn't move a muscle. "Try raising that whip, Moore, and I'll put a bullet through your hand." His gaze never wavered as the men seated at the tables between him and Moore scrambled to get out of the way. "And, Bodine, you keep your hands on the table where I can see them."

"So, MacKenzie, we meet again," Bodine remarked, his mouth curved in a smirk.

"Didn't expect to see you, Bodine. What'd you do, break out of jail?"

"They let me out for good behavior, MacKenzie."

"No accounting for how easy some people are fooled," Flint said.

Garnet spoke up. "Mr. MacKenzie, it's not necessary for you to get involved in this discussion."

Flint kept his gaze fixed on Moore and Bodine. "Get out of here, Mrs. Scott."

"I intend to, but not until I've said all I—"

"Ma'am, please listen to the man," Joey Boone said.

"You two get her out of here," Flint ordered.

Each brother took her by an arm. "Come along, ma'am," Jeb Boone urged.

"Hold up for a minute," Flint called to them. "Moore here still has something to say to the lady before she leaves."

Moore glanced nervously at Bodine. Despite the bully's big talk, Moore had begun to sweat, and after another hateful glare at Flint, he muttered, "Don't pay me no mind, lady. Guess it must have been the likker talking."

It was clear that Bodine's presence was keeping Moore in check. Flint could tell by the big man's stance that Moore wanted to put him to the test. Before there was further trouble, he said to Garnet, "You got an apology, Mrs. Scott, now get out of here."

"But—" she began. Before she could say another word, the Boone brothers forced her through the swinging doors.

"Now that the lady proved you to be the coward that you are, Moore, you and Bodine get on your horses and ride out of town."

Bodine's thin lips curled into a sinister smile as he slowly rose to his feet. "We were gettin' ready to leave anyway, MacKenzie, so don't think you're drivin' us away. But I'm thinkin' we'll meet again." He made no attempt to veil the threat. "Let's go, Bullwhip."

Moore's guys gleamed with malevolence. "Yeah, another time, MacKenzie."

"I can't wait, boys," Flint said with a mocking smile. He stepped aside for them to pass.

As soon as they left, an old-timer at a nearby table spoke up. "You best watch your back, son."

"Ain't hard sniffing a polecat when it gets too close, Pop," Flint said.

He headed for the swinging doors. He'd seen enough of the town. He'd head out in the morning after a good night's sleep—and a final look at the redhead.

He found Garnet alone, standing behind the desk. The moment she saw him, she burst out from behind it snarling like a she-wolf protecting her young.

"How dare you!" she raged. He liked the way her red hair gleamed like flame and her green eyes glowed like emeralds. Deepened with fury, that bedroom voice of hers sounded even huskier.

She was mad. Hopping mad. Sod-pawing, horn-tossing mad!

And so goddamned beautiful, it hurt to look at her. He wanted to double over from the ache in his loins.

"What's scratching at your craw now, Mrs. Scott?"

"Who do you think you are, Flint MacKenzie? How dare you tell those men to hustle me out of the room like a wayward child!"

"I did it for your own good."

"I'm capable of taking care of myself."

"I doubt that, or you'd've had enough sense to keep your mouth shut in there. You still haven't learned, have you? Things are different here. Some folks don't play by the rules. Bullwhip Moore is one of 'em."

"It's no different here than back east. Cowards and liars are the same no matter what part of the country they're in. And as long as people are afraid to speak up to them, they don't go away. I, for one, will not tolerate them."

"What you want to do with your own hide is your business, lady, but you could have gotten those two cowpokes killed for speaking up for you."

As his words sank in, she dropped her glance. "I hadn't thought about that."

"You better start thinking about it, especially if you're planning on settling out here. What happened to those cowpokes anyway? Hate to think of them tangling again with Moore and Bodine out on the street."

"I sent them upstairs to sleep off their drunk. I didn't stop to think that my actions might have endangered someone else." She raised her head and he could see that the fight had gone out of her. "But I can still take care of myself, Mr. MacKenzie, so if I need your help, I'll ask for it."

"Save your breath, 'cause you'll be spittin' in the wind. I've gotten you out of all the fixes I plan to. From now on, Widow Scott, you're on your own. And good riddance!" He slapped down a gold dollar. "Gimme a room. Time I got some sleep."

She shoved the dollar back at him. "Use my room. No sense in letting it go to waste since I have to stay down here all night anyway." She pulled a key out of her pocket and put it on the desk. "Number 6 at the end of the hall."

Amused, Flint arched a brow. "I'd think that would be against the rules, Mrs. Scott."

"Some rules are meant to be broken, Mr. Mac-Kenzie."

Her mischievous grin had a bewitching effect on the dimple in her chin. Which, much to his chagrin, began to have an equally tantalizing affect on his desire for her. He had to get away from the damned little temptress—fast. He clenched the key in his palm. "Number 6. End of the hall." She nodded and he headed for the stairway.

Flint entered the darkened room and closed the door. A shaft of moonlight enabled him to make out the shadowy outline of the bed in the corner. For several seconds he stood still with his back against the wall, letting his eyes adjust to the darkness. Then he became aware of it—a faint scent of roses. Her scent.

As if drawn by a magnet, he moved to the bed and picked up her discarded camisole. He raised it to his nose, then buried his face in the flimsy garment. Cursing himself for being a damn fool, he flung it down and crossed to the window, opened it, and for a long moment stared out at the deserted street. From somewhere in the silent night, he heard a clock toll midnight. Disgusted, he returned to the bed, shucked his gunbelt and hung it on a bedpost. Then he sat down and pulled off his boots and shirt. Yawning, he stretched out.

She just couldn't stay angry with him, Garnet reflected after Flint left. Lord knows he gave her good reason to be angry. Undoubtedly, he was the most unpleasant person she had ever known. He couldn't get along with anyone!

Yet she felt safe in his presence, and confident he would get her through any crisis. She certainly hadn't felt that way about either of her husbands. He was candid to a fault, but he was an honest, straightforward man and despite how much he tried to give a different impression, he lived by a code of honor. Those were good enough reasons to respect any man.

But there was a much deeper, more tangible reason that went far beyond respect, beyond her belief that he was her destiny. Were he the worst rogue in the west, the reason would still exist—her femininity responded to the masculine draw of him. He fascinated her. The way he moved his tall, lithe body excited her. His kiss aroused her.

Why didn't she simply succumb to her body's cravings? Why had she denied the truth to him? Why in the name of common sense had she lied to him? Pretended that his kiss hadn't ignited a fire he continued to fuel with his every touch, with every glance from his mesmerizing sapphire eyes?

And no matter how he tried to disguise it, Garnet knew he desired her just as much. She was woman enough to recognize those signs in him. Even at this moment, he was lying upstairs wanting her. She closed her eyes with the excitement that realization provoked.

And there was a way to make him want her even more.

"I'm sorry, Mr. Closky, for abandoning the post you entrusted to me," she said to herself. "This empty lobby will just have to get by without my company until morning." She shifted her glance to the stairway. "There's a more urgent need for me elsewhere."

She climbed the stairs to the floor above.

When Flint heard the clock strike one, he gave up trying to sleep. Sitting up, he propped the pillows behind his back and stared gloomily into the darkness, cursing himself for being a fool. What in hell was wrong with him? He should have found himself a whore to purge that damn redhead out of his thoughts once and for all.

At the sound of a light creak, he swung his head to the door and reached simultaneously for his Colt. He waited as the door opened slowly. Had Bodine and Moore decided to come back after all? Then he recognized the figure that slipped through the opening and quickly shut the door.

"That's a good way of getting yourself shot. You still haven't learned, have you, Widow Scott?"

Chapter 8

‿‿◦‿○◯○‿◦‿‿

Although it was too dark to see, Garnet could feel Flint's eyes on her as she leaned against the door, letting her vision adjust. Then she saw him sitting on the bed. Moonlight glimmered on his bare shoulders and chest, but his face remained in shadow. He moved his hand toward the lamp.

"No, don't light it," she said.

She began to tremble. Don't let me lose my nerve now, she prayed silently. Her legs were shaking so badly she thought she'd have to sit down. She kicked off her shoes and took a step closer to the bed, feeling all thumbs as she undid the buttons of her bodice.

"Thought I made myself clear downstairs, Widow Scott. I've gotten you out of all the fixes I plan to. You shuck that bodice, and there ain't gonna be no turning back."

"I remember telling you I can take care of myself." She slipped off the blouse and threw it aside.

"You call this taking care of yourself? You've gotta be dumber than a housecat sniffing out a skunk. You ain't got the faintest notion of what kind of trouble you're in right now, do you?"

"Then why don't you tell me, Flint?" she taunted, deliberately releasing the tie on her skirt. It dropped

85

around her ankles and she stepped out of it, moving closer to the bed. Now only her camisole, pantalets, and hose remained.

"I've told you in every way I know how, lady. I ain't young Bobby Joe or ole Freddy. There ain't no wedding strings that go with this. Come morning, I'm out of here."

"So you've said." She reached down and slipped the stocking off one leg, then did the same to the other. Tossing them over the foot of the bed, she moved to the bedside.

"Goddammit, woman! I ain't just chawing wind! I mean it."

"That's a chance I'm just going to have to take." Nudity had never embarrassed her; unhesitatingly, she removed her camisole and pantalets.

She stood naked before him, wondering what her next move should be. Plain determination had gotten her this far, but that resolve was dwindling as rapidly as her confidence. Maybe this was a mistake. What if she couldn't satisfy him? Or worse yet, what if she was so inept, he laughed at her? She'd die! She'd die of mortification right on the spot!

"Your hair. Don't forget your hair, Widow Scott." His composure unnerved her more. She was no longer in command.

He had taken control.

She quickly freed the braid, unwound it, then combed her fingers through her hair. As an added measure, she shook it out. Her hair fluttered around her head then settled on her shoulders. Dropping her hands to her sides, she waited for his next move.

Enveloped in lust, Flint swept his hungry gaze along her nakedness. He had seen her naked in the sunshine, but that vision paled in comparison to seeing her bathed in moonlight. The curves and recesses of her body were cast in mysterious shadows, and her mane of red hair tumbled around her shoulders like a wild vixen's. He was hot and hard. He had never wanted a woman as much as he wanted her.

"By my calculations, Widow Scott, we've got about five hours till daylight. 'Bout time we stop wasting them."

He reached out and pulled her down into his arms, crushing her lips with his own. There was nothing gentle about the kiss. There was no need to be. This moment had been inevitable from the first time their eyes had met across a campfire. Pent-up desire left no need to arouse passion; the explosion came with the first touch of their lips. She was flooded with an exquisite sensation as energizing as it was thrilling.

He pushed her aside, released the belt on his buckskins, and shoved down his pants and underwear, kicking them off impatiently. Then he lay back, pulling her across him, her breasts flattened against the muscular wall of his chest. She stretched out on top of him—flesh against flesh. Reaching up, he buried his hands in her thick hair. "No strings, Redhead."

She raised her head enough to look into his eyes. The sight of his desire only inflamed her own. "None that you'll be aware of, Flint." Driven by a need to taste him, she kissed him.

He trapped her legs in his and rolled her over. When she felt his hard arousal press against her, she opened her mouth in a gasp of pleasure. His tongue slipped in to plunder.

She was breathless when he broke away to trail a path of kisses to her breasts. With a moist rasp of his tongue, he toyed with the hardened nipples until he took one into his mouth. She arched convulsively, thrusting herself tighter against his mouth. Her response became uninhibited, his hands unrestrained.

Hungrily, she opened her mouth to his when he reclaimed her lips. Driven by sensory excitement, she was drawn to a height of passion she had never known and was shocked by her own response—a desire for him that overrode reason. Surrendering control, she allowed her mouth, her tongue, and her hands to explore on their own, discovering his body as he did hers.

Drugged with passion, she swirled in a state of sensation: her ears absorbed his groans, her mind the realization of the male power now unleashed beneath her fingertips and mouth.

She had always been aware of her own sensuality—a lustiness that neither of her husbands had ever attempted to satisfy or even encourage.

Now with abandon she experienced the satisfaction of answering this craving. She was able to fulfill her sensuality with no thought toward a sense of shame or limitations—the reservations she had suffered with her husbands.

For with every move, gasp, groan, and whispered word of approval, Flint encouraged and welcomed this attention, matching it with his own urgent needs, raising her passion to even newer and higher levels.

They touched, tasted, explored—and savored.

Her mouth was throbbing from his kisses, and passion pounded through her mind and body. She felt another moment would be unbearable—yet she prayed it would never end.

Then he drove into her. Tightening around him, she closed her eyes and gasped with consummate pleasure—body and mind ravished by pure euphoria and exquisite sensation.

Together they soared to a rapturous climax.

After several moments, she struggled back to the reality of the mortal confines of her body—aware again of the pain in drawing a breath, of the ache in her chest from the pounding of her heart.

Feeling his touch on her cheek, she opened her eyes and met his baffled stare. He gently brushed back the strands of hair clinging to her face.

"God, woman, if you always made love like that, it's no wonder you're a widow!" He rolled off her and lay outstretched.

Turning onto her side, she leaned on an elbow and gazed down at him. "You're always in character, MacKenzie. I'd think you'd be gallant enough to at least thank me," she said, smiling.

"You should thank *me*," he replied, grinning back at her. "I warned you what coupling with a real man would be like."

"So you claim all the credit? I think this time it was different for you, too, Flint. Remember, I warned you that you'd fall in love with me."

He snorted. "Love! Love had nothing to do with it. We fornicated, Widow Scott. Call it by what it was."

"You can say what you want to, but I know differently," she said smugly.

"Like hell you do, lady. We fornicated!" Irritation had crept into his voice. "That's all there was to it."

She cut off his outburst with a kiss. "We made love, Flint," she corrected, tracing his lips with her tongue.

"Pretty words won't change what it was, little widow. Hope you ain't thinking I'd ever believe otherwise."

"Oh, you will someday," she said and kissed him again.

He slipped his arms around her waist and drew her against him. "I'm willing to admit one thing, Red-head," he murmured in a husky whisper at her ear.

"What?" she asked breathlessly as he nibbled deliciously at her lobe.

"Your mama may have been right about that little diversionary trick she taught you. It sure works like hell when you catch a man feeling horny."

She settled in against him, and to her pleasure, felt his renewed arousal. Raising her head, she grinned at him. "I'll admit something to you, too: a lot can be said for making love with a real man, MacKenzie." Boldly, she slipped her hand down the length of his body until she reached his shaft. Pausing only momentarily, she lightly fondled it. She felt the rise of passion again, sweeping through her like a hot fire, exciting her mind and body. The tempo of her movements escalated until the organ in her hand throbbed with a heat and pulse of its own.

Groaning, he pulled her head down and kissed her hungrily. Raising his mouth from hers, he gazed into her eyes. "Who taught you *that* trick, the kid or the old man?" he asked hoarsely.

"I've been saving it just for you, Flint."

He rolled over, pinned her beneath him, and grinned down at her. "Reckon there's worse ways of dying, but go easy on me this time, will ya, Widow Scott? I've got no hankerin' to join your husbands six feet under."

The sun had risen by the time Flint woke up. Garnet was snuggled next to him. So as not to wake her, he eased himself away, and she settled back. They had touched, kissed, and explored each other throughout the night, until at last, they finally slept.

For a long time, he stared down at her. She sure was a lot of woman. Tempting enough to make a man forget he was the roving kind. Best she not know that he'd never had such sex before. She sure knew how to pleasure a man, all right, and at the same time, let him know how much he was pleasuring her. It was no put-on either, like them faking whores. Every groan and sigh that had come out of her had been genuine. The redhead had enjoyed it.

He dressed hurriedly. He'd be wise to ride off as soon as he could; she was too much temptation for any man. Just thinking about her made him hard again.

After he strapped on his gunbelt, he stopped for one last, lingering look at her face relaxed in slumber.

Asleep, she was prettier than ever. She looked like a young girl, surely too young to be widowed twice.

"You're a real handful, but I warned you—no strings. Take care of yourself, Redhead," he said softly.

He felt his loins begin to knot. Lest he gave in to the urge to crawl back in bed, kiss her awake, and have her once more, he plopped on his hat and departed hastily.

Garnet awoke with a feeling of exuberance. Her lips felt plump from his kisses and her body still tingled from his touch. She turned her head and discovered he was gone; but then, she expected he would be. Flint was not the kind to lie in bed waiting for her to wake. He did what he wanted to do, just like any other man. A man's life had always appeared easy to her— whereas a woman had to toil and struggle day after day with, more times than not, man as the enemy. *Ah, but Flint's not my enemy*, she thought to herself in the glorious afterglow of the previous night.

She got up and glanced down at her naked body. It looked the same, yet it felt different to her. *She* felt different! For the first time in her adult life, she exalted in the knowledge that she was a woman.

Walking over to a wall mirror above the dresser, Garnet took a long look at her reflected image: her cheeks were flushed and her eyes had a glow she had never seen before. She grasped her cheeks between her hands. "You're in love, Garnet Scott." *For the first time in your twenty-six years you are truly . . . deeply . . . irrevocably in love. For the first time in your life you've found someone who can take care of you—yet needs you as much as you need him—whether he's willing to admit it or not!*

"He'll admit it someday," she vowed.

For some reason, she had survived when so many others had perished. And now it seemed that every tragedy in her life had led her to this time, this place— this man. Surely they were meant to be together.

For a brief moment, a sobering thought brought her up short. Could she be fooling herself? Was she being misled by the cravings of her body?

Of course not! She was no blushing virgin. She had lain with two men before Flint. She had experienced arousal. Yet neither of her husbands had left her feeling as she did now.

In the beginning, she might have decided Flint MacKenzie was her destiny simply out of practicality—the same reason she had married Frederick Scott. Flint had been there and she'd needed his help. But now, what she felt for Flint confirmed her belief that their love had been predestined.

She would spend eternity with him.

If she could find him!

Smiling, she turned away to dress. Shortly after, with Juanita's help, she prepared a bath and reluctantly washed away the evidence of Flint's lovemaking. Then she dressed quickly and skipped down the stairway in search of her lover.

Instead, she met a furious Ralph Closky, cigar crammed in the corner of his mouth, waiting at the foot of the stairway. "So there you are!" he declared angrily. "I was just coming up to look for you."

She wondered if the puffs of smoke above his head were fumes of anger. "Good morning, Mr. Closky, how was your son's birthday party?"

"Don't change the subject, Mrs. Scott. Where have you been? You were supposed to stay at this desk until I relieved you."

"I'm sorry, but no one registered the whole evening, so I finally went upstairs to my room."

"Whatta you mean? Two cowboys just came downstairs. I don't see their names on the register."

"Oh, the Boone brothers. Well you see, Mr. Closky, they helped me out of a difficult situation in the barroom, so in gratitude, I gave them a room."

"The barroom?" Two more puffs of smoke floated in the air. "What in hell were you doing in the barroom?"

"I was looking for someone."

"Who?"

"I don't believe that's your concern, sir."

"I told you I ain't running no charity house. You're fired, Mrs. Scott, and you owe me a dollar for the room you handed out to them cowpokes. I oughta charge you for your room too, since you didn't do the job you were hired to do."

"I stayed down here until after one o'clock, sir. That was long enough." She dug into her skirt pocket and slapped a dollar down on the desk. "Here's your money for the room the Boone brothers used, but I'm not paying for mine."

"Well then, pack up and get out of here. I don't want your kind in my hotel."

Garnet put her hands on her hips. "My kind! Please explain just what you mean by that, sir."

"I want you out of here in the next five minutes. Bag and baggage, lady."

"It shall be my pleasure, sir." Garnet spun on her heel and stomped up the stairs. She figured she would find lodging elsewhere until Flint was ready to leave town.

She tied her few belongings and Flint's shirt and trousers in the piece of paper she had gotten at the general store. Then, descending the stairway, she flounced past Mr. Closky without a sideways glance.

Once outside, she had no idea where to look for Flint. Since the town wasn't very big, it shouldn't be difficult to find him. At once, she spied his tall back as he stood talking to a man in front of the stage office. Garnet hurried over and stopped when she picked up the gist of their conversation. Pausing, she stepped into the shadows to listen.

"You'll only have to ride shotgun to Waynesburg,

Flint. Stinger wired here and said they'd have a replacement waiting."

"How's Gallager doing?" Flint asked.

"Doc dug the Comanche arrows out of him and said he should be able to get back to work in a week. I'll be able to pick him up on my return trip. Appreciate your helping me out, Flint," the man said.

"I was heading in that direction anyway, so it's no trouble. Besides, I don't turn down the chance to make some honest money."

"I'm due to pull out in ten minutes."

"Just give me time to get my dun from the livery. I'll tie him to the back of the stage."

So he was leaving town, Garnet thought gloomily. And without even saying good-bye! Rather than face him with the accusation, she sank deeper into the shadows when he passed.

Her course was clear. She knew he would be furious when he discovered she had followed him, but if she didn't act fast, he would be gone. She entered the stage office, bought a ticket to Waynesburg, and was ensconced in the coach by the time he returned. She slouched down in her seat as he tied Sam to the back of the stage. To her relief, he didn't even glance inside before climbing up on the seat beside the driver.

Garnet sat up and smiled at the three other passengers. One looked like a drummer and the other two appeared to be newlyweds.

She flashed them all a bright smile. "Nice day for a ride, isn't it?"

Chapter 9

$\mathbf{G}$ arnet passed the fifty-mile trip to Waynesburg chatting amiably with the whiskey drummer beside her and the newlywed couple who were on their way to Santa Fe. When the driver stopped to rest the horses, she pretended she was asleep and remained inside the carriage.

The stagecoach reached Waynesburg late that afternoon. Garnet remained inside until Flint had entered the coach office, then she climbed out. She had retrieved her bundle of clothing by the time Flint came back out, exchanged a few parting words with the driver, then untied Sam and walked away.

Luckily, the town itself was considerably larger than Comanche Wells, so she was able to stay far enough behind him to avoid being detected.

She was relieved when Flint left Sam at the livery. That meant he intended to remain in town overnight. Toting his saddlebags, he checked into a hotel a short distance away.

Garnet waited until Flint disappeared down a long hallway, then she entered the hotel. She thought it wise not to use her own name until she spoke to Flint, so she registered under her maiden name.

The clerk handed her a key. "You're in room 8 at the end of the hall, Mrs. Pettit."

"I see Mr. MacKenzie registered ahead of me," she commented. "He arrived on the same stage I did."

"Yes, he did. Matter of fact, Mr. MacKenzie's in room 7, right next to yours," he said with a friendly smile. "How long will you be staying with us, Mrs. Pettit?"

"I'm not certain. Most likely, just for tonight." She put down a dollar. "I'll know for certain in the morning."

"The public bath is right next door, but if you prefer to bathe in your room, ma'am, tubs are available for an additional twenty-five cents. Enjoy your stay."

"Thank you, sir, I intend to," Garnet said with more enthusiasm than she was feeling at the moment. The thought of confronting Flint was daunting.

Once in her room, she untied the parcel and picked up his shirt and pants. She left her room and paused outside his doorway. Then, rallying her courage, with all the flair and daring worthy of a cavalry charge by General J.E.B. Stuart himself, Garnet opened the door and sallied into the room.

After shucking his boots and hanging his gunbelt on the bedpost, Flint decided to lay down and grab a few hours sleep. He'd hardly been able to keep awake on the ride in today.

Grabbing the door key off the top of the chest, he walked over to the door. Flint grinned, thinking about the previous evening. The redhead had kept him awake most of the night, but it sure had been time well spent. It'd been hard as hell leaving her. But he knew she had the mettle and courage to get along. What the hell, he rationalized, why should he worry about her when *he* was the one with the worst to come: she'd be tucked snugly in Cousin Milton's bed while he'd still be passing many a restless night thinking about last night!

As Flint leaned down to put the key in the lock, the

door burst open, slammed him in the head, and knocked him flat on his back.

He lay looking up at the thousands of little black circles whirling around on the ceiling. Funny, he hadn't noticed them before.

"Flint darling, are you okay?"

He tried to shake off his dizziness. Of course he wasn't okay. If he were, he wouldn't be imagining that he heard the redhead's voice. If he were okay, he wouldn't be smelling that rose scent of hers, and if he were okay, he sure as hell wouldn't believe that those thousands of whirling circles had settled down into just two big, round, limpid green ones.

"I'm so sorry, sweetheart."

He groaned. *It was her!*

Yep! All the pieces were here: that husky voice that tickled his spine, the two green eyes that could glow with warmth or dim with the pain of heartache, that silken mane of red hair that shimmered like flame in the sun, then deepened with auburn shadows in moonlight.

But he had left all those temptations fifty miles away . . . in a hotel room . . . sound asleep!

There was no possible way they could be here unless. . . . Startled, he realized there was only one logical explanation.

Flint Collingswood MacKenzie, you've died and gone to heaven!

Then, when he recalled how the simplest flash of those eyes, bounce of that red hair, or whisper of that voice could tie painful knots in his loins, Flint reached a different conclusion—apparently the wishes of all the bastards who had told him to go to hell had finally been answered.

He blinked several times, then opened his eyes. His vision had cleared—and there was no redhead. *Imagination could sure make a man feel loco!* he thought, relieved.

He tried to sit up and the redhead suddenly reappeared, shoving him back, putting a cloth on his head, and telling him to lie still.

"You *are* here!" he shouted.

He flung off the cloth and stood up. There wasn't a goddamn thing wrong with him that an explanation wouldn't cure. He walked over to the bed and slapped on his hat—a man had a better chance of thinking straight with his hat on. Long ago he had reached the conclusion that women had figured this out, which was the only reason a woman preferred a man to remove his hat in her presence—to try and gain the advantage.

Outraged, he growled, "You followed me."

"Yes, I did. Matter of fact, on the same stage." She faced him unflinchingly, which only made him madder.

Flint sat down on the bed and folded his arms across his chest. "Goddammit, woman, I meant it when I said good-bye. Why in hell did you follow me?"

She laid the clothes on the chest. "You forgot to take back the shirt and pants you let me use."

Bunching up the pillows, he lay back. He felt a flush of pleasure that she had followed him—he was even flattered. God, she sure was a lot of woman! To his surprise, his hankering for her began to outweigh his anger. Appeared that this thing between them needed a little more time before it ran dry. Hell, there'd been a time or two when he'd found it to his liking to spend more than just one night with a gal.

Tucking his hands under his head, he smirked. "You sure that's the only reason?"

She sat down on the chair and kicked off her shoes. "What other reason could I possibly have?" she asked innocently.

"Come on over here, Widow Scott."

His words sent a blush of expectation through her

and her legs began to tremble. "If you want me, cowboy, you come over here and get me."

As Flint stood up and walked over to her, she felt hot blood surge to her temples, flowing like liquid fire to every nerve in her body.

For a long moment, he stood above her, his gaze locked with hers. Then he reached out a hand to her. She was conscious of how much her own hand trembled as she put it in his and allowed him to draw her to her feet.

"I figured after chasing me for fifty miles, you'd come up with a damn better reason than wanting to return a worn-out shirt and pair of pants," he said huskily, unbuttoning her bodice. As he slid his hand under her camisole and fondled a breast, he lowered his head and took possession of her mouth. The kiss was slow and controlled, sending passion spiraling through her. She gave herself freely to the excitement of his kiss. His lips were firm and moist; his probing tongue sent shivers of desire down her spine.

"Oh God, Flint!" she murmured in a breathless sigh when he freed her mouth. "I want—" The words were smothered as he reclaimed her mouth.

She felt his warm touch when his hands cupped the cheeks of her derriere, pressing her tighter against his heated arousal. He began to rub her gently, hurling spears of exquisite sensation throughout her body.

"I oughta kick this little butt of yours right out of here, but it feels too good, Redhead," he murmured at her ear, pressing her tighter against him.

"I agree," she whispered. "It's never felt so good."

Sliding his hands up her spine, he pulled the bodice off her shoulders to her elbows and trapped her arms in the folds of the sleeves. Then he slid his hand under her camisole, and she felt the divine warmth of his palm on her breast. Suddenly, he shoved up the garment impatiently. She heard it rip. Grasping her by the shoulders, he bent her back enough to take a

hardened nipple between his teeth and began to feast
on her breasts. Groaning with ecstasy, she closed her
eyes and flung back her head, her senses flooding with
wave upon wave of sweet sensation.

She didn't realize her arms were free until he pulled
the camisole over her head. Her bared breasts felt full
and swollen. He lowered his head and sucked at one as
he released the tie on her skirt and pulled the skirt and
pantalets past her hips. They fell to the floor in a heap
around her ankles.

She burned under his slow, sweeping perusal of her
naked body as he hurriedly shed his own clothes.
Unabashed, she examined him with the same scrutiny.
His body was perfection to her—legs and torso
molded in a powerful, proportionate symmetry.

"It's almost completely healed," she said, running
her finger along the fresh scar on his shoulder. She
leaned forward and pressed a light kiss to it, then
traced another scar on his chest. "When did you get
this wound, Flint? It looks pretty old."

"It is." He swooped her up in his arms and carried
her to the bed.

Covering her with his own nakedness, he reclaimed
her lips in a passionate kiss. "You taste so good,
Redhead," he whispered. "I could eat you."

"Don't stop. I want you to," she cried as he ran his
tongue across her breasts.

He licked her breasts, then slowly traced kisses
down her stomach until he reached the core of her sex.
Stunned, she felt him part her legs and raise them to
his shoulders. "What are you—oh God! Oh, dear
God!" she moaned when he covered her with his
mouth.

The erotic sensation was too intense to bear. Writhing beneath him, her body convulsed under wave
upon wave of ecstasy.

When the tremors ceased, she opened her eyes. He

was staring down at her. "You asked for it, Redhead." He ran his roughened fingertips over the tips of her breasts. She felt the instant rise of her renewed passion.

He sensed it too. Taking a nipple into his mouth, he palmed her sex. She gasped and parted her legs. Within seconds, he again raised her passion to a frenzy until she was out of control.

"Please, Flint. Please!"

"Please what?" he asked. "What do you want me to do?"

"You know," she moaned as his hand continued to probe her. "Make love to me," she pleaded.

He raised his head. She tried to slip her arms around his neck to pull him back, but he pinned her arms to the bed above her head. "I don't make love." He lowered his head and sucked at her breasts until she was writhing helplessly again beneath him. "Say it, Redhead. You know what I'm waiting for you to say."

She opened her eyes. She could see the perspiration that glistened on his forehead and felt his muscles taut with tension. "Yes, just do it. Please."

"Do what? Say it, Redhead."

She arched against him, wrapping her legs around his hips.

He had pushed his restraint to the limit and couldn't hold out any longer. Releasing her arms, he raised up and drove into her. She matched the rhythm of his thrusts, and their linked bodies built to an explosive release. She cried out at that second of climax, swirling in a sublime state of rapture.

Flint collapsed on her, and for several moments he listened to the rasp of his own breathing. Finally, he rolled off her and lay back. Garnet turned her head and looked at him. "Well, are you finally convinced, Widow Scott?"

"Convinced of what?" she asked.

"You know damned well *what*," he declared. "You gonna still try to tell me that love had anything to do with our coupling?"

"Will you please stop referring to our relationship as if we were railroad ties?"

"Why not? I've always been willing to call it by what it is."

"Just because you refuse to recognize your true feelings for me, what makes you think you know how I feel?"

"You don't keep it a secret, lady. You sound like a coyote braying to the moon. Reckon you're about the noisiest woman I ever took to my bed."

"And you, Mr. MacKenzie, are about the crudest man I've ever taken to *my* bed. Do you believe for a moment that I would have permitted you to"—her face flamed in a blush—"do the things you did to me if I weren't in love with you?"

"Lady, you're fooling yourself. You'd have done it with the devil himself."

"I thought I just did, MacKenzie!"

She knew he was baiting her, just like he'd tried to do moments ago. She refused to swallow it. Jumping out of bed, she said lightly, "And I'm honest enough to give the devil his due." She began to dress. "I'll admit, it was the most incredible . . . phenomenon . . . I've ever experienced."

"The way you enjoyed it, I figured you found out what you were missing all that time harnessed to young Bobby and ole Freddy. Shame too, Redhead. Same as hitching a thoroughbred to a plow."

She looked at him with amusement. "You're such a boorish philistine, Mr. MacKenzie, but it's not going to work."

"How come in the heat of passion, I'm Flint to you, but in the cold light of morning, I become Mister MacKenzie again?"

"It's not out of respect, I can assure you. If my mama

knew I loved you, she'd turn over in her grave," Garnet declared, shoving the hem of her bodice into the waist of her skirt.

Laughing, he tucked his hands behind his head. "The same mama who taught you that diverting trick?"

She spun around angrily. "MacKenzie, say what you will about me, but don't insult my mother."

"I apologize, Mrs. Scott," he said contritely. "I meant no disrespect to your mother. My ma never raised her sons to insult a decent woman. I just like to rile you to see those green eyes of yours flashing like emeralds."

Brazenly, she ran an assessing glance over him stretched out naked on the bed. "Well, even though you continue to raise the issue about me shedding my clothes, it appears you have no reservations about lying there as bare as a newborn babe."

"I'm more curious to know if it bothers *you*, Widow Scott."

She turned away, unable to look him in the eye. It bothered her, indeed. "And you could call me by my given name, Flint. It's Garnet, you know."

"Reckon I could, Redhead, but isn't a garnet red just like that hair of yours?"

"That's the reason my daddy gave me the name. He took one look at me on the day I was born and called me Garnet." She glanced at him slyly. "You like my hair, don't you, Flint?"

He shrugged. "Reckon I've seen prettier." He got to his feet and slipped on his pants.

"No, you haven't, MacKenzie." She walked boldly over to him and kissed him lightly on the lips. "You're fascinated by it. Oh, I don't think there's anything special about it. And I'm sure there are many women with red hair more appealing than mine. But you know what, Flint MacKenzie? The important thing is that you don't think so." Smiling smugly, she picked up her shoes and paused at the door. "You love it."

"Hey, Redhead," he called out when she started to leave, "I'll buy you dinner."

She gave him a coquettish smile. "I accept, but how about having it later in my room? Right now, I need a nap."

"What for? To regain your energy for later?"

"I advise you to take one, too. Later, you might need all the strength you can muster." The smile she flashed him was enough to rock him back on his heels. She disappeared through the door.

Flint stood shaking his head. The woman was trouble—but just thinking about her heated his loins. He dug into his saddlebags and pulled out the bottle of whiskey he had bought in Comanche Wells. He opened it and took a deep swallow. Yep, that gal sure was trouble. Tomorrow, he'd make sure she didn't follow him. He didn't need any woman crowding him.

He went back to bed. Propping up the pillows behind his back, he sat drinking from the whiskey bottle and thinking about Garnet.

"Yep, she's trouble all right," he reconfirmed, raising the bottle to his lips. "Tomorrow it's good-bye for sure."

But he still had tonight to look forward to.

Chapter 10

W hen Flint joined her in her room a few hours later, Garnet thought his walk looked unsteady. *He's had too much to drink*, she lamented. And she'd just ordered a bottle of champagne to accompany their dinner. If he drank any more, he'd be bound to give her even more trouble than usual.

"Flint, this dinner and champagne are very expensive," she said after the waiter had departed. Flint had opted for a steak, and instead of using the table, they spread a blanket on the floor. Now, sitting across from each other on the blanket, they were devouring the meal greedily. "Just what are we celebrating?"

He raised his glass in a toast. "We're celebrating our last night together, Redhead."

Garnet's lips were curved in a slight smile as she sipped the champagne. "Are you so sure about that, Flint? Maybe you've forgotten that Destiny is a guest at this party, too."

"Destiny only applies to life-and-death situations, honey, so if you're figuring on following me tomorrow, I'd forget it if I were you. You'll end up sniffing your own trail."

She was distressed to hear that he was still determined to leave her behind. Standing up, she walked to the window. "I believe that when the time comes, you'll take me with you."

"You'd be wrong, sweetheart." He drained his wine-glass.

She turned around and watched in silence as he refilled the glass. Rising clumsily to his feet, he staggered over to her, the liquid splashing over the rim and onto his hand.

"Oh, I know what you're up to, sweetheart. You're not fooling me for a minute." His words had begun to slur.

She took his hand and slowly licked the liquid off his fingers. "What am I up to, Flint?" A drop of champagne had settled in the corner of his mouth; rising on tiptoe, she swiped it up with her tongue.

He wove the fingers of his free hand into her hair and drew her against him. As he lightly pulled back her head, she felt his long fingers cup her nape. "You're never going to trap me into doing anything I don't want to do, Redhead."

"Why do you think I'd try to trap you, Flint?" The sting of his words had hurt. "I love you."

"And you'd be so good for me," he said with a smirk. "Isn't that right?"

"That's right. No one could be better."

For a breathless moment, he stared with mockery into her upturned face. Then his mouth swooped down and captured hers in a consuming kiss.

"But your little game won't work," he said when he freed her lips. "We part company in the morning." He released her. "Come on, let's finish the meal. The food's getting cold and it cost too damned much to let it go to waste."

He sat down, and when she moved to sit opposite him, he grabbed her hand and pulled her down beside him. Leaning over, he picked up her plate and set it down in front of her. "This'll do just fine," he said.

After they finally finished the meal, upon seeing

Garnet had barely touched her drink, Flint poured the last of the champagne into his own glass. He gulped it down and smiled wolfishly at her.

"Reckon it's time for dessert, Redhead."

"We forgot to order any."

"'Pears we'll just have to make our own then." Drawing her into his embrace, he kissed her.

As the kiss deepened, she slipped her arms around his neck, and he pressed her back to the floor. She closed her eyes and relaxed, surrendering to the kiss. The feel of his virile manliness, raw and sensuous, aroused her hunger as much as his tantalizing kiss. Desire tugged at her loins as he slid his lips down her neck and his fingers released the buttons of her bodice. She sat up so he could pull it off her arms and heard his chuckle when he discovered she was not wearing a camisole.

"You think of everything," he said.

"You ripped it," she replied. She pulled his shirt over his head and tossed it aside.

They sank down on their knees, and head to head, took time to admire one another. Their movements were slow, unhurried. Each knew they had the rest of the night. He cupped her breasts in his hands and kissed each of the hardened tips. She, in turn, traced a finger around the curves of his nipples, then lowered her head and licked each one.

As he untied her skirt, she released the belt of his pants. Grasping each other's forearms, they stood up long enough for him to shove the skirt past her hips, and for her to pull the buckskins off his long legs.

Neither wore underwear.

Together they sank to their knees, then Flint gently lowered Garnet to the floor. He stretched out beside her, propped up his elbow, and cradled his head in his hand. "If you're not going to drink this, I will," he said, reaching for her glass of champagne. His dark eyes appraised her boldly as he took a deep swallow.

"You would be wiser to just sip that," she warned lightly. Her body had begun to throb with need for him.

"You may be right, Redhead."

Closing her eyes, she waited to savor the return of his hot, tantalizing touch; instead she jerked when she suddenly felt the drizzle of cold drops across her breasts. Startled, she opened her eyes. He trailed more drops of the champagne along her body, then he began to lick up the liquid.

Beneath the fluctuating sensation of cold liquid and the hot ecstasy of his tongue, she basked in a sensory seduction until she realized he was no longer moving. His slumped head lay on her breasts. "Flint?"

When he did not reply, she lifted his head and rolled away. Turning him onto his back, she stared, gaping incredulously at him.

The great lover had passed out!

"Even Frederick didn't do that at such an intimate moment, Flint," she mumbled, thoroughly exasperated.

Grabbing a pillow, she tucked it under his head on the floor. The blanket was still covered with dishes, so she gathered them up and put them on the table, then covered Flint with their recent tablecloth.

Her body felt sticky from the champagne and she needed to cleanse herself of their afternoon lovemaking. Ruling against a sponge bath, she decided to take a proper one.

Garnet put on her clothes and went down to the desk to order a tub. A short time later, two young boys, who appeared to be not much older than ten or eleven, wheeled the tub into the room and proceeded to fill it with buckets of hot and cold water. If they were curious about Flint sleeping on the floor, they said nothing. She had them carry away the dirty dishes.

Locking the door, she glanced at Flint. Throughout

all the commotion, her stalwart plainsman hadn't moved a muscle.

Garnet took a long bath, luxuriating in the warm water. When it began to turn tepid, she climbed out, toweled herself dry, and was about to go to bed when she decided to sew her torn camisole.

She was in need of a needle and thread. Figuring Flint would have them in his saddlebags, she found his room key in his shirt pocket. Once again she pulled on her bodice and skirt and hurried next door. His gunbelt was slung over the bedpost, and his rifle and saddlebags piled on the table along with an empty bottle of whiskey. The whiskey bottle hadn't been there when she'd left his room earlier.

She grabbed his saddlebags, and as an afterthought, decided it would be wise to take Flint's weapons too. Struggling under the weight of the heavy iron and saddlebags, she carried them to her room.

Garnet was about to go back to lock the door when she heard the thud of boots and the sound of voices in the hallway. She waited until it was quiet before peeking out. The door to Flint's room was ajar and she heard voices coming from inside. Sensing something amiss, she strained to listen.

Her eyes widened with shock when she recognized the voice of Bullwhip Moore. "You figure he left town, Bodine?"

"Naw. He wouldn't have paid for a night's bed." Garnet recognized the speaker as the man Flint had addressed as Nathan Bodine.

"Well, maybe he saw us and headed out," another voice added. She had no idea of the identity of the new speaker.

"Whatta you want us to do, Bodine?" To her horror, still a fourth voice entered the conversation. And from the sound of it, he intended Flint no good.

"You men spread out and check the saloons. He's

gotta be somewhere. Most likely holed up with some whore."

Well thank you for that remark, Mr. Bodine! she thought with annoyance. Then she heard Bodine continue. "I'll talk to the bartender downstairs to see if he's seen MacKenzie around. Price, just in case he does try to skip from here, you go to the edge of town past the livery and check out anybody who's leaving."

"I ain't never seen MacKenzie before. I wouldn't know him if I saw him," one of the men replied.

"He ain't hard to miss," Bodine said. "He's a tall man with a big, bushy beard. He's got black hair and wears it tied back with a piece of rawhide. Oh, yeah, he's more run-down and dirtier looking than Bullwhip here. Don't try to take him on alone though. He's faster than a striking rattler with that Colt he wears, and a dead shot—him and his goddamned brothers! So if you find him, round up the rest of us. I don't want the bastard to get away this time. Let's get going."

Garnet ducked back into her room and heard the clink of their spurs as they departed down the hallway. She dared not peek out for fear one of the men might glance back and see her. From what she had heard, there were at least four of them.

Locking the door, she glanced at the guns and saddlebags on the table. Thank God she had gotten them out of the room before those scoundrels had arrived. At least when Flint sobered up, he wouldn't be defenseless. There was no doubt in her mind that Bodine and his cutthroats would not hesitate to gun down an unarmed man.

Garnet hurried over to Flint. Kneeling down, she shook his shoulder to try to wake him. She couldn't budge him. "Flint, please, you've got to wake up," she pleaded, shaking him harder. She had no idea how soon Bodine and his men would return. Flint would be helpless if they discovered him in this condition.

She rushed over to the ewer and found it empty.

Cursing under her breath, she scooped some water from the tub into the pitcher and splashed it on his face. "Flint, wake up!" she ordered in a louder voice.

He jolted up to a sitting position. "Yeah. Okay." Then he flopped back, sound asleep.

"God, deliver me from the addled brain of a drunk!" she mumbled.

She picked up his Winchester. She had never fired a repeating rifle before, but she figured it could only be easier than the Spencer she had always used. However, despite being a good shot, she knew it was unlikely she could hold off four or five men.

Looking desperately around the room, her glance fell on the bathtub. In Flint's current state, she'd never be able to disguise him from Bodine; but what if she changed his appearance so Bodine wouldn't recognize him? She'd have to begin by cleaning Flint up.

"Flint, wake up," she said, kneeling down and shaking him again.

"Yeah. Yeah," he mumbled and went back to sleep.

"Damn you, Flint, wake up," she declared. Frustrated, she threw aside the blanket and grabbed him by the ankles. His head bobbed against the floor as she dragged him over toward the tub, but she knew she could never lift him into it.

"Wake up, Flint," she said, exasperated. "Stand up. Come on, Flint, stand up." He opened his eyes. She helped him get to his feet. "Damn you, Flint, why do you have to be so big?" He appeared to be sleeping standing up. "Don't move. Just stay where you are." Pressing a hand to his chest to keep him from falling forward, she stretched out a leg, hooked her foot through the rung of a nearby chair, and managed to drag it over to them. Maneuvering the chair with her free hand, she got it behind Flint and gave him a light shove. He collapsed in a sitting position onto the chair. She quickly caught him before he fell off.

Garnet took a deep breath and surveyed the situation. Despite all her maneuvering, the tub was still several feet away. She sat down on the floor, grabbed the front legs of the chair, and began to shift it inch by inch toward the tub.

"So . . . help . . . me . . . Flint . . . MacKenzie," she grunted, "if . . . I . . . ever . . . get . . . you . . . in . . . that . . . tub . . ."—she paused to catch her breath— "I'm personally going to drown you."

Her chest was heaving from the exertion and she leaned back on her haunches to catch her breath. He started to slip off the chair, and she jerked forward to catch him. Stopping to gather her strength one last time, she managed to reach the tub.

"Take a deep breath," she murmured and tipped the chair forward, dumping him into the tub.

He came up sputtering, with water dripping from his hair and face. "Wha . . . what's happening?"

"Nothing, Flint. I thought we could take a bath together."

"You coming in, baby?" he asked with a doltish grin.

"Right away, sweetheart. I'll be right in."

His knees were bent up to his chin. Leaning his head on his knees, he was asleep within seconds.

She rummaged through his saddlebags. Considering his bushy appearance, she didn't expect to find a razor, but she did locate a pair of scissors. She'd just have to use his bowie knife to shave him.

"Oh, Flint, you're going to kill me." She sighed and began to clip his beard with the scissors. Finally, not daring to cut it any closer, she worked up a lather with a bar of soap, swabbed his face with it, and began to shave him.

When she finished, she stared in awe at his clean face. "Why, you're a fraud, Flint MacKenzie. There's nothing fierce or menacing about you at all. Under all that hair you are actually quite handsome! And much younger looking than I thought." She reached out a finger and lightly traced the thin scar that ran along his right cheek. "Matter of fact, you're beautiful, Flint," she whispered softly.

Shrugging aside her tender thoughts, she returned to the problem at hand. By the time she finished cutting his hair, which now hung to just below his ears, she had begun to tremble. After sponging the fallen hair off his shoulders and chest, she stepped back to review the effect.

"I think you're beautiful, Flint, but you won't like it. When you see yourself, please remember that I did it to save your tough ole hide."

Now she was faced with the task of getting him *out* of the tub. She took his hands in hers and pulled him forward over the top of the tub. Placing her hands firmly on the cheeks of his rear, she shoved him head first onto the floor.

It took her another fifteen minutes to dress him. Remembering Bodine's derogatory remarks about Flint's apparel, she took a towel and wiped the dust off his boots and hat.

"If I didn't know better, I'd never guess it was you, Flint," she said with satisfaction as she plopped the hat on his head, adjusting it to the angle he liked.

Her smile soon disappeared when it was time to face the next problem: how was she to get him out of town? She'd have to leave him long enough to get a wagon or carriage from the livery. He was in no condition to ride a horse.

Garnet pulled a crocheted runner off the chest of drawers and covered her head, hoping, that if she were seen, she'd be mistaken for a woman on her way to church.

Having followed Flint that morning, she knew where the livery was located. Avoiding the main street, she moved in the shadows along the back streets.

The livery man looked at her curiously when she asked him the rental price of a carriage or wagon. "You a stranger in town ma'am? Don't think I've seen you before."

"Yes," she said, glancing nervously up and down the street.

She noticed his limp when he came over to her. "Do you have a problem, ma'am?"

"Yes . . . yes I do. My husband is ill and I must get him out of here."

"If he's ill, why wouldn't you keep him here for Doc Adams to treat?"

"Ah, the doctor can't help him," she said hurriedly.

"I've got an old buckboard you could use. It's kind of run down, but it's good enough to get you to Morgan's Creek, 'bout fifty miles west of here. My brother runs the livery there and you can leave it with him." He limped over to the wall and grabbed the rigging off a hook.

"Hitch up that dun to it." She pointed to Sam in a nearby stall. She knew it would be bad enough to face Flint in the morning without leaving Sam behind.

"Can't do that, ma'am, it belongs to. . . ." He stopped abruptly, and Garnet saw the sudden gleam of comprehension in his eyes. "This wouldn't have anything to do with the two pistoleros who were here a short time ago, asking a lot of questions about Flint MacKenzie, would it?"

"I don't know what you're talking about," she denied.

"Reckon not." It was clear she hadn't fooled him a bit. He had guessed the truth, but whatever he was thinking, the man kept it to himself.

She was too desperate to continue the facade. "I beg you, sir. Please don't say anything to anyone."

"Don't worry, ma'am. If I hitch two horses to the carriage, you'd have more speed. I've got a mare that takes to a harness."

Garnet thought quickly. Once they were away from

there, she would need a horse. "How much would you sell it for?"

"Well, like I said, ma'am, the mare's a harness horse. I'll let you have her for twenty dollars."

Garnet didn't have the money, but she knew Flint did. "All right. I'll pay you when you bring it. We're at the Cattlemen's Hotel, room 8. I don't dare try to leave through the lobby, so we'll have to get . . . my husband . . . out through the window. It opens onto the road behind the hotel."

"I'll be there in five minutes. Is he wounded?"

"No, he's just passed out."

Garnet hurried back to the hotel and entered through the rear. She stuffed her few belongings into Flint's saddlebags and was waiting at the open window when the livery man drove up. She waved and he pulled up outside the window.

Between the two of them, they managed to lift Flint through the window, then Garnet handed the livery man Flint's saddlebags, rifle, and gunbelt. Glancing back to make sure she hadn't forgotten anything, she saw his hat had fallen on the floor. Grabbing it, she climbed out the window.

"I put his saddle in the back of the buckboard, ma'am, and I threw in an old, worn-out one I had lying around. If it weren't for that scar on his cheek, I'd never recognize him. He sure looks different without that beard," the man said, amazed.

"Hope no one else recognizes him. Getting rid of all that hair was the only disguise I could think of."

After paying the man, she put the rifle on the floor at her feet and the Colt next to her on the seat. Flint toppled over with his head slumped on her shoulder. She put his hat on him to keep his face further concealed.

"Good luck, ma'am," the livery man said, handing her the reins.

"Are there any hostile Indians between here and the next town?" she asked.

"No, they're all east of here. You won't have no problem with Indians."

"I can't thank you enough, sir. Why are you doing this for us?" she asked. "You're risking your own safety, too."

"Couple years back, I tried to stop Moore from beating a horse with that bullwhip of his. So he used it on me instead." He slapped his bad leg. "He gave me this."

Turning, he limped away.

As much as she was tempted to whip the horses to a gallop, she didn't want to attract any attention. She plodded along slowly, staying off the main road until she neared the outskirts of the town several blocks later. Garnet turned onto the trail heading west.

She was on the verge of congratulating herself for evading Bodine and his henchmen, when suddenly a figure rode out of the shadows of a cantina at the edge of town. Brandishing a pistol, he yelled, "Hold up there."

"If you've a mind to stick us up, mister, you've jest rode up to a dry hole. Ben here's spent our last dollar on likker and whores."

"Kind of late to be heading out of town, ain't it, lady?" he asked.

"Reckon that there's my problem, not yours, mister, seein' as how I'm the one has to be doin' the drivin'."

He leaned over for a better look at Flint slumped against her, his scarred cheek concealed against her shoulder. Lifting the hat off Flint's head, he peered closely at him through the darkness. Garnet knew the outlaw was inspecting Flint's face for a beard. "What's wrong with him?"

"I broke a pitcher over his head and I'll do worse if I catch him agin with that blond-haired whore at the Golden Slipper," she harangued, dredging up a name she recalled seeing on the front of one of the saloons. "The cheatin' bastard thought he'd pull one over on me. It'll be a cold day in hell before he sneaks off to town alone agin."

"Okay, lady. I got no hankering to listen to you bickerin' 'bout your marriage." He rode back into the shadows.

Stifling a smile, Garnet flicked the reins and the buckboard moved on.

Chapter 11

The trail was wide and well worn, making it easy to follow even in the dark. Flint continued sleeping peacefully with his head on her shoulder. Although she would have liked to put as many miles between her and Waynesburg as possible, Garnet kept the wagon moving at a steady, even pace.

For the first few miles, she had to fight the reins because Sam was not used to being hitched to the buckboard, but he finally settled down and matched the steady trot of the other horse, a bald-faced roan mare.

When the promise of dawn mottled the sky with gray streaks and patches of dark blue, a dim light filtered through the black shadows that lined either side of the trail. She could see that the way ahead narrowed into a grove of cottonwood and willow trees—an indication that most likely there was water nearby. Reining up, she pulled off at a small clearing on the south side of the road and spied the narrow stream, no wider than a mountain creek.

While the horses drank their fill, Garnet yawned and stretched her cramped muscles, then shook out her hair. It fell disheveled past her shoulders.

At that moment, Flint woke up and saw her.

Suddenly, with breathtaking brilliance, the sun burst

above the horizon, bathing her in a golden glow, and he saw Garnet raise an arm to shield her eyes from the glare.

Oblivious to where he was or how he had gotten there, Flint stared in awe. Her slim figure was pinned in a shaft of sunlight, morning mist swirling around her knees and ankles. The features of her face were an obscure silhouette, but the long hair that clung to her shoulders glinted like copper.

With her arm raised heavenward, she looked like a wild wood nymph worshipping the sun.

As if feeling his stare, she turned and looked at him. "So you finally woke up," she said.

For the first time since opening his eyes, he looked around him and discovered he was sitting in a buckboard next to a creek. Shocked, he saw Sam hitched to the wagon.

"What in hell's going on? Last thing I remember we were—"

"In my room at the Cattleman's Hotel in Waynesburg," she said in disgust.

"Yeah, that's right. Somebody knock me out or something?"

"Not somebody—*some thing*, MacKenzie. You passed out." She folded her arms across her chest and glared at him like a schoolmarm confronting a mischievous child.

With great effort, Flint climbed down from the wagon and knelt on the creek bank. "I sure feel like I've been hit on the head." He started to splash water on his face, then stopped abruptly. "What in hell!" He glanced up at her with astonishment and began to grope wildly at his face and chin. "Am I dreaming? What in hell—"

"It's a long story, Flint," she said, hoping to calm him down.

He jumped to his feet. "My saddlebags. Where are my saddlebags?"

"In the buckboard, but let me explain, Flint."

Without waiting for her explanation, he dug through the saddlebags until he found the mirror and held it up to his face. "God Almighty!" He tossed aside his hat. "My hair, too!"

She watched his expression change from astonishment to anger. Strapping on his gunbelt, he demanded in an outraged voice, "Who sheared me like a goddamn sheep?"

Garnet swallowed hard and took a deep breath. "I did."

He spun on his heel. "You!" he lashed out at her. "You," he repeated with contempt. Seeing the fury in his eyes, she backed up in apprehension, but too late to avoid his reach. He grasped her by the shoulders, his long fingers cutting into her flesh.

"Why?" he asked, stunned. "You said you'd get even with me. Is this your revenge, Widow Scott, or are you just trying to get your own way? You didn't like my beard, but I never took you to be a spiteful woman."

The unjust accusation caught her off guard. He hadn't even bothered to listen to her explanation. She felt her mounting anger sweep through her like a fire. "I did it to save your life," she replied in a low voice taut with anger. "Although, at the moment, I'm hard pressed to believe it was worth the effort."

He smirked sardonically. "And just how did clipping me bald save my life, Widow Scott?" He began to unhitch Sam.

"Well, sir, after you drank yourself into a stupor and passed out, Nathan Bodine and Mr. Moore showed up in your hotel room."

His head snapped around in surprise. Now she clearly had his attention. "You didn't think I could take Bodine and Moore?"

"Hah! In the state you were in? Besides, there were at least two or three others with them."

"Why didn't you just lock the door and stay holed up in the room until I woke up?"

"I figured when they couldn't find you anywhere else, they'd come back to the hotel and begin checking out the rooms. So, I did what I thought would be the wisest thing: I shaved you clean to disguise you and got us out of there."

"You should have woke me. I don't run from a fight, lady—much less sneak out of town. But I reckon you did what you thought you had to, as dumb as it was. I'd be shaming my ma if I didn't thank you for your effort."

"It was the least I could do, since you'd saved my life," she said sarcastically.

"Well, the slate's wiped clean now. Neither of us is beholdin' to the other."

It was the most ungracious expression of gratitude she had ever heard—and her anger only increased. "That's right, my conscience is clear. Just like you said, we're both even now. Except you're still the loser. Your hair and beard will grow back, but what won't come back is *me*, MacKenzie," she shouted angrily. "You've just lost the best thing that ever happened to you, and you're too damn dumb to realize it."

He turned to her, his eyes black with rage. "You don't fool me for a moment," he said, slapping the saddle on Sam, then shaking a finger at her. "Well, it ain't gonna work with me, lady. You've got me shorn, all right, but you ain't never gonna get me trapped. I've got more sense than that." He tightened the cinch, then shoved his rifle into the scabbard.

"What you've got, Mr. MacKenzie, is the intellect of a flea, the manners of an ape, and the disposition of a mule—all combined with an ego the size of an elephant."

"You're a bitter and spiteful woman, Widow Scott," he said as he tied his saddlebags. "I sure as hell will never know why I ignored the common sense the good Lord gave me, to saddle myself with a mean-mouth, viper-spitting Delilah like you."

"Delilah!"

"Yeah? I've read about that Delilah woman in the Bible. She didn't rest either till she had that Samson guy all shorn and under her thumb."

"Oh, what an ego! Mister MacKenzie, I would be a rich woman if I could buy you for what you're worth, and sell you for what you *think* you're worth! And I wish to make something very clear to you. You do not have to fear I will try to trap you into marriage. The thought of wedding you may have once entered my mind, but now I wouldn't marry you even if you got down on your knees and begged me."

Snorting, he swung himself up on Sam. "Yeah! Well, you'll see that day, lady, when mules soar like eagles." He flipped the reins and the horse took a few steps; then Flint stopped and looked back at her. "If I remember, the next town's about ten miles west of this grove of trees. Just stay on this trail."

"Thanks for the directions."

"I'll . . . ah, be cutting off here and heading south."

Now, faced with the actual moment of parting, her anger slipped away, replaced by a sense of loss. "Good-bye, Flint."

"Good-bye, Redhead."

He stared down at her. Her eyes looked as round as saucers and he saw a hint of moisture in them. She looked so damn vulnerable, he wanted to get down, take her in his arms, and make love to her one more time.

Make love to her! Goddammit! Now she had him thinking it too!

He wheeled Sam and rode away.

After a short distance, he reined up on top of a hillside and looked back. He could see Garnet still standing next to the buckboard. In the past, when the time came to ride away, he never bothered to look back. So why should this time be any different? The slate was wiped clean; no strings!

Shaving his beard! Cutting his hair! Before he knew it, the redhead would have him building a cabin and raising a barn!

He wasn't so put out because she had cut off his hair and shaved his beard. She was right—his hair would grow back.

He had lost control—that's what was disturbing to him. Fretting over her, he had drunk himself into a stupor and put his fate in another's hands. And that scared him. He'd never been so careless before. She had sunk her teeth into him like a tick, sucking out his life's blood. He was right to ride away—the time was overdue for him to dig that little redheaded mite out of his hide.

"Let's go, Sam."

He was about to ride on when he caught sight of a large dust cloud some distance away on the trail behind Garnet. Somebody was riding hell-bent for leather, and from the size of the dust cloud, he figured it was more than one rider. Soon after, he made out five riders. His instinct began sending out a signal more ominous than Apache smoke. Glancing back at Garnet, he saw she still hadn't budged from the spot where he'd left her. Within the next five minutes, they'd be at the clearing; Bodine and Moore would be sure to recognize her.

Flint goaded Sam to a gallop.

About to climb on the buckboard and pull out, Garnet glanced up in startlement when Flint on his horse thundered up to her. Grabbing his rifle, he bolted out of the saddle even before Sam came to a full stop. "Bodine and his men are headed this way." He quickly unharnessed the horse from the buckboard and saddled the mare. "Climb on and head for that rise."

"What about you?" she asked.

"I'll catch up with you. Just keep heading south."

"Flint, I can handle a rifle. I'm a good shot, too."

It was too late to argue—the five riders had come into view. "Get going, Sam." The horse trotted into the trees. He gave the mare a whack and it followed Sam. Flint took cover in the bushes behind the buckboard, pulling Garnet down beside him. "Stay low," he warned.

Flint put a shot on the road in front of the riders, and they reined up. "That's close enough, Bodine," he shouted.

"That you, MacKenzie?" At a nod from their leader, the riders headed for the trees on the north side of the road.

"Keep low," Flint ordered as bullets started to strike the trees behind them. He pumped several shots at the scurrying outlaws. "It'll take them a couple minutes to regroup. They can't get a clear shot until they work themselves closer. I figure they'll leave their horses behind when they do. Stay low and start pulling back to that rise."

"What about Sam and the mare? We can't outrun Bodine on foot."

"Don't worry about them." He drew his Colt and handed it to her. "Use this if any of them slip past me."

"Aren't you coming with me?"

"No. I'll be along. Just keep moving." Flint fired several more shots in the outlaws' direction. Bullets ripped into the trees above his head as the gang returned his fire.

"What do you have in mind, Flint?" she asked suspiciously.

Suddenly Bodine called out to him. "Hey, MacKenzie. Never thought you'd take to hiding under a woman's skirt just to avoid a fight."

Flint threw Garnet a disparaging look. "I don't know what you're talking about, Bodine."

"Took me awhile to figure out that the redhead called herself by another name at the hotel and then got you out of town," Bodine shouted.

"Guess you're smarter than I gave you credit for, Widow Scott," Flint whispered.

"I'll remind you of that when we get out of here, MacKenzie," she replied.

"I reckon you will." *That damn grit of hers*, he thought. He couldn't help admiring it; she hadn't said *if*, she'd said *when*.

He suddenly thought of an idea that might get them away. "Gimme the Colt, and you take the rifle. Fire at them every couple of minutes to keep their attention."

"Where are you going?" she asked when he slipped the pistol into his holster.

"They can't follow us without horses, can they? Just stay low and keep firing."

He started to crawl swiftly through the trees. Although the thick grove offered him some concealment, it was still too light to have the advantage of darkness—and speed was important; he couldn't give them too much time to move in on Garnet. She was doing her part by firing sporadically, forcing them to keep their heads down.

Flint saw that all the gunfire was coming from trees on the opposite side of the road. Hoping he wouldn't be spotted, he continued to crawl.

"That you, Norton?" Bodine called from across the road.

"Yeah, boss," a voice replied nearby. Flint saw a figure step out from behind a tree several yards ahead of him and dart forward to the cover of another one. Apparently, the man had not seen him.

Flint cursed under his breath. He should have guessed there'd be a shooter on the same side of the road as he was, even though none of the gunshots, as yet, came from this direction. He'd have to take him out, but he didn't dare expose his position with a gunshot. He slid behind a willow clump and drew his bowie, crouched to spring. As soon as the gunman passed, Flint jumped him. The outlaw never had a chance to utter a sound.

"We're moving forward, Norton, so don't get wild with any shot," Bodine called out in a low voice. "And stay on that side of the road so you can take 'em by surprise."

"Yeah, boss," Flint answered with a muffled tone.

Hearing a whinny, he crawled forward. Soon, he could clearly see the five horses clustered across the road. One man with a rifle was guarding them.

The gunfighters had their backs to him, but Flint realized he couldn't cross the road without being seen by the guard. Time was running out; Bodine was getting ready to close in on Garnet. His decision was made for him when the guard saw him and raised a rifle. Flint rolled over, drew his Colt and fired. As the gunman fell back with a bullet through his head, the rifle fell from his hand, discharging when it hit the ground. Neighing and flailing in panic, three of the spooked horses broke free and bolted away.

Flint dashed across the road as surprised shouts sounded from the gunman. "What in hell is going on back there?" Bodine yelled.

Flint slashed the reins of the remaining horses and fired several shots in the air. The frightened horses took off. He saw Bodine and Moore running back. They hadn't seen him yet, and as much as he would have liked to take them on, it'd be too risky. He had to consider Garnet's safety, so he dashed into the trees.

As Flint skirted the three gunmen, who were scrambling to catch the horses, he encountered a new danger—Garnet's shots. She had begun firing more frequently, and the bullets were bouncing off the trees around him.

Throwing caution aside, he dashed across the road. The gunmen saw him and opened fire. "Get going," he shouted to Garnet as he got nearer. "Get to the hill."

Jumping up, she started to run. Flint caught up with her, snatched the rifle from her, and grabbed her hand. They continued to dash through the trees with bullets falling at their heels.

He glanced behind them and saw that Bullwhip had given up the chase, but Bodine and his henchman were still in pursuit. If he and Garnet weren't out of rifle range before they crested the hill, they'd be sitting ducks.

Garnet's steps had begun to slow. "I . . . can't go . . . any farther." She staggered and slumped to the ground.

"You don't have to, babe. I think we made it." He gave two sharp whistles.

She turned her head in surprise at the sound of a heavy thrashing. Sam came thundering out of the trees, followed by the mare.

Flint picked her up and swung her onto the mare. "Yaw," he shouted and slapped the mare's flank. The horse bolted up the hill. He leaped onto Sam's back and goaded him up the hill. The shots that followed fell uselessly behind him.

When Flint crested the hilltop, he looked back to see Bodine throw down his rifle and kick angrily at a pile of dried manure.

Chapter 12

"Flint, where are we headed?" Garnet asked after about a thirty-minute ride. They were crossing a flat plain of grama grass and sagebrush with few trees and no trail.

"South."

"I know that, but why south?"

"That's where the Triple M is—near the headwaters of the Red."

"How far away is it?" she asked.

"We should be there by nightfall tomorrow."

"And you're taking me there?"

"Don't have much choice. Guess I'll have to." She was unsuccessful in suppressing a grin. "What are you smirking about, Delilah?"

"Nothing. Nothing," she repeated when he looked at her askance.

By midday, Flint was convinced that Bodine wasn't trailing them, so they stopped to eat in a small cluster of piñon and cottonwood. "Why are you so sure Bodine isn't trying to follow us?" Garnet asked as they took turns sipping coffee from the same cup.

"Well, by the time they caught up with us this morning, they had already been riding their mounts hard. Rounding them up would tire the horses more. Sam and the mare had been rested and watered, and the others would never be able to keep up with us. Besides, Bodine couldn't follow a trail if it had a white stripe painted down the middle of it."

"But Moore is with him. He's a wagon scout, isn't he?"

Her remark only produced a snort from Flint. "Yeah, but Bodine's calling the shots. And I know Bodine: he's lazy, he don't like surprises, and since he lost a couple of his men, he don't like the odds." For a long moment, he stared silently into his cup. "Most likely I'll be the one who'll kill him someday. Should have done it a long time ago."

Garnet studied him as he stared gloomily into the distance. He had made the statement sound so matter-of-fact. Killing seemed to be a part of life out here. One man destroying the life of another seemed as common in the West as going to church on Sunday was back East. Indians slaughtered white settlers . . . gunmen shot or beat one another at a blink of an eye. Did the wildness of this country produce such men—or was the West the product of their wildness?

And Flint was a part of this West. Was that why he fascinated her—that edge of ruthlessness about him that was so different from Bobby Joe or Frederick? For other than his fierceness, what did she know about Flint MacKenzie? What drove her to abandon the moral concepts she had always lived by to come so shamelessly to his bed? Even now, looking at the silent, brooding figure, she felt her pulse begin to throb, the quickened beat of her heart—the rise of passion.

She glanced at him and discovered that his disconcerting, dark-eyed gaze was turned on her with the brooding intensity she had come to recognize—probing and stripping her of the privacy of even her own thoughts. Flustered, she folded her arms across her chest and turned her head away.

"Hungry?"

He was taunting her. She jerked her head around to vent her anger, then felt her face flame with a hot blush when she discovered he was holding out a piece of jerky he had just cut.

She took it from him, started to bring it to her mouth, then paused to glance at the knife in his hand. "Ah . . . Flint, do you ever sterilize that blade?"

"Think I did when you got snakebit."

She glanced skeptically at the knife. "And when did you last use it?"

"Just now." He took a bite of the jerky and began chewing on it.

Garnet continued to hold the meat gingerly between her fingers. "I mean prior to just now."

"This morning." He had caught the gist of her concern, and she saw amusement gleaming in his eyes. Grinning, he said, "But you don't want to hear how I used it."

"I thought so!" She handed back the piece of jerky. "If you don't mind, would you please bite off that cut end for me? I'll take a chance on you rather than that knife."

He bit off the end of the strip and handed the meat back to her. "When we were running from those Comanche, you weren't so finicky, Widow Scott."

Garnet began to chew on the strip of beef. "Having survived that ordeal, MacKenzie, I figure I used up all my luck. Just trailing along with you is tempting the gods enough."

He shook his head in good humor. "Gotta admit, you're pretty handy in a fight. You handled that rifle real good, Widow Scott."

"Praise coming from you?" she said.

"Thought you believed in giving the devil her due."

"*His* due, MacKenzie. But since we're fessing up, as Mama used to say, I didn't mean all those things I said to you this morning."

"Figured you didn't. People tend to say a lot of things when their feathers are ruffled."

"I suppose I should take that as your apology, too."

His mouth slashed into a grin. Reaching out, he hooked a hand around her neck and pulled her to him. "You know, Redhead, you're a good sport." His lips hovered inches from hers. "Gotta admit, trailing with you ain't as bad as I make out."

She felt her heart hammering in her chest, and the feel of his fingers splayed along her neck was sending erotic shocks to her spine. "Is that an invitation, Flint?"

The grin left his face. "Didn't say that." He quickly released her and stood up. "We best get moving. We're wasting good daylight."

They rode in silence the rest of the afternoon. She began to feel the effect of the sleepless night and was glad when he finally called a halt.

Later that evening, after they finished their meal of jerky and dried biscuits, Garnet sat staring drowsily into the fire. Flint poured another cup of coffee and handed it to her. "You first."

She smiled, took several sips of the hot brew, then gave it back to him. After taking a long swallow, he offered the cup to her again, but she shook her head. "I've had enough."

"Don't know if I can finish all this," he said lightly. "Kinda gotten out of the habit of having a whole cup to myself." There was more affection than censure in his voice.

"All right, you've convinced me." He chuckled when she reached for the cup.

"Flint, why did you come back for me this morning?" The question had been on her mind most of the day.

He met her fixed look, and for a lengthy moment they stared at each other in silence. Finally, he shifted his gaze back to the fire. "Reckon I didn't want to see you hurt, especially since you tried to help me."

"Is that the only reason?" she pressed.

He looked over at her. "Don't try to make it more than it was. I don't much guess that I'd leave any woman to the likes of Nathan Bodine and Bullwhip Moore."

She put a hand over her mouth and yawned. "I suppose not." Her eyes began to droop as she thought over what he had said. Maybe deep down he believed gallantry was the only reason, but she knew he had feelings for her that he just wouldn't admit. Yawning again, she closed her eyes.

Realizing Garnet had fallen asleep, Flint sat staring at her and thought about what she had gone through the previous night to save his hide. *Other than Ma, I don't know any woman with her grit, except maybe Honey.* He fondly recalled his sister-in-law's actions when his brother Luke was in danger. Yeah, he could see that Garnet was like his mother and Honey, the kind of women who would stand by a man they loved at the risk of their own lives. He always figured women of that breed were few and far between. He'd misjudged the redhead about a lot of things.

He tossed more wood on the fire, dumped the coffee grounds into the ashes, then stood up and walked over to Sam to get the blanket. After spreading it out near the fire, he slipped an arm under Garnet's knees and lifted her into his arms. She raised her eyelids. "There's still only one blanket, Redhead."

"That's fine with me," she said in a husky voice. Nuzzling her head against his chest, she fell back to sleep.

After laying her down gently, he removed her shoes, sat down on the blanket, and pulled off his own boots. Stretching out beside her, he slipped an arm around her and drew her into his arms.

Reflexively, she snuggled against him. Her body felt warm and soft, and smelled of roses. He lay awake holding her and looking up at the stars.

"What are you thinking about, Flint?" she suddenly asked.

"Thought you were sleeping," he said, surprised.

"I was, but something woke me."

"What was it?"

Raising her head, she leaned across his chest and looked down into his eyes. "An awareness of you."

He twined his fingers into her hair. "God, woman, you know just what to say to fire a man's blood, don't you?"

"If that's true, why are you so willing to get rid of me?"

"It's not your fault. A man like me just don't make good company, Redhead. I'm ornery and I like my solitude. If I didn't, I'd have found me a saddle mate a long time ago."

"Or a woman?" she said softly.

"A woman?" He shook his head. "Naw, I've never kept a woman for more than a night or two."

"Not just *any* woman, Flint." She moved closer, making him more aware of her warmth, her soft curves. His arm tightened around her. "Feel me in your arms, Flint. I feel good, don't I?" she whispered in his ear. "And you like that feeling." She stroked his chest and could feel his rapid heartbeat. "Feel what my touch does to you, Flint. You're too much man not to have a need for this comforting at the end of the day."

His nearness and the feel of his muscled body beneath her fingertips had again inflamed her passion. She found herself caught in the web of her own making. The intimacy of the moment had transformed her love into an escalating, irreversible need for him.

Having lost her own battle of restraint, she knew he was fighting his own. She slid her hand lower. Through the thickness of his buckskins, she could feel the heat from his hard, pulsating erection. "And you need this too, Flint, just as much as you need that solitude you cherish so much. I think you need this even more."

With a low, feral growl, he rolled over, trapping her body beneath him and pinning her hands to the ground. "Damn you, woman, you're shameless."

"Shameless, or just honest? I thought you liked honesty, Flint, so why not be honest with yourself? Look me in the eye right now and tell me you can ride away."

"You know I ain't going anywhere right now," he grumbled as he unfastened the buttons of her blouse. "Especially now that you've got me fired up like a rutting bull in a passel of heifers. If this is what you want . . . what you're willing to settle for, I'd be a fool to try to drive you off. I'm willing to let you trail with me, but take it for what it's worth, Redhead. No strings—either one of us is free to ride on whenever we hanker to."

"No strings, Flint," she managed to whisper just before his lips smothered hers in a powerful, dominating kiss that sealed the bargain.

Toward sunset on the following day, they reined up on a hillside. Garnet used the moment to appreciate the view. The arrival of spring had carpeted the valley below with tiny, white blossoms that appeared to stretch to the distant purple mountains. Smoke drifted from the chimney of a log house nestled in the shelter of a stand of white birch and Ponderosa pine. A stream in the sage-covered valley snaked past a pine-fenced corral that contained a dozen grazing horses.

"There's the house where I was born and raised," he said somberly. "My dad built it."

"It all looks new, especially the outbuildings."

"The outbuildings *are* new. The original ones were all destroyed in the raid. Some of the house too. Luke rebuilt them when he moved back here last year. Cleve brought in stock and—needless to say—a most fertile bull. There's plenty of grass and water. Between his own and what he's been able to round up from the breaks, Luke's been able to build up a good-size herd."

"What do you mean by, 'round up from the breaks'?" she asked.

"A lot of steers stray from other outfits and end up roaming wild in the draws or gullies that are overrun with scrub. If the cows are old and not wearing a local brand or currently registered brand, they're free for the taking. You can cross out the old brand and put on your own. Trouble is, it's a hell of a job trying to round them up out of those places because the ground's steep, overgrown, or swampy—but more than one herd's been started that way."

"Sounds close to stealing."

"Not if it's a dead brand or from one of the herds that may have been driven north in the last couple years." He leaned across his saddle and took another long, sweeping look. "The old place sure looks good. Luke and Honey must have worked themselves thin to shape the place up the way they have."

Garnet looked fretfully toward the house. "Flint, do you think your family will mind that I'm with you?"

"Why do you ask that?"

"Well, under the circumstances, I've got no right to be here."

"Little late to be fretting over that. 'Sides, no one will be happier than Honey. She's probably hankering for some female companionship."

The sound of a slamming door drew Garnet's attention toward the house. She saw that a young boy, followed by a grayish-black dog, had come out on the porch. The dog started barking and the youngster looked up toward them.

"Quiet, Amigo. Daddy, somebody's coming," he shouted.

"That's Josh," Flint said. "Luke's son."

The door slammed again and two men stepped onto

the porch. Both were tall and broad in the shoulders
like Flint. The taller of the two stayed back and leaned
against the wall. The other man stepped to the boy's
side, his right hand riding casually on the pistol
strapped on his hip.

Then the slim figure of a woman came out of the
house, walked up behind the boy, and put her hands
on his shoulders. Her long blond hair was tied back
from her face with a bright red ribbon and hung
loosely past her shoulders. In the glow from the setting
sun, her hair looked like spun gold. The man casually
slipped an arm around her shoulders.

So that's Honey, Garnet thought. Even without seeing
her face, Garnet could sense she was beautiful.

Flint lightly flicked the reins and Sam started to
amble down the hillside toward the house.

To bolster her courage, Garnet reached instinctively
for her locket, remembering too late its loss. She
swallowed to moisten her throat, which had suddenly
gone dry. Then she followed.

Chapter 13

━━━━━━◦❯❮◦━━━━━━

As they neared the house, one of the men exclaimed loudly, "My God! I don't believe it. It's Flint!"

"Flint!" Honey cried joyously, running forward.

Flint dismounted and she threw herself into his arms. After they hugged and kissed, Flint stepped back and looked at her. "You're prettier than ever, Little Sister."

"Oh, it's so good to see you, Flint." Garnet could see tears glistening in the woman's blue eyes as she smiled up at him. "I didn't even recognize you without that horrible beard. You're downright handsome, Flint MacKenzie. Almost as handsome as your brother," she enthused, glancing impishly at the man who had walked up behind her.

"It's good to be home. Howdy, Luke," Flint said, shaking hands with his older brother. Grinning, the two men slapped each other on the back.

"Well, I'll be damned!" The tallest of the three men had approached, reaching out for a handshake.

"Good to see you, Cleve," Flint said. "When did you get here?"

"A couple days ago." Once again a series of backslaps followed. "Did some Comache lift that hair off your face, Brother Flint?" Cleve asked.

"Came pretty near to, Little Brother," Flint remarked before he bent down and swooped Joshua up into his arms. "Hey, how's my little partner doing?"

Joshua squeezed him in a bear hug. "Hi, Uncle Flint. Sure glad you're back. Now you can teach me how to rope like you promised."

Flint took off his hat and plopped it on the youngster's head. "How old are you now, Josh?"

"Seven years old. Don't you remember?"

"Seven years old, and your daddy or Uncle Cleve haven't taught you how to rope yet?" Josh shook his head. "How do they expect you to earn your spurs?"

Josh's eyes widened with excitement. "You mean when I learn to rope, I can wear spurs? Oh, boy!"

Flint glanced down at Amigo, who was leaping excitedly around his legs, the dog's tail wagging furiously.

"See you still got this lame dog." He patted the dog's head.

" 'Course! Amigo's my best friend, Uncle Flint." Quickly shifting to another subject, he asked, "How come you shaved off your beard? You sure look like my daddy now."

Engrossed in watching and listening to the family's reunion, Garnet failed to notice that Cleve had walked over to her until she heard him ask, "May I help you down?"

She found herself looking into the face of the handsomest man she had ever seen. A dark, full moustache above a wide, sensuous mouth accentuated the masculinity of his deeply-tanned face, which had been spared from prettiness by a slight hook at the bridge of his nose. Her previous apprehension over meeting Flint's family dissolved at the sight of Cleve's friendly smile.

"Oh, I'm sorry. I didn't see you." Instantly, she saw the resemblance between Flint and Cleve—especially in their dark hair and thickly-lashed, sapphire-colored eyes. They differed, however, in one aspect: Cleve had an open, affable expression, unlike Flint's enigmatic, guarded look.

Cleve's hands spanned her waist and he swung her to the ground. "I'm Cleve MacKenzie, Flint's younger brother."

"How do you do. I'm Garnet Scott," she said, returning his smile.

A dark brow arched quizzically. "Miss or Mrs.?"

"Mrs. Scott."

"Oh." Disappointment registered in his voice. "For a moment, I thought maybe Brother Flint had—"

"I'm a widow, Mr. MacKenzie," she interjected.

Once again his eyes sparked with pleasure. "Is that right? Are you and Flint—"

"Flint rescued me from a Comanche massacre."

"Oh, I'm sorry. Forgive me, Mrs. Scott. Seeing you with him, I guess I got overzealous in hoping that my brother had finally fallen in love."

Then Garnet did something which, a few weeks earlier, she would have considered scandalous. She winked at him and whispered, "I'm working on it, Cleve."

He threw back his dark head in laughter. "Garnet, anything . . . *anything* I can do to help you, you be sure to ask."

He tucked her arm in his, and they turned to discover the others were all staring at them.

"Honey . . . Luke. I'd like you to meet Mrs. Garnet Scott. Flint rescued her from a Comanche attack."

Instantly, Honey sprang into action. "Oh, you poor dear!" she exclaimed, hurrying over, her baby-blue eyes warm with compassion.

Luke followed his wife. "My pleasure, Mrs. Scott."

He's certainly a handsome man, too, Garnet thought immediately, observing the same dark hair and riveting, sapphire-colored eyes as his brothers'. Both character and strength were reflected in his rugged face.

He's known deep sorrow, she thought, upon looking deeper.

Slipping an arm around her shoulder, Honey led her toward the house. "Please come in and sit down. You must be exhausted."

Garnet felt overwhelmed by all the attention. Nervously, she glanced back at Flint. "I'll be along as soon as I take care of the horses," he said.

"I'll help you, Uncle Flint," Joshua said eagerly.

As they reached the house, Garnet looked back again and saw Flint leading the horses toward the barn. Joshua was perched on the back of the mare and Amigo limped behind them.

Within minutes, Luke and Cleve had wandered outside to join Flint. Honey took the opportunity to show Garnet the house. Other than the large rectangular room that served as a kitchen and parlor, the house had two bedrooms and a loft. Although sparsely furnished, the interior had a pleasant coziness.

"Josh and I made the rug," Honey said proudly, pointing to a braided rug in front of the fireplace. "We spent the whole winter braiding the scraps I could collect and those left over from the kitchen and bedroom curtains. This coming winter, Luke's going to build another chair for the parlor."

"He must be very handy," Garnet said.

"Oh, Luke can do anything he sets his mind to," Honey said with a worshipful glance out the window, to where the three men were talking in front of the barn. "When we sell the cattle, we're going to buy a cookstove. Then I won't have to use the fireplace for cooking. Next year, he's going to add another room. There's just been too much to do since we came here. When Flint and Cleve come, there's hardly room to move around. Not that I mind having them," she added with another loving glance out the window.

Garnet walked over to the doorway and looked at the three tall men as the low drone of their voices carried through the darkening evening. She couldn't help thinking that, individually, each one looked formidable enough, but together they looked invincible.

"Amazing, aren't they?" Honey said. "An army unto themselves."

Garnet jerked around in surprise. "How did you know what I was thinking?"

"Because I thought the same thing the first time I saw the three of them together. I've always wondered what their father looked like. He died at the Alamo, you know."

"Yes, Flint told me." Garnet returned her glance to the three men, who were now standing near several crosses in a small, fenced burial plot. "Their mother must have been a remarkable woman. Flint seems to worship her."

"They all do. So he told you about her, too? I'm surprised; Flint is the most reticent of the three. Then I imagine you know about Sarah MacKenzie, and that Josh isn't my son."

Garnet nodded. "Yes. He also said that seeing the two of you together, no one would ever guess it."

"Flint really said that, did he? I think I loved Josh from the first moment I saw him." She hastily wiped away her tears with a corner of her apron. "Oh my, what must you be thinking! I usually don't tear up so easily." Honey hustled over to the fireplace and stirred a pot bubbling on the hearth. "We're going to have to consider sleeping arrangements. You can take our room, Luke can bunk with Flint and Cleve, and I'll share the loft with Josh."

"I won't hear of it," Garnet declared. "I refuse to shove you and Luke out of your bedroom. I can sleep out here or in the barn."

"In the barn! Heavens, you don't know Luke MacKenzie. He'd never consider letting a woman sleep alone in a barn."

Garnet thought there was no time like the present to

say what they would all soon discover for themselves. She drew a deep breath and looked Honey straight in the eyes. "I wouldn't be alone. Flint would be with me."

It took a long moment for the words to sink in, then Honey's eyes widened with surprise. "I can't believe it! Flint MacKenzie has actually fallen in love!"

"Oh, please, don't say that to him. He'll deny he loves me, but I believe he just won't admit it to himself."

"Are you in love with him?" Honey asked gravely.

"I wouldn't be with him now if I weren't, Honey," she replied just as solemnly.

Honey reached out, clasped her hand, and squeezed it. "I understand."

In that single moment, Garnet knew a bond had been formed between them.

"I guess I better think about getting some supper on the table. I'm sure everybody's hungry," Honey said.

"What can I do to help?" Garnet asked.

"Well, you can slice up a couple loaves of that bread over there. You'll find a knife in that drawer on the right."

As they began to work side by side, Honey glanced sideways at her. "Where are you from, Garnet?"

Garnet quickly shared the important details of her life, including how she had met Flint. "Thank goodness you followed him when you did, or else you'd be dead now, too," Honey replied compassionately.

"I knew Flint was my destiny the moment I saw him," Garnet declared. Out the window she saw Flint swing Josh up on his shoulders. The men started to walk back to the house.

"They're coming," she said, turning to Honey with a smile.

"We're going to have to eat in shifts. We only have four chairs."

"I can sit in front of the fireplace."

"I will, too. The men can sit together and hash over old times." She leaned forward and whispered, "Confidentially, I've heard all the stories before."

The two of them were giggling like schoolgirls when the men came through the door. Stopping just inside it, they crowded together. All had washed their hands and faces, and their hair had been slicked back with water.

"My, how handsome you all look!" Honey exclaimed as she hurried over to them. "Especially this one." She swooped Joshua up, and he giggled with pleasure when she nuzzled her nose in his neck. Then she plopped him down on a chair at the table.

"Dinner's ready. You men sit. Garnet and I are going to eat over at the fireplace. I want to see an empty plate in front of you when I come back, young man," she warned Joshua. "And that doesn't mean you're to feed your food to Amigo."

"I'll eat it all up, Mama. I promise," he said. They all broke into laughter when he added with childish innocence, "No matter how bad it tastes."

Honey and Garnet picked up their plates and settled in front of the fireplace. When Cleve glanced over at them a short time later, both women's faces were flushed and animated as they chatted and giggled with their heads together.

"Looks like a lot of female talk going on over there. Reckon the ears of one of you should be ringing about now," Cleve said, grinning at his brothers.

Luke chuckled, but Flint cast a suspicious glance at the two women.

"Daddy, what does Uncle Cleve mean by ringing ears? You and Uncle Flint s'pose to wear rings in your ears like ladies do?"

"No, son, it's just an expression that means someone is talking about you."

"That's sure a dumb s'pression, ain't it, Amigo?" he said, reaching down and giving the dog a bite of meat.

"They should say fingers are ringing, 'cause you wear rings on your fingers."

"And bells on your toes," Cleve chimed in.

"Bells on your toes? What does that mean, Daddy? Who wears bells on their toes? Cassie, our cow, wears a bell around her neck, but not on her toes. I don't even know if she's got toes. Does Cassie have toes, Daddy?"

Luke's long-suffering look fell on Cleve. "I warned you, Little Brother. Choose your words carefully around your nephew or *you* can spend the night explaining them."

Flint's fixed stare had remained on the two women—particularly Garnet. "Wonder just what those two gals have found to talk about. 'Pears like they sure have hit it off."

"After spending two weeks alone in your company, Brother Flint, poor Garnet is probably desperate for the sound of a human voice," Cleve joshed good-naturedly.

"Daddy, I'm finished. May I be 'scused?" Joshua asked, shoving back his chair.

"Take your plate to the sink, Josh. Don't expect your ma to do it for you."

Joshua carried away his plate, then ran over and sat down on Honey's lap. Reflexively, she hugged him and pulled him closer as she continued talking to Garnet.

"I'm just happy for Honey," Luke said. "She's been out here with no female to talk to. I'm glad you brought Garnet here, Flint, instead of leaving her behind in some cowtown."

"Might as well tell you now; me and her have decided to trail together till one of us gets tired of the arrangement."

Cleve had just started to relax. Hearing Flint's words, he sat up straight. "Did I hear you right? What happened to your life of solitude? You must have finally figured out there's a way of staying warm on winter nights without having to throw logs on the fire."

Flint grinned at him. "I don't see any woman on your arm, Little Brother."

"You will when I find the right one. I'll know it the first time I see her. For now, I'm spreading myself around trying to keep them all happy."

"Well, don't make more of what's between the widow and me than there is." He glanced warily at Cleve. "You're the one with all the book learning, Little Brother. You ever read much about Destiny? The redhead sure puts a lot of stock in it."

"Destiny . . . God's Divine Plan . . . Kismet. Call it by whatever you want. It's all the same," Cleve said.

"Well, like I told you outside at the barn, I was heading back here when I stopped in Dos Rios to buy some grub. That's when I heard about these two guys who rode with Charlie Walden. If I hadn't picked up their trail and followed it, I'd never've been anywhere near that wagon train Garnet was on." He shook his head. "Sure makes a man wonder about the what-for of it."

"I wonder what happened to the guy you said got away."

"Never saw any sign of his track again. Could be the Comanche got him."

"Well, I'll tell you what I'm wondering," Luke declared. "I'm wondering what happened to Charlie Walden. He seems to have dropped out of sight. He ain't been raiding up this way, and Cleve just came back from Dallas; Walden ain't been raiding in those parts. I've wired a couple of the lawmen I knew in California. He ain't raiding there either. So where in hell is he?"

"Maybe somebody's killed the bastard," Cleve said.

"No, he ain't dead," Flint answered. "That goddamn snake in the grass is out there somewhere—just waiting to strike."

Another outburst of laughter from Honey and Garnet caused Flint to look toward the women. "Sure is puzzling, just what those gals are finding to talk about for so long." He looked at Luke. "Figured you're crowded enough in here, so when I was stabling Sam, I fixed a place for me and Garnet in the loft."

"You don't have to do that," Luke said. "You two can have the loft right here in the house. Or Josh and Cleve can take it and Garnet can take Josh's room."

"Naw, we'll do just fine out in the barn."

"Bet you will, Brother Flint," Cleve said, tongue-in-cheek.

"See that grin on our little brother's face, Luke? Remember how we used to wipe it off him when we were kids? Reckon it's about time to do it again."

Cleve laughed and raised his hands. "Save your strength. Sounds like you need it."

"Well, as soon as we finish supper, I think we should sit down and discuss the cattle drive," Luke said. "I want to hear what the two of you have to say."

"How about waiting until morning, Luke? It's been a long day. Reckon Garnet's pretty tired."

"Fine with me. We'll discuss it right after breakfast. You all can sleep on it."

By the time the dishes were done and Garnet had helped Honey set the dough for the morning bread, everyone was ready to call it a night. Flint grabbed a lantern. "Let's go, Redhead. We'll see you all first thing in the morning," he told the others.

Flint had laid out a snug bed with blankets in the hayloft and surrounded it with bales of hay. "Ain't no hotel, but it's under a roof in case of rain. What do you think, Redhead, would you rather stay in the house? The offer's been made, you know."

"No, this will do just fine, Flint. I'd rather have the privacy. Wouldn't you?"

"That's why I did it."

"I like your family, Flint," she said as she slipped out of her bodice and skirt.

" 'Pears like they've taken a liking to you, too." He lay waiting for her to join him.

When Garnet lay down beside him, he gathered her into his arms and kissed her. She pulled away quickly. "Ouch! Your whiskers sting." Flint rubbed his fingers over the sharp bristles. "Flint, we're going to have to add another provision to our agreement. If we stay together, you've got to shave. I don't want my face rubbed raw."

"You should have thought of that before you skinned me."

"I never liked that beard of yours any more than I do these whiskers. Well, what's it gonna be?"

He raised up on an elbow and looked down at her. "One thing I'll say about you, Redhead," he whispered as he pulled the camisole over her head, "you sure catch a man at the proper time to do your bargaining— when his blood's all fired up and all he's thinking about is tasting you." He lowered his mouth to her breasts.

She slipped her fingers into his thick hair. "Then it's a deal?" she asked breathlessly.

"Reckon so, Delilah," he murmured, and captured her mouth.

Chapter 14

The nip of spring was still in the morning air when the MacKenzies assembled after breakfast to listen to Luke explain the seriousness of the family's financial situation. Garnet had remained at the sink, lingering over the breakfast dishes, but she could hear the discussion.

"Right now, Texas is glutted with beef. I can only get three dollars a head, four at the most. I can't keep the Triple M running with those prices."

"At that price, I'd say it doesn't even pay to run cattle," Cleve agreed. "Might just as well be a farmer. You can get more for your crops,"

"Or go back to being a sheriff," Luke said. He swung a guilty glance at Honey and caught her distressed look. "Don't look so worried, Jaybird. I promised you I wouldn't go back to being a lawman."

"What do you have in mind, Luke?" Flint asked.

"If we drive the herd north to Abilene," Luke said solemnly, "we can get forty dollars a head for them."

Garnet turned toward them and put aside the towel. All were looking with surprise at Luke, especially Honey, whose mouth was agape as she stared at her husband.

Cleve finally broke the silence. "The Chisholm Trail."

Luke nodded. "Once we cross the Red, it'd be six hundred miles straight north."

"Yeah, but three hundred of those miles are through the Nations." Flint's words sounded to Garnet like a warning.

"I know, Flint, but the Comanche and Kiowa are the only hostiles; the other tribes aren't bothering the drives. And I heard that even most of the Comanche bands have headed north to Wyoming. I was talking to Ben Ward last week in town. He rides for the Bar K. Last year they trailed a herd of longhorns up to Abilene. He said there's good grass and water the whole way. The only trouble they had was from a gang of Jayhawkers, not Indians."

"What are Jayhawkers?" Honey asked.

"They operate in Kansas and are as bad as outlaws," Luke said. "They claim to be the law and demand a levy for crossing Kansas. If they don't get what they ask for, they take cattle instead. And don't care who they kill doing it."

"Why, that's just plain rustling!" Honey exclaimed.

"That's exactly what it is," Cleve agreed. "But by the time they reach Kansas, most trail bosses don't want trouble, so they give them what they want rather than risk their drovers' lives."

"How big was the Bar K drive, Luke?" Flint asked.

"About a thousand head."

"And who was the trail boss?"

"Dallas Fenton," Luke replied.

Flint shook his head. "Hell, Luke! Fenton's the best trail boss in Texas. He can sniff out water before a steer can."

"Well, Ben Ward said there's a guy named McCoy in Abilene who's cut a deal with the railroad and is buying up Texas beef as soon as it reaches the town. In '67, only thirty-five thousand head were driven north, last year over seventy thousand, and this year they're figuring over three hundred thousand!"

"Well, how many riders did Ward say the Bar K used?" Cleve asked.

"He said there were ten of 'em, besides the cook and Fenton."

Cleve never changed his expression. "And how many head have you got, Luke?"

"Figure by the time they're all rounded up, there should be over four hundred head."

"Four hundred head!" Cleve emitted a long, low whistle.

"Now you can see why selling them here or selling them in Abilene could be the difference between sixteen hundred dollars and sixteen thousand."

"Where the hell did you get four hundred head?" Cleve asked, still astounded. "I only brought in a couple hundred last year."

Luke grinned rakishly. "I'm counting calves, too. That bull you brought in has been keeping himself busy. Right now, I've got about three hundred head rounded up on the north range. And I know there's at least a hundred more in the breaks."

Flint snorted. "You sure they're all yours? Stealing cows is still against the law in these parts, ain't it?"

"Sure, there's strays wearing other brands among 'em. We can cut them out of the herd. But we've got the right to slap a Triple M brand on any maverick or cow we find on our range."

"But, Luke, how can you vent a cow if you don't know whether the brand's still active?" Honey asked.

"I got a copy of a stockgrowers' brand book that's just been published. It'll be easy enough for us to check out a brand we don't recognize. If it's not registered, we can cross out the old brand and put our own on the cow."

"How do you do that Daddy?" Josh asked.

"We just put an 'X' over the old brand and put our brand right next to it. That's called venting, son."

"Wow!" Josh exclaimed. That sure must hurt the cow!"

"When did you have in mind to get started, Big Brother?"

Luke turned to Flint. "I was hoping about the middle of June. I need another month to finish the round-up and do the branding."

"And how long you figure this drive will take?" Flint asked.

Luke unfolded a map. "The Kansas Pacific's been handing out this guidebook showing the trail. That's the railroad that's shipping the stock east."

Flint and Cleve bent over the table for a closer look as Luke began to trace the route with his finger.

"If we follow the Red east we could reach Red River Station in about ten days—you both know that's the easiest spot to ford the river."

"Yeah, quicksand and all," Flint said sarcastically.

"Then I figure it'd take about another fifty days to reach Abilene." Luke straightened up and looked at them hopefully.

"Four months there and back, and good trail all the way. Doesn't sound too bad to me," Cleve said.

"Well, there are a few rivers to cross," Luke confessed. He leaned over again and pointed to the map. "After the Red, 'pears like there's the Wichita, the Canadians, Cimarron, the Arkansas, and the Kansas."

"And three of us and four hundred cattle," Cleve scoffed. "I take back what I said about how easy it sounded."

Luke folded up the map. "Sure, I'd like one or two more riders, but they've all been picked up by the bigger spreads."

"I can ride," Garnet said.

Up to now, she had been listening in silence, figuring this was MacKenzie family business—not hers. She could see both sides of the argument: Luke had to be optimistic because, most likely, the Triple M's survival depended on this drive; on the other hand, Flint and Cleve were right in saying it would be almost impossible for only three men to accomplish it.

Surprise registered on their faces as they continued to stare at her.

"I can ride," she repeated. "I've never herded cattle before, but I've done my share of riding—and handling a rifle, too."

"And I could drive the chuck wagon," Honey piped in. "Remember, Luke, I drove a wagon from Missouri to California."

"And me and Amigo can help Mama cook," Josh said excitedly. "I can make the biscuits." Honey beamed at him and slipped her arm around his shoulders.

Garnet saw Flint and Cleve exchange a meaningful glance. "No women or children," Flint declared.

"We'll just see about that, Flint MacKenzie," Honey challenged.

"I agree with Flint on this, Honey," Cleve interjected. "I'm sure Garnet will be willing to stay with you while we're gone. Won't you, Garnet?"

"Don't you dare use that patronizing tone with me, Cleve MacKenzie," Honey said. "You're not talking to one of those saloon whores you're used to dealing with. They're only good for one thing!"

"Now, now, Little Sister, don't go getting all riled up," Cleve cajoled.

Flint winked at Cleve. "We're only thinking of your welfare, little Honey Bear," Flint added.

Honey looked near to bursting. "What did I warn you about calling me by that ridiculous name?"

Holding back his laughter, Flint scratched his head. "Reckon I don't recall. You remember what she said, Little Brother?"

"I think she said she prefers Sugar Bear to Honey Bear," Cleve responded.

Honey put her hands on her hips. "You two are

worse than little boys. I'm going to have to take a broom to you."

"What does that mean, Mama?" Josh asked.

"You'll find out soon enough, Joshua MacKenzie, if you start acting like your uncles."

Grinning, Luke pulled her down on his lap. "Hey, cool down, Jaybird." He looped his arms around her waist and kissed her lightly. "You know how they like to see you riled."

Honey slipped her arms around his neck. "I know. But you wouldn't leave me behind, would you, Luke?" she asked worriedly.

Luke sobered. For a long moment he stared deeply into her eyes, then he said solemnly, "No, baby, I'd never leave you behind." He looked up at the two men. "I mean it, boys. I'm not leaving my family behind. Remember what happened to Sarah and Ma?"

"Flint and I never figured you would," Cleve said. "We just thought it'd be worth suggesting."

Garnet felt Flint's stare and looked over, meeting his gaze. "Well, Redhead, I reckon you've got a vote on this matter, too."

"It's not my place to say what's the right or wrong thing to do. But speaking as a woman, I can't imagine how Honey and Josh could be any safer here than with Luke. And as for the hardship on the trail. . . ." She winked at Honey. "It takes a couple of bachelors to underestimate the endurance of a woman."

"Well, I think the lady's made her position pretty clear," Cleve said with a wide grin. "Looks like you've got yourself a crew, Big Brother. Look out Abilene— here come the MacKenzies!"

Honey jumped to her feet and rushed over to them. "Oh, I love you two! I love you! I love you!" she enthused, hugging and kissing the two men.

"Does that mean you won't whomp us with your broom?" Cleve asked. He spanned her waist, lifted her off her feet, and swung her around in a circle.

"I'd never be foolish enough to promise *that*," she said, squealing.

When he put her down, she looked up at him and smiled. "Thank you, Cleve," she said emotionally. Turning to Flint, she reached out and stroked his cheek. "And you, too, you old fake." Her eyes suddenly flashed with impishness. "Oh my, you need a shave!" Rushing back to Luke, Honey plopped down on his lap and slipped her arms around his neck.

"And you, Luke MacKenzie, I love you more than I can ever say." She kissed him. His hands slipped to her shoulders as the kiss deepened.

Cleve went over to Josh. "Come on, nephew, let's you and me ride out and count cows. Your daddy and mama need some time alone."

"Why do they—" Cleve's hand clamped over the youngster's mouth before he could say more. Picking him up, Cleve carried Josh outside with Amigo following at his heels. Garnet turned to Flint. He nodded and they slipped out, closing the door behind them.

Joshua raced ahead of them as Garnet walked between the two men toward the horse corral. They stopped and leaned on the fence.

"I think we'll need a lot more than a dozen horses on the drive," Flint said. He hooked his heel on a rung. "Riding in yesterday, I thought I caught a glimpse of some mustangs. Think I'll ride out and try to spot them again."

"Well, I'd go with you," Cleve said, "but I told Josh I'd take him out to the north range to see the cattle. Why don't you and Garnet ride along? I'll hunt mustangs with you tomorrow."

"You feel like a ride, Redhead?"

"Sure, why not?" she said. She was amazed at how quickly Flint conceded, since he usually offered an argument first. Then it occurred to her how much more relaxed he appeared around his family. Perhaps she shouldn't intrude on this chance for him to spend time with his brother and nephew.

"On second thought, you all go without me. I'm kind of all rode out," she said lightly.

"You feeling okay, Redhead?" Flint asked. She detected an unusual note of concern in his voice.

"I'm fine, Flint."

"Sure you don't mind us leaving you alone, Garnet?" Cleve said a short time later, when they were ready to ride out. Joshua was sitting in front of Cleve on the saddle.

"Oh, I'll find something to do, don't worry about me," she said as she waved good-bye to them.

Garnet went back into the barn. Seeing some tubs and a washboard in the corner, she was reminded of the soiled clothing stuffed in Flint's saddlebags, and decided that now would be the ideal time to wash them.

Garnet dragged out the wash tubs and placed them on the metal grill obviously intended for outside use. After filling the tubs, she built a fire under the grill. While she waited for the water to heat, she strung a clothesline between two trees. Then, climbing up in the loft, she picked up Flint's saddlebags.

Once outside, Garnet dumped the contents on the ground and put back everything except the pile of dirty clothes.

She cast a disparaging look at the clothes she was wearing. Clearly, they could use a washing. Since Flint had more to wear than she did, she ducked into the barn, shed all her clothes, and put on the shirt and pants of Flint's that she had worn before.

She washed the underclothing first, along with her skirt and bodice. After stringing them on the line, she returned to scrub Flint's shirts and trousers.

Whistling contentedly, she picked up one of his

shirts. She recognized it as the one he had worn the morning he had the knife fight with the two Indians. She held it up and saw it was heavily bloodstained.

As she shook it out, an item fell from the pocket. Stunned, she stared in disbelief at her locket—the cherished locket she believed had been lost forever. Joyously, she sat down on the ground and opened it, her gaze consuming every detail of her family's beloved faces.

Through the rush of happiness, she became struck by the implication of finding the locket in his shirt pocket. Her heart seemed to sink to the pit of her stomach.

Flint had had her locket all the time!

How did he get it? Why didn't he tell her? He knew how much she cherished the locket. Was it some reprehensible joke? Did he enjoy witnessing her grief over its loss? Surely he didn't do it as a prank.

He had his own family. He could see them, talk to them, hear their laughter. But she would never know such precious moments again.

It broke her heart to realize that this didn't matter to him. Despite what they had gone through together— the intimacy they had shared—the cold, hard truth was that it didn't matter one bit to him.

She buried her head in her hands. No, this went much deeper than malicious humor. This was cruelty. He was all that she had once declared him to be—a mean man. A cruel and heartless man.

Once, she had believed she could love this man! Despite all his boorishness, she had believed Flint MacKenzie had some kind of redeeming grace—and that he would come to love her through the sheer force of her love for him.

What a foolish belief! What a naive, girlish, foolish belief! Her eyes weren't closed any longer, or clouded with fantasies. She finally recognized the one truth that had been before her lovesick eyes all the time: Flint MacKenzie was incapable of love.

When she had exhausted all the names she could think of calling him, she was left with only heartache. A deep-down heartache. The kind that left a wrenching pain in her chest and hurt every time she tried to breathe.

She started to cry—hot, scalding tears that stung her heart as much as they did her cheeks. "I loved you, Flint," she sobbed. "I thought I could change you . . . to make you start believing in love. But I was wrong. You'll get your wish. I won't bother you anymore. I'm riding away and leaving you alone.

"You're not worthy of my love, Flint—and God pity the next woman who's foolish enough to fall in love with you."

Chapter 15

Garnet waited until she saw Luke ride away to join the others, then she saddled up the mare, tied her tiny bundle of clothes to the saddle, and led the mare to the house. She had stayed to have a private good-bye with Honey—and now the moment she dreaded could no longer be put off.

Her steps dragged as she entered the house. Honey was at the sink and looked up with a bright smile. "Hi, are you hungry? Thought I'd start dinner. There's no telling when those men might return."

"I'm leaving, Honey. I came to say good-bye."

"Leaving?" Honey's surprise and disappointment were evident. "Oh, I'm sorry. I thought that . . ." She put her head down and continued to peel potatoes. "I guess I thought that you and Flint were—"

"Well, it's . . . ah . . . not working out."

"Oh," Honey said. She sighed and turned her head away. "It's the cattle drive, isn't it? I guess I can't blame you. There's no reason why you should put yourself through that if you don't have to."

Garnet did not intend to tell Honey her real reason for leaving. Flint was a brother-in-law Honey loved dearly; nothing would be gained by bad-mouthing him. Garnet hoped they could part friends. "Well, I

158

didn't want to leave without thanking you for your hospitality."

Honey looked sorrowfully at her. "Where are you going, Garnet?"

"Santa Fe, I guess." Garnet shrugged. "I'm supposed to get married, you know."

"No, I didn't know that. You never mentioned it; neither did Flint."

"I thought I did. That was my purpose in coming west."

"Do you have any money, Garnet?" Honey asked worriedly. "You did tell me you lost everything you owned in the Indian massacre."

"I'll be fine. I'll find something to do in the next town to earn enough for a stagecoach ticket to Santa Fe." Garnet laughed lightly. "How far is the next town? I have no idea."

"It's about twenty miles from here. You turn right at the top of the hill and head due west. There's kind of a worn wagon path you can follow. Before you leave, will you sit down and have something to eat?"

"No, I'm really not hungry."

"Well, at least let me pack you a lunch to eat on the way."

"Oh, Honey, you don't have to do that." Garnet wanted to stop her, but Honey had already sliced the bread and was now piling beef on it. Then she filled a canning jar with water.

"Will you sit down and have a cup of tea with me?" she asked.

"I think it would be better for me to get out of here in case Flint comes back."

"You didn't tell him you were leaving, did you?"

Garnet shook her head. "No, but I don't think it matters much to him one way or another."

"I think you're wrong. Flint's changed. And I think you're the one who's changed him." Honey finished wrapping the sandwich and her fingers lingered on the string after tying it. "I don't suppose I can convince you to stay."

"No, Honey," Garnet said firmly.

"I don't like you riding off alone. You don't even have a weapon to protect yourself. Why don't you wait until the men get back? Then one of them can ride into town with you."

"I'll be okay. I can't imagine anything happening to me that hasn't happened already. I did take Flint's blanket, though. Please tell him so when he gets back."

"Is there anything else you want me to tell him?" Honey asked.

"Tell him . . . just tell him good-bye for me."

Suddenly the two women were hugging each other. Honey stepped away, drew a hankie out of her pocket, and blew her nose. "It's been so nice having you here."

Arm in arm, they walked outside. Garnet climbed up on the back of the mare. "Be careful, Garnet, and I hope you'll be happy in your new marriage. Maybe when you get settled, you could write me a letter."

"I'll do that, Honey. Good-bye, and thanks for everything."

She rode up the same hill that, just yesterday, she had descended at Flint's side. When she reached the top, she reined up the mare and looked back. Honey stood at the door. She raised her arm and waved.

Garnet waved back, then she turned the horse westward.

Flint felt uneasy. He didn't know why, but from the moment he had ridden away from the house that morning, he felt something was going to happen. Something to do with Garnet. It made no sense to him why he should be fretting over her.

Last night when they made love—"Goddammit,

there I go again," he cursed softly—last night had been better than their first time. And he'd never have believed it was possible. Hell! Each time with her always seemed better than the time before. He had never enjoyed sex with any woman as much as he did with her. Her intensity and uninhibitedness added an extra something special that he'd sure never gotten from any two-dollar whore. Just thinking about the feel of her in his hands . . . the way she tasted to his tongue . . . the smell of her . . . were tempting enough for him to ride back and have her again. *Goddamn!* he thought, grinning, that little wild, redheaded vixen had dug her spurs into him—he was hurting.

"Lot of cows, aren't there?"

Cleve's voice snapped him out of his reverie. He saw that his brother had dismounted and Josh had scampered away.

Flint climbed off Sam. "Yep, sure are. And Luke says there's another hundred to round up." He took a moment to take a long look at the cattle strung out on the slopes and floor of the valley below.

"What's your gut feeling about this drive, Cleve?"

"I don't see why we can't make it. I'd be a lot more comfortable with a couple more riders, though. We could use the iron—especially with those women along."

"You figure Luke's lost his edge?"

Cleve looked at him, surprised. "Why would you say that?"

"I dunno," Flint said, shrugging. "Once a man gets himself tangled up with a woman, it seems to take something out of him. His mind's not on what it should be. He keeps thinking about that woman or kid who's depending on him. Those seconds could get him killed."

"You running into that problem, Brother Flint?" Cleve asked, grinning.

"Me? Hell no! I'm talking about Luke."

Cleve nodded slowly. "Oh, I thought maybe you might be speaking from experience."

"Don't be looking at me with that goddamn grin of yours, Little Brother."

"Well, if Luke's lost his edge, I don't see a sign of it. I saw him draw on a rattler yesterday. He's as fast as he ever was."

"Well, I ain't talking about his draw. Leastwise, a rattler warns you before striking. When a man loses his edge, he's not as quick to sniff out that snake before it starts its rattle."

"Come on, Flint, Luke can take care of himself," Cleve said. He slapped Flint on the shoulder. "It's not like you to be worrying. Something else on your mind that you're not saying?"

"I reckon not."

"Thought maybe you were concerned about Garnet coming along on the drive."

"I don't much like the idea of Honey coming, either. I can say though, Garnet don't scare easy. And she can ride and handle a rifle all right."

"She sure is likeable."

"Little Brother, that redhead's been trouble from the moment I met her . . . but I kinda like trailing with her. She's a good sport."

"Is that the only reason, Brother Flint?"

"What are you getting at?" Flint asked belligerently.

"I thought maybe you were thinking of getting married."

He snorted. "Not me, Little Brother. I'll leave the women to you and Luke. I don't need no wife in my life!"

"Have you told Garnet that?"

"I remind her of it every day." He swung back up on Sam. "We best be getting back to the house. Reckon our big brother's ready to talk ranching."

Cleve whistled for Joshua. "Let's go, Josh."

Clutching a handful of early-blooming bluebonnets, the youngster came running back with Amigo barking at his heels.

As soon as Flint arrived back at the ranch, he unsaddled Sam and put the horse in one of the stalls. He climbed up to check the loft, not really expecting to find Garnet there, then headed for the house.

Luke and Cleve's guarded looks when he entered were all he needed to know that something was wrong. Seeing no sign of Garnet, he asked Honey where he could find her.

"She left, Flint. She told me to tell you good-bye."

Flint felt as if he had been punched in the stomach. "She say why she was leaving?"

"Only that it wasn't working out between the two of you. She was gonna catch a stage to Santa Fe to get married."

"Oh. I see." Flint slammed the door on his way out of the house. That deceiving floozy! That conniving, redheaded little liar! How come she didn't say so that morning, if that was what she had in mind? She'd even promised to join them on the drive.

He felt the rise of anger. Goddammit! How come she didn't face him down and tell him she was leaving? To just ride off the way she did without even a good-bye sure didn't seem right—especially after they had just agreed to trail together.

The more he thought about it, the angrier he got. She should have told him. Instead, she made him look like a fool in his family's eyes. For damn sure, he didn't need her—but he'd sure like to tell her as much before she had a chance to climb on that stage.

Having worked himself up into a fever pitch, he spun on his heel and stormed back into the house. "How long ago did she leave?" he shouted.

Honey dropped the dish she was holding and it crashed to the floor. "I'd say around noon." She bent down and began to pick up the broken pieces of crockery. "If you used that same tone on her as you just did on me, it's no wonder she left you, Flint MacKenzie."

Flint knelt down and began to help her. "I'm sorry, Honey. I didn't mean to spook you. Did she say where she was heading?"

"She did ask the directions to Calico."

"Did you give her any money?"

"I didn't have any to give her, Flint, or I sure would have tried. All she left here with was a sandwich—and your blanket."

"My blanket! So, she's a thief on top of everything else."

"Ah, come on, Flint," Cleve objected. "A damn blanket!"

Flint stood and hurried to the door. "She ain't gonna get away with that."

Honey looked at Luke and Cleve. "You don't think he'll harm her, do you?"

The two men exchanged amused glances and began chuckling.

Grinning widely, Cleve replied, "I think it's safe to say that Brother Flint's fallen in love."

Garnet was relieved when she saw the lights of the town. The first thing she did was go to the livery. After a lengthy argument with the livery man, she sold the mare for ten dollars—ten dollars less than she had paid for it. Then she went to the Wells Fargo office and discovered she was still fifteen dollars short to buy a ticket to Santa Fe. Well, it was still early enough for her to look around to see if there were any jobs available. With the blanket roll in hand, she surveyed the town.

Several blocks long, Calico looked to be nothing more than a dusty road lined with wooden buildings on either side.

"Don't people out here ever bother to pave a road?"

she grumbled as she recalled the cypress and magnolia-lined streets of Georgia, with their lamp-posts and gracious homes.

Garnet walked past the hotel and the gunsmith next to it. Her goal was a storefront bearing the name Jenkins Dry Goods. When she entered the small store, she smelled the scents of new leather and candle wax. A thin-faced man with gray hair fringing his bald crown regarded her through a pair of glasses perched on the end of his nose.

"I'd like to speak to Mr. or Mrs. Jenkins," she said.

"What can I do for you?" he asked.

"Mr. Jenkins, I'm wondering if you need any help. I'm looking for a job."

He shook his head. "Can't say that I do. Heard that Maud Malone, over at the diner, had been looking to take on some help. Might have some luck trying over there."

"Thank you, I will."

When she started to turn away, he asked, "You a stranger in town?"

Garnet nodded. "Yes, I'm passing through on my way to Santa Fe."

"Uh-huh," he said, regarding her with more curiosity. "Passing through from where?"

"Georgia."

"Georgia?" He scratched his bald pate. "Is that one of them towns near El Paso?" Garnet was already halfway out the door and didn't bother to respond.

She crossed the street to a small building bearing a sign that read MAUD'S EATERY—BEST HOME-COOKING IN TEXAS. As she entered, a bell tinkled above the door and she was met by the tantalizing aroma of fried steak. Apparently, the sign was not an exaggeration; all the tables but one were occupied. A heavy-set woman with gray hair and skin that looked as tough as saddle leather hurried past carrying a tray laden with two plates, each heaped with steak and potatoes.

"Just sit yourself down at that table in the corner, honey. I'll be with you as soon as I can."

Garnet walked over and sat down. Shortly after, the woman came back and set a cup of coffee in front of her. "Steak and potatoes is the special tonight."

"Are you Maud?" Garnet asked.

"That's right, honey. Maud Malone."

"Well, Maud, I really didn't come here to eat. I was told you're looking for help."

"Hold on, honey. I'll be back," Maud said.

Garnet sipped the coffee and watched as Maud took the order of two cowboys seated at a nearby table. When Garnet saw Maud hurry back to the kitchen, she got to her feet and began to clear the dishes from a table that had just emptied. She carried them into the kitchen, where Maud was ladling soup into two bowls.

The woman glanced at the dishes in Garnet's hand. "What's your name, honey?"

"Garnet Scott."

"Okay, Garnet, job pays a dollar a day—two dollars on Saturdays and Sundays—and you get to keep all the tips you earn. And there's always somethin' to eat around here. Grab that tray and take these bowls of soup to the table by the window." Wordlessly, Garnet nodded and did as she was told.

The two women worked nonstop for the next three hours. Finally, after the last customer had departed, Maud locked the door, put a Closed sign in the window, and pulled down the shade.

"Got a couple pieces of apple pie left, if you've got a mind for it."

"That sure sounds good to me," Garnet said.

Exhausted, they sat down with pie and coffee. "I have to be honest with you, Maud. I intend to leave for Santa Fe as soon as I earn enough for a ticket."

"Well, I can use the help until then," Maud replied, resigned. "Is that where you're from, honey?"

"No, I'm from Georgia."

"Knew your accent didn't sound like any Texas gal. How'd you ever end up here in Calico?"

"I'm the only survivor of a wagon train that was wiped out by a Comanche attack."

"Sounds like you were plumb lucky, gal. Ain't too many been attacked by the Comanche and live to tell about it."

"I was rescued by a man riding through, and by chance I ended up here."

"Who was this fella?" Maud asked.

"Flint MacKenzie."

"Flint MacKenzie!" Maud slapped the table with her hand. "Hell, honey, I'd say you were downright blessed! A person's luck don't fall any better than that. If anyone can dodge a Comanche arrow, it's Flint MacKenzie."

"Oh, you know him," Garnet said.

"Land sakes alive! I've known Flint from the time he was a boy. All of the MacKenzies. Some folks say Flint's the most thin-skinned of 'em—the meanest— but I've never seen him kick a dog or beat a horse. And he's a fair man in a fight; he ain't ever been known to bite or gouge eyes. Now, Cleve!" Maud rolled her eyes. "There's the rogue! I love that young'n. He could charm the skin off a snake. That boy's broken the hearts of more gals than there's stars in the sky." Maud paused for a moment, then her tone became more thoughtful. "Luke's the most serious of the three. Kind of had to take over and fill his pa's shoes. Spitting image of his pa, too." She reached over and patted Garnet's hand. "I'll tell you a secret, honey, one I've never told to another soul. Makes no sense why I'm telling it to a stranger now, 'cept that I've held the ache inside me all these years and I 'spect it ain't going away less'n I let it out. I was in love with Andrew MacKenzie. It near broke my heart when he up and married my best friend."

"Andrew was Flint's father?" Garnet asked.

Maud nodded. "When the young fool died at the Alamo, my heart broke same as Kathleen's. Then, when she was killed the way she was, it sure saddened a lot of us folks around here. She was a good woman. Can't fault Andy for lovin' her." Maud shook her head sadly. "Reckon those three boys ain't gonna rest till they find the bastards that did it."

She rose wearily to her feet. "Well, morning comes sooner than I like, so we best get going on those dishes or it'll be daylight before I get these old bones in bed. Where are you staying?"

"I just arrived tonight, so I haven't had a chance to find a place yet."

"You can have the couch upstairs, if you've a mind to. It ain't the best, but it's a place to rest your head."

"Maud, I've been sleeping in everything from a cave to a hayloft. A couch sounds like a real comfort. And I insist you go up to bed right now. I can do the dishes."

"Lordy, gal, there's a passel of 'em."

"That doesn't bother me."

"Well, if you're sure you don't mind. Guess I'm getting too old for this business. Gotta be thinkin' 'bout givin' it up one of these days. Goodnight, honey. I'll lay you out a quilt and pillow."

"Goodnight, Maud. And thank you."

Garnet watched the old lady climb up the stairs, then she hurried out to the kitchen.

Chapter 16

It was almost midnight when Flint rode into Calico. By that time, his anger had cooled and he had figured the whole thing out. This was another one of Garnet's tricks to get him to marry her. He should have guessed it earlier, instead of losing his temper. He rode immediately to the livery stable and found the doors closed, but not locked. He opened one of the doors just wide enough to slip through. After lighting a lantern, he checked the stalls and found the mare. It was a good sign; Garnet had made it this far, anyway.

Wanting to make certain she was safe, Flint went next door and woke up the livery man. The two men were well acquainted. "Curly, there's a bald-faced mare in one of the stalls. Where'd you get it?"

"I bought it from a redheaded gal that rode in here. Why'd you ask?"

"The mare belongs to the Triple M."

"Hell, Flint, I didn't see no Triple M brand on it."

"Haven't had time."

"Haven't had time? That mare's five or six years old."

"Just bought the mare a couple days ago from a livery in Waynesburg and paid twenty dollars for it. How much did you buy it for?"

"Ten dollars," Curly said. "Hell, Flint, that mare's been rode hard and put away wet. It wasn't worth any more than that to me. If you got it from a livery, the mare's had a lot of different riders."

"What happened to the gal who sold it to you?"

"Saw her later at Maud's when I ate. 'Pears like she's working there."

"Thanks, Curly. Sorry to wake you."

"You want that mare back?"

"I'll let you know. If I do, you'll get your ten dollars back."

"Cost you twelve dollars. Man's got to make a living," Curly said slyly.

"Wouldn't try doing it by buying stolen horses, Curly."

"Told you, Flint, I didn't know the horse was stolen. You gonna get the sheriff in on this?"

"No. But I am gonna stable my dun for the night. That'll make us even."

Flint went back to the stable, and as soon as he finished taking care of Sam he headed for the diner. He wasn't through with the redhead yet. Seeing the place was closed, he went around to the back and looked in the window. He pounded on the back door.

Sighing with relief, Garnet finished drying the last skillet. When she heard a pounding at the door, she spun around in startlement. "Who is it?"

"Open up," Flint shouted.

"Oh good Lord!" She had no trouble identifying *that* voice. She put the skillet down on the table and went to the door. "Who is it?" she asked purposefully.

"You know goddamned well who it is!"

"The diner's closed. And be quiet or you'll wake up Maud."

"Goddammit, Garnet, open the door or I'll wake up the whole blasted town," he warned at the top of his voice.

Garnet knew it wasn't an idle threat. She unlocked the door and walked away. He entered and slammed the door shut behind him.

"What do you want this time of night?" she asked without giving him a glance.

"I came to get the mare and the blanket you stole from me."

She looked at him just long enough to glare. "Oh, don't be ridiculous."

"Stealing a horse is a serious offense in these parts. So is stealing a man's personal possessions."

Garnet continued to ignore him as she stacked the dishes and kettles she had just washed onto the rows of floor-to-ceiling shelves. "It appears like everything other than killing a man is an offense in these parts. Maybe I should have done that instead."

"The horse belonged to me, Widow Scott. Have you forgotten the mare was bought with my money? That makes you a horse thief, lady."

"All right, hang me!" Picking up a heavy kettle, she climbed up on a stool to put it on a top shelf near the ceiling.

The stool began to wobble, and for several seconds she tottered perilously. Flint saw her plight and rushed over. He managed to get one hand on her hip and the other on her rear in time to keep her from falling.

"You lecher! Take your hands off me!"

"Okay, if that's the way you want it, lady." He removed his hands.

As soon as she leaned forward and put the heavy kettle on the shelf, the stool started rocking again. With a frantic yelp, she reached out with both hands and grabbed the shelf just as the stool toppled over. Holding on with her fingertips, she dangled from the top shelf. She groped unsuccessfully with her foot, trying to make contact with a lower shelf. Wild-eyed, she turned her head and saw that Flint was leaning casually against the table, his arms folded across his chest.

"Well, are you going to help me, or just let me hang here!"

"In answer to your first question, you've already declined my help. As for the second one, I warned you stealing horses was a hanging offense."

"You're an insufferable, pitiful excuse for a human being, MacKenzie. A shame your humor has to be wasted on me." She returned to toe groping.

She glanced down to see him below her. "What are you doing besides looking up my skirt?"

"Now, Widow Scott, we both know how that thought excites you, so you've gotta try to keep a cool head. I've analyzed your predicament, and I've a suggestion."

"I have one for you, too," she fumed, puffing at the hair that had fallen over her face. Her arms had begun to ache.

"If you work yourself down to the end of the shelf, I'm sure with a hefty swing of those long legs of yours, you oughta be able to make it over to the table."

"I've already thought of that," she snapped belligerently. She gave the hair in her face several more hasty puffs of her much needed breath.

"Then how come you haven't done it?"

"I was waiting for you to get out of the way. I'd feel real bad if I kicked you in the face in the process."

She started to inch her hands slowly along the shelf.

With half the distance still to go, she was feeling the ache and strain on her tiring muscles. She was on the verge of swallowing her pride and asking Flint again for his help when she suddenly froze. A soul-rending shriek burst from her throat as, horrified, she stared eye-to-eye into two glittering eyes.

Her fingers slipped off the shelf's edge and she fell. Shutting her eyes, she waited for the painful contact with the floor. Instead, she landed in firm arms that closed around her so securely that not even an earthquake would shake her free.

It took her several seconds to realize she hadn't crashed to the floor—and several more to make her aware that the arms holding her so securely belonged to Flint MacKenzie.

"Good Lord, Garnet, what's up there? A snake?"

"It was . . . it was—"

"What?" he asked, concerned by her fright.

She drew a shuddering breath. "It was a mouse."

"A mouse!" He dumped her on the stool. "God, woman, I'll never understand you. Snakes and Indians don't scare you—but look out for those killer mice!"

"Have you ever tried to stare down a mouse, Mac-Kenzie?"

"No, I've always been faint-hearted, so I've limited myself to bears and buffalo."

"Oh, get out of here!" She jumped to her feet. "I've listened to all your sarcasm that I intend to."

He drew back with an exaggerated look of alarm, which only infuriated her more. "But if I leave you, who will protect you from the gnawing jaws of Monster Mouse?"

His last remark pushed her to the limit. "I warned you, MacKenzie!" Garnet picked up the skillet from the table—and bopped him on the head!

For several seconds Flint couldn't see, and he leaned against the table to keep from falling. When the room stopped spinning, he clutched his aching head. "You hit me!"

"Yeah, with the skillet, and I should have hit you harder," she declared with a hostile glare.

"You are loco, woman—plain loco! You might have killed me!" He approached her slowly, his eyes black with rage. She backed away. She had seen that angry look enough times before.

Garnet swallowed past the lump in her throat. "Nonsense, I barely tapped you. If I had wanted to kill you, you'd be on that floor right now."

He appeared not to give her explanation much

credence, because he continued to stalk her around the table. She managed to stay out of his arm's reach. "What in hell did you hit me for?" he asked, rubbing his head. "I've got a bump!" He felt his head again and looked at her incredulously. "Lady, you raised a knot on my head!"

"Oh, for heaven's sake! Stop whining like a little boy. It's not that big."

"Not big!" He lunged across the table, but she managed to step back and evade the attack. "Maybe not as big as the knot I'm gonna tie in your neck as soon as I get my hands around it."

How dare he threaten her! He knew damn well she refused to be threatened. She had told him time and again that she didn't back down from a bully. "I dare you to try it, Flint MacKenzie." She changed her direction and charged right up to him, defiantly lifting her head right in his face. "Here it is. I just dare you to try it!"

He grasped her by the shoulders. "What in hell has gotten into you?"

"You dare ask me that, after what you've done?"

"What the hell did I do?"

Indignant, she shoved his hands off her shoulders, then dug the locket out from under her bodice, and held it up to his nose. "That's what!"

"A locket?"

"Not just any locket, Flint MacKenzie. *My* locket. The locket I believed had been lost to me forever."

"Oh, yeah. I forgot all about your locket."

"I guess you did." Her eyes blazed with contempt. "Or maybe you didn't expect me to find it in your shirt pocket."

"I reckon you're right about that," he said, irritated. "A man's shirt pockets are his own business. I don't hanker after you going through them, Widow Scott."

"And I don't hanker after your kind of cruelty, MacKenzie. You knew what my locket meant to me."

"I figured I did. That's why I went back to find it after you dropped it on the trail."

"Oh, don't try to weasel out of it now. If the real truth were known, I probably never dropped it. You had it all the time."

"A man's word means something in these parts, lady. I don't know who put a burr up your butt, but I've listened to all I'm gonna from you."

"I didn't tell you to come here, did I? And you won't have to listen to me much longer. As soon as I earn enough money, I'll be on that stage heading for Santa Fe."

"That's fine with me! Be sure and give my regards to Cousin Milton." He strode toward the door, but the move was too quick considering the blow he had just received. He hadn't taken more than two steps when the room started to spin again.

He turned. Staggering, he held out his hand to her. "Redhead. . . ." he murmured, then his knees buckled and he fell forward into her arms.

Garnet caught him but could not hold him up. They both went down, her fall breaking his. "Flint. Flint, are you okay?" she cried out. She squeezed out from under him and turned him over. "Flint, please say something."

Maud came shuffling down the stairs. "What's going on down here?"

"It's Flint! I think I killed him," Garnet cried.

Maud stared at her, appalled. "God, child! What happened?"

"I hit him in the head with a skillet."

"Lord, child! I'll get the doctor."

"I can get there faster. Tell me which house is his."

"It's a white house with black shutters. Right next door to the bank. 'Bout a block up the street from here."

Garnet ran as fast as she could up the block. Five minutes later, she was back with the doctor in tow.

Flint was awake and sitting in one of the chairs, holding a wet cloth to his head.

While the doctor examined Flint, Garnet paced the floor. "I never meant to hurt him, Maud. I love him too much to ever want to see him injured. And now he's hurt—and by my hand! If I've seriously hurt him, I'll never forgive myself, Maud. Never."

"Honey, I don' think he's hurt that bad," Maud said patiently.

A short time later, the doctor called them out of the kitchen. Garnet cast a fretful glance in Flint's direction. He sat in the same chair, holding his head.

"How is he, Doc?" Maud asked.

"Right now he feels like he's been kicked in the head by a mule, but his pulse is normal and he's not running a fever. Reckon he'll be just fine. He's got a thick skull and a tougher hide; it'd take more than a tap on the head with a skillet"—he glanced pointedly at Garnet—"to lay him up for long."

"Oh, thank God." Garnet sighed in relief.

"I don't want him riding back to the Triple M tonight. Best he stay in town for what's left of the night. Can you put him up here, Maud?"

"Wish you'd all stop talking like I ain't in the room," Flint grumbled.

The doctor gave Flint a censuring glance of dismissal, then spoke again to Maud. "He might tend to be a little ornery 'cause he's got an aching head."

"Damn right I've got an aching head!" Flint glared at Garnet, which only made her feel more guilty.

"He can have my bed, Doc," Maud said.

"That's not necessary. I'll put up at the hotel tonight," Flint announced, rising unsteadily to his feet.

"I'd rather you weren't alone, Flint," the doctor said. "Wouldn't hurt to have someone checking on you a time or two."

"I'll stay with him, Doctor," Garnet offered.

Flint regarded her warily. "What for, Widow Scott? You figure you can finish me off while I'm sleeping?"

"Flint, please, I'm sorry," she implored. "I didn't mean to hurt you."

"Yeah, like I said, you're dangerous, lady."

"I've missed too much sleep already to stand here the rest of the night and listen to the two of you argue," the doctor said. "Fight it out between you; just don't settle it with any more frying pans." He removed a stethoscope from around his neck and put it in his black bag. Then he closed the bag and picked it up, preparing to leave. "You heading for the hotel or not, Flint?"

"Yeah, I guess so," he said, resigned.

"And I'm going with him," Garnet added with an emphatic toss of her head.

"Well, then let's get going. I'll help to get him there, then you're on your own, Mrs. Scott." He went over and assisted Flint to his feet. "You feel strong enough to walk a short distance, Flint?"

"Sure, Doc."

The doctor took his arm and the two men went out the door. Garnet halted long enough to say a quick good-bye to Maud, and apologize for all the trouble she had caused her.

"I'll be back in the morning," Garnet said as she hurried after Flint and the doctor.

"What did you go back for?" Flint asked when she caught up with them.

"The frying pan," she replied, straight-faced.

Once in the hotel room, and after the doctor had departed, Garnet felt awkward undressing Flint for bed. She could feel his steady stare as he sat on the side of the bed, not saying a word when she knelt down and pulled off his boots and socks.

She cleared her throat and lifted her head. "I'll . . . ah, have to remove your gunbelt, Flint." His expression remained inscrutable as he lifted his arms. On bended knees, she unbuckled the heavy belt and hung it on the bedpost the way he liked it. "Now your shirt." He raised his arms again and she quickly pulled it over his head.

Now the temptation of his taut, muscled body was only inches away: wide, corded shoulders, hard biceps, a powerful chest with its generous spattering of dark, crisp hair—and his vital, rugged energy so near she could feel its magnetic pull. All she would have to do was lean forward and let it envelop her.

She raised her head. His dark eyes were fixed on her face, and he seemed to be enjoying her struggle to maintain control. She willed her voice to remain steady. "Now your pants."

She fumbled with his belt but could not release the buckle. Leaning forward, she bent her head lower, her hair brushing his bare chest. She could feel his tension. Finally the buckle gave. Taking a deep breath, she unbuttoned the fly of his pants. Now she felt his heat. Hurriedly, she pulled the pants off his hips and legs.

Relieved to have gotten through it, she almost jumped to her feet. "There, Flint. Now lie back and relax."

"You mean it's not my turn now?" he asked with a mocking grin, but lay back compliantly. He yawned, and she could see he was drowsy. "Getting sleepy, Redhead. Remember, we didn't get much sleep last night. This bed's mighty comfortable. Sure you wouldn't like to join me?"

She smiled despite her effort not to. "You misled me, Flint MacKenzie. I really thought your head was harder."

His teeth flashed in one of his rare smiles. "Never figured you for a barroom brawler, Redhead. 'Pears like you can hold your own with the best."

"I imagine I'll become famous now as the woman

who brought down that notorious gunslinger, Flint MacKenzie."

"With only one shot to the head from . . . her . . . iron-handled . . . frying—" His voice completely faded. He had fallen asleep.

Garnet sat down on the edge of the bed and stared at him for a long while. She wasn't going to leave this man. She loved him too much to willingly ride away. He would have to be the one to do it—not her. She gently brushed back the hair that had fallen over his forehead. "What's going to become of us, Flint?" she whispered softly.

Now that her anger had cooled, she realized how wrong she had been. Maud had summed him up perfectly—he was a fair man in a fight. "Too fair to have done what I accused you of doing," she said to him. "Oh, yes, at times you can be cantankerous . . . arrogant . . . mulish . . . and just about the most unpleasant man I've ever known." She smiled tenderly. "But you're not a cruel man, my love. I should have remembered that before I accused you of it." She leaned down and lightly kissed him. "I love you, Flint."

She sat at the bedside throughout the night, listening and watching for any change, but his breathing remained steady, his sleep peaceful. Daylight had already begun to filter through the window when her head slumped to the bed and she slept.

Flint awoke and found her that way. He reached out a hand and fondled the red head lying so near. She began to stir, and he quickly jerked his hand away and closed his eyes.

Garnet awoke slowly. She knew she had been dreaming of Flint, because she could still feel his touch. Glancing quickly at him, she saw he appeared to be sleeping peacefully. Yawning, she stood up and stretched, closed her eyes, then rolled her head back and forth several times to try to work the stiffness out of her neck. When she opened her eyes again, she saw that Flint had awakened.

"How are you feeling this morning?" she said cheerfully. She fortified herself for his reply—Flint was never his best in the early hours.

"I'm okay." He made a big show of lifting the blanket and peering under it.

"What are you looking for?"

"The last time I went to sleep depending on your mercy, I woke up and found out you had cut off my hair. Thought I better check something out in case you got hold of my knife again."

Garnet decided to give it right back to him. "Flint MacKenzie, you don't think my mama raised a daughter that dumb, do you?" With a nasty smile, she leaned over him, pressing a hand into the pillow on either side of his head. "Why would I damage my favorite plaything?"

"If you mean that, Redhead, get your butt in this bed."

She didn't budge or blink an eye. "What makes you think I'd consider climbing in that bed with you, MacKenzie?"

"Because you're not any more ready to ride away from what we've got than I am."

She straightened up and walked over to the window. "Well, you're wrong about one thing, Flint. Whether I'd be ready or not, I'd never stay with you if I ever lose my respect for you. Yesterday, I was ready to ride away."

"So what happened to cause you to change your mind?"

She turned back to him. "I'm thinking more clearly now. My mama always warned me never to allow hot anger to burn away cool reasoning."

"Your ma and me would have gotten along just fine," Flint said. "She makes good sense."

"When I found that locket in your shirt, I was angry enough to think you deliberately hid it from me. I didn't stop to remember my mama's words. If I had, I would have realized you have too much character to have done what I accused you of."

He didn't say anything for a long moment. Then, looking up at her, he said, "I plumb forgot about the locket, Redhead." Had she not already believed he was being honest, the remorse in his eyes would have convinced her. "While you were sleeping that morning, I went back a couple miles along the trail and found it. I put it in my pocket, and after that Comanche nicked me, I took off the shirt and haven't worn it since. I forgot all about the locket."

She sat down on the bed. "Why'd you go back for it, Flint?"

He looked embarrassed and turned his head to the side. "Ain't figured it out myself. Damned fool thing to do."

"No, don't turn away. Look at me, Flint." She lightly cupped his cheek and turned his head to face her. Her anxious gaze probed his, trying to reach his soul. "It's time for the truth, Flint. I have to know why you went back."

For an instant she thought she saw a flicker of compassion in his blue-eyed gaze before he lowered his eyes. "Because I knew that locket meant a lot to you."

Her voice dropped to a mere whisper. "I thought so." She pressed her mouth to his in a slow, passion-arousing kiss. He slid his hands into her hair and held her head firmly to his.

"Then I'm forgiven?"

"Not quite. I thought we made a pact," she whispered into his parted lips. "You agreed to shave."

He traced her lips with his tongue. "I intended to yesterday when I came back from the range, but I got sidetracked."

"No time like the present." She trailed a string of light kisses along the scar on his cheek.

"I don't have a razor."

She pulled away lightly. "Yes, you do." Withdrawing from his arms, she walked over and picked up his bowie knife. "How about this?"

He laughed lightly. "Thanks to you, I don't think my hand's steady enough right now."

"Mine is," she replied with an alluring smile.

She picked up the pitcher and poured water into the basin. Reaching for the bar of soap that lay next to it, she brought it to her nose and breathed in the scent of bay rum.

"You're really going to try to shave me, aren't you?" he said when she carried the basin over to the bed.

"Just the rough spots." She leaned down and pressed two light kisses on his bare chest, then tucked a towel under his chin. "There, this will keep the water from dripping on you."

"Or the blood," he quipped.

Garnet soaped his face and picked up the knife. "Now, lie perfectly still," she warned, holding the bowie poised above his cheek.

"And you were the one talking trust, lady!"

With her tongue curled over her upper lip, she carefully began to scrape the edge of the razor-sharp knife along his chin. As she attacked the whiskers with cool deliberation and a steady hand, not a muscle flexed in his cheek.

Five minutes later, she laid aside the knife, rinsed away whatever soap remained on his face, and stepped back to admire the result. "Not a nick in sight." She ran her hands over his cheeks. "That's much better. I like you with bare cheeks."

He drew her into his arms, and she felt the slide of his hands down her spine. "I like you with bare cheeks, too," he said in a husky murmur into her ear. Without warning, he rolled her over onto her back.

"You know what else I like bare on you, Redhead," he whispered, unbuttoning the front of her bodice. "I don't have to say it."

Smiling seductively, she arched against him and slipped her arms around his neck. "Yes, say it, Flint. Say it. I love hearing you say it," she implored with an ecstatic sigh just before his mouth plummeted down on hers.

Chapter 17

The morning rush had ended by the time Garnet and Flint entered the diner. They found Maud in the kitchen.

"I've been worried sick about you. Didn't know if the two of you had killed each other or not. Tempted to send Cal Ellis up to the hotel to check out your room."

"Who's Cal Ellis?" Garnet said sotto voce to Flint.

"The sheriff," Flint whispered back to her. "Don't worry, he's so old, he couldn't have climbed the stairs."

"Maud, I'm sorry," Garnet said, "but I won't be staying in town after all. I'm going back to the Triple M with Flint."

"Figured as much the first time I laid eyes on the two of you together," Maud mumbled. She poked Flint in the ribs with her elbow. "You don't fool me, sonny."

"Dammit, Maud! You ever gonna stop meddling in other folks' business? I'll have four or five eggs and a slab of bacon. I need a pot of strong coffee, too. My head feels like it was whomped with a frying pan." He walked out of the kitchen and sat down at one of the tables.

"Love that boy like my own son," Maud said fondly. "But he can be the orneriest fella in the whole state of

184

Texas when he puts his mind to it." She began to slice off strips of bacon.

"Let me do that, Maud. You sit down and rest for awhile." Without an argument, Maud handed her the knife and plopped down in a nearby chair.

"How does Flint like his eggs?" Garnet asked when she finished frying a dozen strips of the bacon.

"Just flip 'em over easy, honey. And give him a hunk of that fresh-baked bread. He likes to sop up the egg yolk with it. Whatta you gonna have?"

"Just coffee and a couple slices of bread with some jam or honey."

"Got some apple butter I just made. It's still warm."

"That sounds good to me." Garnet deftly began to flip the eggs over.

"You look like you're at home in a kitchen, gal."

Garnet laughed lightly. "I like to cook. Funny, the things you least expect to are the ones you miss the most. I never thought I'd miss having my own kitchen—and someone to enjoy my cooking."

"If you ever take a mind to it, there'll always be an openin' here for you. I'd like to find me a partner."

"Thanks, Maud. I'll keep that in mind," Garnet said, flipping the eggs onto the plate. "There's no telling when I might have to take you up on that offer."

"You and Flint fixin' to tie the knot?"

Garnet shook her head. "No. Flint's pretty outspoken on that subject. It'd take a miracle to get him to change his mind." She added the bacon and a scoop of grits to the plate.

"Well, I ain't one for tellin' folks how to live their lives," Maud said. "Lord knows I'd do one or two things different if I had it to do over, but you know what they say, gal—why buy the cow when you can get the milk for free?"

Garnet picked up the coffee pot. "What would you do in my place, Maud?"

Maud peeked into the dining room and stole a

glance at Flint, who sat staring out of the window. Slouched in the chair, he had shoved his hat up to the top of his forehead, his fingers were hooked in his belt, and his long legs were stretched out in front of him.

Maud shook her head. "Well, honey, I sure can't fault you. If I was a young'n like you, I'd let that boy hang his gunbelt on my bedpost anytime he took a hankering to."

Garnet paused in the doorway between the two rooms. "Even if he made it clear he had no intention of marrying you?"

"Well, I reckon you just have to hang in there 'til he gets some horse sense. Trouble with men, gal, is that they've got nothin' under their hats but hair—and sometimes that's pretty thin."

Garnet winked at Maud and carried out the plate and coffee to Flint. Then she went back for her own. "Is that all you're gonna eat?" he asked when she sat down at the table.

"I live on love," she replied drolly.

"No wonder you're so thin."

"The pickings are poor, MacKenzie."

"Now if you could fry eggs like this, you wouldn't have a problem. I'd even marry you myself."

"They're that good, huh?" Garnet asked, amused.

"Fried to perfection! Best Maud's made yet. Here, taste it." He fed her a forkful.

"Yes, it's very tasty." Turning her head aside, she tried to hide her grin.

He glanced up and saw her amusement. "What?" he said.

"Huh?" she asked innocently.

"Why the look like the cat who swallowed the canary?"

No longer able to stare him in the eye, she took a bite of the bread and jam. "Hmmm, this is good!"

He looked over and grinned. "You're wearing your hair different this morning."

Self-consciously, she raised a hand to her hair. "Oh, I just pulled it back and tied it with a ribbon. Easier than braiding it."

"Looks right pretty."

"Okay, Flint, what are you buttering me up for?"

He flashed a broad grin. "For a taste of that apple butter. Bet it's fresh made."

Garnet broke off a corner of her bread and spread a daub of the jam on it. She held it out to him, and he sucked it into his mouth, then raised his brows in approval. "I suppose you want another bite," she said.

"I'll swap you a piece of bacon for it." He held out a bacon strip in his fingers. "Here, take a bite."

They continued feeding each other. He'd offer her either a forkful of egg or a piece of bacon, in return for the pieces of bread oozing with apple butter that she popped into his mouth. By the time they were through, Garnet realized she had eaten at least one egg and a couple strips of bacon.

"Flint MacKenzie, you duped me into eating a big breakfast!" she exclaimed.

Laughing, he tipped back his chair. "Gotta fatten you up, Redhead. Sure wouldn't want to see my favorite *plaything* wasted down to skin and bones."

She broke into a light laugh. Clearly pleased with himself for getting back at her, he stood up and tossed several coins on the table. "We've got a long ride ahead of us."

"I'll take these dishes back to the kitchen and say good-bye to Maud," Garnet said.

"I'll bring the horses around."

Other than having the comfort of knowing he was near, Garnet figured she could just as well make the ride alone. Flint set a steady pace, but maintained his usual silence as they rode. She wondered what he thought about in these long stretches.

When they arrived at the Triple M, what might have

been an awkward moment for Garnet was made easier by the welcoming smiles of the rest of the MacKenzies. No one questioned the reason for her departure or return—not even Joshua.

As they did the supper dishes, Honey appeared nervous. "What's wrong?" Garnet asked in a low voice.

"Oh, Garnet, Luke told me to sit down and write out a list of what I need for the drive. I haven't got the slightest idea. Sure, I drove a wagon from Missouri to California, but I only had to feed myself—not a whole crew." Honey glanced at her hopefully. "Do you have any idea?"

"I'm afraid not. I only had myself to worry about, too. And more times than not, one of the families on the wagon train would invite me to join them."

"Luke wants to go to town tomorrow and talk to the banker about a loan to make the drive. He expects me to let him know how much I think we'll need for food." She shook her head. "I don't know what to tell him."

"I bet Maud would know. She's used to cooking in large quantities. Maybe we could ride into town with him and talk to her. She probably can give us a lot of good advice."

"I bet she can," Honey said, sighing with relief. "I'll tell Luke we're riding to Calico with him."

"Anyone else want to come along tomorrow?" Luke asked after Honey told him what she and Garnet planned.

"I do! I do!" Joshua exclaimed.

"Not me," Flint said. "Thought I'd ride out and try to put a rope on some of those mustangs I saw."

"What about you, Cleve? You want to ride along with us?" Luke asked.

"No, I'll head out with Flint. Besides, when we go into town next Saturday for the railroad celebration, I'm planning on spending the night."

"What are you going to do there all night, Uncle Cleve?" Josh inquired.

There was a long silence as everyone looked with amusement at Cleve. Finally, he answered, "I just don't want to tire my horse."

Joshua frowned. "So . . . that's why Uncle Flint and Garnet stayed there all night," he decided. Puzzled, he looked at his father. "Daddy, how come we don't stay all night when we go to town? Don't our horses get tired, too?"

Throwing his younger brother another suffering look, Luke replied, "Well, son, we've always had to think about getting back and feeding the stock. I think you better get to bed. We'll be starting out early in the morning."

Bright and early the following morning, Garnet again found herself on the road heading to Calico, this time in a wagon being driven by Honey. Josh sat between them and Amigo was trailing along beside the wagon. Luke rode his gelding.

"Is there a particular reason why you and your brothers all ride dun geldings, Luke?" Garnet asked.

"'Cause they all like the same kind of horse," Josh piped in. "Asked them that already."

"How do you tell the horses apart? I haven't noticed any individual marks on any one of the geldings."

"'Cause it's not hard to know your own horse. Asked him that already," came the reply.

Luke chuckled. "Actually, Garnet, it is easy to recognize your own horse. It's the same as picking out your own child in a crowd." He glanced at Honey. "Or finding your woman in the dark." The couple's gazes met and held.

Observing the exchange, Garnet thought, *The sapphire eyes of these MacKenzie men can be as lethal as the Colts they wear on their hips.*

As soon as they reached Calico, they went to Maud's

diner. After hugging the women and Josh, Maud insisted they sit down and eat. She set a heaping bowl of chili and a huge slice of chocolate cake in front of each of them. When they finished, Luke took Josh with him and went off to speak to the banker.

Garnet and Honey explained the purpose of their visit to Maud. She began to list the foodstuffs they would need to take along. They hadn't even scratched the surface by the time Luke returned.

One look at his downcast face brought Honey to her feet. She hurried over to him at once. "What's wrong, Luke?"

"Oh, just a little setback. Kiefer said he's got to think hard before he lends me any more money. I've already got a note against the ranch."

Maud looked at him slyly. "So you're drivin' your herd to Abilene." She grimaced and looked at Garnet and Honey. "I'd be happier than a weasel in a chicken coop if I could be in them gals' boots."

"For God's sake, Maud, why would you envy them? If I do figure out a way to go, it's gonna be a long, hard trip."

"Don't reckon you need another cook?" she asked.

"Another cook? Maud, you're plumb loco. A trail drive's no place for women and kids. We wouldn't be taking our womenfolk along if we didn't have to."

"Stop talkin' like I never looked down the barrel of a rifle before, Luke MacKenzie. I was born in this here town over fifty years ago—and I ain't sayin' how many years over fifty. I've had to fight off Comanche, Mexicans, border gangs, and any saddle tramp who thought I'd be easy pickings. Over fifty years! In that time, I've seen more different flags flying over Texas than I can keep count of. But I've never seen a big city, Luke, or this railroad I've been hearing so much about. I ain't done nothin' 'cept let my money pile up in Stover Kiefer's bank."

"What's stopping you from taking a stage to Fort

Worth, or a train to St. Louis, Maud?'' Garnet said gently.

"Nothing, gal. Might do that if you take me with you to Abilene," she said with a glance at Luke. "Or even go to San Francisco if I've a mind to, now that they're finally finishin' this railroad they've been buildin' across the country."

"Ah, come on, Maud. Don't try to make me feel guilty now." Luke grinned. "You're the most independent woman I know. Nothing would stop you from doing what you set your heart on. You could have gone any time."

She squared her shoulders and looked him right in the eye. "Well, Luke, I've just set my heart on going on that drive."

"What about your diner?"

"Got a Closed sign for the window and a lock for the door. Folks here can try eatin' at the hotel for a spell."

"Well, Maud, if we make the drive, I'll talk to my brothers about you. It's not just my decision."

Maud winked at Garnet and Honey. "I'll make you a deal, Luke. Forget that tightfisted Stover Kiefer. I'll lend you the money, son. My interest charge is that I drive the chuck wagon."

When Luke still appeared hesitant, Maud's tone became more persuasive. "Land sakes alive, Luke, I've already got all the kettles and the like right here. A lot of the grub you'd be needin' to take along, too."

"You're making your offer sound more appealing by the minute, Maud."

"So what's stoppin' you from sayin' yes?"

"I told you. I've got to talk it over with Flint and Cleve. They've got an interest in this, too. I don't know how they'll feel about taking another woman along."

"You tell them two scalawags for me, Luke MacKenzie, that I'm just part woman. The other half of me is a she-wolf from Hell. I'm tougher and meaner than most men, and I can hold my own in any turkey shoot."

Garnet and Honey exchanged anxious glances as they waited for Luke's decision. "Luke, if Maud drove the chuck wagon, I could drive an extra wagon," Honey said.

"Yeah, I can see where it'd be an advantage to have an extra wagon," he said, deep in reflection. Finally, he looked at the older woman. "Maud, reckon I can't speak for my brothers, but other than Flint and Cleve, I can't think of anyone I'd rather have watching my back." He reached out and shook her hand. "We've got a deal, partner."

Honey and Garnet rushed over to Maud. For several moments, the three women hugged and kissed. Luke and Josh listened to them jabbering away excitedly.

"What do you think, son?"

Copying his father's pose, Josh put his hands on his hips and shook his head. "I don't think Uncle Flint's gonna like this idea." He grinned, revealing a gap from two missing front teeth. "Daddy," he said, glancing up at his father, "if Maud comes with us, are we gonna have chocolate cake on the drive?"

"All right, gals, let's sit down and figure out what we're missin'," Maud said. "First off, we need a chuck wagon." Maud looked over at Luke. "You know Ben Franks of the Flying F. He was in here earlier. Told me he's goin' to New York to live with his daughter. He's sellin' off the Flying F. Bet you could buy his chuck wagon for under a hundred dollars."

"I'll talk to him when we come back next Saturday for the railroad celebration," Luke said. "Ben'll be here for it, won't he?"

"Lordy, Luke! The whole county's comin' in for it," Maud replied.

"Well, come on, Josh. I've got some supplies to pick up, then we'll be heading back, ladies. If you don't finish up with Maud today, you can always do it Saturday."

As soon as he left, Maud put the Closed sign in the

window and locked the door. "We've got important business to discuss and we don't want any interruptions."

She turned and faced them, put a hand on each hip, and grinned broadly.

"Yahoo!" she shouted.

Chapter 18

As they anticipated, Flint did not take the news about Maud calmly when they returned home. "We need a wrangler, Luke, not another cook—and a female one at that!"

"Will you calm down and let me try and explain," Luke declared. He described the financial crisis they faced, and using the same arguments Maud had used on him, proceeded to defend his reasons for accepting her offer. "I can't see how Maud would be any different from old Ben Franks."

"I can!" Flint shot back angrily. "At least an older man can fill in as a night rider sometimes. We sure as hell can't use a woman to ride night duty. The three of us are gonna be sleeping in our saddles before we're even halfway to Abilene."

"I'm sorry, Flint, there's no other way. The bottom line is we need the money."

Flint started for the door and stopped with his hand on the knob. "Ain't just me, Luke. I'd ride into hell if you asked me to. But we're undermanned, and we don't need to see any of them get. . . ." He took a long look at the women, then turned on his heel in frustration.

"Wish I could help you out," Cleve said after Flint disappeared through the door. "I broke myself buying the bull and heifers. I don't even have enough to buy myself into one of those high stakes games in Dallas, or I'd try to win some quick cash that way."

Honey jerked up her head. "High stakes game?"

"Don't even think it!" Luke declared emphatically. "Remember: Luke, no sheriff; Honey, no card game."

"Well, I guess I better get back to helping Flint bust those broncos," Cleve said.

Luke nodded. "Yeah, I'll come with you." A silent Josh, accompanied by Amigo, followed the two men.

"Honey, what did you mean about the card game?" Garnet asked.

"Oh, when I was younger, I traveled with a medicine show and learned how to play poker. Matter of fact, I'm real good at it. So is Cleve. I'd say it's a toss-up between the two of us. I used to deal poker in Stockton where Luke was the sheriff. Even sat in a game with Charlie Walden once. Do you believe it! Well, Luke doesn't want me in any more card games with strangers. He says there's too many unsavory characters around and I could get hurt. So we made a pact: if he promised not to go back to being a lawman, I'd give up poker."

Honey sat down at the table and cradled her head in her hands. "Garnet, do you think Luke's making a mistake trying to drive the herd to Abilene? Maybe we should forget it and take what we can get right here."

Reaching across the table, Garnet grasped her hand. "I don't know what to tell you, Honey. I trust Luke's judgment. He strikes me as being a very practical man."

Surprised, Honey glanced up at her. "Don't you trust Flint's judgment, too?"

"About some things. But Flint tends to play devil's advocate, so he often approaches a problem expecting the worst. Luke appears more methodical, but once convinced, he's totally committed. The two men are a perfect balance on any issue."

"And where does Cleve fit into your equation?" Honey asked.

"Cleve MacKenzie doesn't fool me for a moment. Under all that charm and easy manner is a cool-thinking, level-headed mind that never shuts down. I think if Cleve believed this cattle drive was impossible, he'd say so and would have come up with a different solution to Luke's problem by now."

Honey rose wearily to her feet. "Well, I hope between the three of them, they'll decide to do whatever's right."

Garnet walked down the hill to the corral. A bridled mustang, its front legs hobbled, was tied to a post with the reins. Flint was trying to put a saddle on the wary animal. He grabbed the saddle blanket and approached the horse. The animal backed away until it was stopped by the fence.

Flint moved in on the animal. Using his own body strength, he managed to keep the horse pinned against the fence as he held the blanket on its back with his left hand. Grabbing the heavy saddle with his right hand, he hoisted it onto the horse's back. As soon as the mustang felt the weight, he started to thrash.

Garnet flinched when she saw a heavy shove send Flint falling backward, but before the horse could shake off the saddle, Flint was back on his feet, snatching the cinch and tightening it.

Flint untied the reins and grasped them firmly in his hand. When the mustang began to balk, Flint grabbed the horse's ear and twisted it.

Garnet saw that the shock of pain seemed to momentarily stun the animal. Flint took those precious seconds to swing up into the saddle.

"Okay, cut him loose," Flint shouted.

Luke pulled the hobble rope off the horse's front legs. Instantly the mustang reared up, then thumped down, bending itself almost in half trying to buck off the weight on its back.

"Ride him, Flint," Luke shouted.

Whistling, Cleve applauded. "Keep it tight, Brother Flint. Don't let that bangtail get its head down."

The fight was on between man and animal—nine hundred pounds of snorting, bucking horsepower against almost two hundred pounds of stubborn determination. The arm-wrenching, teeth-jarring duel continued for many minutes. Finally the horse tired, and Flint reined the mustang to a stop. Climbing down, he tethered the reins to the fence.

"It's all yours, Little Brother," he said, draping himself over the fence in exhaustion.

Cleve went over and climbed on the back of the tired animal.

"What's he going to do now?" Garnet asked.

"Cleve's gonna start hazing it."

"I hate to sound stupid, Luke, but what do you mean by hazing? Some of this western jargon is a mystery to me."

"It's just whipping and snapping a blanket near its head while you're riding it. These horses have to be trained as cow ponies and be taught not to bolt or shy away from any sudden movement," Luke explained. "Unfortunately, we don't have time to teach them how to cut in and out of a herd. They'll have to learn that on the drive."

"This all sounds kind of cruel, Luke," Garnet said sadly.

"Well, if we had more time, we could let the horses get to know us. But we're running out of time, and we can't start the drive without at least thirty mounts. We should have more. All we can do for now is break 'em to a saddle and give 'em a little hazing."

Luke went over and hobbled the next mustang. Garnet watched as the process began all over again. Shaking her head sorrowfully, she walked back to the house.

* * *

Honey's doubts about the drive drifted in and out of Garnet's thoughts throughout the rest of the day. Later, as she and Flint prepared for bed, Honey's words were again on her mind as she rubbed unguent on Flint's aching body.

"God! I ache in places I didn't know I had," Flint complained. He lay on his stomach in the hayloft with his cheek resting on his hands. "I'm gonna shoot the next horse that throws me. Now I remember why I gave up ranching."

His flesh felt firm and warm beneath her fingertips; they tingled from the contact. Slowly, she kneaded the tight muscles across his shoulders and back, then ran her fingers along the bunched cords of his neck, working the tautness out of them.

"A man's a damn fool to tie himself down trying to keep a spread going. Look what's happening to poor Luke."

"I don't think of him as poor Luke. He looks like a pretty lucky man to me. He has a wife and son who worship him."

"And depend on him," Flint quickly responded.

"I don't hear him complaining." She dabbed some more salve on him and began to massage the back of his thighs and calves, then moved to the cheeks of his rear. The muscles felt hard and tight; she could feel them contract beneath the stroke of her fingers.

"God that feels good, babe," he groaned. "Ain't ever had anyone do this for me."

"I bet *poor Luke* has, especially after a hard day when he comes in all tuckered out from being *burdened* with responsibility. I bet you Honey's right there for him—to rub his aching bones or comfort . . . whatever needs comforting. I don't think you realize Luke is the kind of man who relishes responsibility. The signs are all there. He's the only one of you three brothers who married by choice, started a family . . . even became a lawman. To me, that speaks of a man who welcomes obligations with open arms."

"Well, he's sure carrying around a load of those obligations right now. Sure glad I'm not in his shoes."

"I'm confident that if anyone is up to facing the task ahead, it's Luke. Okay, turn over," she said, giving his rear a light tap.

He flopped over. Surprised, she saw he had the start of an erection. Arching a brow, he said in amusement, "You missed a part."

"You fraud! I thought you said you were aching."

His eyes gleamed with devilishness. "I said I was aching, Widow Scott, I didn't say I was dead!" Grasping her by the shoulders, he drew her down to him.

The next morning as Flint pulled on his buckskins, Garnet watched him worriedly. "Flint, why don't you forget about the horses for a day? Ride out and round up strays, or some such thing, until you're not so sore."

"No. We should finish breaking the rest of those mustangs today. That way we oughta have the soreness out of us by the time we're ready to start the drive." He plopped his hat on at the usual cocky angle. "Luke figures the way things are moving, we'll be able to leave in another week. You still game for it?"

"Why do you ask?"

Flint shrugged. "You seem to have something on your. . . ." He cut off his words abruptly when the barn door opened. "No reason." He quickly climbed down from the loft.

Garnet lay listening to the three men talking and laughing as they gathered up their saddles and reins. Then they left and all was quiet again.

For a few minutes, Garnet lay there grappling with her troubled thoughts. Did Flint suspect what she herself feared? Her menses was two weeks late. Although it wouldn't be the first time—she had been late

before—her instinct told her this time was different.
What would she do if she were carrying Flint's child?
Knowing how he felt about marriage and children,
how could she tell him?

She shrugged aside the fretful thought. She was just
being panicky. It was more likely that the frightful
events of the past several weeks had affected her
menses. She doubted she could even conceive a
child—after all, two marriages hadn't produced one.

Of course, neither of her husbands had Flint's
virility—nor had either of her husbands ever aroused
such an all-consuming passionate response from her.
Perhaps those two factors were necessary to make
babies!

Shrugging off her worry, she got up and began to
dress. She wouldn't let herself dwell on it.

She walked outside and looked around. The air bore
the promise of another warm day. As the sound of
Cleve's voice carried to her, her gaze swung to the
corral.

"He's a bucker, Flint," Cleve said. "Keep his head
up. Keep his head up."

Smiling, she strode toward the house. It was going to
be a beautiful day. Too beautiful to worry about sore
bones, cattle drives—or babies. And tomorrow there
was a dance in town to celebrate the completion of the
transcontinental railroad. When was the last time she
had been to a dance? Her step quickened almost to a
skip.

Later that day, Honey and Garnet sauntered down to
the corral to welcome Ben Franks, who had ridden up
in a chuck wagon. "Heard you boys are fixin' to drive
your herd to Abilene," Garnet heard him say.

Honey leaned over to whisper in Garnet's ear. "I
can't believe how everyone calls them 'boys.' I wonder
if the people in town will ever get around to thinking
of my husband and his brothers as men."

"That's right, Ben," Luke replied. "Figure we'll be ready in another week."

"Luke, Maud Malone told me you're lookin' to buy a chuck wagon," the old rancher said.

"Yeah, I was going to talk to you about it tomorrow at the celebration in town."

"Oh, that there celebration's been called off 'til Monday."

"Monday!" Flint exclaimed. "That's sure a hell of a day to be holding a celebration. How come?"

"Heard tell they was flooded out in one of them canyons up there in Utah. Keepin' some of them bigwigs from the East holed up from arrivin' on time."

"Yeah, I read there's dignitaries coming from several foreign countries," Cleve said. "We're so far from the excitement here in Texas, we don't stop to think of what a great accomplishment building a transcontinental railroad is."

"It sure sounds better than crossing the country in a wagon," Garnet quipped. "Guess I should have waited a little longer to come west."

"Me, too," Honey agreed.

Cleve looked at them, dismayed. "Had you done that, dear ladies, what do you think the odds would have been that you'd end up here at the Triple M?"

Garnet was unable to resist the opportunity to tease him. "That's what I mean."

"You give up in believing in that destiny hogwash you've been spouting?" Flint asked.

Garnet had thought Flint wasn't even listening, since he and Luke had begun to check out the chuck wagon. She flashed him a mocking smile. "Well, I guess it certainly would have put my belief to a test, now wouldn't it?"

"Makes no sense to me why, as long as that railroad's been built, we can't go ahead with our dance tomorrow," Ben grumbled. "Who cares if a couple of them greenhorns ain't there for a ceremony."

"From what I read, Ben, it's my understanding that
the railroad will not actually be completed until the
ceremony at Promontory Point in Utah," Cleve said.
"That's where they intend to drive in the last spike.
They'll certainly wait to do that until everyone of
importance is present. So I expect none of us should be
celebrating until the last spike is driven."

"Then how come we didn't go to that Utah place?"
Josh asked, looking up at his father. "You're a 'portant
person, Daddy."

Luke tousled his hair. "Only to you, son. And to
your mother," he added with a wink at Honey. "Wagon looks good, Ben. If the price is right, I'm willing to
buy it."

"Well, what's your offer?" the old man said. "Near
spankin' new. Only used it on two roundups."

"Seventy dollars."

"Eighty-five, and I'll throw in that there water
barrel." Garnet glanced at the object Ben was pointing
to. Strapped to the side of the wagon was a wooden
barrel with a metal spigot extending from its base.
"Holds two days' supply."

"All right. Here's my hand on it," Luke said. The
two men shook hands.

Garnet had barely glanced at the wagon. She had
seen her fill of wagons coming west! But now she took
a longer look at the canvas-covered vehicle. It appeared to be sturdier than she'd been accustomed to.
The water barrel rested on a shelf that extended from
one side of the wagon, and what looked to be a coffee
grinder was hung a short distance away. The wagon
bed had several compartments, and from where she
stood, there appeared to be another one protruding
under the wagon at the rear. Extending from the other
side was a large, rectangular box that ran the full
length of the chuck wagon.

Ben Franks began to unhitch the big chestnut har-

nessed to the wagon. "You selling that chestnut, Ben?"
Luke asked.

Ben patted the horse. "Nope. Ole Red and me's rode
a lot of trails together. Ain't ready to part with him jest
yet."

"I'll saddle him for you, Ben," Cleve said.

"No, I can do it."

Garnet didn't miss the note of pride in the old man's
voice. Apparently Cleve didn't either. He dropped the
subject and slapped the old man lightly on the shoulder, then lounged back against the fence post.

"You boys hear that I'll soon be movin' to New York?
Daughter says I'm getting too old to be left on my own.
Reckon ranching's for young men like you boys. Ain't
got no sons to take over the Flying F, and with my
Molly gone these past ten years, reckon it's time to sell
out. Lookin' for a buyer, if you hear tell of one."

Garnet felt a rise of sympathy. She suspected that
the cloying walls of a big city would soon suffocate this
aged range rider, who was being uprooted from the
only life he had ever known.

"I've got a couple hundred head that's strayed over
to the draws on the west end of my ranch. If you boys
are willin' to round 'em up, I'll sell you the herd for five
hundred dollars."

"That's less than three dollars a head, Ben," Luke
said, astonished.

"Hell, by the time I'd hire a couple of punchers to
round 'em up and drive 'em to Fort Worth, figure I
wouldn't be out any by sellin' 'em to you. 'Sides that,
then I'd not be worryin' if them fellas would show up
back here with my money."

"What do you think, Flint?" Luke asked.

"Right now, I'm thinking eight thousand dollars
more. Reckon we can drive six hundred cows as well as
four hundred."

"Okay, Ben. Seeing as how there's no dance tomorrow, we'll ride over in the morning." Luke shook Ben's hand. "Good luck in finding a buyer for the Flying F. It's a good spread, Ben. If I could afford it, I'd buy it myself. Wouldn't mind expanding the Triple M."

"Well, keep it in mind, Luke. Can't think of leavin' it in better hands than a MacKenzie's," Ben said. "You take care, ladies," he said, bringing a finger to the tip of his hat.

"Won't you stay for dinner, Mr. Franks?" Honey asked. "We'd love for you to join us."

"Nope. Gotta get back and feed my stock. But you gals be sure to save me a dance at that there shindy on Monday."

Honey walked over and kissed his cheek. "We sure will, Ben."

Chuckling with pleasure, Ben winked at Garnet. "I can still kick up my heels with the best of 'em."

"I bet you can, Mr. Franks," Garnet said, smiling.

The old man climbed slowly onto the back of the chestnut and urged the animal into a slow walk home.

With hands on hips, Honey surveyed the wagon. "Looks like this wagon could use a good cleaning."

"I'm game if you are," Garnet agreed.

"Well, there's no sense in going to the trouble of hitching up that wagon," Luke said. "We can push it up to the pump."

"Figured you'd say that," Flint mumbled.

Garnet and Honey lifted the long tongue and began to pull, while the three men put their already aching shoulders to the wagon.

"Hey, Little Brother," Flint grunted to Cleve as they pushed the big wagon up the hill. "You ever stop to think why there's more horses' asses than there are horses?"

"Why?" Cleve asked, puffing.

"'Cause none of the horses have a big brother named Luke."

After settling the wagon on level ground near the

pump, they all took several minutes to examine the wagon. Josh crawled in it for a better view.

"Mama, bet me and Amigo could sleep in here on the trail if we wanted to," he called out excitedly.

"Think you better ask Aunt Maud about that, sweetheart," Honey said. "She might have the same idea for herself. But I'll be driving a wagon, and you and Amigo can sleep in that one."

"This contraption is called the chuck box, ladies," Luke said. He released a hinged lid on the box, and it dropped down to form a worktable on a swinging leg. The box now resembled a rolltop desk, for the lid had concealed at least a dozen compartments or drawers. "When you're not using it, you just shove up the leg and close it . . . like this." Then, to demonstrate how easily it worked, he released the hinged lid once more and again the lid and swinging leg dropped down to form a table.

"My goodness, all of the comforts of home!" Honey exclaimed.

When the three men left to resume their bronco busting, Joshua lost interest in the wagon and followed them. Garnet and Honey continued to inspect all the various compartments and drawers.

"It *is* a coffee grinder!" Garnet exclaimed after a closer look at the machine attached to the wagon.

"And will you look at this!" Honey called out to her. "These drawers on the chuck box are actually marked with what should go into them. See, this one says flour; there's another that says pinto beans. One for sugar, dried fruit, coffee beans! There's even one for needles and thread, and medicines! Josh will love to hear there's room for the castor-oil bottle."

"I have to say, the whole thing is very well thought out, isn't it?" Garnet agreed, peeking into the compartments in the wagon bed. "Looks like this compartment could hold bed rolls and blankets. This one's divided into bins. I bet it's for potatoes and bulky foods like that." She opened another section of the wagon bed. "Oh, good heavens, will you look at this, Honey? There's even an extra wagon wheel stored in here."

"Well, I guess we've got our work cut out for us," Honey declared. "Every one of these compartments and drawers we've been admiring now has to be scrubbed clean."

Grimacing, Garnet stepped back and surveyed the wagon. "Well, I do have to say, it's certainly lacking something very important."

Honey's eyes rounded in surprise. "Lacking? What could it possibly be lacking, Garnet?"

"A cookstove and a kitchen sink."

For a moment, Honey looked at her, bemused. "You could never expect to have. . . ."

Garnet could no longer hold back her laughter.

"Well, why not a bath tub?" Honey suggested. "With hot running water!" She began to giggle.

"We're really getting silly," Garnet scolded, trying to muffle her mirth. She lost the battle.

Grabbing each other, the two women howled with hilarity.

Their laughter carried to the ears of the men below.

Luke looked up and wondered what had amused the women.

Flint stopped to listen, his face inscrutable.

Cleve grinned.

Chapter 19

The following morning, Josh was just scurrying away from the table when Garnet entered the house.

"Morning, Auntie Garney." He grabbed his hat. "Come on, Amigo, let's go or we'll get left behind." Garnet smiled as boy and dog scrambled out the door.

"Good morning, Honey."

"Morning," Honey called back cheerfully. "Sit down and have a dish of oatmeal while it's still hot."

Garnet stood in the doorway and watched the boy and dog racing to the barn. "They certainly are attached to each other, aren't they?"

"They have been from the beginning," Honey said. "Amigo helped us to break through to Josh."

"What do you mean?"

"Oh, it's a long story. I'll save the telling for one of those long days on the drive. I think you'll enjoy hearing it. But it definitely was love at first sight between them."

"Sounds like Flint and me," Garnet said drolly, pouring herself a cup of coffee.

Honey giggled and shook her head. "I remember the first time I saw Luke." She sighed deeply and clutched her breast. "My poor little heart set to thumping and it's been going full steam ever since." Honey set a dish of the hot cereal in front of Garnet, then sat down at the table. "What are you wearing to the dance Monday?"

"All I have is what I've got on. I don't have a fancy gown. Everything I owned, I lost."

"Well, as soon as you finish eating, we'll look through mine. We're darn near the same size. A stitch here or there should do it. Matter of fact, I've got a green gown that will look perfect with your red hair and green eyes." She hurried to the bedroom. "I'll show it to you." Honey came back carrying a gown of pale green silk chine. "Let's try this on you."

After shedding her bodice and skirt, Garnet stepped to the mirror to appraise her appearance. The fitted bodice had a low, round neckline trimmed with a wide, ivory-colored lace ruffle embroidered with tiny pink and white flowers. Each sleeve was fitted to below the elbow, with a flounce of the same embroidered lace cascading almost to the wrist. The embroidered pattern was repeated in the gown's full skirt, which dropped in swirling folds to her ankles.

"It's almost a perfect fit," Honey exclaimed after tying the satin streamers into a big bow at the back of Garnet's waist.

Garnet ran a hand across the soft, silky fabric. "Oh, Honey, this gown is exquisite."

"Luke bought it for me in San Francisco. The dress was imported from China. I've only had a chance to wear it one time."

"Then *you* should wear it Monday," Garnet insisted.

"No, I intend to wear my black gown. It's very seductive." She giggled wickedly. "It drives Luke wild! Of course, I'll have to add something to the straps and bodice for modesty's sake, or the citizens of Calico will probably run me out of town. I have a piece of material that'll be perfect."

Garnet took another long glance in the mirror. "I

never owned a gown this elegant, even before the war."

"Don't move. I'll get my sewing pins. I think it just needs a few tucks under the arms; my breasts are slightly fuller than yours."

Garnet cast a sideways glance at Honey's voluptuous curves. "My dear, your breasts are considerably fuller than mine."

"I wouldn't say that," Honey remarked. She scurried away to get the pins.

Garnet glanced down at the curve of her bosom. She had never considered herself generously endowed. Leaning forward for a closer examination in the mirror, she noticed her breasts did appear slightly fuller.

Honey returned carrying a pin cushion. "With the men and Josh heading out to the Flying F, we have all day to ourselves. As soon as I finish with you, you can help me tack this lace on my gown. Monday, Miz Garnet, you and I are going to stand the citizens of Calico on their ears!"

On Sunday, the men rode to the south range to begin branding cattle. Honey unpacked their suits and shirts, which she kept in a cedar chest. Meanwhile, Garnet polished their good boots and dusted off the Stetsons Honey kept wrapped in paper for special occasions.

The afternoon was spent pressing the clothes they intended to wear at the celebration. After supper that evening, all of the males were ordered to bathe in a tub in the barn, while Garnet and Honey enjoyed the luxury of a hot bath and shampoo in the house.

Bright and early Monday morning, with the wagon hitched, the horses saddled, and the men properly dressed, all was in readiness waiting for the women to appear.

Garnet gave Honey a final inspection. She looked

elegant in the black gown, which enhanced her blond loveliness. The lacy black capelet Honey had added to the dress covered, but did not conceal, the ivory luster of her shoulders and arms. After sweeping up Honey's hair into a chignon on the top of her head, Garnet tucked a black plume into the honey-colored hair.

Having donned the green gown, Garnet brushed her own hair until it shone. Pulling the hair off her face, she allowed it to hang loosely to her shoulders, and pinned a narrow woven band of pink apple blossoms and white satin ribbon to the crest of her head.

When Garnet and Honey emerged from the bedroom, the three men stared awestruck at them.

Instantly, Garnet swung her glance to Flint. Seeing the look of approval in his eyes, she smiled, but couldn't tear her gaze from him. Cleanshaven, his bronzed face contrasted dramatically with his white shirt and narrow string tie. Unlike Luke and Cleve, he was not wearing a dark suit, but rather a dark, open vest and black trousers. His virility seemed to reach out and wrap around her in an embrace.

Cleve's long, low whistle broke the spell. "Ladies, you both look lovely."

Luke walked over to Honey. "You look beautiful, Jaybird." Smiling up at him, she slipped her arm into his.

As soon as the women were settled on the wagon seat and the men mounted on their horses, a new crisis developed.

"Daddy, you forgot Amigo," Joshua said.

"I think it's better to leave him here, Josh. The town's no place for him today," Luke said.

"Amigo's just as 'cited about the railroad as we are," Josh argued.

"I'm sure he is. But the town's going to be full of people."

"Amigo don't take up as much room as Uncle Flint

or Uncle Cleve do. They're much bigger than he is,"
the boy declared with a petulant pout.

Garnet turned away from the sorrowful sight of
Amigo standing with his tail wagging, waiting to be
lifted into the wagon.

"Luke, other than an hour for church on Sundays, I
don't remember a time when Josh and Amigo have
been separated," Honey interjected.

"Amigo doesn't have to be a part of everything this
family does."

Josh's brow crimped into a determined frown not
unlike the one his father now wore. "Amigo's a
member of this family, too. If he can't go, then I don't
want to go either." He folded his arms across his chest.

"Don't use that tone with me, young man." Luke
clearly had lost his patience. "You heard me. Amigo
stays home."

"Want to bet?" Honey whispered to Garnet.

"I don't suppose we could solve this problem by
some sort of majority rules kind of vote?" Cleve said
lightly.

"It is solved," Luke responded with a dark glare at
his younger brother.

"Good God! What harm is there to the dog coming!"
Flint suddenly exclaimed.

This surprised Garnet. She thought that Flint would
be the last person to express an opinion—much less
care whether or not Amigo joined them.

"Well, do you have anything to say on the matter?"
Luke asked, turning to Garnet.

She shook her head. "It's not my business to say."

"Why not, everyone else is. Let's get going to this
damn celebration," Luke declared. "Amigo, you stay,"
he ordered.

The confused dog trotted to the porch, stretched out,
and lay down with his head on his paws.

Luke goaded his horse and started off at a trot. Flint

and Cleve followed. Honey flicked the reins and the wagon rolled forward. Amigo emitted a mournful whimper.

"Bye, Amigo." With tears streaming down his cheeks, Josh raised a hand and waved.

"This is heartwrenching," Garnet murmured to Honey.

They hadn't gone more than a quarter of a mile when a furry figure appeared limping on the trail behind them.

"Look, Mama. It's Amigo."

Honey reined up. "Oh, Luke?" Her eyes beseeched him.

"Okay! Goddammit! What choice does a man have when even a goddamned dog won't listen to him?"

"Yippee!" Josh cried. Amigo trotted up to the wagon. "Come on, Amigo, Daddy said you can come." He opened his arms and Amigo jumped up into them. Puffing, he stretched out on Josh's lap, his tongue lolling out of his mouth, and regarded the boy with adoration.

Arching a brow, Honey exchanged a meaningful glance with Garnet. "What did I say?"

No one else uttered a word, but Flint's and Cleve's laughter said it all. Within seconds, Luke was shaking his head and laughing with them.

As he watched the dancers, Flint was only half listening to the conversation of the small group of men gathered around the beer barrel. He didn't give a damn who was president of the United States. Last time he allowed himself to give it a mind, he ended up going off and fighting the goddamned war. So what if it was Ulysses Simpson Grant! He hadn't voted, so he figured he couldn't complain.

His eyes were on Garnet, smiling up at Cleve as he waltzed her around the dance floor. The music ended and he returned his attention back to the men. The conversation had shifted to the topic of Texas beef.

When the clamor of music and the stomping of dancers' feet on the wooden floor resumed, he looked for Garnet again. In that fancy gown of Honey's, Garnet stood out against the homespun clad women like a peacock in a gaggle of geese. Excitement had brought an added glow to her face, and her red hair bounced on her shoulders as she whirled around the floor in the arms of a new partner.

Flint figured if she didn't sit down soon, he'd have to rub salve on *her* aching muscles for a change. He grinned to himself, thinking of how good she'd feel under his hands.

When the men began commenting on how the transcontinental railroad would affect the Texas herds, he moved away and leaned against the wall. He sought out Garnet again among the dancers. This time her partner was the top hand from the Lazy D spread. What the hell! She'd already danced with him!

"Haven't seen you out there on that dance floor."

Flint gave Cleve a sideways glance. "Reckon you won't either."

"You ought to try it, Brother Flint. You might be surprised to find you like it."

"Not much chance of that. Nothing looks dumber to me than a bunch of grown men prancing around on their toes like they're suffering with a case of St. Vitus' dance."

Luke and Honey had just come up to them when the call came out for a lively square dance. "I've been waiting for a chance to get you away from that brother of mine," Cleve said. He grabbed her hand and led her out on the floor.

"Dancing sure works up a thirst," Luke said. "I need a beer." He headed for the beer barrel and the circle of men. Flint had had enough of their talk. It was no wonder he liked his solitude. Restless, he wandered outside.

"You leaving without us even having one dance together?"

He recognized Garnet's husky voice at once. He stopped and turned around.

"I figure we do enough dancing in the hayloft."

Garnet frowned at him. "Flint, there are other ways of having fun."

"Like hopping around in there like your drawers are itching."

He was tempted to weaken when she grabbed his hand. "Oh, come on, Flint. Just one dance."

"I don't dance, Widow Scott. When you're in my arms, I figure there's something better to do than swing you around on the dance floor."

Instantly, her smile disappeared and she dropped his hand. "Can't we ever have a conversation without you reminding me of the only reason we're together?"

"I'd hate to have you forget it," he said with a smirk.

"Oh, I won't forget it, Flint, but are you sure you're not trying to convince *yourself?*" She kissed him lightly on the lips, then turned and walked away—her red hair bobbing on her shoulders.

Flint grinned. The damn little temptress! She always got in the last word.

Figuring to get a cup of strong coffee and some peace and quiet, Flint headed for Maud's diner. He saw Luke and caught up with him. "You have enough of the dancing or the bullshit, Big Brother?"

"Honey asked me to check on Josh. He was going over to visit with Maud."

"I was just headed there myself," Flint said.

As they walked toward the diner, they heard a young boy say, "Thanks, misters. I'm sure grateful to you."

"That sounds like Josh," Luke said.

They hurried around the corner. Away from the

dancing, the town was dark and deserted except for two men and Josh, holding Amigo in his arms. "What's the problem, Josh?" Luke asked.

"Daddy, these men saved Amigo. A big, red dog, 'bout as big as you, was gonna fight him. Amigo wouldn't of had a chance."

"Well, we was just ridin' by and saw what was happenin', so we drove off the other dog," said one of the men. "Your boy's lucky he didn't get bit by that big red when he tried to pull this little fella away." He patted Amigo's head.

The men looked familiar to Flint. It took him several seconds to remember he had seen them in the bar at Comanche Wells.

"I'm grateful to you," Luke said. "The dog means a lot to my boy."

"Reminds me of the dog we had back home, don't it, Jeb?"

"Yep, we called him Stranger, 'cause he just showed up at the door one day," Jeb said. "Say, ain't you Flint MacKenzie?" Flint nodded. "Remember us, sir? We saw you in Comanche Wells."

"Yeah, I remember," Flint said.

"I'm Jeb Boone. This here's my brother Joey."

"And I'm Luke MacKenzie, Flint's brother." After they shook hands, Luke stepped back, grinning. "You two look enough alike to be twins."

"We are, sir," Joey Boone replied. " 'Cepting I'm the oldest."

"By five minutes," Jeb spoke up. "That's about the longest we've ever been apart."

"Well, it's sure been a real pleasure meetin' you folks," Joey said.

"Thank you, mister, for saving Amigo." Josh put the dog down when Joey reached out to shake hands.

Jeb hunched down and began to scratch Amigo behind his ears. "You take care of this little guy, Josh."

"I sure will, mister."

Garnet and Honey walked up just as the two men were about to climb back on their horses. "Why, it's the Boone brothers," Garnet exclaimed as soon as she saw them.

Both brothers broke out in wide grins and doffed their hats. "Well, howdy, ma'am," Joey said.

"Right pleasure seein' you again, Mrs. Scott," Jeb added. "You're sure lookin' mighty pretty, ma'am."

"Whatever brought the two of you to Calico?"

"We was just passin' through," Joey said. He wore a sheepish grin. "When we heard about the big celebration, we figured we'd hang around for a free meal. Then we was just ridin' out when we saw the dogfight and Josh there in trouble."

"For heaven's sake, what happened?" Honey asked, hurrying over to Josh. "Are you okay, sweetheart?"

"He's fine, Jaybird," Luke answered. "I already looked him over. Where are you boys heading for?"

"We've been lookin' for work. Fella told us that the Block L near Mission is taking on riders," Joey said.

"We ain't lookin' for handouts," Jeb interjected. "Me and Joey are willin' to work for our keep. Seems most folks around here don't have no call for two men. And we ain't gonna break up."

"You been around cattle much?" Flint asked.

"Hell, yes!" Joey said. "Our pa ran a few head afore he died. He and our ma were burned out by some goddamned Jayhawkers after the war. I apologize, ladies, for my bad language."

"Our folks never owned a slave in their lives, and would never have owned one if they could have," Jeb said bitterly. "But them Jayhawkers burned them out just because they hid a couple Rebs from a lynching party. Ma and Pa both died in the fire."

"So Kansas is your home?" Garnet asked kindly.

"Yes, ma'am. 'Cepting we ain't got no home."

"In another week, we're driving a herd to Abilene," Luke announced. "We could use a couple riders if you're interested. Job pays forty dollars a month, plus a fifty dollar bonus when we get there."

The Boone brothers exchanged glances. "That sounds mighty good to us," Joey said.

Luke shook hands with them to seal the agreement. "You can come back to the ranch with us. Our brother Cleve's in on the drive, too, and we're just on our way to meet our other partner. Grab your mounts and come along with us."

Once at the diner, Luke explained the situation to Maud. "You goin' on the drive, ma'am?" Joey asked.

"Hell, yes, son! And call me Maud."

"Garnet and I will be going, too," Honey said.

"So will me and Amigo," Josh added.

"Still game to come along?" Flint asked.

Joey and Jeb exchanged another glance. "We sure are, Mr. MacKenzie."

"Hot dog!" Maud exclaimed. "How would you boys like a big piece of chocolate cake?"

"Chocolate cake? Never had any chocolate cake before, ma'am," Jeb said. "But me and my brother sure like cake. Don't get much chance to have it."

"Well, you're gonna have some now." She glanced at Josh, who had listened engrossed to the conversation. Winking, Maud said, "Been savin' a piece for you, too, sweetheart."

"Sure was our lucky day when we rode past and saw that dog," Joey commented. "Else we would have kept riding."

"See, Daddy," Josh said. "Amigo helped you, didn't he? Good thing he didn't stay home."

Chapter 20

On Tuesday morning, the five men rode out to continue the branding. Later, Garnet and Honey loaded up the buckboard and took them their lunch. The dust-filled air was rent with the sound of heifers bellowing in protest as their bawling calves were cut away from them. The acrid smell of singed hair permeated the air.

The branded cattle were driven into a makeshift corral constructed of fallen pines that had been crudely hewn into lodgepoles and lashed together with rawhide.

Flint and Jeb Boone were cutting out the cattle and driving them up to the fire. If necessary, Cleve clipped off their horns, then Luke and Joey would brand and castrate the males.

Noticing that not all the cattle were being dehorned, Garnet asked Honey the reason why.

"Luke said only the males are dehorned," Honey said. "The heifers need their horns to protect their calves from being trampled on when the herd bunches up."

Somewhat appalled by the sight, Garnet asked, "Does it hurt them when their horns are cut off?"

"I guess not."

Garnet watched as Flint rode up with a roped calf. In

what appeared to be almost a single motion, he leapt from his horse and flipped off the rope. Grabbing a fistful of the calf's side skin, he pulled on it as he kicked the foreleg out from under the animal. Cleve immediately clipped off the calf's horns, then pushed the calf's underside hind leg forward and pulled up its top hind leg to stretch the skin taut. He held the animal down and Flint remounted his cow pony. Joey put a hot iron to the calf's left rear flank while Luke castrated it and sealed the cut with a hot iron. By that time, Flint was waiting to drive the bellowing calf into the corral in search of its mother.

"That little guy doesn't sound too happy," Garnet murmured.

Grinning, Cleve looked up at her. "I sure can't blame him. Dirty trick to pull on any male."

"Well, that's what separates the steers from the boys," Luke joshed, tossing the calf's severed male pouch onto a nearby pile of cut-off scrotums.

"You have just destroyed all of the romance of ranching for me," Garnet said as Jeb rode up with a calf. She turned away and walked over to the water barrel.

Garnet continued to watch Flint and Jeb separate the calves from their mothers and drive them up to the fire. Despite the earlier teasing, she could see it was grueling work, particularly in dealing with the older and larger cows. Both Flint and Jeb had to rope and wrestle a strong animal to the ground. When a cow's horns were too big for clipping, it took both of them to hold down the cow while Cleve chopped or sawed off the horns.

If the animal already wore a brand, Luke had to check it out in the stockgrowers' book. He'd either shout "A throw back," and Joey would release the animal, or "Brand it," and Joey would then take an "X" iron to vent the old marking, and right next to it, brand the cow with a Triple M iron.

In the weeks Garnet had been on the Triple M, she had found every facet of ranch life fascinating. As she watched Flint continuously cutting in and out of the herd, she wondered if she'd ever see the day when he'd want to settle down to such a life.

A short time later, he rode over to her. Covered with dust, his sweat-stained shirt clinging to him in wet patches, he showed the effects from his labor and the heat of the afternoon. Dismounting, he removed his hat and wiped the perspiration from his forehead with his forearm as he filled a ladle from the water jug.

After gulping down the water, he pulled off his shirt, refilled the ladle, and dumped the water over his head.

Her breath caught in her throat. Mesmerized, she stared at him. He lounged against the cow pony and draped his arms loosely across the saddle, his hat dangling from his hand. His eyes were hooded against the sun by thick, spiky lashes. He was bare from the waist up, and his wide, sinewy shoulders sloped to powerful biceps, slickened with water. Dark, curly hair narrowed in a seductive trail that tapered down the muscular brawn of his chest to a lean, flat stomach, then disappeared into the faded buckskins hugging his slim hips and long legs.

As she stared blatantly, she felt his eyes on her. She lifted her gaze and discovered he was studying her just as intently. Garnet knew how easy it was for him to read the undisguised hunger in her eyes. Heated blood surged through her, and she wondered if she could ever look at him without wanting him.

His mouth curved into a grin and he plopped his hat on at the familiar jaunty angle. "I'll be glad to take you up on your invitation, Redhead, as soon as I get back and wash off this trail dust."

Blushing, Garnet turned away and hurried over to Honey's side. She glanced back. Flint was still standing where she had left him—and still grinning.

* * *

Every rising sun brought the day of their departure closer. On Wednesday, while the men continued the branding, the two women rode into Calico to purchase the rest of the supplies needed for the drive. Since Josh had ridden out earlier with the men, Garnet and Honey were able to spend a leisurely time shopping and picking out more practical clothes to wear on the drive.

Knowing she would be on horseback, Garnet wanted pants. "I sure would turn a lot of women's heads back home if they saw me in these," she said with a giggle as she tried on a pair of tight-fitting jeans.

"I'm sure you'll turn a lot of heads here too, but I think they'll be male ones," Honey teased. "But I'm getting a couple of pairs, too. I'm not going to mess with long skirts and petticoats on the trail. I made that mistake when I came west."

By the time they left the dry goods store, each had bought two pairs of jeans, two shirts, several pairs of wool socks, drawers, and camisoles. Garnet had also picked out a nightgown, a Spanish style cowboy hat with a low crown, and a pair of cowboy boots. Her woman's boots were not high enough for western wear.

"Oh, Honey, I'm sure Flint's going to be upset when he hears how much these clothes cost," Garnet fretted.

"Nonsense, he told me to see that you're properly outfitted. Besides, it's all part of the cost of the drive."

They made several more stops at the saddler, the blacksmith, and the gunshop before pulling up the wagon in front of Maud's.

"Land alive, gals, you've already got a wagonload," she said as they added several crates of pots and kettles.

"I'm officially closing the diner Saturday night. I'll drive out Sunday with the rest of the supplies and we can pack up that chuck wagon," Maud announced. "Lord, gals, ain't this excitin'?"

"Maud," Garnet said, "there are more exciting things to do than being jostled around in a wagon. Believe me, it's not that much fun."

"You mean not as exciting as being jostled around in a hayloft?" Honey teased.

Garnet tried not to laugh. "That would depend on who's in the hayloft with you."

Honey rolled her eyes. "I guess the same could be said about the wagon."

"Listenin' to you two ladies, reckon I'm gonna have to take along an extra bar of soap to wash out your mouths."

Honey kissed her on the cheek. "Good-bye, you old dear. We'll see you Sunday." She climbed up on the wagon seat. Garnet hugged and kissed Maud, then climbed up beside her.

Honey handed her the reins. "Seeing as how I'll be driving a wagon for the next couple months, you can have the pleasure."

The two women laughed as they shifted around each other to change positions. Then they both waved good-bye again and started to ride off.

Shaking her head, Maud Malone stood in the road and watched the wagon roll away. "Lordy, Lordy," she mumbled affectionately, a smile breaking the weathered lines of her face. "Considerin' all those two gals have gone through, I'd have thought both of 'em would have forgotten how to laugh." Then she thought the better of it. Cocking her head, she grinned wickedly. "No. I reckon if I was a young'n cuddlin' up to one of them MacKenzie boys each night, I'd be smiling, too."

True to her word, Maud arrived on Sunday with a wagonload of additional supplies. "How are we going to squeeze three wagons of supplies into two wagons?" Garnet questioned as the three women rolled up their sleeves and set to work.

While Maud loaded the foodstuffs in their respective drawers on the chuck wagon, Garnet packed away the skillets and pots in the compartment extending below the wagon at the rear. Maud put Joey and Jeb to loading the shovels and branding irons, and the other heavy tools, into the long rectangular side box.

With Josh's assistance, Honey put the bedrolls, blankets, rain slickers, and other clothing in her wagon. Joshua packed his collection of *Leatherstocking Tales* in the back of the wagon to make sure they would not be left behind.

Honey came out of the house with both hands full. "Here's a bottle of calomel and a couple tins of unguent," she said.

Maud pointed to one of the drawers in the chuck box. "Put them in that drawer with the rolls of bandages."

"Don't forget the matches," Garnet warned.

"I've got enough matches to set the whole state of Texas to burning for a year," Maud replied.

"Josh, bring me my guitar," Honey shouted from the back of her wagon. "And a deck of playing cards."

By dusk, almost everything was packed into the two wagons. Garnet headed to the barn to gather her clothes. She was about to climb the ladder to the loft when she saw Flint in the horse stall that had once held her mare. A buckskin mustang stood in its place.

"Where's my mare?" Garnet asked, perplexed.

"I put her with the other horses in the corral. I figure this cow pony will be better for you to ride. I broke her gently and trained her when I had the free time. She's surefooted and not skittish."

"You didn't have to do that, Flint. I could have ridden my mare."

"That mare's almost swaybacked and she shies away from cows. You'd be fighting the reins all the time trying to keep her in line." He bent down to examine the mustang's shoes.

"When did you ever find the time?" she asked. She had been on the ranch long enough to know how many hours it would have taken him to break and train the animal.

"I've got something else for you," he said. He took her hand, led her over to a pile of hay, and picked up a wrapped package.

"What is it?" she asked excitedly. She smiled up at him as she released the string tied around the package. Peeling aside the paper, she discovered a Colt revolver and a leather belt and holster. "Flint!" she exclaimed. "I don't know what to say."

"Let's adjust that belt."

She raised her arms to enable him to slip on the belt and buckle it. "It's just a little too loose." He took it off her and began to work on it with his bowie.

With a loving smile, Garnet studied his face. He looked boyishly appealing as he concentrated on poking a hole in the leather. "There, that should do it," he said. He buckled it back on her. "Now slip the Colt into the holster so that it rides against your thigh."

Garnet slipped the pistol in and out of the holster several times. "It feels good to me, Flint."

"I don't want you to go anywhere without it."

"Why?" she asked softly.

"For your own safety."

"No, I mean, why did you do all this? The horse? The pistol? I'm not used to anyone looking out for me like this." She felt the rise of tears and turned away.

He turned her around and tipped up her chin. "You're not going to get all teary-eyed on me, are you?"

"Yes, I am," she said, sniffling. "Why do you do things like this? Just when you convince me you're an uncaring lout, you go and do this. Damn you, Flint! I never know whether to hit you or kiss you."

He grinned down at her. "There's never a question in my mind. Besides, I've got an investment in you."

"You're not fooling me. One of these days, you'll admit that you're in love with me, Flint MacKenzie."

The smile suddenly left his face and eyes. He cupped her cheeks in his hands and for a long moment stared down into her upturned face. "I just don't want to see anything happen to you, Redhead."

He released her and walked away.

He loves me, she told herself. *I know he loves me.* "The man I love, loves me!"

That evening, Luke called them all together for final instructions. "I figure Flint should ride point when he's not scouting. That leaves four men and Garnet to trail the herd—I figure two flankers, two drag men, and a wrangler. Garnet can ride the right flank and the rest of us can alternate between the other positions I've mentioned. The flankers will just have to work as swing men, too. How does that sound to the rest of you?"

Cleve did some quick calculating. "If we keep the herd bunched and move it four or five cows abreast, we'd only be strung out a little over half a mile. That would keep the riders closer together in case of trouble."

"And a wagon in the front of each flank would help those flankers when it came time to swing the herd," Flint added.

"Do we all agree?" Luke asked. His gaze moved from one to the other. "Maud, how are we set for supplies?"

"Got a good two months' supply, Luke. Flour, coffee and pinto beans, dried fruit, sugar, salt, baking powder, vinegar, molasses, honey. Plenty of onions, potatoes, salt pork, and smoked bacon. Got some sourdough fermentin' in a keg right now. Can't think of anything else."

"Ain't you bringing along any chocolate, Maud?" Josh moaned, disappointed.

" 'Fraid not, sweetheart. You're gonna have to hold off 'til we get back. Promise to bake you a chocolate cake the first day we do."

"What about grain for the wagon teams?" Flint asked.

"I filled up a couple of them bins in the chuck wagon with oats," Jeb spoke up.

"Can anyone think of something we might have missed?" Luke asked. "Shovels . . . axes . . . extra reins? Enough lanterns?"

"Everything's all set, Luke," Flint said quietly beside him. "Cleve and I checked it all out."

"Honey, did you pack enough blankets and slickers?"

"Between Maud's and ours, there are more than enough, Luke," Honey replied.

"Well, just don't forget the coffee pot, Maud. That's the most important thing as far as I'm concerned," he said lightly.

"I've already warned her about that," Honey teased. "Knowing you, we even brought along an extra one just to be safe."

Luke slipped an arm around Honey's waist. "Now, I figure Maud can sleep in the chuck wagon. Honey, Garnet, and Josh in the covered wagon. The rest of us either under the wagons or around the fire."

"No offense to Garnet or Josh, but I'm not so certain I like the sleeping arrangements," Honey announced candidly. "I've gotten kind of used to cuddling up next to you. Maybe we ought to open that up for further discussion."

"Jaybird, by the end of the day, you'll be so tuckered out, you won't care who's cuddling up next to you."

She arched a brow provocatively. "Speak for yourself, MacKenzie."

"Well, other than our little Honey Bear's disgruntlement with the sleeping arrangements, everything else sounds good to me," Cleve said.

"Well then, let's go to bed and all try to get a good night's sleep." Once again Luke paused and his gaze swept the faces in the room. "We'll move out at first light."

Chapter 21

If the weather was an omen, they were going to be lucky, Garnet thought. As dawn gave way to morning, the warm spring day glowed with bright sunlight filtering through the trees and sparkling on the stream. A faint breeze carried the scent of pine off the hillside.

She felt the flutter of butterflies in her stomach as she took her place on the right flank of the herd. The five men had already rousted the cattle and had them bunched together, moving east toward Red River Station where they would pick up the Chisholm Trail north to Abilene.

She could see Luke in front of the herd and Cleve on the left flank. Joey was rounding up strays at the rear, and Jeb was driving the horses in the remuda. At the head of the herd, she could see the chuck wagon on the left flank and Honey's wagon on the right flank.

Flint rode up to her. "I'll be riding ahead now. Probably won't see you till sundown." He leaned across his saddle and tied a red bandanna around her neck. "Here, drover, use this when you have to. It'll help to keep you from eating dust. Take care, Redhead."

"You too, Flint."

For a moment, his gaze lingered on her face, then he

228

wheeled Sam and galloped away. She watched until he disappeared.

As they started to move out the cattle, Garnet spied the lone figure of Ben Franks watching from a distant rise. She raised a hand and waved good-bye to him. The old man's white hair ruffled in the breeze as he took off his hat and waved back.

Luke set a slow, easy pace for the cattle. Occasionally, when a steer would start to drift, just a flick from the rawhide lariat would drive the animal back to the herd. As Garnet ambled along, her thoughts constantly drifted to Flint.

Giving no thought to Luke's warning about getting a good night's sleep, which she was sure Luke and Honey had ignored too, she and Flint had spent the major part of the night making love—like two lovers who were about to be separated for the rest of their lives. They had alternated between urgent passion and tender lovemaking until they both finally succumbed to exhaustion.

Flint was such a paradox, she thought warmly—a tender and considerate lover who made certain she reached the same satisfaction as he, so sensitive and vulnerable in those glorious moments. A far cry from the indifferent lover he claimed to be.

Would he ever admit his true feelings?

Luke halted the herd at noon and rode back to her. "How are you doing, Garnet?"

"Fine, so far," she said. "This is easier than I thought it would be."

He chuckled. "I hope you feel the same way by the time we finish the drive. I'm gonna let the herd graze for a couple of hours. Relax and get yourself something to eat."

When Garnet rode up to the chuck wagon, Maud and Honey already had a fire started, a kettle suspended above it on a tripod, and the coffee pot brewing.

"Hmmm, something sure smells good here," she said, climbing down and stretching.

"Grub'll be ready soon," Maud told her. "How're you doin' back there, gal?"

"Just fine, Maud. As I told Luke, it's much easier than I thought it would be."

"Well, I'm sure it'll get harder. At least the saddle sure will." Maud snorted at her own joke then bent down to stir the pot of chili.

"Need any help over here?" Garnet asked, moving over to where Honey was rolling out biscuit dough on the worktable.

Winking at her, Honey shook her head. "I've got a helper." She nodded toward Josh, who waited with a glass in hand to cut out the biscuits.

"I sure feel useless watching you and Maud do all the work," Garnet said.

"I'm grateful I'm not on horseback," Honey said. "I barely know how to ride one. Luke's been trying to teach me, but so far, I haven't been a very apt student. Okay, partner, it's all yours." She bent down and dug out a pan to hold the biscuits. "Garnet, why don't you go over and stretch out in the shade of my wagon?"

"Think I will." Taking Honey's suggestion, Garnet lay back and closed her eyes. The next thing she knew, Honey was gently shaking her awake an hour later. By then, the rest of the crew had eaten.

As Garnet ate, Jeb rode up leading a fresh pony for her. "Howdy, ma'am," he said with a wide grin. "Do you need a fresh mount?"

"No. The one I'm riding is fine."

"Okay. You have a good day, ma'am."

"Jeb, I hope you don't intend to call me ma'am the whole drive. My name's Garnet."

"All right, Miz Garnet." He galloped away.

Shortly after, Luke felt satisfied the cows had eaten their fill and they started the cattle moving again. By the time the rear of the herd reached the wagons, Maud and Honey had finished cleaning up and were ready to pull to the front. As Honey drove past, she waved and shouted at Garnet. "See you at supper."

Throughout the afternoon, Garnet kept a sharp eye open to prevent any cow from straying. That morning, she had observed that when cattle broke from the herd, they tended to return with very little coaxing. Still, she took her responsibility seriously. The thought of how easily the loss of cows could add up to a tidy sum of money preyed on her mind. Determined not to let any loss be attributed to the right flank of the herd, she maintained a steady vigilance.

Upon seeing a calf break away, Garnet goaded her horse toward the stray, but had not anticipated the reaction of the calf's mother to her sudden move. The heifer came charging to get between the horse and her calf.

Garnet's cow pony had been trained to anticipate such sudden moves and wheeled to the left. Garnet gasped with pain when the heifer's horn caught her leg, ripping her pants and breaking the skin. Responding as it was trained to do, the horse instantly turned to block off the cow from leaving the herd. With this threat between her and her calf, the heifer mewled in outrage and dogged behind the horse. The horse stopped in its tracks, wheeled again, and continued to cut off the cow from the calf, trying to drive the heifer back to the herd.

Garnet realized the heifer was just trying to get to the calf. She jerked the reins, moving the horse out of the path of the cow. The heifer trotted over to the calf, nudged the young calf, then heifer and calf trotted back to the herd.

Blood had begun to soak the leg of her jeans. She

checked the wound and saw the injury was bloody but not deep. The medical supplies were in the chuck wagon, so she removed the bandanna looped around her neck, wet it with water from her canteen, then tied the bandanna over the injury. Since that was all she could do for the moment, she returned to her post.

The sun had set that evening by the time she unsaddled her pony and turned the mare over to Jeb. She carried the heavy saddle over to a spot near the campfire, dropped it on the ground, then slumped down—stiff, sore, and exhausted.

With the exception of a couple hours at midday, she had been in the saddle from sunrise to sunset. Expelling several deep breaths, she allowed herself a few moments to relax until she felt sufficiently rested. Garnet was about to get up and go over to the chuck wagon when Flint rode back into camp.

He unsaddled Sam, came over and dropped his saddle beside hers, then sat down. "Hi, Redhead. How did it go today?"

"Sitting on a horse doing nothing can be very exhausting," she said with a sigh.

"What happened to your leg?"

"It's nothing, Flint. Just a surface scratch."

He knelt down to examine it. "What did you scratch it on?" he asked as he untied the bandanna.

"On the horn of a heifer. My horse zigged, and the cow zagged."

"Stay here. I'll get something to clean it with." Garnet was too tired to protest.

Flint was back shortly carrying a bandage roll and a bottle of whiskey. Honey hurried after him with a bowl of hot water and a cloth. "Garnet, are you okay?" she asked. "Flint said you hurt your leg."

"It's just a scratch, Honey."

"Oh, my!" Honey exclaimed after looking at Garnet's leg. "Let me clean it with this hot water."

"I can do that," Flint spoke up. "You and Maud have your hands full."

"All right, but if you need anything, call me." Honey hurried back to the chuck wagon.

"You gotta take off those jeans," Flint said.

"I can't take my pants off here. Anyone could come along and see me."

"Where's your blanket?" he asked impatiently.

"In Honey's wagon."

He untied the bedroll from his own saddle and handed her a blanket. "Here, use this one while I clean up that scratch. Infection can set in easy here." After Garnet removed her gunbelt, Flint immediately spoke up. "Be glad to give you a hand in getting your pants down."

"You always have," she retorted with a laugh.

Grinning, he said, "Just drop down your pants over the top of your boots, Redhead."

Glancing around to make sure they were alone, she did as he told her, then covered her hips. Frowning, Flint studied the injury after he finished rinsing away the blood. "That's a long gash." He uncapped the whiskey bottle. "This will disinfect it, but it's gonna hurt."

He hadn't exaggerated. She clenched her teeth as he poured the stinging liquid over the injury.

"At least it's not deep, or we'd have to sew it closed," he said.

"Flint, I can tell a surface scratch when I see one."

He wrapped and tied a bandage around her leg. "There, that oughta do it." He leaned over and kissed her knee.

"And what was the kiss for?" she asked skeptically.

"Thought you were supposed to kiss it to make it well."

"My knee wasn't hurt, Flint." She pulled up her jeans and buttoned them.

"I don't want the pain to spread." He kissed her

again, this time on her mouth—a tender, lingering kiss. She savored every second of it.

"Heard Garnet was hurting." The statement came from Luke.

Flint broke away and glanced up at his brother. "I took care of it." He stretched out, bracing his head on his saddle.

"What does it look like ahead?" Luke asked.

"I found a spot with good grass and water about fifteen miles from here. We're making good time, so it shouldn't be a problem tomorrow."

Cleve walked over and joined them. "Is it safe to come over now? I held off in fear of interrupting. Joey's taking the first night watch. I'll take the second."

"Where's Jeb?"

"He's stringing a corral for the horses."

"Then you better eat and bed down. Midnight comes around before you know it."

"Yeah, I intend to. Soon as I eat," Cleve said.

"Well, if you three will excuse me," Garnet said as she stood up. "I have to find a needle and thread to sew up my ripped pants."

"Shame on you, Brother Flint," Cleve scolded.

"Good-bye!" Garnet said, grimacing at the remark. She started to walk away.

"Hold up, Redhead. I'll come with you. Gotta take care of Sam before I get too comfortable."

After eating supper, Garnet changed into her night-gown. Then, wrapping a blanket around herself, she went out to the fire and sat down to mend her jeans. She was upset that her new pants were damaged already.

The camp had settled in for the night. She saw that Cleve and Jeb Boone were asleep in bedrolls near the campfire; Flint and Luke were both stretched out close to the wagon; and Josh had fallen asleep cuddled against Luke's side. Honey and Maud were quietly moving around at the chuck wagon by the light of a lantern.

She heard Maud and Honey say goodnight, then Maud took the lantern and climbed into the chuck wagon. Having hung around for the possibility of any final food scraps, Amigo came trotting over to the sleeping figures, stretched out, and laid his head across Josh's lap.

"Aren't you in bed yet?" Honey asked Garnet in a half-whisper.

"I'm just finishing up mending these pants."

"Oh, look at him!" Honey said fondly when she saw Josh sleeping peacefully at his father's side. "I hate to wake the darlin' to move him."

"Are you talking about Josh or Luke?" Garnet teased lightly.

"Guess I mean either one."

"Why don't you just leave Josh where he's at? He's in good company," Garnet said.

"Guess I will. When are you coming to bed?"

"I'm almost done here."

"Well, it's been a long day. Goodnight, Garnet," Honey said, climbing into the wagon.

"Goodnight, Honey."

After adding the last stitch, Garnet inspected the mended pants. Satisfied with the result, she sat motionlessly, enjoying the quiet night. The voice of Joey Boone singing softly to the herd drifted faintly on the evening breeze.

She smiled with contentment.

On the afternoon of their tenth day of the drive, they reached the border town of Red River Station. The following morning, they would be crossing the river—leaving Texas and entering the Indian Nations.

The MacKenzie brothers talked over the next day's travel plans as they got rid of their trail dust in the public bath. When they finished, they returned to the herd and gave the Boone brothers the night off from any responsibilities. Joey and Jeb were free to seek whatever pleasure they preferred. After a little haggling, Flint convinced Luke that he should remain with Honey and Josh, so Flint and Cleve tossed a coin to see who would stay with the herd. Flint lost.

"Sorry about that, Brother Flint," Cleve said, slapping him on the shoulder. "Hey, fellas, wait for me," he shouted to the Boone brothers as they headed for the nearest saloon.

Upon registering at the rundown structure that served as a hotel, the women headed for the public bath. After ten days on the trail, the hot water and soap suds felt divine on their tired bodies. Maud left with a declaration that she was returning to her room and intended to get a full night's sleep for a change.

"What's Flint eating for supper?" Garnet asked as she shared an evening meal with Honey and Luke at the diner.

"He grabbed some jerky out of the chuck wagon and the makings for coffee," Honey said.

Garnet toyed with her food for several minutes. "I think I'll take him some of this chicken. It's delicious."

"That would be nice of you," Honey said, tongue-in-cheek. Garnet knew she wasn't fooling her friend for a moment.

"And listen, you two, since we have connecting rooms, why don't you put Josh in my bed? He can sleep with me tonight."

"You mean it?" Honey asked hopefully. "You're sure it wouldn't be an inconvenience to you?"

"Of course not."

"Did the two of you ladies cook this up in the bath?" Luke asked with a skeptical glance.

"Certainly not," Honey said, aghast. Then her face broke into a dimpled smile. "But we would have, if we'd thought of it then."

Josh was entirely in the dark regarding the drift of

the conversation. "Auntie Garney, is it okay if Amigo sleeps with us? He can't sleep 'less he's in bed with me."

"Yes, Auntie Garney," Honey said. She held a straight face, but her eyes were dancing with devilment. "Joshua has observed that poor Amigo has this serious sleeping problem. I haven't noticed Amigo's problem, because I'm always tripping over him while he's stretched out sleeping on the floor."

"Well, maybe if somebody gave me a kiss on the cheek, I might consider letting Amigo join us, Josh," Garnet said.

"Yeah, Amigo, give her one of your big slobbering ones," Luke said. "Most likely the kind she's used to getting from Uncle Flint."

"Daddy, Auntie Garney meant me," Josh declared.

"Oh, you give slobbering kisses, too?" Luke asked.

Now, Josh was completely confused. Perplexed, he looked at Honey. "Mama, do I give slobbering kisses?"

"Of course not, sweetheart. Only your father does."

"Hey, Jaybird, whose side are you on?"

Laughing, Garnet shook her head. "I think we've all been out in the sun too long—we're beginning to sound tipsy."

"Well, tipsy or not," Honey said with a squeeze to Garnet's hand, "we love you for this."

"Yeah, we do, Garnet," Luke said sincerely. "So why are we sitting here wasting time?"

Garnet had the diner pack a basket containing several pieces of fried chicken, two hard-boiled eggs, two corn muffins, and a piece of blackberry pie. After saying good-bye to the MacKenzies, she rode the short distance out of town to where the herd was grazing for the night.

"I brought you something to eat," she said when she rode up to Flint's small fire. Dismounting, she took the basket of food off her saddle and spread it out on his blanket.

"I was hoping you'd ride out," he said after they sat down. She wrapped her arms around her bent legs, rested her chin on her knees, and watched him eat.

"If you wanted me to come, why didn't you just ask?"

"Guess I figured you'd want to spend the night in town in a decent bed for a change."

He handed her his cup of coffee. She took a sip and handed it back to him. His gaze on her face felt powerful and compelling.

"Sometimes a bed isn't all it's given credit for— unless the right person's in it with you."

Grinning, he reached out and began to toy with several strands of her hair. "You're about the most straightforward woman I've ever known, Redhead." His voice was low, seductive. A shiver raced down her spine.

"I wish you could be just as honest with me." Coping with a rising ache in her chest, she was unaware of the pensive tone that had crept into her voice.

"I have been." He finished the coffee and put the cup aside.

"I'm not ashamed to admit that I love you, Flint."

"I am."

Surprised, she glanced up, searching his face to try to comprehend the meaning behind his unexpected admission. "Why? Why would you be ashamed?"

"I don't understand what love is all about. Yeah, I love what we have together. It's good. It's never been better. But it ain't love. At least not the kind of love you mean . . . the kind of love Luke and Honey have." His gaze caught and held hers. "The kind I ain't capable of. Reckon what I'm trying to say, Redhead, is that there're some men who just aren't fit to be loved because they can't love back."

"No, you're wrong, Flint. That's not true." She put her fingers over his mouth. "Don't say that." Lying back, she pulled him down into her arms. "Don't even think it."

"I'm not like Luke, Redhead." His tongue traced the soft fullness of her lips. "I could never settle down. Never have children."

She was reminded of the fear she had shoved to the back of her mind. "Don't you like children, Flint?" she asked, hoping she sounded casual.

"Sure I do, but when I get that itch to move on, I gotta scratch it."

Then he kissed her, and any thought of the future was obliterated by the swell of passion as she breathed her love through her parted lips.

Later, as she lay beside him, Garnet gazed up at the stars. They looked so close, she felt as if she could reach up and pick one out of the sky. "Which one do you want?" she asked.

"What?" He had been lying toying with the locket that lay on the swell of her bare breasts. Glittering in the moonlight, the locket was a golden beacon gleaming against the ivory globes. He lowered his head and kissed each of the dusky rose peaks.

"Which one do you want?" she repeated.

"I've got no preference. I'm attached to both of them."

"I'm talking about a star, silly."

"A star?"

She turned her head and smiled at him. "Which star would you like to have as your own?"

Lying back, he tucked his hands under his head and looked up at the sky. "I think you ought to leave all of them right where they're at. The sky is their range to ride."

"Which is the North Star?" she asked. "Maybe that's the one I'll choose."

He pointed to a single brightly shining star. "Now look to the left. See those seven stars strung out there?

That's the Big Dipper. Soon it'll be sliding around the star. And that's how we tell time."

"What time is it now?"

"About eleven o'clock. In a couple more hours, the dipper'll start swinging under the star. When the dipper gets directly under the star, it'll be time to raise the herd."

"But you can't see the stars when the sun comes up, so how do you tell time then?"

"By the position of the sun. But that dipper is still turning away up there. If you look up in the sky this time tomorrow, you'll see that big ole dipper in the same place."

"Where did you learn so much about stars, Flint?"

"Just the Big Dipper. Even if you fall asleep riding herd at night, all you have to do is locate that dipper to know what time it is. Man don't need no watch."

"Well, maybe I'll just leave that North Star up there where it belongs."

"That's good. 'Fraid I was gonna have to learn how to tell time all over again."

"More likely, you weren't taking me too seriously." Unwisely, she shifted suddenly and winced aloud. "Ouch!"

He raised his head. "What's wrong?"

"I don't think my body will ever stop aching. It's been sore since the first day on the drive."

"Why didn't you say something sooner?" He slipped on his buckskins and walked over to Sam. After digging through his saddlebags, he returned carrying a tin of unguent. "Turn over."

She shifted over on her stomach, and Flint began to rub in the salve. She groaned as he started at her shoulders and worked down her spine, then her thighs. His long, strong fingers felt like an aphrodisiac.

"Your behind's actually bruised, Redhead! My God, you must have been riding in pain!"

"Just rub some of that salve into it." She groaned. "It

feels good." He leaned down and lightly kissed each bruised cheek.

And she continued groaning, this time with pleasure, long after he put aside the tin.

Chapter 22

Low, gray clouds loomed ominously above the small huddled group waiting on the southern bank of the Red River. Sitting astride her mare, Garnet watched anxiously as Flint slowly stepped Sam through the swirling water. Spring rains had swelled the river, but at the moment, the Red looked low enough to be fordable—the danger lay in the quicksand bed underneath the brown, sludgy water. She glanced fretfully toward a nearby cluster of crude wooden crosses marking the resting place of those who had tried unsuccessfully to cross.

"Soft sand here," Flint called out as Sam sank several inches. For a moment, horse and rider fought both the force of the rapidly flowing current and the grabbing pull from below, until at last, they plodded forward. Near midstream, the water deepened to the height of the horse's flanks, then gradually lowered again as it neared the river bank. "Bad sand over here," Flint called out from the opposite bank.

Many of the townsfolk had come out of their stores and stood in scattered groups on the boardwalk to watch the operation. "All right, let's take the herd across," Luke said, galvanizing the small group around him into action. "Jeb, drive the remuda over first. That way Flint can corral them before we move the cattle.

Then come on back. We'll need your help with the herd."

Jeb rode back to the remuda. Whistling and hazing the horses with his lariat, he drove the band of mustangs into the water. The fleet cow ponies proved to be good swimmers and crossed easily. Once on the opposite bank, Flint immediately rounded them up and drove them into the makeshift corral he had strung between the trees. When he finished, he took off his hat and waved it as a signal to start the herd across.

"Cleve and Joey, go downstream about twenty-five yards and catch any calves that might float away," Luke ordered. "Jeb can take the left flank; I'll take the right. Garnet, you drive them from the rear. Be sure to keep the cattle moving so they don't get mired down in the quicksand or start to mill around in midstream and turn on us. The wagons can go over last, after the herd's out of the water."

Cleve and Joey galloped downstream as Luke started the cattle moving. Garnet rode to the rear of the herd, which was strung out for half a mile. Then she started to press the cattle forward. She could hear the shouts and whistles of the men above the bellowing cows and mewling calves already in the water. Cold water splashed on her legs and in her face when she reached the river bank. Ahead of her, she saw the long stream of cows and the noses of calves sticking above the water as they swam next to their mothers. Occasionally, a few lost the battle with the current and drifted away, but Cleve and Joey were there to catch them downstream and get them headed toward the river bank.

When several of the cows would stop swimming and begin to mill in a circle, Garnet or one of the men rode in among them, and several stinging slaps from their lariats would get the cows moving again.

The gruelling, nonstop work took almost two hours. Finally Flint had the herd rounded up and beginning to graze on the far bank, as wild-eyed, bawling calves ambled around in search of their mothers.

Sitting between his father and mother, and clutching Amigo tightly in his arms, Josh's face glowed with excitement as Luke drove Honey's wagon across the river. Now, all that remained was the chuck wagon. Flint and Joey each tied a rope between the front axle of the wagon and his own saddle horn, and started the wagon across.

"Keep moving, you two old swaybacked broomtails, or so help me, the both of you are gonna end up in tonight's stew," Maud shouted, whipping the reins of the two-horse team. But despite the pull of four horses, the heavy-laden wagon sank up to the axles in quicksand.

Cleve jumped off his horse and shouted to Jeb. "Get a rope on that rear axle." The two men quickly tied ropes to the rear, and then their mounts. With the power of six horses, the wagon was wrenched from the quicksand and pulled to the opposite bank.

As Garnet's horse lumbered out of the water, she heard a bawling calf nearby. Glancing over, she saw that the critter had strayed back to the river and was mired in quicksand.

She rode over to it and dismounted. "What's the matter, little guy, you lose your mama?" she cooed. Looping a lariat around the calf's neck, she tried to tug it out gently so as not to strangle the thrashing animal. Mewling for its mother, the calf struggled and finally freed its front legs, but the rear legs remained trapped in the sand.

Garnet moved to the rear of the animal. Hoisting and shoving the calf from behind with her hands and shoulders, she managed to shake the little fellow loose. As the calf bolted away, Garnet's hands slipped off its back and she landed on her hands and knees in the quicksand. She felt the sand immediately grab and hold her. Looking up, she saw a heifer break from the herd and head for the calf. Reunited, they trotted back to the herd.

She quickly turned her attention to her own predicament. In her awkward position, she could not get any leverage to pull free.

Flint and Cleve rode over and peered down at her. "Well, what have we got here, Brother Flint?" Cleve asked.

"Looks like a little doggie," Flint replied.

Cleve shook his head. "Well, it don't look like any of ours. Must be a stray from another herd."

"Too bad," Flint said. "Right cute little heifer, too."

Garnet gritted her teeth as they dismounted and walked around her, stroking their chins as they studied her.

"'Bout the leggiest calf I've ever seen," Flint reflected, "but it's sure got a right pert little rump, Little Brother."

"Don't see any MacKenzie brand on it though," Cleve replied.

"And you never will!" Garnet lashed out, not amused.

"Sure it's a calf, Brother Flint? Sounds more like one of them big snapping turtles."

They climbed back on their horses and started to ride away.

"Get back here and get me out of this sand right now!" she shouted.

Flint wheeled his horse and looked back at her. "Aw, that little heifer's too cute to leave. Maybe we oughta help her out, Little Brother."

Once again they climbed down and walked around her. "Don't see any place where we can get a rope on her. Figure we'll have to lift her out. Which end do you want?" Cleve asked.

"Both ends look good to me," Flint replied.

"When I'm out of this and my hands are free, you two had better ride clear of me—way clear!" she warned.

"Must come from good stock. The little heifer's still got fight in her," Flint said. He hooked an arm under her breasts. Cleve did the same around her stomach near her hips. Together they lifted her out, and set her feet on the river bank.

Garnet glared at them. Then, shaking hunks of sand off her hands and arms, she turned and walked away with the sound of their laughter ringing in her ears.

Flint rode up beside her, leaned over, and scooped her up into his saddle, setting her sideways in his arms.

"Little heifer, indeed!" she grumbled.

He cut off any further tirade with a kiss, then goaded Sam to a loping gait.

Everyone's spirits were high. Even though they faced fifty more days on the trail, one of the biggest hurdles was behind them—the Red River—and they hadn't lost a single cow!

They stopped there for several hours, to give the crew a chance to rest and change their soiled and sodden clothing.

Garnet took immediate advantage of the opportunity. The wet, grimy sand had oozed into her boots and she couldn't wait to get them off.

After the midday meal, they prepared to move out, now faced with the second major threat—three hundred miles through the Indian Nations. Luke called them all together with a warning that from this point on, it was important to keep the herd bunched, and no one was to stray off alone.

"There's safety in numbers," he warned just before he rode to the front.

"If a wagon train didn't discourage the Comanche from attacking, why wouldn't they attack the few of us?" Garnet asked Flint.

"The wagon train was attacked by a war party on a killing raid," Flint explained. "They may be in Wyoming by now. The Comanche Nation is divided into many small bands. Not all of them are out on killing raids. And if we run into a Kiowa or Apache, who knows, maybe we can negotiate."

"Negotiate for what?" Honey asked.

"Oh, maybe the two of you gals and a mustang," he said lightly, then galloped away.

Garnet and Honey exchanged a distressed look. "Flint really has a peculiar sense of humor, doesn't he?" Honey said.

"Very peculiar," Garnet agreed. Then she rode to her position on the flank.

Several hours later, Flint rode back and told Luke that the best grass and water he had seen was a mile ahead, so they stopped earlier than usual and made camp.

Later that evening, Garnet sat by the fire and watched Luke say goodnight to Honey and Josh before he rode off for night duty. The couple so openly adored each other that Garnet felt like a voyeur. She couldn't help but yearn for such a relationship with Flint. True, he had begun to show signs of affection to her in the presence of others, but it was a far cry from a man in love.

"What are you planning to do when we finish the drive, Joey?" she heard Flint ask.

"Me and Jeb'll probably look for a job punchin' cows. Sure would be nice if someday we could have a little spread of our own. Pretty hard to get enough money to get started."

"Why don't you go back to Texas with Luke? I'm sure he'd like to keep you on."

"Figure he's got enough hands with you and Cleve."

"Oh, we won't be staying," Flint said. "Soon as this

drive's over, we'll go back to searching for Charlie
Walden and the others who raided the ranch and killed
Ma and Sarah. Cleve'll be following a lead south, and I
was on the trail of a couple of 'em when I caught up
with the wagon train that Garnet was on. I had to cut
away then."

"How do you figure on pickin' up their trail again?"
Joey asked.

"I just keep asking until I hear a word here and
there. Before I know it, I'm sniffing at their heels.
That's why Cleve's heading south. He heard that some
of the Mex with the gang might be working the
border."

"Isn't it possible that some of that band of Comancheros are dead?" Garnet asked.

"Sure. I've killed a few of them myself. So have Luke
and Cleve. But we've never got the man who led
them."

"Luke has a family, Flint," she went on. "How can
he go after any outlaws? He wouldn't even leave
Honey and Josh behind on this drive."

"I know, and I understand why—but I reckon he'll
want to be there in the end. Josh's real mama was
killed in that raid; Luke would want to make it right by
her."

"Even if Honey wouldn't want him to go?"

"A man's got to do what his conscience tells him."

"And if he's killed, Flint, what will his conscience
matter? Will he be any less dead?"

"Reckon not. But women have no role in this matter
'til it's all over."

"No role? What does that mean? Isn't this all about
avenging the murders of the two *women*? If women
have no role in it, what are you avenging—your honor
or your pride? Obviously, it's not for love of the
women you lost." She walked away.

An uneasy silence followed her departure. Joey
stood up. "Reckon I'll get me a drink of water," he

said. Jeb got up and followed him. Flint remained, staring into the fire.

Garnet was too worked up to consider going to bed. She started to stroll, calmed by the beauty of the night. A warm breeze, drifting in from the south, carried the smell of rain. She glanced skyward; there was no indication of an approaching storm. A bright moon streaked the earth with silvery patches of light, and the sky glimmered with a myriad of stars. She leaned back against a tree and folded her arms across her chest.

The conversation had disturbed her. Flint was on a mission—he had said so himself. Once this drive was over, he'd return to pursuing his mother's murderers. Garnet didn't believe he'd ever consider allowing her to accompany him. She'd only get in his way. So he must be intending to leave her when they reached Abilene—to ride away with no strings, as he so often said. What would be his reaction if she told him that she was carrying his child? Would that prevent him from leaving her? And if it did, would he resent this interference in his pursuit of those killers? She didn't know what to do except wait until she was certain she was pregnant.

She glanced heavenward. She needed some sign— some assurance—that she meant more to Flint Mac-Kenzie than a good romp in a bedroll! *Please, God. Please give me some sign.*

"What are you doing out here alone?"

The sudden intrusion startled her, even though she recognized the speaker immediately.

"It's frightening how you manage to move so silently, Flint."

"So does a Comanche. You heard Luke's warning this morning." His tall body blocked out the moonlight as he approached her.

"I don't think you'd let anything happen to me."

Flint gathered a few of the coppery strands of her

hair and rolled them between his fingers. "Someday I might not be around when you need me most, Red-head, so don't wander off like this." He took her hand. "Come on, let's go back."

Unresisting, she let him lead her back to the camp-fire.

All but Luke, who was on night watch, and Josh, who had been put to bed, were seated around the fire. Everyone's attention was on a card game being played by Honey and Jeb.

"Okay, Jeb, now supposing there's just the two of us in the game and we're playing five card draw." She dealt each of them five cards. "Now what are you holding?" she asked.

"I've got a pair of eights, the deuce of spades, the six of diamonds, and a king of clubs. So I'd open for five matches." He grinned as he shoved five match sticks into the center of the pot.

"All right, since I have a pair of sixes, a four and nine of diamonds, and a queen of spades, I'd cover your bet."

She put down her hand and picked up the stack. "So, how many cards are you going to draw?"

"Reckon it'd have to be three," Jeb said, grinning across the blanket they were using as a table. He saved his pair and tossed away the other three cards.

"And the dealer will take three cards also," Honey announced. She too, saved her pair of sixes and tossed the other cards into the center of the pot. Then she dealt each of them three new cards.

"All right, now what do you have?"

"I caught a pair of fives and a jack of diamonds," Joey said. "I'll bet ten matches this time."

Honey turned over her hand for all to see. "And I caught a three, a seven, and a jack. Neither of them help my hand, right? But I'm going to see your bet and raise you five more." Honey shoved fifteen matches into the pot and picked up her five cards.

"Yeah, but I'll call you," Jeb said adding five matches, "because my two pair beat your pair of sixes." He grinned broadly at Joey.

"But not my full house," Honey said. She turned over her cards and there were now three aces and the pair of sixes.

Maud slapped her knee. "Well, if that don't beat all!"

Jeb looked astonished. "How'd you do that, Miz Honey? We all saw your hand." Honey pulled the three missing cards out of her left sleeve.

"Neatly done, Honey," Cleve commented.

"Well, where did the three aces come from?" Jeb asked, scratching his head of thick blond hair.

"Most likely from her right sleeve, Jeb," Cleve said.

"Dammit, gal, you're good!" Maud said.

"Just don't try that unless the game is down to two players and you're dealing," Honey said.

"Don't try it at all," Cleve corrected, "unless you want that hand to be buried right along with the rest of you in the same pine box. Where'd you learn to stack a deck like that, Honey?"

"I used to travel with a medicine show."

"You ever try winning honestly?" Cleve asked, challenging her.

Honey's eyes flashed with amusement. "Dear Cleve, I did this for fun, but I don't have to cheat to win at poker. I've probably forgotten more about playing poker than you'll ever know."

"That sounds like an invitation, Little Sister. Move over, Jeb," Cleve said. "Miz Honey is about to get an education."

"Are you in for a surprise." Honey laughed, picked up the cards, and shuffled them. "Name your poison, Cleve MacKenzie."

As their play continued, one by one, they all wandered off to bed. Only Honey and Cleve remained at the fire.

Chapter 23

T hey woke the next morning to rain. It continued off and on, following them in their trek across the level plain. By the third day of the inclement weather, conversation had been reduced to a minimum. They rode huddled in their saddles during the day. At night, they strung a tarp on poles and built their fire. Camping beneath the temporary shelter kept them dry, but it wasn't enough to keep the dampness out of their bodies and spirits.

Luke turned somber, Honey reserved. Josh became whiny and bored, Maud ornery, Joey withdrawn—and Flint taciturn. He and Garnet barely spoke. Even Cleve's usually affable nature seemed stretched to the limit. The only one who managed to keep his good humor was Jeb. He had a laugh or good-natured grin for everyone whatever the weather conditions.

Garnet found herself brooding. No matter how many encouraging talks she gave herself, she spent her days in the saddle feeling sorry for herself—a state of mind she had never suffered before.

And as each day passed, Garnet knew there was no doubt that she was carrying Flint's child. The day the sun finally broke through, everyone's spirits lifted but hers. She was faced with a truth she could no longer deny.

"Luke, how about stopping right now and drying out?" Honey suggested when they had halted for water near a stream. "Everything is damp and we can spread it out in the sunshine."

"Jaybird, we've got a half day of light left."

"It sure wouldn't hurt to give these teams a good rest, too," Maud added. "They've been carting these wagons through a lot of mud."

"We'll never finish this drive if we don't keep moving," Luke reminded them.

Honey sighed and walked over to him. "You're right. It just seemed like a good idea for everybody to kind of relax. But nothing's as important as the drive." She clasped his hand.

"You always roll with the punch, Jaybird. That's one of the reasons I love you." He slipped an arm around her waist. "Reckon we can pull up for the rest of the day. It'll do us all good to have an afternoon of doing nothing." Squealing with pleasure, Honey threw her arms around Luke's neck.

"Hey, Big Brother, looks like you're getting mellow in your old age," Cleve said, grinning.

Luke nodded. "Yeah, I reckon so. But what the hell will one or two more days matter, anyway."

Flint looked up and grumbled, "It'll matter a lot if we have rain those last one or two days on the drive."

After spreading out their blankets, Honey and Garnet went down to the stream to wash their clothes. "I think we need washing more than these clothes do," Garnet grumbled, glancing at her mud-splattered pants.

A dimple formed in each of Honey's cheeks as she said impishly, "Let's bathe in the river."

"Do we really dare? A bath would sure feel good, even if it's a cold one."

"Let's do it. The men are all occupied right now with the cattle and horses. We won't get a better chance."

She hurriedly stripped down to her pantalets and camisole and waded into the water. "Come on in, Garnet, it's not too bad."

"I might believe you, if your teeth would stop chattering," Garnet said. She shed all but her underclothes and followed. Before long, the girls were cavorting merrily in the water, any concern for modesty forgotten.

On the verge of returning to the river bank, Garnet looked up to see Cleve approaching. "You gals want any company in there?"

"If you're referring to yourself, the answer is no," Honey called out to him.

"I knew someone would see us," Garnet said, a blush creeping up her cheeks.

"We're beginning to turn blue," Honey shouted past her chattering teeth. "Are you going to leave, Cleve MacKenzie, so we can get out of this water?"

"What's stopping you?" Cleve asked innocently. "I've been standing here for the last ten minutes watching you gals."

"I'm going to tell your big brother on you," Honey warned.

"Don't worry, Little Sister, I've just been watching Garnet," he yelled back.

"Flint's not gonna like that much more than Luke would," Honey shouted.

"Then maybe he'll get concerned enough to correct his mistakes." Laughing, he strolled away.

"I wonder what he meant by that," Garnet said.

"I'm sure Cleve probably doesn't like Flint's . . . arrangement . . . with you any more than Luke does. You're a wonderful gal, Garnet, and we all love you. We'd like to see Flint make—"

"Make an honest woman of me," Garnet intoned drolly. "Not any more than I would."

"Let's get out of here before we freeze." Shivering,

they ran out of the water and wrapped themselves in towels. "I've got to go back and help Maud, so I'm going to change in the wagon," Honey said. She picked up her clothes and ran back to camp.

Wrapped in the towel, Garnet managed to shed her wet underclothes, rubbed herself vigorously, then put on a dry shirt and pair of pants. Feeling clean and refreshed, she was brushing her hair when Jeb approached.

"Hi, Miz Garnet. Looks like you had yourself a bath," he commented pleasantly.

Garnet patted the ground beside her. "Come on over and sit down." He sank down beside her. "Water's cold, but refreshing." Tilting her head to the side, she studied him intently. "You know, you don't look comfortable. Is it me, or are you sitting on a cactus?"

A slow grin crossed his face, giving him an even more youthful appearance. "I guess you're right, Miz Garnet. I sure feel more at ease on horseback than I do with a lady."

"You shouldn't feel that way. You and Joey are very appealing. Women find it easy to take a liking to men like you."

"Me and Joey's never had much call to be around real ladies, 'ceptin' Ma."

"Well, speaking as a woman, I can assure you, Jeb, neither of you will have a problem when you find the right woman."

"Reckon I'll never see that day, Miz Garnet. Joey and I stay together. Him being the oldest and all, he figures he's gotta look after me. And I wouldn't want it any other way. Can't see any gal comin' between us."

"Oh, you say that now," Garnet teased, "but you'll both think differently when you meet the right gals."

"You and Flint are sure sweet on each other," he said in a forthright manner. "He's a good man, Miz Garnet. I sure admire him. Luke and Cleve, too."

"Yet, had you been old enough, you would have fought them on opposite sides during the war," Garnet said.

"Yep," Jeb drawled reflectively. "Reckon every man's got his own reasons for what he does. You're not a Texan, are you, ma'am?"

"No, I'm from Georgia, Jeb."

"That's what I mean. It don't pay to condemn a man for defendin' what he believes. Heck, Miz Garnet, even I kin tell them MacKenzies don't believe in slavery any more than I do. Did you own a slave, ma'am?"

"Heavens, no! Yankees have the misconception that everyone in the South owned slaves. You'd be amazed to find out how many did not. It was a shameful war, Jeb. So many men dying over an issue that should have been resolved without going to war."

"Yep. My Pa always said that's the reason for votin' for them there politician fellas. But they can't stop fighting among themselves, much less keep the states from doing it."

Turning to a lighter subject, Garnet said, "But speaking of good men, I've taken quite a shine to that brother of yours."

At the mention of his brother, Jeb's eyes warmed with affection. "Yeah, Joey's always been the one to look after the two of us."

"Well, we better get back, Jeb, or we'll miss the meal." She stood up and bundled her clothing in the wet towel.

"Let me carry that, ma'am," Jeb said.

When they returned, a large fire was blazing in the center of the camp. The horses had all been tethered for the night, and the men were beginning to settle down, waiting for their evening meal.

Maud had made a pot of stew and freshly baked biscuits. Garnet looked around for someplace to sit. Luke and Honey were seated away from the group.

Josh, with Amigo at his feet, was chatting with Cleve. Deciding not to join any of them, Garnet sat by herself near the wagon and began to eat. She realized she was hungrier than she thought, and consumed her food ravenously.

Flint came over carrying his plate and cup, and settled down beside her. "The way you're shoveling down that food, it looks like you're figuring on not eating for the next couple of days."

She began to nibble on a piece of beef. "I'm sorry if I've offended you with my eating habits."

"You don't offend me, Redhead." Flint chuckled. His eyes roamed her appreciatively. "You must have gotten in a bath. You sure look rosy, and you smell like a flower garden."

"More blue than rosy. Cleve had Honey and me trapped in the water and we couldn't get him to leave."

"He was most likely making sure you two gals were safe. Ain't smart for the two of you to be off bathing alone. Next time you want a bath, take me along for protection."

"And who would protect me from you?" Garnet asked sarcastically.

"Well, it's for sure you wouldn't turn blue from the cold," he said, laughing.

Suddenly Garnet resented his cavalier attitude toward her. It wasn't the long week of rain, or even her suspicion that she was carrying his child. She was irritated that he continued to view their relationship as nothing other than sexual. He never asked her how she was feeling, or how her day had passed. And he sure didn't have a problem discussing different topics with the others. But with her, the conversation always revolved around the same topic—sex!

"I'm beginning to believe Luke is the only one of you MacKenzies who isn't a womanizer. The only difference between you and Cleve is that he admits to being one, while you ride around claiming you don't want anything to do with women. You know what I've just realized, Flint? You're a hypocrite."

"What in hell's eating at your craw?" he asked, surprised.

"Nothing that you'd understand, MacKenzie."

With an angry toss of her head, Garnet returned to the chuck wagon, where she began helping Maud clean up.

"Hey, gal, what're you doin'? You've got a long day tomorrow. Go set yourself down and rest."

"I've got to work off some of my energy, Maud."

"What's got you riled, gal?"

"Men, Maud! Just men."

"You and that boy spatting again?" Maud smiled tolerantly.

"No, we're not arguing. It's me, Maud. I agreed to an arrangement that I no longer seem able to live with. And I'm blaming Flint for it when I knew what I was doing from the beginning. I've got no one to blame but myself."

Maud stopped washing the dishes and regarded her solemnly. "Just tough it out, gal. I know it'll all work out for the best."

"I wish I had your confidence, Maud," Garnet said. Sighing, she picked up a towel and began wiping dishes.

After Garnet left Maud, she avoided any further contact with Flint by going to bed early. She realized her mistake too late: she was too worked up to sleep. She lay awake thinking about Flint, and the more she did, the more she became convinced that she had no one to blame but herself.

Honey and Josh came into the wagon and bedded down. Long after they fell asleep, Garnet remained awake. She finally started to doze when she heard a rifle blast. She bolted up to a sitting position as the night suddenly erupted with shouts, gunfire, and blood-chilling shrieks.

Startled, Honey sat up. "What's happening? Have the cattle stampeded?"

Garnet peeked out the back of the wagon. Bare-chested, Flint dashed over in his stocking feet. "Get under the wagon!" he shouted.

Startled and confused, she grabbed Josh and handed him to Flint. Amigo jumped out to follow as Flint shoved the frightened boy under the wagon. Then Flint hurriedly pulled Garnet out of the wagon bed. She scurried under it as Flint reached up and did the same to Honey.

"Stay under there and don't move," Flint ordered. A figure moving among the trees sent him spinning on his heels and firing into the underbrush. Then he crouched down by a wagon wheel.

"What's happening?" Honey asked, her eyes wide with fright.

"Kiowa. I don't know how big their party is."

"Where's Luke?" Honey cried frantically.

"He was on night watch," Flint said. "He's over somewhere with the herd."

"Oh, dear God! They may have killed him!"

"Honey, he's returning their fire, so he's still alive."

Suddenly remembering her pistol, Garnet crawled from cover and climbed back into the wagon. She groped around in the dark until she found her gunbelt.

In the flashes from the blasts of Maud's Henry rifle, coming from the chuck wagon, Garnet saw Joey and Jeb on their stomachs snaking their way toward the horse corral. She scampered back under the wagon as an arrow slammed into the wood of the wagon bed above their heads.

"Dammit!" Flint swore. "They have us pinned down here. They're after the horses, not us." With pistol in hand, Garnet crawled to the opposite end of the wagon.

Barking at the sudden appearance of an Indian in the
nearby trees, Amigo raced out from under the wagon.
"Amigo, come back!" Josh shouted.

"Josh!" Honey screamed.

Garnet heard the anguished shout just as Josh
dashed past her in pursuit of the dog. A backward
glance revealed that Flint was firing in the opposite
direction and had not seen the boy's actions.

Garnet didn't take time to consider the risk to her
own life. She bolted after Josh, her white nightgown a
beacon in the dark.

Amigo had sunk his teeth into the arm of an Indian
who was about to cleve the dog's skull with a tomahawk. Garnet fired, and the savage fell. Josh scooped
up Amigo in his arms just as Garnet reached them.
"Get back to the wagon!"

Clutching Amigo, Josh raced back with Garnet a few
steps behind. One of the Indians dashed out of the
trees in pursuit.

"Goddamit!" Flint cursed as he turned just in time to
see her predicament. She appeared unaware of the
savage behind her. Flint shoved his rifle at Honey.
"Here, use this if you have to, and for God's sake, keep
Josh down." He drew his Colt and sped toward
Garnet.

She screamed when the savage leapt at her from
behind, shoving her to the ground. He yanked her
head back by the hair and raised a knife to slit her
throat.

Unable to use his gun because of Garnet's proximity,
Flint made a flying tackle at the redskin, knocking him
off her. As the two men rolled on the ground, Flint
fought to release the Indian's grasp on the knife.
Garnet picked up her fallen pistol, but the constantly
shifting positions of the two men in their life-and-
death struggle prevented her from getting off a shot.
By the light of the moon, she could see a red stain had
begun to darken Flint's shoulder.

He succeeded in shoving the Indian off him, but the savage still clasped the knife. "Shoot!" Flint shouted. Garnet fired and the Indian slumped back.

Flint scrambled to his feet, grabbed her hand, and they dashed for the cover of the wagon.

The gunfire ended as suddenly as it had begun.

Garnet started to examine Flint's wound before Honey and Josh had even crawled out from under the wagon. Blood streamed from Flint's shoulder as Garnet knelt beside him and ripped a strip of cotton from her nightgown. "Sit still, Flint," she cautioned. She wadded the cotton strip and pressed it against the flowing wound. "I'm so sorry," she said.

"Why the hell didn't you listen to me?" he demanded. "I told you to stay under the wagon!" His rage obliterated every thought except the sight of that Indian about to slit her throat. What if his shot had missed? Or what if he had been a couple seconds too late? "Damn it, woman, when are you going to learn to obey an order?"

Garnet cowered under the scathing attack, believing his anger was caused by her responsibility for his injury. "I said I was sorry," she said, her eyes misting.

"Flint, it was Josh's fault, not Garnet's," Honey interceded.

"No, Mama, it was Amigo's fault." Josh spoke with a quivering lip. "I didn't want him to get killed."

"Women and children and dogs have no place on a cattle drive," Flint ranted.

Cleve was the first to reach the wagon, followed by Maud. "How bad are you hurt?" Cleve asked Flint.

"I'm just nicked."

"Luke? Has anyone checked on Luke?" Honey asked.

"He took an arrow in the leg, Honey. Joey and Jeb are bringing him in." At Honey's gasp of alarm, Cleve put an arm around her. "He'll be fine, Little Sister," he said gently.

"Oh, thank God!" Honey sighed and buried her head against his chest.

Flint was just as relieved to hear his brother was not seriously wounded. "How many horses did they get away with?"

"Only three," Cleve said. "I found some good cover and was able to hold them off until Jeb and Joey showed up to help."

"Well, let's get you over to the fire and tend to that shoulder 'fore you bleed to death while we stand here jawin'," Maud said.

A closer examination of the wound in the light brought a reassuring response from Maud. "Looks like you got lucky again, boy. You've got more lives than a damn cat. But we best get this cleaned and bandaged."

She wiped away the blood, then poured whiskey into the wound. "It'd heal faster if I closed it up with a couple stitches."

"Oh, no you don't!" Flint protested.

"Stop your bellowin' like a castrated bull!" Maud complained. "Never figured you'd get cold feet over a couple tucks of skin."

"I don't need any of your tucks of skin, Maud. Besides, I heal fast."

"Well, let the gal here put a bandage on it." Maud handed Garnet the bandage roll and tape.

Garnet quickly dressed the cut, then helped put a shirt on him. Over his objections, Garnet placed his arm in a sling. "Just wear it until morning. It will take the pull off that injured shoulder," she insisted.

"I best get a pot of coffee goin'," Maud said. "Don't reckon there'll be much more sleepin' around here tonight."

"I'll give you a hand, Maud," Garnet offered. "Honey will want to be here when Luke gets back." She hurried after Maud.

The coffeepot was perking on the fire by the time Joey and Jeb rode in with Luke. After being helped down from his horse, Luke shrugged aside their hands and limped over to the fire, the shaft of an arrow protruding from his right leg. He lowered himself to the blanket Honey had spread out for him.

"Thought you'd have more sense than to be using that leg till you found out if there was poison on that arrow," Flint said.

Luke cast a quick glance at the sling on Flint's arm. "How bad are you hurt?"

"Just a nick from a knife."

"Well, let's get this goddamned arrow out of me," he said to Cleve.

As they huddled around Luke, Cleve drew his bowie and ran the tip of the sharp blade along the seam of Luke's pant's leg, peeling aside the fabric. The arrow was embedded in the fleshy part of Luke's muscular thigh. He cut off the feathered shaft of the arrow. "I'll warn you now, Big Brother, I've never dug out an arrow before."

"Reckon I can do it. I've dug out my share of arrows," Maud said.

"Go to it, Maud, it's all yours," Cleve said, relieved.

Maud leaned over the wound to study it. "Well, I've seen deeper, but it'll take some diggin', Luke."

"Figured as much," Luke said. "Where's that whiskey bottle you've been toting around?"

"I'll get it," Garnet said and hurried over to the chuck wagon.

"And bring back that small knife we use for peelin' potatoes," Maud yelled after her.

When Garnet returned, Maud put the knife in the fire and waited while Luke took several swallows of the whiskey. "Reckon I'm as ready as I'll ever be," he said, handing the bottle to Cleve. He lay back with his head resting on Honey's thighs.

"You men are gonna have to hold him still," Maud warned. The Boones each grasped one of his legs, Cleve his right shoulder. Shoving off his sling, Flint

firmly grasped Luke's left shoulder. Honey reached for
Luke's hand and pressed it between her own. Luke
looked up and grinned at her. Honey smiled back
through her tears.

Maud took a deep swig from the bottle of whiskey
and handed it to Garnet.

Garnet held the bottle up to the light. "I hope the
two of you left enough to sterilize the wound," she said
lightly, breaking the tension.

Maud began to dig at the arrowhead with the sharp
tip of the knife. Perspiration dotted Luke's brow, and
his hand tightened around Honey's in a crushing
grasp.

"You wanta wipe away some of that blood, gal?"
Maud said. Garnet quickly mopped it away with a
cloth.

"Seems like this arrow don't wanta part company
with you, Luke," Maud said lightly. She pressed
deeper into the wound.

"You ever notice, Flint . . ." Luke grunted through
gritted teeth, ". . . how our little brother . . . always
comes through these skirmishes without a scratch?"

"That's because I have enough sense to duck," Cleve
replied. "Unlike my two older brothers, I don't believe
in defying the gods."

"Figure you'd have a good reas—goddammit,
Maud! Get it over with," Luke cried out. The four men
strained to hold down the powerful man as Luke
thrashed under the pain.

"I'm hurryin', son," Maud said. Perspiration dotted
her brow and her hands were trembling. "Just hold on.
One more time oughta do it."

All the men were straining to hold the big man still.
"Please, sweetheart, it'll soon be over," Honey sobbed,
cradling his head to her breast.

As Maud probed deeper, Luke's powerful body
jerked from the pain, then suddenly he lay still. "Oh,
dear God! Luke! Luke!" Honey cried frantically.

"He's okay, Honey," Flint said. He and Cleve exchanged a relieved glance over their brother's still
form. "He's just blacked out, Little Sister."

"Got it!" Maud cried victoriously. She held up the
arrowhead. "You take over, gal," she said to Garnet.

Garnet immediately poured whiskey into the
wound, then covered it with a compress. Pale and
exhausted, Maud sank to the ground next to Josh.

From the time his father had been brought back
wounded and bleeding, the youngster had sat wide-
eyed and frightened, clutching Amigo in his arms.
"See, Amigo, I told you Daddy would be okay," Josh
said in a quaking voice. He rushed over to Honey.

"Your daddy's going to be just fine, sweetheart," she
said, hugging the trembling boy to her side.

When Luke opened his eyes a few moments later,
Garnet had already neatly bandaged and wrapped his
thigh. Honey leaned down and kissed him lightly on
the lips.

Luke grinned up at his wife and son. "Hey, what're
the two of you looking so serious about?"

Then he closed his eyes and slipped into slumber.

Chapter 24

～✦～

One day passed into another, as they traveled north on a prairie of brown grass broken by an occasional high, open hill.

In the last week in June, after thirty-five days on the trail, they crossed the Cimarron into Kansas, leaving behind the threat of an Indian attack. The men's wounds had healed, and everyone looked healthy—if not well-rested. Garnet's usually light, freckled skin had deepened to a smooth pecan.

Other than the earlier week of rain, the weather had been sunny and pleasant, with plenty of water and good grazing grass for the herd.

A week after entering Kansas, they caught a glimpse of a wild buffalo herd for the first time since starting the drive. The animals numbered in the thousands. Garnet pulled her bandanna over her nose. They smelled worse than the cattle or horses. Being downwind from the buffalo, their party was able to pass close alongside of the grazing herd without the animals being aware of their presence. It seemed to her that despite the gargantuan size of the lumbering creatures, they were devoid of any natural instinct for self-preservation. However, she still felt intimidated by the huge beasts, and was relieved when they left the buffalo behind without any serious incident.

They'd put the Kiowa attack behind them. Everyone's spirits were high, and a close camaraderie had grown among them. With one exception: Garnet and Flint.

Since there was no longer a danger of Indian attack, Flint stayed with the herd, riding ahead only a few hours a day to scout out the next grazing site.

Garnet had not decided whether to tell Flint about the baby, and until she did, she intentionally avoided being alone with him. Due to the lack of privacy, they had not been intimate since the evening before they crossed the Red. But each time their gazes met, the tension built between them, and she knew a showdown would soon be inevitable.

With the smell of buffalo still in her nostrils, later that evening as she tried to concentrate on reading one of Josh's *Leatherstocking Tales*, Garnet found herself repeatedly shifting her gaze from the page to Flint, who was lounging against the chuck wagon drinking a cup of coffee.

Everyone else sat around the fire, except Joey, who was riding night guard. Honey strummed "The Blue-Tailed Fly" on her guitar. She and Jeb sang the words, and Josh sat on his father's lap as they clapped along to the music.

Shuffling to the rhythm, Cleve came over to her. "Come on, gal, we're wasting some good foot stompin' music here." He pulled Garnet to her feet and began to whirl her around in a sprightly step. Laughing, Garnet relaxed and surrendered to Cleve's infectious gaiety.

Before long, Jeb had Maud on her feet and the four of them were dancing together in a lively square.

Flint's gaze was on Garnet as she laughed and clung to Cleve when he swung her off her feet. He'd be as blind as a bat not to have noticed how close Garnet and Cleve had become on the drive. Often in the past weeks, when he'd ride in, he'd catch the two of them laughing or chatting together. Cleve always seemed to be able to make her smile or bring a warm glow to those green eyes of hers.

But Cleve had that way about him, Flint reflected. Gals flocked to him—even though it might look to be the other way around. Luke was popular with the gals, too. They took to Luke 'bout as easy as they did to Cleve.

He was the one the gals shunned. Women were so different from men, he didn't really know how to talk to them. Not that he enjoyed talking to men, either. The redhead was the only woman who'd ever said she loved— He shook aside the thought. The way she'd been avoiding him lately, she'd probably had a change of heart about that, too. What the hell was he thinking? He didn't want a woman in his life anyway!

His gaze followed Garnet as Cleve whirled her to the music. He didn't have to see her eyes to know that they were sparkling with warmth, the way they did when she laughed. Those eyes of hers. They tended to say more than any words could, everything she was feeling: anger, sorrow, happiness . . . passion. Lord! He could see them now—glowing like melted emeralds when she was aroused. God! How he loved looking into them then. They heated his blood as much as the touch of her hands or mouth.

"Land alive!" Maud said breathlessly. "I've gotta sit me down, son, and rest." Jeb plopped down beside her.

Garnet and Cleve joined them to listen when Honey changed the tempo of the music. In her mellow, husky voice, she began to sing the words to an old, sentimental ballad. " 'Believe me if all those endearing young charms, that we gaze on so fondly today. . . .' "

Flint's gaze remained on Garnet. Firelight flickered on her profile and turned her hair into burnished copper. He fought an overwhelming need to be close to her, to feel her presence beside him, to smell her sweet rose fragrance.

She turned her head, and for a long moment, their gazes held. Then he tossed away the coffee that had long since turned cold and walked away.

Garnet wanted to chase after him. Overwhelmed with love for him, she knew that she was hurting him—and it was breaking her heart. He was so proud. Too proud to ever admit this to her. But she understood him. And felt his pain. It was the same as hers.

How much time did they have left to be together? she reflected. Once they reached Abilene, he would pick up the search for his mother's murderers, but at least they could spend these remaining days together. She started to rise to go to him.

"Will you be goin' back to Calico, Garnet?"

"I'm sorry, what did you say, Maud?" she asked, sitting back down.

"I asked if you'd be goin' back to Calico."

"Oh, I don't think so."

"You give up the idea of takin' over the diner for me?" Maud asked.

Garnet thought about the baby, and how difficult it would be to raise the child where everyone would know it was a bastard. "I think it would be wiser if I didn't return to Texas."

"Well, I ain't hankerin' to go back to runnin' that diner. Reckon I wouldn't mind having a little spread." Maud turned to Jeb. "If you and your brother have a mind to, maybe we could think about becomin' partners. There's a ranch right next to the Triple M that oughta be just right for us."

"You mean that, Maud?" Jeb said.

"Gosh, that sure would be nice. Maybe Joey wouldn't have to worry over takin' care of me then."

"Reckon I could do it for him, Jeb. When we get back, we'll go over and talk to Ben Franks. Maybe we could fix up a spot for Ben, and then he wouldn't have to leave the Flying F. You and Joey talk it over. With what you boys earn from this drive, you could buy your way in with a bull. How does that sound to you?"

"I'm gonna saddle up and ride out right now and tell Joey," Jeb said. "I love you, Maud." He kissed her cheek and hurried off.

"That's a fine thing you're doing for those boys, Maud," Luke said.

"They're good boys, Luke. Joey's so serious, he kinda reminds me of you when you were a young'n. And that Jeb, he's sure like you were, Cleve. He can win a gal's heart with just that grin of his."

"Well, my little bronco here has gone to sleep," Luke said, smiling down at his son sleeping in his arms. "Time to carry him back to the wagon and bed him down."

"I'll come with you," Honey said. Luke shifted Josh and slipped his arm around her shoulder. They left with Amigo trotting at their heels.

"Yeah, reckon I'll go and clean up the coffeepot, then grab some shut-eye myself," Maud said. "Daylight comes around soon enough as it is. Good night, all."

Garnet and Cleve both wished her a good night and she went over to the chuck wagon.

"I guess I better be thinking of getting some sleep, too," Garnet said. "And I don't want to keep you awake."

"You're not keeping me awake, Garnet," Cleve said. "I'm enjoying the company."

"I just want to give Honey and Luke a chance alone to say good-night." She glanced longingly toward where Flint had disappeared.

There was no sign of Flint when Maud woke them the next morning. Garnet asked where he was and Maud said he had already ridden out, which only added to Garnet's depression. She missed the special good-bye Flint used to give her before leaving.

Early in the afternoon, he came riding back. After he exchanged a few words with his brother, Luke called them all together. "I'm afraid Flint just rode in with some bad news," he informed them. "You want to tell them, Flint?"

Flint sat relaxed with his right leg slung over the saddle horn. "We're coming up on a stream that's full of alkali."

"And the cattle are thirsty," Luke said with a worried frown. "They're gonna want to drink."

"Any way we can skirt it?" Cleve asked.

Flint shook his head. "I checked it out for five miles to the east and west. It's all the same."

"I figure we're gonna have to stampede the cattle across it," Luke said.

Cleve voiced what the rest of them were thinking. "They'll still try to turn back to get to the water."

"Reckon it'll be up to us to keep 'em from doing it," Flint said.

"Yeah," Luke agreed. "Once we get the herd across, we'll just have to keep 'em running."

"Hell, you know they won't run for more than four miles," Cleve argued. "That's not far enough to keep them from trying to get back to the water."

"There's a small stream about five miles past," Flint said. "If we drive them hard, we can reach it."

Luke still wore a worried frown. "At best, we'll lose only a few calves. The worst is that it'll take about fifty pounds off each beef. If they look scrawny, we won't get as good a price for 'em when we get to Abilene."

"Still be a lot more than if they're sick or dead from bad water," Flint said.

"Well, if we find some good grass, we can always rest 'em for a day and hope they fatten up on it," Cleve suggested.

Luke nodded. "Yeah, that's what I've been thinking, too. Here's what I have in mind. In the next couple miles, the cattle're gonna pick up the scent of the water and start breaking for it. Keep bunching and squeezing 'em together. When I give the sign, we'll stampede 'em across the stream. Keep the wagons at the rear and out of the way. And, Jeb, keep the remuda moving, too. We don't want any of those horses drinking that salt water either."

He glanced at each of them. "Does everyone understand what to do?" They all nodded.

"Garnet, I think it'd be better if you ride in one of the wagons. I don't want you getting hurt."

"You'll need riders to keep the herd moving, Luke. I'll be careful," she said.

"All right. But don't take any chances," he warned. "Stay clear of 'em. And remember, after a hard run, those cow ponies are gonna be as tired as the cows. They're more apt to stumble and fall, so stay out of the center of the herd. Keep alert and good luck to all of you."

As predicted, when the thirsty cows smelled water they quickened their pace, but the six riders were able to keep the cattle tightly bunched. As they approached the riverbank, Luke fired several shots in the air. In one thundering mass, the cattle bolted forward.

Garnet galloped alongside the stampeding herd, waving her slicker and shouting. Above the sound of the thundering hooves, she could hear the shouts and whistles of the men and the explosive sound of gunfire. She caught a glimpse of Luke on the opposite flank and knew that Cleve was somewhere over there too. In an undulating swirl of sight and sound, she was aware of the horses in the remuda galloping past. Now set in motion, this driving phalange of bodies and horns couldn't be halted. Water splashed in all directions as the cattle pounded across the shallow stream and up the opposite bank. Still, they were not permitted to stop, but continued to be pushed onward. After several more miles the herd gave up running, but rather than move ahead, they tried to turn back to the water.

Whistling, shouting, and pressing them forward, the weary riders fought to keep them moving north. Then, while Joey was roping a cow, another determined heifer charged him and ripped open his horse's stomach. As Joey jumped clear, the hapless horse bled profusely and finally collapsed and died.

The descending darkness made the job even harder, until at last the lead steers smelled the water ahead. Then the arduous task grew easier.

As the herd now forged willingly ahead, Garnet pulled away and reduced her horse to a trot. Easing her hold on the reins, she leaned back in the saddle and relaxed. Suddenly, the reins slipped through her fingers and she was pitched forward as her horse stepped in a prairie dog hole and stumbled. She cried out, instinctively trying to cushion her fall with her shoulder in an effort to protect her unborn child. In that infinitesimal moment, she realized her fear was not for herself, but for her baby.

With the herd of disgruntled cows milling past her, Garnet lay on her back in the dirt of the Kansas prairie and came to the realization that nothing was as important as protecting the child she carried in her womb. Granted, she had arrived in Texas with nothing more than the clothes on her back, but she had left it with the greatest wealth God could ever bestow upon her.

Beset by anxiety over the past few weeks, she had not considered that blessing. She curved a hand protectively around her stomach. As if she could feel this new life within her, with a mother's intuition she knew her child had not been harmed by the fall. She raised her eyes heavenward and said a prayer of thanks.

Flint came galloping over and leaped off on the run. "Are you hurt?"

"No, I'm fine." She looked him in the eyes and smiled with a serenity she knew would only further puzzle him. "Better than I've been for weeks."

However, the pony wasn't as lucky. The horse's leg had been broken. After stripping off the saddle, Flint shot the suffering mare. However, Flint would not hear of her climbing onto a horse. She finished the rest of the ride next to Honey on a wagon seat.

It was almost dawn by the time the cattle had their fill of water and settled down to sleep. The bedraggled riders rode up to the chuck wagon. Maud had a pot of coffee on the fire. They attacked it voraciously, but were too exhausted to eat anything other than a hot biscuit.

A short time later, Garnet awoke as Honey leaned over her by the campfire and took the coffee cup out of her hand, then covered her with a blanket. "Good night, dear," Honey said softly. Garnet smiled at her, then fell back to sleep.

Maud and Honey continued to move cautiously around the campfire, covering up the other five weary riders who had fallen asleep wherever they had sat down. Then they moved to their wagons and their own beds.

The cattle were grazing peacefully when Luke rode out at eight o'clock in the morning to cover the first watch. The men had decided to divide the day into four-hour shifts, with the intention of moving out at six o'clock the next morning.

Everyone in camp moved lazily. Garnet ached slightly from the fall, but since starting the drive, she had grown accustomed to aches and pains. The kettle was kept boiling on the fire all day, as the men shaved or did laundry. Honey started out the day cutting Josh's hair, and then Luke's when he returned. Before she could put the scissors and comb away, she had trimmed Cleve's and both Boone brothers' as well. Flint showed no interest in getting a haircut, but Garnet noticed he did shave. If he intended it to be an unspoken message, she decided to accept the invitation. They had wasted too much time already.

In the afternoon, Maud and Josh went off with burlap bags to gather cow chips for the morning fire. Honey and Garnet did laundry, and while Cleve rode watch, Luke and Flint went out and tallied up the herd. In all, there were 595 steers and heifers—only four had been lost on the drive. From what they could count, there also appeared to be about 150 calves. By the time they finished, Joey rode in to relieve Cleve. The MacKenzie brothers rode out to the site of the stampede. They found the bodies of three dead calves, one steer, and the two horses.

"I reckon it could have been a lot worse," Luke said.

"Yeah, someone could have been seriously hurt. Garnet took a bad fall from a horse, and Joey could have been severely gored."

"Well, it was some run," Cleve said with a more upbeat attitude. "None of us will be forgetting it for a long time."

Before leaving they cut a hunk of beef off one of the dead cows, and Luke took it back to camp for supper while Cleve returned to camp and Flint rode north to check the trail ahead.

Maud had not returned, and when Garnet saw the big slab of beef Luke had brought back with him, she decided it would be a way of breaking the ice between her and Flint.

Hastily, she began to prepare the evening meal. She dug the big cast iron Dutch oven out of the chuck wagon and put the hunk of beef into it. Adding water, she seasoned the meat and threw in a couple of bay leaves, then covered the kettle and set it on the fire to roast.

Garnet peeled potatoes and soaked them in water to add to the pot a few hours later. Unfortunately, she would have to make do without carrots. By the time

Honey noticed Garnet's fervid activity at the chuck wagon, Garnet was in the process of peeling onions.

Honey wandered over to inquire what she was up to.

"Thought I'd give you and Maud a rest from cooking tonight," Garnet told her.

"What are you making?"

"Pot roast."

"Oh, Luke loves pot roast," Honey exclaimed.

"Uh-huh."

Honey looked at her askance. "How did you know?"

"Just like his mother used to make, I bet."

"That's right." Honey continued to look perplexed.

"Look, Honey gal, I may not have worked in a medicine show, but that doesn't mean I don't have psychic powers."

"Garnet, what's this all about?" Honey demanded.

"Pot roast and the predictability of the MacKenzie brothers," Garnet replied, with a smug smile. She went over, lifted the lid off the kettle and took a deep breath. "Ah, it smells delicious. I really should throw in some Attar of Rose and a few hunks of my hair, but I'll save those two items for the dessert."

Honey looked distressed. "Garnet, you're beginning to worry me. Are you sure you didn't hit your head when you fell yesterday?"

"I'm fine. Just fine. Never felt better."

"Then why are you talking so strange? Who ever heard of Attar of Rose and hair in a dessert? Sounds like some kind of witch's concoction."

"You silly girl—it's one of Flint's favorites! But I'll serve it to him when we're alone. Now be off, you little twit," she cackled in the voice of an old crone. "I've got woman's work to do." She nodded toward the wagon and added in a whisper, "And so have you, me pretty. Aren't you aware your son is gone and your husband isn't? I agree that one of us must have been hit in the head, but it's not me!" She winked at Honey and returned to peeling onions.

"You're right!" Honey exclaimed. She didn't even glance back as she hurried over to the wagon.

An hour later Luke rode back to the herd, and Jeb remained in camp with them. Garnet and Honey had just removed the dried clothes from the line Luke had strung that morning when Maud came hurrying back to camp carrying Josh. "He's been bit by a scorpion," she said breathlessly, handing him to Honey.

Jeb ran over to lend a helping hand. "Give him to me, Miz Honey. I'll take care of him."

"I'm coming with you," Honey declared as Jeb headed for the chuck wagon.

"Maud, sit down and catch your breath," Garnet insisted.

"It's my fault. I should have watched the boy closer."

"Stop blaming yourself, Maud," Garnet said. "Josh will be fine."

"I told him not to pick up one of them chips without kicking it over first."

"Did I ever tell you about the time I was bit by a cottonmouth in Georgia?" Garnet said in an attempt to divert Maud's attention. "And not too long ago, I got bit on my way to Texas. That darn Flint killed the rattler and then had the nerve to try and feed it to me."

Despite her anxiety, Maud broke into laughter. "If that don't beat all. I heard tell of biting the hand that feeds you. Leave it to Flint to figure out a way to bite back."

Jeb was carrying Josh when they returned from the chuck wagon a short time later. "Put him in the wagon, Jeb," Honey said. "And you, sweetheart, are going to spend the rest of the evening resting," she told Josh.

"Am I gonna die, Mama?" he asked solemnly. He looked so scared, Garnet wanted to pick him up and hug him.

"Heck no," Jeb said. "Shucks, I know how to suck

out a bite of poison, and I've even been scorpion bit a time or two, myself. Once I put on my boot without shaking it out, and one of 'em big old scorpions was in it. My foot swelled up so big, my ma thought they was gonna have to cut it off." When he saw the look on Josh's face, he added, " 'Course, that didn't happen."

"You may be a little sick for a couple days, sweetheart. That's why I want you to stay in bed," Honey said.

"Will you read to me, Mama?"

"I sure will."

Garnet glanced down at Amigo and saw that his head was drooping and his tail wasn't wagging. He appeared to be barely able to walk. "Was Amigo bit, too?" she asked, alarmed.

"That faker!" Honey scoffed. "He acts like this if Josh so much as catches a cold. I end up with two patients instead of one." She lifted the dog into the wagon. "Poor little pooch," she cooed, rubbing his head. It was enough to produce a weak wag of his tail.

Darkness had long descended by the time the excitement over Josh had quieted enough for everyone to relax and sit down to eat. However, much to Garnet's consternation, Flint had not returned to camp.

Everyone had finished their meal by the time he rode in. Garnet grabbed two plates and put several slices of beef, potatoes, and onions on each of them, then carried the plates over to where Flint had plopped down near the horse corral.

She handed him a plate, seating herself beside him. "I waited to eat with you."

Surprised, but pleased by her attention, he started to eat. "This tastes good."

"Luke and Cleve claim it tastes just like the kind your mother used to make."

"Reckon it'd be hard to tell them apart," he said, and continued to consume the food hungrily.

When he finished, Garnet handed him her plate. "Here, you can have mine."

"Aren't you hungry?"

She shook her head. "I've been eating all day."

"Well, if you're sure you don't want it, I'd hate to see it go to waste."

Enjoying this quiet moment alone with him, she sat back and watched him eat, recalling the many nights they had spent together when they were fleeing from the Indians.

"There's more if you want it," she said when he finished and put the plate aside.

"No, I've had plenty."

"I remember you said you'd marry the woman who could make pot roast like your mother."

"Reckon Maud's a little old for marriage," he said, grinning. When she continued to smile mysteriously at him, his smile slowly dissolved. He regarded her for a long moment. "Reckon I've been bushwhacked. Maud didn't make that pot roast, did she?"

"No, I did. Does that mean we're engaged?" she said lightly.

"I was hoping you came over here for something other than arguing."

"What, for instance?"

He shifted his glance from her eyes to her mouth. "Maybe for this."

He pulled her against him and his mouth covered hers hungrily. Parting her lips, she returned his urgency with that of her own. His tongue explored the recess of her mouth with heated, tantalizing probes, sending currents of desire rushing through her. Sliding her arms around his neck, she curled into the curve of his body.

"Oh God, Redhead, I need you," he groaned as he rained kisses on her face and neck, then reclaimed her lips.

"I want you, too, Flint. I want you so badly," she

said breathlessly. He slipped his hand inside her shirt and she moaned when his warm palm cupped her breast. It had been so long since she had felt his touch—her body ached for more.

He raised his head and glanced toward the campfire. Everyone appeared to be dozing. "Let's get out of here."

"We can't. They'll know."

"I need you, Redhead," he growled in a low, husky voice that sent a shiver of excitement down her spine.

Josh's sudden cry galvanized the camp to action. Honey appeared at the back of their wagon and hurried over to the chuck wagon. Luke left the campfire and chased after her.

"I'm sorry, Flint," Garnet said regretfully. She slipped away from him. "Is there anything I can do?" she asked as she hurried over to Honey.

"No, he's just restless and he's running a little fever. I thought I'd get him a drink of water."

By this time, everyone in camp was huddled around the chuck wagon, concerned and listening. "Luke, if you want to be with them, I can sleep outside tonight," Garnet said.

"I'd appreciate that, Garnet," Luke answered. He took the pitcher of water Maud had filled, then he and Honey returned to their wagon.

"You all best be gettin' some sleep," Maud advised. She climbed into the chuck wagon. One by one the others drifted back to the campfire. Garnet and Flint exchanged a meaningful glance, then followed the others.

A short time later, Garnet fell asleep with the contented feeling of knowing Flint lay only a few feet away.

She was unaware when he got up at midnight, stood for a long moment looking down at her, then saddled Sam and rode out to take his shift on night watch.

Chapter 25

Josh was still running a fever the next morning, and Honey did not want to move him. Luke agreed to lay over for another day, and decided to use the time to shoe a couple of the horses.

"Sure wish we had some quinine salt or an antipyretic," Honey said. "It would sure help Josh's fever."

"Looks like there's a town about twenty miles from here," Flint remarked as he studied the map. "I'll ride in and maybe get some there."

"I've a mind to kick myself," Maud grumbled. "I was gonna bring some and out-and-out forgot to."

"Don't feel bad, Maud," Garnet spoke up. "We were bound to forget something."

"Why don't you ride in with Flint?" Maud suggested. "I could use more sugar and molasses."

"Do you mind, Flint?" Garnet asked, feeling uneasy in case Flint would rather be alone.

"I'll saddle the horses," he said.

While he was gone, Maud added a couple more items to the list. "We're not taking a pack mule, Maud," Flint retorted when he saw the list.

"As long as you're going, why not get what we need?"

"Makes sense to me," Honey agreed.

"I'll take saddlebags, but not another horse," Flint conceded.

If Garnet had learned anything about Flint MacKenzie, it was that he did not talk on the trail. He was his usual reticent self; he didn't even bring up the subject of the previous night.

Newton appeared to be typical of most of the small western towns. Every business was stretched out on a main street about two blocks long. A couple of soddies and wooden shacks were scattered around the town. As they passed the cemetery, Garnet saw preparations were being made for a funeral. The cemetery appeared to be as big as the town itself.

They rode up to a wooden trough in front of the livery and let the horses drink. A tall, big-boned man came out to greet them. "Will you folks be needin' a stall?"

"No, just passing through," Flint said. "You got a doctor in this town?"

"Yeah, but I wouldn't take a sick horse to him, myself."

"Where can I find him?" Flint asked.

"If he's sober, you'll find him in his office at the end of the block. Otherwise, try the saloon."

"Thanks." Turning to Garnet, Flint said, "I'll go look for him while you get the supplies Maud needs."

Garnet had the saddlebags packed and there was still no sign of Flint, so she walked down to the doctor's office. Finding it closed, she went to the saloon. As soon as she entered, a big man stepped into her path. Dark-jowled, he had a square head, a thick neck and wide shoulders heavy with muscle.

"Ain't seen you around here, little lady."

"Just passing through, sir. Would you mind stepping aside please."

"And if I don't, I s'pose you'll draw that Navy Colt you're packin' there, little lady."

"Mister, I don't want any trouble, so why don't you just step aside so I can go about my business?"

"Hear that, boys?" the big man declared. "Sounds like the little lady's gettin' short tempered. Must go along with that red hair of hers."

Garnet had lost her patience. "If you don't get out of my way, I'm going to call the sheriff."

"Sheriff?" the big man said. The other men all burst into laughter. "'Fraid he ain't gonna hear you. They're plantin' him right about now. I'd say you've got a problem, little lady."

"I'd say, mister, that you're the one with the problem," Flint said coolly, from where he stood at the bar. He picked up the whiskey glass in front of him and downed the drink.

The man glanced at Flint, who was leaning against the bar with one foot hooked over the rail. The very casualness of his pose generated a veiled threat far greater than any words.

"She your woman?" the man asked.

Flint turned slowly, his expression inscrutable. "Well, mister, she's a very independent woman, so I don't think she'd take too kindly to being called my woman. But I thank you for the compliment. One thing I can tell you about her for sure—you're gonna have to come through me to get her."

"I don't want no trouble, stranger," the man said. He stepped aside hurriedly.

Flint walked over to Garnet. "Let's go, Redhead."

"Did you get the quinine?" Garnet asked as soon as they were outside.

"The doctor doesn't have any." Flint glanced at the sky. "Looks like it's fixing to rain. We'll eat something and get out of here."

It couldn't be soon enough for her.

* * *

Thirty minutes later, they were passing the cemetery on the way out of town when Flint suddenly reined up. "Well, what do you know? I see an old friend. You ride on, Redhead. I'll catch up with you."

Garnet had no intention of leaving without him. She followed him to where he had dismounted near a small crowd gathered around the open hole of a burial plot. A pine box had been set on the ground ready to be lowered.

"Didn't expect to see you up here, Moore," Flint said.

Bullwhip Moore spun around in surprise. Seeing Flint, he blanched, and for a brief moment fear flickered in his eyes. Then his mouth curved into a smirk. "MacKenzie!"

"Don't suppose that snake Bodine is with you?" Flint asked. "I've got a score to settle with both of you."

"Don't see him, do you? But I see you got your whore with you."

Unaware that Garnet had followed him, Flint turned his head and saw her. "Garnet, get out of here," he shouted. It was enough time to give Moore the chance he needed. With a shrug of his shoulder, the handle of the bullwhip landed in his hand.

Flint drew his Colt just as Moore flicked the whip. A bloody gash slashed the back of Flint's hand and fingers, and the gun fell to the ground. Moore drew back his arm to render another stinging blow, but Flint made a flying leap at him, knocking the whip out of his hand. The two men rolled on the ground, and for the length of a breath, tottered on the brink of the hole before they both dropped the six feet into it.

Surprisingly fast for his bulk, Moore regained his feet, a drawn knife in his hand. Flint drew his own knife as Moore lunged at him, the man's huge body almost filling the hole from side to side. As Flint dodged the blow, he sank his knife into the big man's chest and the fight ended as quickly as it had begun. Moore fell back, his beady black eyes staring lifelessly up at the people crowded around the grave peering down at him.

Flint wiped off the blade of his knife on the dead man's pants, then found himself faced with a new dilemma—how to get out of the deep hole.

Garnet drew her pistol. "Couple of you men either toss him a rope or give him a hand," she ordered. She didn't have to ask twice. One of the men hurriedly threw a rope into the grave. Flint grabbed it and climbed out.

"Say, mister, you just killed the man who done in the sheriff," the man said. "You interested in the job?"

"Not me. I just did all the sheriffing I intend to," Flint said. "Just pile that dirt back on him. He ain't worth the cost of a pine box." Flint walked over, picked up his Colt, holstered it, then climbed on Sam.

Still stunned by the swiftness and savagery of the action, Garnet felt nauseated. The whole incident had taken less than five minutes to play out. How easily it could have been Flint lying lifeless at the bottom of that grave. Death—be it man's or animal's—appeared to be so common in this tumultuous country that most folks seemed unaffected by it. Flint had been fighting for his life, but the others watching. . . . She shook her head in bewilderment. Would she ever become so jaded as to accept this finality with such a cavalier attitude? Was killing the only method of survival?

Sickened and dazed, Garnet followed him.

In the afternoon, brilliant forks of silver streaked the distant sky and the low rumble of thunder reverberated across the valley. "Better put on your slicker," Flint warned. "That storm's gonna be on us before we know it." They quickly donned ponchos, then goaded their horses to a faster gallop.

Still dazed by Moore's death, Garnet rode beside

Flint in a state of numbness. She glanced at him and
his expression was inscrutable. Was he thinking about
the incident? Just a short time ago he had brutally
killed a man in hand-to-hand combat, then climbed
back on Sam and rode away as if nothing had
happened. She had seen his capacity for brutality
when he had killed the two Comanche—but that had
been to save her life.

He had initiated this fight with Bullwhip Moore,
coolly and deliberately. His intention was to kill the
man when he walked up to him. Had Flint felt one bit
of remorse afterwards? How could she tell when his
face showed neither sadness nor joy?

A deafening boom of thunder jolted her out of her
musing. Driven by the rise of wind, huge raindrops
began to splatter the dusty trail. As if pierced by the
jagged lightning bolts, the sky exploded with a thun-
derous clap and the rain poured down on them.

The storm struck with a rapacious fury that seemed
to turn day into night. Streaking from the sky, the
silver spears bombarded the earth, lashing out at
anything in their path.

"We've got to find some cover!" Flint shouted to her.

Hunched in her saddle, Garnet drew a frightened
breath each time one of the terrifying thunderbolts
struck home. They seemed to have ridden into the jaws
of hell. The air smelled like sulphur. Rocks and even
the ears of her horse glowed with the blue flame.
Luminous balls of lightning rolled along the ground,
spooking the horses. Fighting to keep a tight rein on
the mare, she struggled to repress her mounting hysteria.

Another brilliant flash, accompanied by a thunder-
ous crash, struck the top of a nearby tree. Transfixed,
she watched a glowing stripe of fire streak down the
tree trunk and across the ground in front of her before
the pouring rain extinguished the flame.

Visibility had been reduced to only a few yards as they searched for refuge. "Over there," Flint shouted, pointing to a hillside ahead. She saw the round opening outlined in an incandescent glow.

They dismounted and dashed into the small cave. Relieved to be out of the storm, Garnet slouched down on her knees. Removing her hat, she brushed the soggy strands of hair off her face. Now, sheltered from the downpour, she knelt in silence, staring out at the raging turbulence.

"I bet you the herd is scattered over most of Kansas by now," Flint said beside her.

For the first time since the storm began, Garnet thought about the herd. Remembering the frightening experience of the earlier stampede, she could imagine what it would be like in this terrifying storm to bring the stampeding cattle under control.

"Oh, dear! What will happen to them?"

"The cattle can only run so far," Flint said. "It's for sure we'll have to spend a few days rounding them up." He looked up at the sky. "Looks like the storm is passing over. We should be able to leave soon. Too bad we don't have some firewood. We could dry out."

Another crash of thunder caused her to wince. "At least we're under cover. I'm just glad to be out of that storm." Another bolt of lightning illuminated the darkness and she glanced up at the roof of the cave.

Her eyes bulged in horror, and she started to scream. The sound bounced off the walls like a siren. At once, the cave filled with the sound of beating wings.

Instinctively, Flint dove for her and knocked her over. Throwing himself on top of her, he covered her mouth with his hand to stifle her screams and shielded her body with his. She buried her face beneath him and heard the fluttering increase as thousands of small, furry bats took wing.

Trying to get free and bolt, Garnet squirmed under

Flint as the bats fluttered around him, filling the cave until the swarm finally flew outside. Flint raised himself and released her. "They're gone, Redhead."

Garnet was gasping for breath. "Let me go! I have to get out of here!" Her eyes were wild with panic.

"Relax, Redhead. The storm's almost over."

"No. I have to get out of here!" She shoved his hands away and ran outside. The rain had slowed to a drizzle. Even the dark sky had begun to lighten. Driven not by fear as much as hysteria from the abhorrent violence of Moore's death, Garnet climbed on her horse and raced away. Whipping and goading the animal to a gallop, she raced across the countryside, mud and gravel flying in all directions beneath the pounding hooves.

Flint finally rode her down and pulled up on the reins of her horse. "For God's sake, Garnet, you're going to have an accident. That mare's already been spooked by the storm." Garnet climbed down and began to lead the mare.

"Let's sit for a few minutes," he said, walking up beside her. "How about right over there." He pointed to a nearby tree.

"All right." She led her mare over to it, and after Flint tethered the horses and loosened the cinches, he spread his poncho on the ground and covered it with his blanket. Garnet sat down.

"Now what's wrong, Redhead?" Flint asked, seating himself beside her.

"It was those bats. I hate them."

"They wouldn't have hurt you. They eat insects, Garnet."

"I know." She began to tremble. She knew it was more than just the bats. She wanted to scream out that she was carrying his child, that the knife fight had horrified her, that the storm had frightened her, and the bats. . . . She didn't say any of those things. Instead, she simply said, "There were just so many of them."

He gathered her into his arms and held her tightly. "Thought you told me you believed I wouldn't let anything happen to you."

Garnet slipped her arms around his waist and buried her head against his chest. Just feeling his arms around her gave her a sense of security. Her trembling eased. "I do."

As she relaxed, he asked softly, "Feeling better?"

Garnet simply nodded and cuddled tighter against him. "I don't know what got into me. Or what I would have done if you hadn't been there." She raised her head. Lacing her fingers through his thick hair, she smiled up into his dark eyes. "I love you, Flint."

He lowered his head and kissed her. He had intended for the kiss to be gentle, but as soon as he felt her soft lips part beneath his own, his good intentions were shattered by the hunger of passion. Moving his lips on hers, he devoured the sweetness of her mouth. "I've missed you, babe," he whispered tenderly, sliding his lips to the hollow of her ear. He opened her shirt and slid it off her shoulders. After pulling the camisole over her head, he eased her back.

His mouth on her breasts became exquisitely unbearable. "I missed you, too, Flint. Oh, God, how I've missed you," she said, moaning.

He raised his head, and for a long moment, stared into her emerald eyes before he finished undressing her. Reclaiming her lips, he probed the sensuous chamber of her mouth. Her breathing began to come in quick, short gasps as he trailed his tongue down to her breasts.

"Hurry, Flint, hurry," she pleaded when he laved the turgid peaks. Reaching for his shirt, she quickly pulled it over his head. Her hungry gaze rested on the wide expanse of his shoulders and chest. She felt her fingertips tingle as she ran them down the muscular wall.

Her eyes gleamed, watching his every move as he divested himself of his remaining clothing. Then they clung together—mouth to mouth, flesh to flesh. She savored his every kiss, every touch, her senses spinning with awareness of him—his male essence, the taste of his lips and body, the sound of his whispered words of encouragement to her exploring hands and mouth.

Then the moment came when his firm hands slid down her spine, cupped the cheeks of her derriere, and pulled her to his loins. Together, they rode to a tumultuous release, cutting off each other's moans of rapture with a soul-melding kiss.

Both knew that once was not enough to satisfy the passion they had been suppressing for weeks. They lay entwined, savoring the contact until his potent virility was rejuvenated. Then they made love again.

Finally, regretfully, they dressed. But before leaving, Garnet felt there never would be a better time to tell him about the baby. Yet, her conscience struggled with the right or wrong of it.

"Flint, we'll be reaching Abilene soon. What are your plans when we finish the drive?"

"There's something I have to do," he said.

"You mean tracking down your mother's killers." He nodded. "And where do I fit in to your plans?"

"I was hoping you'd go back to the Triple M and stay with Luke and Honey."

"And wait for you to come back. How long, Flint? Six months? A year? Six years?" she said sarcastically.

"I've got no way of knowing how long it will take. But it's something I've got to do."

"I know—your honor's at stake. And you expect I'll sit by and wait indefinitely for you to come back. Then what? We make lo—we fornicate—and you leave again. Is that the plan?"

"I can't take you with me. It's too dangerous. You could get hurt—or worse."

"I don't want to go, Flint. And I don't want you to go either."

He clasped her by the shoulders. "Don't think I haven't put my mind to it in these last couple of weeks. A man's a fool to ride away from a woman like you, Redhead."

She shrugged off his hands. "I don't want to hear how wonderful you think I am, Flint. I want to hear what's wrong with me that you can let me go."

"It's not anything to do with you. It's me. I don't have a choice."

"Then I guess you don't leave me any choice either," she said. She got up and walked over to her mare. After tightening the cinch, she climbed on and started to ride away.

Flint folded up the blanket and poncho, stuffed it into the saddlebags, and rode after her. He had until they reached Abilene to resolve the problem between them.

The sun had set by the time they arrived back at camp. Most of the herd had been rounded up, but they were missing about twenty head. The good news was that no one had been hurt when the cattle stampeded, and, in addition, Joshua's fever had broken.

We didn't have to go to that town after all, Garnet thought. And if they hadn't, how would it have changed the doubts she now suffered? She wandered to the river and sat down near the riverbank. With her elbows on her knees and her head in her hands, she stared reflectively into the swiftly flowing water. What had set her off so emotionally that afternoon? Was it the storm—or seeing Flint kill Bullwhip Moore? Most certainly the combination of the two had been enough to cause her hysteria in the bat cave.

"Hi." Garnet glanced up and saw that Honey had

wandered down to join her. "What's wrong, Garnet? Did you and Flint have a serious quarrel?"

"Well, we seem to do that frequently," she said lightly.

"That's a good sign. Luke and I fought like cats and dogs when we first met. Now we rarely exchange a cross word. Get all the misunderstandings out of the way before you get married."

"I don't think there's much chance of that happening," Garnet scoffed.

"What—getting the misunderstandings out of the way or getting married?"

"Both."

For a long moment, Garnet tottered on the brink of a confession. She followed her instinct. "Honey, if I tell you something, will you promise not to breathe it to another soul?"

"Of course." Honey sat down beside her. "What is it, Garnet?" she asked gravely.

"I'm going to have a baby."

Honey was speechless for a few seconds, then she clasped Garnet's hand. "That's wonderful, Garnet. How does Flint feel about it?"

"I haven't told him, and I don't intend to."

"But you can't keep something as important as this from him, Garnet. He's the father. He has a right to know."

"I almost told him today. Then we started to talk about his intentions to pursue the hunt for his mother's murderers as soon as we finish the drive."

"Well, once he finds out he's going to be a father, I'm sure he won't leave."

"That's my problem, Honey. Flint's obsessed with this mission. He'd never forgive me if he couldn't pursue it."

"Garnet, Luke believed the same thing until we were married. Oh, I don't doubt he'll be there for the final

showdown whenever Flint and Cleve catch up with
Charlie Walden. And as much as I don't want him to
go, I know in my heart I'll have to let him or he'll regret
it all his life."

"Luke is very different from Flint, Honey. Luke
admits the importance of having you and Josh in his
life. Flint, on the other hand, is convinced he doesn't
need a woman, much less a child."

"Garnet, you're being naive. You wouldn't be on this
drive right now if Flint MacKenzie didn't want you
with him."

"He didn't ask me. I made the choice to come."

"But if he didn't want you, you sure as heck
wouldn't be here. And what about the time you left
him in Calico, and he followed you? You don't know
these MacKenzies. They don't bother with anything or
anyone that doesn't interest them."

"You don't understand our relationship. We both get
a great deal of pleasure from, ah—"

"Making love together," Honey said.

"Well, Flint has a less delicate term for it."

Honey laughed lightly. "Knowing Flint, I'm sure he
does. But what you don't understand is that these
MacKenzie men can be the most stubborn, bullheaded
breed you could ever meet. They're convinced that
nothing's worth pondering unless one of them came
up with the idea. But Lord, Garnet, when they love,
they love deeply. I think they're almost ashamed to
admit this vulnerability to anyone, much less to themselves."

"That's probably true of Luke, Honey. And I'm sure
you're right where he's concerned. But Flint's very
different from his brothers."

"He may appear so on the surface, but underneath,
they're very much alike. Do you love him, Garnet?"

"I love him so much, I'll give him up rather than
force him into a marriage he'll regret. Flint doesn't love

me, Honey. Luke was in love with you when he married you. That's the difference. All I am to Flint is someone he enjoys sleeping with."

"I once believed the same thing about Luke, and I was wrong. I think you may be listening so hard to hear him say he loves you that you're ignoring the signs that show his love. He's committed to you, Garnet. I'm not referring to marriage, or even sex," she said. "Sometimes a few men and women are fortunate enough to make a commitment that goes beyond physical limitations. You and Flint have such a commitment, whether you're willing to admit it or not."

Garnet shook her head. "Honey, what Flint feels for me is simply passion. I'm his whore."

"Luke, Cleve, and Maud—people who have known him all his life—believe differently."

"Let them believe what they want. Flint and I are the only two who know what's between us, Honey."

"A very wise woman once gave me some advice. She told me no one knows a man as well as the woman who sleeps with him. Think about that, Garnet. And if you still believe he doesn't love you, then maybe you're right and the rest of us are wrong." Honey stood up. "I think he'd want to know about his child." She squeezed Garnet's shoulder and departed.

Chapter 26

 ⌒◯◯⌒

Later that night, Garnet was about to get ready for bed when Honey popped her head in the wagon. "Whoever said a woman needs a man has never tried to reason with Luke MacKenzie. He's the most bull-headed, stubborn, unreasonable man in the world. If I don't see him for a year, it'll be too soon."

"A short time ago, you implied your marriage was practically made in heaven. What did he do to make you change your mind?" Garnet asked.

"It's what he won't do," Honey said, climbing into the wagon.

"Which is?"

"He won't let me ride out with him tomorrow in search of strays."

"I thought you were afraid of horses."

"That's his argument, too. He said a horse can tell if the rider's afraid, and he's got enough on his mind without having to worry about me getting thrown."

"He has a point, Honey."

"Not you, too," Honey moaned.

"Is that a whiskey bottle you're carrying?"

Honey raised the bottle. "Oh, yeah, I forgot. Maud sent this over. She said you look like you need a good, stiff drink of rotgut."

Garnet swung her gaze to Honey in alarm. "You didn't tell her about the baby?"

"Of course not. Maud just thinks you're feeling blue."

"She's got that right, for sure."

Honey held up the bottle again. "Well, Maud says this cures more than colds."

"She wants me to drink it?" Garnet asked aghast. She gingerly put the bottle to her mouth and took a few sips, then handed it back to Honey. "I don't understand the appeal of the taste of whiskey. Besides, it burns the throat going down. Taste it and see what I mean."

"My father always claimed it could cure what ails you," Honey said. "What ails me is Luke MacKenzie. Maybe he should be the one drinking it. He needs curing more than I do. The damn tyrant!"

She took a few tentative sips. Her lovely face screwed up in a grimace. "It tastes horrible." She handed the bottle to Garnet. "Just why do men enjoy drinking down one glass after another?"

Garnet took a swallow. "Well, I think they see it like their passing into manhood," she said, giving the bottle back to Honey. "Their first drink of whiskey, you know." She smirked in contempt.

"I thought they felt that way about the first woman they had." Rolling her eyes, Honey took another deep swallow from the bottle. "That's a *big* source of masculine pride."

Taking the bottle Honey handed her, Garnet took another swallow. "And we can't forget the first man they kill," she said sarcastically. She took another drink. "Big feather in their caps. Big . . . big . . . feather." She sat with the bottle dangling from her hand. "First notch on the gun and all that."

"How come women don't put such empha . . . emphasis on passing into womanhood?" Honey asked, reaching for the bottle. "What have we got to look forward to, except developing breasts?"

"That sure was a big disappointment for me," Garnet said. She started to giggle. "Or I should say, a small *development* in my life." Honey joined in her laughter.

"Well, womanhood brings our monthly menses, too," Honey said as Garnet took another drink. "I'd like to know what men would think if we women went around bragging about *that* first time."

"I don't have to worry about that either—at least for six more months." This caused another round of laughter between them. "Or what if we strutted around bragging about—" She hiccupped. "'Scuse me—bragging about *our* first time."

Honey leaned over, her eyelids appearing too heavy to lift. "Who was your first, Garnet?" she asked conspiratorially.

"Bobby Joe Renfrew."

"B-B-Bobby Joe!" Honey giggled. She took another drink and cast aside the empty bottle. "Who wuz . . . Bobby Joe Renfrew?"

"My first husband. He was eighteen years old."

"Wuz . . . he good?" Honey asked, trying valiantly to lift her eyelids again.

"Heavens no!" Garnet started to giggle. "Like Flint said, it was the first time he discovered it could. . . ." She began laughing uncontrollably.

"Could what?" Honey asked expectantly.

"Could be used for something other than peeing with!" The two women began laughing hysterically. Clutching each other, they slumped to the floor. "What about your first time, Honey?" Garnet asked when they finally paused to breathe.

"His name wuz Robert . . . Robert. . . ." She frowned with concentration, then shook her head. "I can't remember his last name. He wuz a lawyer and I wuz in love with him."

Garnet sat in a stupor trying to analyze Honey's words. "Well, why didn't you marry him?"

"After about a week, he remembered he had a wife!" That brought another lengthy outburst of laughter. "But I had the last laugh." Putting a finger to her lips, she leaned forward. "I faked it every time," she whispered.

Garnet's eyes rounded in surprise. "Really!"

Honey nodded. "I only pretended because Robert considered himself a great lover. I wuz so innocent, I believed him. He said I'd never want another man after him." Honey giggled and grabbed Garnet's arm. "He was right! I sure *didn't* want another man after him. It wasn't 'til I met Luke. . . ." Honey broke off with a sigh and looked deeply into Garnet's eyes. "Did I ever tell you how much I love ole Luke?"

"You kind of hinted at it, dearie."

"Admit it, Garnet. Don't you think he's beautiful?" Honey said with a wistful sigh.

"Yesh. He's very handsome. So are his brothers. Es . . . speshly Flint. And esspeshly since I shaved off his beard."

"Shaved off your beard!" Luke whispered. He and Flint had arrived in time to overhear the end of the conversation.

"She did it to save me. I was drunk and passed out," Flint explained. "My God, they're soused in whiskey!" he exclaimed as he and Luke continued to listen.

"Who's soused?" Cleve asked, walking up and joining them.

"Honey and Garnet," Luke replied.

"Well, you could stop it instead of standing here eavesdropping," Cleve remarked. The three men moved to the fire.

Luke chuckled warmly. "I was kind of enjoying listening to them. I never figured I was *that* good in bed."

"That's got to be the whiskey talking, Big Brother," Flint commented. At the sound of another outburst of laughter, he shook his head. "They're not gonna find much to laugh about tomorrow morning."

"Ah, let them enjoy themselves," Cleve chided. "Both of them have been working hard and deserve to let their hair down."

"Yeah, you're right," Luke agreed. "Those two gals sure get along. And they're good for each other. Honey was madder than hell at me a short spell ago. Now listen to her. Sounds like I couldn't do wrong if I tried."

" 'Pears like this is the right time to break it up, so the two of you can kiss and make up," Flint joked.

Luke gave Flint a long look. "Speaking of making up, what are you and Garnet at odds about?"

"Who said we're at odds?"

"She's been looking kind of down in the mouth lately," Luke said. "Now, I've never tried to tell you how to run your life, but—"

"Like hell you haven't," Flint interjected. "Ain't that right, Cleve?"

"That's for damn sure," Cleve agreed, chuckling.

"Well, reckon I did," Luke said sheepishly, "but I figured Ma needed some help. At times the two of you were real troublesome."

"And you were a real pain in the ass," Flint joshed.

For a long moment Luke grinned at him. "Sure would be nice if you'd settle down one of these days. Kind of got my hopes up when you brought Garnet back with you this time."

"Matter of fact, since the drive I've been kind of thinking about it."

"Did you just hear what I did, Big Brother?" Cleve asked. "Did Brother Flint just say he was thinking about unsaddling his dun and kicking off his spurs?"

"Can't believe he's quit wondering what's on the other side of the mountain," Luke added.

Flint took their teasing good-naturedly. "I've been noticing lately that the other side of the mountain don't look that much different."

"Must be Garnet who helped you to notice."

"Yeah, reckon so." Flint shook his head. "Never figured a woman as fine as her would ever give me a second thought. She's got a lot of Ma's strengths. . . ." His voice drifted off as he smiled. "But she's all Garnet."

"Hallelujah!" Cleve exclaimed. "I never thought I'd see the day when Brother Flint would let a gal rope and hogtie him."

"You forgetting Ma always warned us not to go leaping any fences till we was sure the horse was broke?" Flint asked. "Could be Garnet's still fixing to marry that cousin of hers in Santa Fe."

"Heck, Flint, anybody can see how the two of you feel about each other," Luke said.

"Don't know about that. In the last month, Garnet's been kind of short-tempered with me. And today she plumb broke down."

"What do you mean?" Luke asked.

"During the storm, we took cover in a bat cave and she started screaming and couldn't stop."

"You can't blame her for that," Cleve said. "Even Maud was scared spitless during that storm."

"And you can't fault her for screaming," Luke added. "Most women would. Bat's are pretty ugly critters, Flint."

Flint shook his head in denial. "I've seen her take on a rattlesnake to save a squirrel. And she was ready to do the same with two painted Comanche. Even when Nathan Bodine and his gang tried to bushwhack us near Waynesburg, she covered me with a rifle rather than try to save her own hide." He shook his head again. "No, she don't scare easy. She's a strong woman, and don't let nothing beat her down. She's a survivor no matter what. But lately, she ain't been herself.

Something's chewing at her craw, and she ain't saying what it is."

"Have you asked her what's wrong?" Cleve said. "Or have you even told her that you want to settle down?"

"Well, no. And now I reckon she just wants out. Can't blame her if she does. I ain't the best company, you know. Besides, there's still Charlie Walden to be thinking about. Speaking of bastards, today in town I ran into one of the scum that hangs out with Nathan Bodine."

"Who was it?" Luke asked.

"Bullwhip Moore."

"Wasn't he one of the men who bushwhacked you and Garnet?" Cleve asked.

"Yeah, but he won't be bushwhacking anyone again. We fought and I killed him with my bowie."

"Did Garnet see you do it?" Cleve asked.

"I warned her to keep riding, but she never listens to me. She saw the whole fight."

Cleve emitted a long, low whistle. "And you're wondering why she broke down!"

"If it's not gunfights, it's knifings! Goddammit, Flint, when are you gonna settle down and quit wandering the way you do?" Luke asked.

"I can take care of myself, Big Brother. Besides," Flint said, slapping Luke on the shoulder, "it's harder to hit a moving target. Reckon I'll bed down."

Luke and Cleve watched him spread out his bedroll. "What do you think?" Cleve asked after Flint was asleep.

"I think you're right. It's not a pretty sight to see two men going at each other with knives. That probably did upset Garnet. But there's been something bothering her before today. Bet she told Honey. Those gals are real close." Luke stood in thought for several seconds. Then, grinning, he turned his head to Cleve. "And I can't think of a better time to find out."

Luke went over and picked up Josh, who had fallen asleep by the fire.

"You best be beddin' down that little guy or he'll soon be all slept out," Jeb said.

"I think you're right. Good night, all." Luke carried Josh over to the wagon. "Hey, you two decent in there?" The question produced an outburst of giggles.

"No, we're not. So you can come in," Honey called out.

Luke winked at Cleve and handed him his sleeping son. "Bed him down as soon as I get Honey out of there." Luke opened the flaps. The wagon reeked of whiskey.

"Hi, sweetheart." Honey greeted him with a wide smile and slipped her arms around his neck. "You're just the man I wanta see. Have I told you how much I love you?"

Luke grasped her around the waist and drew her into his arms. "Tell you what, my drunken little wife, how about me making you a bed next to mine right under this wagon? Then you can tell me all about it."

Honey sighed. "Oh, I'd love that." As Luke lifted her into his arms, she turned her head to Garnet. "I'm sorry, dear, I have to go now. I'm sleeping with my husband tonight. He wants to know how much I love him."

Garnet didn't answer. She had already passed out.

Cleve laid Josh down and covered him up, then did the same to Garnet. Amigo jumped up into the wagon. Lifting his head, he sniffed the air, then buried his snout under Josh's blanket until only his furry back end stuck out.

The next morning Garnet opened the wagon flaps and immediately shoved them back together. Groaning, she grabbed her head.

"What's the matter, Auntie Garney, are you sick?" Josh asked.

Garnet sat down on the stool and cradled her head in her hands. "Quiet, Josh, I just want to sit here and die."

With Amigo at his heels, Josh jumped down from the wagon. The first person he saw was Flint. "Uncle Flint! Uncle Flint!" he shouted, running up to where Flint was shaving near the chuck wagon.

"What's wrong, Josh?" Flint asked, putting aside the razor. Seeing the youngster was trembling, Flint picked him up.

"It's Auntie Garney, Uncle Flint. She's real sick and said she's gonna die."

"Oh, don't worry. She's gonna be fine, Josh. She's just feeling a little under the weather. I'll take care of her. You go on over to Auntie Maud and she'll give you some breakfast."

"Where's my mama and daddy?"

"They're down at the river. Your mama's throwing up, but I wouldn't go down there. It's not a pleasant sight."

"Is Mama feeling under the weather, too, same as Auntie Garney?"

"Reckon so, Josh."

"Is under the weather worse than a scorpion bite, Uncle Flint?"

"Reckon it can seem so."

"Poor Mama and Auntie Garney," Josh said sadly, shaking his head as he walked away.

Flint finished shaving, rinsed off his razor, and dumped out the water. Then he took off his hat long enough to put on his shirt, and walked over to the wagon. Garnet didn't even turn her head to look when he shoved the flaps apart.

"How are you feeling, Redhead?" he asked gently.

"Please don't shout. I have a headache."

"You gals really had a good time last night, didn't you? Maud said the two of you polished off almost half a bottle of whiskey."

"If you don't mind, I do not wish to discuss it," Garnet replied.

"Your best bet is to throw up and get it out of your system. That's what Honey's doing right now."

"I do not have to throw up. I have a headache, that is all." She stood up, and carefully putting one foot in front of the other, walked to the back of the wagon. Ignoring his proffered hand, she climbed down slowly.

"They always say that a fast night makes a slow morning," he said, grinning.

Avoiding any quick movements, she turned and looked him in the eyes. "If you don't get out of my sight, Flint MacKenzie, I shall draw this Colt on my hip and shoot you right where you're standing."

He raised his hands in surrender. "Okay. Okay, I'll leave." Laughing, he hurried over to the chuck wagon.

Fortunately, Garnet didn't have Honey's upset stomach. Maud fixed her a foul-tasting concoction that almost did make her ill, but it somehow managed to alleviate the worst of the headache. Garnet was able to ride out with the men.

They agreed to split up to search for strays, and return no more than four hours later. Luke headed south, Cleve east, Garnet and Flint west, and Joey and Jeb north.

Garnet and Flint worked the draws for a couple hours but saw no cattle. Flint thought it was unlikely any cows could have wandered farther because of a high ravine that ran along the western edge of the trail for several miles.

"We might as well head back to camp," he said. "We're not gonna find stray cattle here."

As they rode back, he noticed some cattle tracks that went off to the north. "These must belong to our strays. Let's take a look in case Joey and Jeb miss 'em."

* * *

Having rounded up fifteen head of the strayed stock, Joey and Jeb were driving the cattle back to the herd when three men rode up to them. Figuring the riders were from another drive, Jeb grinned at them with his usual friendly manner.

Joey felt uneasy when the strangers did not respond to his brother's greeting. "What outfit are you fellas from?" he asked.

"Reckon that ain't your problem, boy," one of the men said gruffly. " 'Pears like you two are startin' your own little herd here."

Jeb laughed. "Naw! We're just rounding up strays after the storm."

"Yeah, maybe rounding 'em up to sell for yourself," one of the men said. Before either of the brothers could guess his intent, the man drew a pistol. "Drop that iron you're wearin'." Looking around, Joey saw the other men were pointing pistols at them, too.

"Tie 'em up and let's take 'em to the boss," the man said.

"There's no call for this," Joey tried to explain as their arms were jerked behind them and their wrists bound with rawhide. "Just ride back about five miles. That's where you'll find the herd we're drivin'."

The men didn't listen. They took the two boys to a nearby patch of cottonwood where three more men waited. Joey and Jeb were hustled up to a man seated on a stump. Joey figured this was their boss.

"Howdy, boys," he said in a friendly way. His voice was low, with a hint of southern honey. He continued to pare his nails with the thin blade of a stiletto. His hands were tanned and long-fingered, with clean, clipped nails that made Joey think the man hadn't done a lick of hard work his whole life.

"Mister, this is all a mistake," Joey said.

"I hope so," the man said. His wide grin revealed a row of perfect, even white teeth. He stuck the knife into the top of his boot, pulled on a pair of leather gloves, then stood up. Small boned and of medium height, the stranger did not appear to have a speck of dust on him, even though he began to brush himself off.

Joey felt uneasy as the man studied him through gray eyes. He didn't look like any rancher or cow man Joey had ever seen before. The man had fine features, and his yellow hair looked to be as thick and silky as Miz Honey's. If it weren't for the man's moustache, Joey thought, he was pretty enough to pass for a woman.

The man sat down and looked solemnly at them. "What are your names, young men?" he said in his soft-spoken southern drawl.

"My name's Joey Boone and this is my brother Jeb," Joey replied.

"The two of you look enough alike to be twins."

"We are twins, mister," Jeb spoke up.

"Where are you from, Mr. Boone?"

"From Kansas, sir," Joey replied.

"Well, it's regrettable that we have to meet under such unfortunate circumstances."

"Ain't I seen you two fellas somewhere before?" one of the men asked. Joey glanced at the speaker: there was a familiarity about him.

"I swear, mister, me and Jeb ain't cattle thieves," Joey said.

"You're driving cattle with other brands. That looks to me like you're thieves."

"Them's vented cows, mister," Jeb said. "We didn't steal 'em."

"So you're denying you stole them and intended to sell them." His face dropped in sorrow. "I wish you hadn't said that," he said kindly. "I hate to see this happen to such fine young men like the two of you. And twins yet!" He shook his head. "So sad! How your poor mother will grieve."

"Our ma and pa are dead, mister. Me and Jeb's just got each other," Joey said.

"Soon the devil will have you both," one of the men said with a snort of contempt. The other men joined in his mocking laughter.

"Now, now, men. Don't make light of the situation," their leader scolded. "These men are soon to face their Maker." He turned to Joey. "I'm afraid, young Mr. Boone, my men here are having a difficult time accepting your alibi."

"But it's the truth," Joey cried out.

"What are you gonna do with us?" Jeb demanded.

"Well, the crime you're accused of is a hanging offense, young man."

"There's no call to hang us," Joey pleaded. "I swear we ain't done nothin' wrong. We're just drovers tryin' to earn an honest dollar."

"Aha, so you're confessing. I've heard that confession is good for the soul."

Confused, Joey looked around him at the ring of faces. "Confessing to what?"

"To the crime you're accused of, Mr. Boone— earning an honest dollar. You see, we don't take kindly to honest men. Isn't that right, men?"

"Yeah, boss," the man beside him said as the others broke into a round of laughter.

"Tsk! Tsk! Tsk!" The man sighed deeply. "So sad."

"You ain't ranchers, you're rustlers," Joey accused.

"That's right, Mr. Boone." Then, to Joey's horror, he saw the leader's gray eyes glitter maniacally. "Hang them," Charlie Walden snarled malevolently.

"Run, Jeb!" Joey shouted.

The two boys took off, but with their arms tied behind their backs, it was a simple task for the outlaws to overtake them. Knocked off their feet, the two men kicked and thrashed, but outnumbered and bound, they could not prevent their captors from also binding their legs.

The outlaws dragged them over to the tree where two nooses had been tossed over a limb. Eager hands reached out to hoist the brothers up on their horses.

"Please, mister, don't hang us," Jeb pleaded.

"Don't beg 'em, Jeb. They ain't gonna listen," Joey said as one of the men climbed up on the tree limb and slipped the noose around his neck.

"But I'm afraid to die, Joey." Jeb started to sob quietly as the man slipped the other noose over his head and tightened it.

"Don't worry, Jeb, I'll be there to take care of you," Joey said.

"Bye, Joey," Jeb sobbed.

"Bye, Jeb," Joey replied.

Then Nathan Bodine slapped the flanks of the horses.

Chapter 27

"**L**et's give the horses a rest," Flint said to Garnet as they followed the cattle tracks into a cottonwood grove. Dismounting, he glanced around but saw no cattle. He could tell by the tracks that some had been there, though, and decided to check further among the trees. Flint hadn't taken more than a dozen steps when he saw the two bodies hanging from a tree. Immediately recognizing the red shirt that Jeb Boone had been wearing that morning, he froze in shock.

"What is it, Flint?" Garnet asked, walking up behind him.

"Stay back, Garnet. Don't come—"

His warning was too late. She saw the two figures hanging from the tree limb. Through the nightmare of shock and horror, she recognized them, their faces now blackened and bloated.

"No!" she mumbled in a whisper wracked with pain. "Oh, God, no!" She sank to her knees. Folding her arms across her chest, she clenched her hands together and stared in disbelief. "Oh, please. No, no, no." Lowering her head, she rocked back and forth, repeating the litany over and over. "No, no, no. Please, God. Please!"

Flint cut the ropes and lowered the bodies of Joey and Jeb. Gently, he laid them on the ground and pulled the ropes from around their necks. For as long as he could remember, he had seen men die, and was responsible for some of those deaths himself. But this time he felt as if he were choking—as if the hangman's noose had been tightened around his own neck. He fought to make his aching lungs draw in a breath.

Turning away, he hurried over to Garnet, who was still rocking back and forth. Kneeling, he gathered her into his arms. "Hush, baby." He cradled her head to his chest and held her close.

"Why, Flint? Why would anyone hang them?" Garnet finally asked through her grief.

"They probably came upon some border gang rustling our steers," he said.

"But why kill them? And by hanging—" She broke off and began to sob.

He rocked her in his arms. "Cry it out, baby," he cooed tenderly.

"I can't stand any more, Flint," she whimpered. "I thought I was strong. That whatever happened, I was a survivor. But I hate this life. It's cruel and merciless. There's no civilization out here—death and destruction are all that exist."

He continued to let her vent her sorrow.

"There isn't a spot on this western plain that's worth shedding a drop of blood over. Why must men kill and die for it? Give it back to the wolves and jackals—and the white and red savages who want to claim it. Let them kill one another."

"A man can find a good life here, Garnet. It's not all like this."

"Yes, it is. All a good man can find is an early grave." She beseeched him with her eyes. "They were only eighteen, Flint. What did they ever do to deserve to die in such a manner?"

"The manner in which a man dies, Garnet, is not as important as the manner in which he lives."

Her eyes flashed in anger as she shoved him away.

"Don't you dare start to preach that warped philosophy to me. You're just like the others, Flint. You live by a so-called code of honor that you're so proud of. Yet yesterday I saw you run a knife into a man and think nothing of it, because in your judgment he deserved killing. Your judgment! Who are you, or any others like you, to make that kind of judgment?" She raised her voice in an impassioned cry. "Who was the man who judged that Joey and Jeb had to die?"

"Garnet, you're getting hysterical."

Tears streaked her cheeks and she brushed them aside. "Am I, Flint? Then aren't you afraid I'm liable to draw my Colt and shoot you because you've just insulted me—or, God forbid, because you don't live by my code?"

"What's gotten into you? You sound like you're blaming me for Joey and Jeb's deaths."

"Oh, I'm not blaming you. But their deaths give you an excuse to go out and kill the men who did it. The only difference between you and those killers, Flint, is you think you're justified. But the result is still the same—someone dies. And the list keeps growing, doesn't it? There's Charlie Walden for killing your mother and Sarah, Nathan Bodine for trying to kill you and me. Now you can add these new names, however many there may be, for killing Joey and Jeb. Oh, yes, and while you're at it, be sure and kill any Indian who might get in your way," she ranted. "Conscience. Integrity. You've convinced yourself that those virtues separate you from the Charlie Waldens and Bullwhip Moores, because you're on a mission. Well, they don't, Flint." She shook her head. "Oh, for a while, you almost had me believing it too. I thought you were a Sir Galahad."

"I don't know what the hell you're talking about! Sir Galahad? You're raving, Garnet. But blame me if it makes you feel better."

He walked away and led their horses over to the tree.

After tying the bodies over the saddles, he began to check out the footprints in the dirt. Bending down on a knee, he studied one more closely. Then he stood up. "I'm leaving. Are you coming? We're gonna have to walk back."

Heartsick, Garnet got up and followed.

Joey and Jeb Boone were buried as they had lived and died—side by side, in a single grave. Cleve and Flint chose a site on the top of a knoll overlooking the stream that ran past the campsite.

Maud was heartbroken. When they returned from the burial, Garnet led her over to the fire. "Sit down, dear."

"I loved them two boys like they were my own sons," Maud said, slumping down on a chair. Garnet sat down at her feet and held the grieving woman's hand. "When we got back to Calico, I was gonna buy Ben Franks's spread, and me and the boys was gonna go into ranchin'."

Garnet ached for Maud. Trying to console the grieving woman helped to lessen some of the sorrow she was feeling.

They finally persuaded Maud to go to bed. Honey and Garnet undressed her, and after unraveling the braid Maud always wore wound on the top of her head, Honey brushed out Maud's long gray hair.

"Leave her alone to mourn, Jaybird," Luke said gently, slipping an arm around Honey's shoulders. "You and Garnet better get some sleep now, too," he said. "Joshua's fallen asleep at the fire. Leave him there; he can sleep with me tonight." Unresisting, the two women climbed into the wagon.

Garnet felt numb, physically and emotionally spent. She had no more fight left in her. For the time being, she believed she had no more tears left to shed.

She lay awake staring up at the top of the wagon, and knew that Honey was doing the same. Neither one felt like talking.

Once the women had retired, Flint called Luke and Cleve over to the fire. "I have something of interest to tell you, but I didn't want the women to hear. I saw a familiar track in that grove today."

"What do you mean?" Luke asked.

"Remember I told you when I was in Dos Rios, I got on the trail of two men from Charlie Walden's gang? One of them had been riding a horse with a slit in the right rear hoof. I saw that same print today."

"You saying you think the hanging of Joey and Jeb is tied up with the Walden gang some way?" Luke asked.

"I don't believe in coincidence, Luke. If I cross a wolf's path, I'm on its trail, but when I find it behind me later, I know it's on mine. I think I should follow this track and see where it leads."

"You mean now?" Luke said.

"Yeah, while the trail's hot."

"Lord, Flint, there's only three of us as it is. If you go off chasing this lead, there'll only be Cleve and me to protect three women, Josh, and six hundred cows. This just isn't the right time."

"We ought to reach Abilene in about five days, Flint," Cleve said. "If Walden's around these parts, we should be able to pick up some word. Then I'll go with you."

"I reckon you're right. But Walden's so close, I can smell him," Flint replied. He went over and climbed on Sam. "I'll take the night watch." He rode off without any further word.

"What do you think?" Cleve asked.

"Flint's too good at reading signs to doubt his judgment. He's on to something, all right."

"Well, you can bet he won't give any more thought to settling down now. Where will that leave Garnet?"

"Cleve, what I'm about to tell you is not to be repeated to anyone," Luke said solemnly. "I found out from Honey what's been bothering Garnet, and I promised Honey I wouldn't tell anyone."

"I won't say anything," Cleve agreed impatiently.

"Garnet's going to have a baby."

Cleve let out a low whistle. "Has she told Flint?"

"No. And she swore Honey to secrecy. I got it out of Honey by promising not to tell anyone. You've got to do the same."

Cleve shook his head. "Dammit, Luke, this situation is ridiculous. This shouldn't be kept from Flint. Goddammit, he's the baby's father! And are you forgetting, he's our brother?"

"Of course not," Luke said. "I figure we can straighten it out in Abilene. Right now, we gotta concentrate on getting the women and the herd safely there."

"Okay, but once we're in Abilene all promises are off."

Luke nodded. "We best get some sleep."

"Yeah. I'll check to make sure Maud's okay, then I'll be back," Cleve said, and the two men went their separate ways.

Josh opened his eyes. "Did you hear that, Amigo?" he whispered to the dog curled up beside him. "Auntie Garney and Uncle Flint are gonna have a baby. Maybe they'll let me be the godfather just like our friends Auntie Cyntia and Uncle Doug back in Stockton did with baby Melissa." Confused, he frowned. "But how can Auntie Garney be having a baby if Uncle Flint don't know about it? Sure don't make sense to me, Amigo." He hugged his beloved pet, closed his eyes, and went back to sleep.

When Garnet awoke the following morning, she saw that Honey was still asleep. Dressing quickly, she climbed out of the wagon. Maud had already opened the chuck box, but there was no sign of her. Flint, Luke, and Josh were sleeping near the fire. She figured Cleve was with the herd.

Garnet knew she owed Flint an apology for her outburst the previous day, but she didn't want to wake him. She had heard him ride in from night watch just a couple hours earlier. Without Joey and Jeb, they would all be working harder and longer hours, and Flint needed all the sleep he could get. Most certainly, her help would be needed now more than ever. She'd eat and hit the saddle.

When she couldn't find Maud, she looked around in alarm, then caught sight of her up on the knoll at the grave. Garnet climbed the hill and put her hand on Maud's shoulder.

"How are you feeling this morning, Maud?" she said softly.

The older woman looked up at her and managed a smile. "Reckon I can tough it out, gal. Had to more than one time in my life. Person ain't got much choice, if you want to keep your faith in the Almighty."

"I guess so," Garnet said. She realized that she had lost sight of that belief lately.

"Thought I'd come up and say my good-bye now before it's time to pull out."

Garnet smiled gently. "That's a good idea."

"Kinda nice up here, ain't it?" Maud said, looking around. "Real peaceful-like. Figure them boys will like it here."

Garnet lifted her head. A gentle breeze lightly stirred the hair on her nape. She swung her gaze toward the plain of grass that stretched to the horizon. Most of the cattle were still down, and she saw Cleve riding slowly among them, rousing them to their feet. Morning sunlight glistened on the silent, flowing water below, and in the distance she could see a doe and its fawn standing on the bank, drinking from the stream.

"Yes, it's very peaceful, Maud."

"Well, I best get back to my cookin'. There's beans and grits on the fire and bacon already fried."

Garnet slipped an arm through Maud's, and arm-in-arm they walked back down the hill.

"This'll wake you up," Maud said, pouring Garnet a

mug of coffee when they returned to the chuck wagon. "Made it extra strong 'cause I figure we could use it this morning."

"Flint'll sure appreciate it," Garnet said lightly. "You know how he likes coffee that you have to practically chew before you can swallow it."

One by one the others began to stir and quietly came over to eat. After Luke rode off, Cleve came in and ate his breakfast too. Within the hour, they were moving the cattle: Luke on the point, Cleve on the drag, and Flint and Garnet on the flanks. The horses ambled along beside the cattle.

Five days later—fifty-nine days from the time they had left the Triple M—they drove the herd into the sturdily constructed stockyard pens at Abilene, Kansas.

Garnet still had not gotten up the courage to apologize to Flint for the unkind remarks the day they discovered Joey and Jeb's bodies. She hadn't told him about the baby, either.

Chapter 28

A young man came running out of a nearby office. His excited manner and custom-fitted three-piece suit contrasted greatly with the languid, jeans-clad westerners. As soon as he spoke, it became clear he was from the East. "Drive them right in those pens, gentlemen."

Luke dismounted, and the man reached out to shake hands. "I'm Joe McCoy. I've been expecting you. Your herd was spotted earlier coming in. Looks like we can do some business together."

"Sure hope so," Luke said. As if a burden had been lifted from his shoulders, Luke grinned over McCoy's head at Cleve and Flint. "I'm Luke MacKenzie. These are my brothers, Flint and Cleve."

"Pleasure to meet you, gentlemen," McCoy said, offering a handshake.

So this was the famous Joseph McCoy, Garnet thought, studying the young man intently. Luke had told them about this young entrepreneur, who had turned Abilene into the most famous cattle town in the West. After the war, the young visionary had anticipated the fortune that could be gained from shipping the thousands of cattle glutting Texas to the eastern cities now crying for Texas beef. He had chosen

317

Abilene, Kansas, as the logical site for this merger of
cattle and railroad. The result had exceeded even his
expansive expectations.

"You're the sixth drive in this year. How far have you
come?" McCoy asked.

"About seven hundred miles. We've got a ranch in
west Texas near the Red."

McCoy stuck his hands in his pockets as he looked
over the herd. "Well, these cows look healthy. Looks
like you've got well over five hundred here."

"Closer to six hundred, Mr. McCoy, and over a
hundred calves," Luke said.

"Let's go into the office and we'll get down to
business." Noting the wagons, McCoy hurried over to
them. "How do you do, ladies."

"My wife," Luke said, introducing Honey. "And this
is Mrs. Scott and Miss Malone."

McCoy greeted each of them. "Our business will
take hours, and I'm sure you ladies would like to relax.
Why don't you go to the Drovers' Cottage and get
settled in."

Luke nodded to Honey. "No sense in your waiting
around here, Jaybird. We'll join you as soon as we
finish."

"Be sure and tell the desk clerk that I sent you,"
McCoy said. "Tell him I said to make sure he takes
good care of you."

As they left the stockyards, Garnet said, "That's the
noisiest place I've ever heard. The sound of all those
train whistles and clanging railroad cars, mixed with
the thud of the cattle hooves on those wooden chutes,
was just about all the noise I can take for one day."

"And just think, this goes on all summer," Honey
remarked.

"I wonder if they close up the town during the
winter," Garnet said drolly.

They reined up in front of a three-story, yellow
building trimmed in bright green, bearing the name

Drovers' Cottage. "Some cottage!" Garnet commented as she dismounted. Upon observing the several dozen men sitting on the veranda, she whispered to Honey, "If you feel like you're being stared at, you're right."

"In those eastern suits and derbies they're wearing, they sure don't look like the drovers I'm used to seeing," Honey replied.

"And in these dusty pants and shirts, we don't much look like the women they're used to seeing back East." Garnet giggled.

"I never expected to see anything like this in a Kansas cattle town," Honey commented as they entered the hotel. "This place looks as fancy as some I've seen in San Francisco and Chicago."

As Honey stepped up to the desk to register, Garnet took a longer look around. Several doors led to lounges and a large, formal dining room.

"Do you have luggage, madam?" the clerk asked, noting their appearance with a long, disapproving look.

"We left it in the wagon," Honey said.

"I'll send a bellboy for it." He motioned to a young man nearby.

"No sense in emptying out the whole wagon," Maud said. "I'll go with him and point out what we'll be needin'."

"And how many rooms will you require, madam?" the desk clerk asked disdainfully.

"Well, my husband and I will want a connecting room for our son." Honey turned to Garnet. "How many more rooms do you feel we will require, Mrs. Scott?" It was clear that Honey was uncertain if Garnet intended to share a room with Flint.

"I would say one for Cleve, one for Maud, and one for Flint and myself. That would be three more."

"So that would be five rooms—two of which are connecting. Is that correct, madam?" the clerk asked officiously.

"Sounds right to me. Doesn't it sound right to you, Garnet dear?" Honey said.

"There are tubs with running water and a water closet in each room."

"In each room!" Honey shook her head. "Amazing, isn't it? Do you have five such rooms available, sir?"

"Madam, we have eighty rooms in this hotel."

"Well then, there certainly doesn't appear to be a problem, does there?"

"It's just that we do have a two-room suite available, which I suggest would be more suitable for you and your son, madam."

"Is that two bedrooms, sir?" Honey asked sweetly.

"No, madam. A bedroom and a sitting room."

"Well, tell me. . . ." Honey paused. "What *is* your name, sir?"

"Theodore Danvers, madam."

Honey crooked her finger and motioned him closer. "Tell me, Mr. Theodore Danvers," she said in a confidential whisper, "if you were me, and were married to the handsomest man in the whole state of Texas, and you had just spent two months sleeping in wagons and bedrolls surrounded by a half-dozen other people . . . would you want your son sharing a bedroom with you and your husband?"

Danvers turned beet red. Honey flickered her long lashes at him and smiled. "We'll take connectin' rooms, if you please."

Danvers rang for another bellboy. Handing him the keys, he said, "Show these ladies to their rooms." Casting a disdainful glance at Amigo, Danvers asked, "Do you wish that animal to be stabled along with your horses and wagons?"

"Amigo? Oh, heavens no!" Honey said with feigned shock. At the mention of his name, the dog's ears perked up and his tail began to wag. "You see, sir, Amigo can't sleep in anything other than a bed with fine cotton sheets. The beds do have fine cotton sheets, don't they, Mr. Danvers?" They started to climb the stairway, and Honey turned her head back to look at him. "Oh, by the way, Mr. Danvers, I forgot to give you a message from Mr. McCoy. He said you were to be sure and take good care of us."

Danvers blanched. "Mr. McCoy?"

"That's right."

"I hope you and your family enjoy your stay in Abilene, Mrs. MacKenzie," Danvers said with a sickly smile.

"I'm sure we will . . . now."

"You're outrageous!" Garnet whispered as they followed the bellboy upstairs.

"Well, don't you think he was rather pompous?" Honey replied. "Who did he think he was dealing with? Some backwater sodbuster whom he thought he could intimidate? Luke told me that before McCoy came here and built up this town a couple years ago, Abilene was nothing more than a prairie village with just a dozen log huts."

"Well, the prairie village sure has changed," Garnet said a short time later, glancing out the third story window of Honey's room. "I don't think this town's wanting for anything. I see everything from a hardware store to a dentist's office. There's even a photograph studio. Let's go out and look over the town."

"Not now," Honey replied. "I'm going to soak in a hot bath."

"I wonder if Maud's willing."

Honey shook her head. "She said first she's taking a bath, then she's going to stretch out on that feather mattress in her room and sleep 'til we're ready to leave Abilene."

"Well, how about Josh and Amigo? I can't believe they wouldn't be game for a walk."

"Josh went back to the stockyards to watch the men load cattle. I don't have to tell you where Amigo went."

"Well, I guess I can either go for a walk by myself or go back to my room and take a bath," Garnet said.

"Now, when Luke gets back here, if you want to take Josh for a walk *then*. . . ." Honey trailed off, smiling suggestively.

"I'd love to, dearie, but I just might be occupied myself." She left the room laughing.

"Twenty-four thousand dollars!" Luke exclaimed as they left McCoy's office. He slapped Flint on the shoulder. "Do you believe that, Brother Flint! And we oughta get close to another thousand for the remuda and wagons. No sense in driving them wagons back to Texas." He put his arm around Cleve's shoulders. "Come on, Little Brother, I'll buy you a drink."

They stopped in front of the hotel to send Josh upstairs. "Why can't I come with you and Uncle Flint and Cleve?" he asked. "I'm thirsty, too."

"A saloon's no place for a youngster, Josh MacKenzie," Luke declared. "If you're thirsty, you go and tell your mama. She'll get you a drink of water."

"Is that what you're gonna have?" Josh asked.

"No, it isn't. Now get going," he said, tapping him on the butt. "And tell your mama I'll be back in thirty minutes."

As soon as Josh disappeared into the hotel, the men headed for the glass doors of the Alamo Saloon. Glancing around at the polished brass fixtures and the walls lined with mirrors and paintings, Cleve emitted a long whistle. "This place looks as fancy as some I've seen in San Francisco."

Luke hardly noticed. His mind was back in Texas and his plans for spending the money. "First thing I'll do with my share is buy Honey a decent cookstove.

After we pay Maud and Garnet what they've got coming, we'll split up the rest."

"Forget any split for me, Luke," Cleve said. "I just want a couple thousand to get started. You'll find plenty use for the rest around the ranch. You're going to have to restock it, you know."

"Yeah, but I'll be buying beef back in Texas for three dollars a head. Remember?"

"I won't be needing much either," Flint said. "Ain't got no use to be toting a lot of money around."

Cleve and Luke exchanged a meaningful glance. "Thought you were thinking about settling down with Garnet," Luke said. "Why not talk to Ben Franks so you and Garnet can set up a spread on the Flying F? We'll expand the Triple M."

"Don't think Garnet would be interested. She ain't got much use for me since the hanging."

"Whatever's wrong, I'm sure it's not anything the two of you can't talk out," Cleve said. "I think the time's past due to tell you that—"

Before Cleve could finish, six men walked up to them. "Been told you Texas boys just drove in that herd of beef." The speaker was a tall, thin man with small black eyes. His mouth had a sour look to it, due to his slightly protruding front teeth. But the Colt .44 hanging from each hip was a good indication he was not to be ignored. "Which one of you does the speakin' for the others?"

Having been a lawman, Luke could make quick judgments about strangers. He decided he didn't like this one at all. "Reckon we're all old enough to speak for ourselves, mister."

"How many head you drive in here today?" the man said.

"Enough," Luke replied.

"That ain't what I asked."

Leaning back with his elbows on the bar, Flint

hooked a heel over the fancy, polished brass rail. "Could be you ask too many questions for a stranger."

"Case you Texas boys haven't figured it out, you're the strangers here, or you'd know who I am."

"So, who are you?" Luke asked.

"Me and the boys here represent the Abilene Cattle Protectors' Society."

"Never heard of it." Luke turned his back to him and motioned to the bartender for a refill.

"You could say we represent the law here."

"That right?" Flint remarked. "Heard there was no law here in Abilene."

"Not officially. But sometimes we citizens have to take matters into our own hands."

"You saying you're vigilantes?" Luke asked.

"Wouldn't say that either. Our job is to keep an eye on the town's legal transactions."

"Legal transactions?" Luke asked. "Heard there was no government here either. No mayor or city council. So, what legal transactions are there, mister?"

"You know—fines . . . levies."

"Levies on what?"

"For instance on that herd you just drove in. We'll have to charge you five dollars per head."

"For what?" Luke asked.

"You drove them across Kansas land, didn't you? We can't afford to allow you to do that without imposing a little levy."

"Sounds a mite high to me," Flint said. When one of the men shifted over on his right, Flint quickly waved him back. "I don't like crowding, mister. Move back to where you were." The veiled threat was enough to cause the man to do it. Flint turned his head back to the leader of the gang. "Now as I was saying," Flint began. "By the way, mister, you got another name other than 'Ugly'?"

"Your smart mouth's just cost you another dollar a

head. You goddamned Rebs are too dumb to know when to keep your mouths shut."

"Maybe so, but we ain't too dumb to recognize a goddamned gang of crooked Jayhawkers," Flint said.

"You've been fixing for a fight since we came in here," the man said. He gave Cleve a long, contemptuous look. "How come you ain't said a word?"

"I listen well." Cleve looked distressed. "Is this fight going to be with fists, Colts, or knives?"

"We don't need nothin' but fists against you Texas Rebs. You in this fight or not?"

"I'd really rather not."

"First smart Reb I've met. Move your ass out of here then."

Cleve walked over to the nearest table and sat down. "You don't mind if I stay and watch, do you?" he asked with his wide, friendly grin. "It's been a long time since I've seen a good fight."

"You ain't gonna see one now, Reb. This one's over before it starts. There's six of us to two of them."

Cleve nodded. "I know. Terrible odds. That's why I stepped out. It wouldn't have been fair for all three of us to take you on."

Anger glared in the Jayhawker's eyes. "I've heard enough talk from you smart-assed Rebs. The levy's just gone up to ten dollars a head."

"Hey, Luke," Flint said. "Didn't the Boones say their pa and ma were killed by Jayhawkers? They must have talked the poor folks to death with threats."

From a table in the corner of the saloon came a loud burst of laughter. A tall, buckskin-clad figure rose to his feet. There was an air of confidence in his walk as he crossed the room. Flint's glance fell immediately on the pair of Colts shoved into his waistband. The way he wore the pistols with the butt to the front, Flint figured the man would be fast and use a cross draw. He was the real threat in the room, not the big-mouth Jayhawker and his gang.

Flint braced for violence. If this stranger was in cahoots with the Jayhawkers, he and his brothers were in for trouble—and not the kind that was settled with fists.

Flint studied the stranger, trying to discern a weakness. The man was hatless and had long hair that hung to his shoulders. It wasn't red like Garnet's, but a dark, auburn shade like hers looked sometimes in the moonlight. The stranger had a large crook in his nose like an eagle, and a steady stare to him—the kind you'd hate to be looking into if you were on the wrong end of a Colt. His eyes weren't blue, but Flint saw they weren't gray either. Kind of a mix of both colors. At the moment, they were fixed on the Jayhawker he had walked up to.

"Pitiful," he said with contempt. "You're pitiful." He shook his head. "Anyone can see these men can cut you passel of skunks to ribbons. Not that you wouldn't have it coming. You attempt this kind of holdup often?"

"Who the hell are you?" the Jayhawker asked. "Another one of these goddamned Rebs?"

"Not at all, big mouth. I had the pleasure of serving with the Union army during the war. Obviously you didn't, or you'd have sense enough to know what you're up against by taking on these Rebs. Maybe then you wouldn't be so loose with your name calling."

"Yeah. Well, I'd say you ain't much smarter, 'cause you just cut yourself into the same trouble they're in."

"I'm really curious to know how a swaggering little asshole like you has managed to stay alive so long."

As soon as the Jayhawker started to draw, Flint's Colt cleared the holster. "Don't try it," he ordered. Cleve and Luke already had their pistols trained on the other men.

The stranger hadn't made a move toward his own guns. His stare remained fixed on the Jayhawker. "See what I mean about how lucky you are? You owe these men a debt of gratitude; they just saved your life." He tapped one of the butt handles at his waist. "If I'd have drawn on you, I'd have shot you." The man's gaze became as cold and hard as steel. "Take your own advice and get your ass out of here, 'cause next time you're not going to be so lucky."

The Jayhawker hesitated momentarily. "Let's go, boys." He hurried away, followed by the other five men.

Luke extended his hand. "Well, we owe you a drink, stranger. You saved us the trouble of beating the hell out of those assholes. Name's Luke Mackenzie. This mean-looking critter on my right is my brother Flint, and the other is my brother Cleve."

"My pleasure, gentlemen. Name's James Hickok. Most people call me Wild Bill though," he said, after shaking hands with all of them.

"I'd say it's a proper sobriquet," Cleve said.

"A proper what?" Flint asked.

"Nickname, Brother Flint. Nickname," Cleve said, bellying up to the bar.

"You've got the look of a lawman about you, Luke," Hickok said.

"Could say the same about you, Wild Bill," Luke replied.

Hickok winked. "Forget that—sobriquet—crap and just call me Jim. That's what my friends do."

"You're right, Jim, I was a lawman for a couple years in California."

"I'm sheriff of Ellis County right now. Couple years back, I was a deputy marshal at Fort Riley."

"What brings you to Abilene?" Cleve asked.

Hickok grimaced with disgust. "In the last couple years, this town's gotten so wild every lawman in Kansas is concerned about it. Drifters and scum like that gang of Jayhawkers end up crossing other parts of Kansas to get here. This town needs a lawman to clean them up."

"You look like you could handle it, Hickok," Flint said.

"Never can tell. Might consider it someday. Right now, I've got my hands full with Ellis County." He finished his drink. "Well, I came here to do some gambling. Looks like a chair's opened up at one of them tables. It's been a pleasure talking to you," he said with a round of handshakes. "If I were you, I'd get out of Abilene as soon as I finished my business here."

"We're planning to," Luke said.

"You fellas take care and watch your backs. Ain't seen so much riffraff in one town as long as I've been a lawman." He nodded and sauntered over to a distant gaming table.

"Reckon we better get this check in the bank, and then get to that hotel and see what the women have been up to," Luke said.

"I think we ought to take Hickok's advice," Cleve remarked. "The sooner we get them out of this town, the better."

Flint agreed. "Yeah, this town's got the smell of trouble to it."

Chapter 29

Nathan Bodine sat on the lumpy mattress in the flea-ridden hotel and continued to sniffle. The tears streaking his cheeks were caught by his upper lip, where they lay like raindrops on a leaf. He swiped his arm across his nose, then raised the whiskey bottle to his mouth and took a deep draught. Setting aside the bottle, he drew his Colt, took careful aim, and blew the number 12 off the calendar on the opposite wall. He shoved the gun back in its holster and reached again for the bottle.

For the past five years, he had spent the anniversary of this date in a similar manner. "It was your fault, Sarah. All your fault." He swiped his nose again, then raised the bottle to his mouth.

His dazed vision focused on a cockroach crawling across the floor. Once again he drew his Colt. His hand shook as he centered the insect in the sights and pulled the trigger. The roach splattered against the wall.

The whore in the room below pounded on the ceiling. "Goddammit, quit shooting off that gun! You're gonna kill somebody down here."

"Shut your whoring mouth!" Bodine shouted back.

Women were all alike. Willing to sell themselves for a few dollars or a handsome face and body. Whatta they care about the man who loves 'em? He resumed his sniffling.

"Your fault, Sarah. Your fault!" he shouted at the top of his lungs.

"Shadup," an angry male voice bellowed from the next room. The complaint set up a hue and cry from other rooms. Bodine snorted, his mouth twisting into a derisive smirk. He didn't care whether the other sons of bitches liked it or not. He had never cared what anybody thought about him except Sarah—his beautiful Sarah. Beautiful, blue-eyed Sarah. He had loved her from the time they were children.

His eyes narrowed into a malicious glare. And the deceiving little bitch had led him on with her shy smiles and kind words. She had no right doing that to him. Pretending to be kind to him. Most likely she had herself a good laugh behind his back with that goddamned Luke MacKenzie.

"Well, who had the final laugh, Sarah?" he shouted.

Now the MacKenzie bastard was right here in Abilene. He had seen him with his own eyes—him and those goddamned brothers of his!

He finished the whiskey and hurled the empty bottle against the wall. The glass shattered, and the shouted complaints started up again. "I'm coming in there and blowing your goddamned head off," a voice sounded gruffly from the next room.

"Come ahead," Bodine said quietly. With a mouth now curved in a maniacal smile, he fondled the hilt of the knife in his boot. "Come ahead."

At the sound of a knock, he swung his glance toward the door. "Bodine, it's me."

Recognizing the voice, he mumbled, "Cum'n."

Charlie Walden opened the door and slipped through it. "What the hell are you doing, Bodine?" he asked angrily. "We came to this flea trap to stay unobserved, and you're going to have everyone in the place pounding on the door."

"I'll do what I want," Bodine grumbled. "My business."

"What happened? You weren't like this when I left you a couple hours ago."

"I was thinkin' of Sarah." He began to blubber again. "Been five years since she died."

Walden was disgusted. He loathed any man who was weak enough to wail over a woman. "Who the hell is Sarah?"

"Don't you go talkin' about her that way." Bodine's voice had risen to a bellow. "She was beautiful. My beautiful Sarah. I loved her."

"Okay, okay. So you loved her." Charlie straddled a chair. "How'd she die?" He didn't give a damn, he just wanted the son of a bitch to quiet down.

"I cut her throat."

"You killed the woman you loved!" Charlie shook his head. "Now I've heard it all. You sure are a strange one, Bodine. Sitting here blubbering over the same woman you killed."

Bodine swung his legs over the edge of the bed. "I've gotta have a drink."

"You can get one later." Charlie wanted Bodine to settle down. He figured the best way to do it was to keep him talking. "So why'd you kill this Sarah?"

Bodine sat on the edge of the bed staring at the calendar. "Remember that ranch we raided in Texas five years ago? There was a couple of women. An older one and a young gal with dark hair."

"Hell, no. How'd you expect me to remember a raid that long ago? But what about them?"

"The young gal was Sarah."

Charlie frowned. "You're not making sense, Bodine. I thought you said you loved this Sarah."

Bodine swiped his nose as tears streamed down his cheeks. "I did. That's why I told you we should raid that ranch."

"You wanted her dead?"

"I was hopin' the bastard she married would have been there. But him and his brothers had gone off to the war. I gave her a chance. I wouldn't have raped her, or let the rest of 'em do the same, if she would have admitted it."

"Admitted what?"

Bodine had gazed off into space. "Even when I held the knife to her throat she wouldn't say it."

"Say what?" Charlie asked impatiently.

Bodine turned his head and looked at him. He appeared to have sobered up, even though his face was puffy and his nose red from crying. His eyes appeared to Charlie to be glazed, but not from alcohol. In a voice edged with an indifference that brought a slight chill to even Charlie's impassive mien, Bodine said, "That she loved me, of course. She just wouldn't admit it. But I knew there was no way she could love Luke MacKenzie more than she did me. So I slit her throat."

"Luke MacKenzie!" Charlie exclaimed. "Are you saying this Sarah was married to a man named Luke MacKenzie? And this MacKenzie had brothers?"

"Yeah. A couple brothers. So what?"

"So what? My brother Beau was killed by a sheriff named MacKenzie."

"Thought you said Beau was killed in California."

"He was. And later me and some of my boys shot it out with the MacKenzies. That's when we headed to these parts."

"Yeah, well, MacKenzie's a common name." Bodine snorted. "Don't have to mean it's the same man."

"God, you're an idiot, Bodine! A sheriff with the same first and last name—who also happens to have two brothers—*has* to be the same MacKenzie!"

Bodine got an injured pout on his face. "You got no call to call me names. I wasn't with you in California, so how was I to know the MacKenzie that shot Beau was the same one from Texas? I saw him today."

Charlie jerked up in surprise. "Saw him?"

With a cocky smile, Bodine nodded. "Yep. Him and his brothers. They drove in them cattle. Funny, ain't it? Same date as the day we raided their ranch."

"MacKenzie know you killed his wife?" Charlie asked.

"Don't know how he would."

"Then stay out of sight 'til I have time to think about this."

"I ain't staying holed up here." Bodine stood up and walked to the door.

"Where are you going?" Charlie demanded.

"To get a drink."

"Well, try to stay out of trouble," Charlie ordered. Bodine slammed the door and with heavy footfalls, strode down the hall.

"Imbeciles!" Charlie mumbled, returning to his own room. He was surrounded by imbeciles. He dug the pipe and pouch of brown powder out of his saddle-bags. If only he had someone intelligent to talk to in quiet moments. Since Beau's death he had no one. Instead, he was confronted daily with scum like Bo-dine whose only aptitude was a propensity for killing. Sitting down on the bed, Charlie packed the bowl and lit it, then took a deep, covetous draw on the pipe.

For a short while he had believed Nathan Bodine might be someone with whom he could sit down to discuss a book or fine line of poetry. He had been mistaken. Bodine was as deranged as all the others he had associated with for the past few years. Perhaps the time had come to give up this way of life, and settle down and become respectable. There was only one thing to deal with before he could consider it—Luke MacKenzie, the man who had killed his brother Beau and arrested his other brother Billy Bob. Beau had been like a son to him, and for the past year Billy Bob had languished in prison. And all because of Luke Mac-Kenzie.

But before he killed Luke MacKenzie, he would

make certain the ex-sheriff saw his brothers die. He wasn't crazy enough to take on all three of the MacKenzies at the same time. If that idiot Bodine had said something sooner, he could have picked them off one at a time on that cattle drive.

After he settled that score, then he would find a new life away from the slime and dregs of the past seven years—and the company of idiots like Nathan Bodine.

As the opium began to seep in soothing relief through his bloodstream, Charlie could feel the tension ease from his body. Smiling, he recalled the good ol' days when he rode with William Quantrill. Quantrill was an intelligent man, someone like himself who could sit down and converse intelligently. But there weren't any more like Quantrill. There were only the Nathan Bodines and Bullwhip Moores, the kind of men who would just as soon slit his throat as that of a stranger.

He continued to drag on the pipe. Yes, Charlie thought, curving his handsome face into a smile, as soon as he took care of this unfinished business, he would set this life behind him and settle down to a respectable one. He had enough money stashed away in the bank to live comfortably for the rest of his life. That is, if some bastard didn't rob the bank. Charlie started to chuckle. That was funny. He was a funny man.

Leaning his head back against the headboard, he began to float in a dreamy euphoria free of any Nathan Bodines or Luke MacKenzies.

As soon as they finished at the bank, Flint couldn't wait to get to the hotel and see Garnet. They had a lot to talk over. He had to convince her to go back to the Triple M with Luke and Honey, until he settled up with Charlie Walden. Cleve and him were sure to catch up with Walden. There'd be no escape for the bastard this time. The trail was too hot! Then it would all be over, and Garnet and him could marry and settle down on the Flying F just like Luke suggested. Ranching was a good life—if the redhead was there to share it with him. He'd meant it when he told his brothers he was over his wanderlust, and Garnet was the reason. But like Cleve had said, why hadn't he told her this?

Because he was scared, that's why. He had pretended she didn't matter to him, had kept telling her he could ride away from her anytime he had a mind to. Maybe he had said it too often, and she'd gotten tired of hearing it. He knew he was pretty dumb when it came to females, but it seemed she'd begun to shy away from him in the last month.

He wasn't any prize, and he'd never been any good with words. But she'd always seemed to understand what he wanted to say. He grinned. More times than not, she'd put the words in his mouth for him.

But this time, he'd have to be the one to say those words.

That he loved her. That she'd come to mean a lot to him. That he no longer could imagine a day dawning without knowing he'd see her face or hear her voice.

Grinning, he shook his head. Yep, the little filly had crept into his heart exactly like she had warned him she would. The smile dissolved. Knowing the stubborn redhead, he'd have a real fight on his hands to convince her. He'd given her good cause not to want to stay with him.

Flint was about to enter the hotel when he spied her head far down the street. "I'll see you boys later," he told his brothers and hurried over to where he had seen her. Looking around, there was no sign of her now. Then he saw her come out of a boutique on the corner and walk away empty-handed. Following a hunch, he entered the store.

"Ah, ma'am, there was just a lady in here . . . redheaded," he said awkwardly.

"Oh, yes. Mrs. Scott," the proprietress said.

"Was there something special she admired?" he asked.

"As a matter of fact, there was. I'm just wrapping it now." Flint glanced down and saw a green plaid gown in the box. "Mrs. Scott said she would pay for it when she picked it up tomorrow morning. Along with this bonnet." The woman opened a hat box and held up a flowered straw bonnet. "Isn't it delightful!" Flint thought it was ridiculous looking, but withheld his opinion.

"I'll pay for them and take them with me now," he said. "Kind of like to surprise her."

The shop owner finished packaging the gown and added a big bow to the box. Then she smiled with pleasure as she gave him the boxes. "Do I detect the fragrance of *amour*, young man?"

Flint lifted his head and sniffed the air. "I don't smell anything."

He hurriedly paid for the purchases and snatched up the parcels. When he left the shop, he saw no sign of Garnet. Hoping she had returned to the hotel, he hurried back there.

The desk clerk gave him the room numbers of their party, and Flint took the stairs two at a time. Much to his disappointment, Garnet wasn't in the room. He put the boxes on the bed and headed next door. Honey answered his knock.

"Garnet said she was going for a walk, Flint. I'm sure she'll be back soon."

"Yeah, I saw her, but I lost sight of her," he said. "Reckon I'll go looking for her to hurry her along."

After leaving the dress shop, Garnet decided to return to the hotel. She had thoroughly enjoyed her tour of Abilene. The town abounded with a variety of stores and shops that offered a wide assortment of goods. To her amazement, she had even counted seventeen saloons.

Garnet walked past the stockyard, but seeing no sign of Flint or his brothers, she crossed the railroad tracks and headed for the Drovers' Cottage. As she passed one of the saloons, a man stepped outside, blocking the walk.

"Excuse me," she said, attempting to step past him.

"Well, if it ain't the redhead," he said.

Recognizing the voice, Garnet jerked up her head in surprise and looked into the leering face of Nathan Bodine. She tried to bolt, but he grabbed her arm. "Not so fast there, sister."

"Take your hand off my arm," she declared, "or I'll scream for help."

"Won't do you much good in this town. The folks are used to yelling and shouting." Grabbing her by her arm, he hauled her against him. She turned her head aside to avoid the foul odor of whiskey on his breath. His fingers felt like knives cutting into her flesh, and she tried to squirm out of his grasp. He squeezed harder. "Where's your boyfriend, bitch?"

"I don't have a boyfriend." The wild look in his eyes was frightening, and the pain in her arm was becoming unbearable. He had tried to kill her and Flint once before, and she knew he wouldn't hesitate to try again.

"Whatta you call MacKenzie?"

"Certainly not a boyfriend, Mr. Bodine. Besides, I haven't seen him since we arrived this morning. We parted company."

Bodine shoved her up against a chestnut horse hitched to the rail. "Get up on that horse," he ordered gruffly.

Rubbing her arm, she refused to budge. "I'm not going anywhere with you, Bodine." She shoved him away and started to run. He grabbed her arm, yanking her to an abrupt halt. Wrenching her arm behind her back, he twisted it until she gasped with pain. "Try that again, sister, and I'll cut your throat."

"Please stop. You're hurting my arm," she cried. She

bent forward, dizzy from the pain. He lessened his grip, but did not release her.

"Do what I tell you, or I'll break it," he said.

"All right."

He released her arm. It ached all the way up to the shoulder. She cradled the throbbing arm in her other hand. "What do you want of me?" she pleaded. "I can't help you."

"I'm usin' you as bait, bitch, to draw out your boyfriend."

"I told you, we've split up. I only stayed with him to get to Abilene."

"Well, you better hope he thinks enough of you to come after you. Get up on that horse."

She suddenly felt a surge of hope when she saw Joseph McCoy come out of his office. She opened her mouth and started to scream. "Help! Please help me!"

"Hey, what's going on there?" McCoy shouted.

"You little bitch!" Bodine snarled. Before she could scream again, he raised his fist and punched her in the jaw.

She saw stars. A shock of paralyzing pain shot to her head, and she stumbled back against the horse. She felt him pick her up and sling her over his saddle as a wave of blackness swelled up and engulfed her.

Having had no luck upstairs, Flint came down and stepped out on the veranda. Where the hell could Garnet be? There were a dozen stores she might have gone into. He didn't know where to begin to look. Only a woman would spend time shopping without a penny in her pocket, he grumbled to himself.

"Mr. MacKenzie!" Hearing his name, he turned his head to see Joseph McCoy bearing down on him. The man was winded from running. "Mr. MacKenzie, I just saw Mrs. Scott being abducted. The man rode off with her toward the red light district."

"Where the hell is that?" Flint asked. He had already unhitched Sam and was swinging into the saddle.

"It's about a half mile down the road," McCoy said breathlessly. "The man was riding a chestnut stallion."

"Go tell my brothers," Flint shouted. Goading Sam to a gallop, he rode off in the direction McCoy had indicated.

Within minutes, he reached the cluster of bordellos and run-down boarding houses, hotels, and saloons that was Abilene's red light district. At the sight of a big chestnut hitched to a post in front of one of the saloons, he reined up and dismounted. He ran his hand along the horse's neck. It was wet and the animal was breathing hard. He had found what he was looking for.

Entering the saloon, he saw a half-dozen men sitting around the room. A couple more were standing at the bar. He recognized one of the men at the bar as the Jayhawker who had tried to shake them down earlier.

Flint walked over to the end of the bar. The bartender immediately put a shot glass down in front of him. "Whiskey?"

Flint shook his head. "Where'd the man go who just came in here with a redheaded woman?"

"Don't know what you're talking about, mister," the bartender said.

"I ain't got time for games. I'll ask you nice like one more time, then I get nasty."

The bartender shifted his eyes to the stairway. "Mister, I ain't seen no redheaded woman come in here."

"You don't mind if I take a look for myself." He headed for the stairway.

There were a half-dozen doors on the second floor. Flint opened the first door; the room was empty. He moved to the next door and opened it.

"What the hell do you want?" a man growled,

rearing up his head from the bed he was sharing with a frizzy-haired blond.

Flint quickly closed the door and moved on to the next one. His search was unsuccessful and he climbed the stairway to the third floor. There were only four doors on the top floor. The hall was dark, but he saw a light shining from under one of them. He tried the handle and found the door was locked. Acting on pure instinct, he drew his Colt and kicked in the door.

In an instant's glance, he saw Garnet staked out on the bed with her hands and feet bound to the bedposts. A gag was tied around her mouth.

Flint dived through the doorway, getting off a shot at the same time that smoke belched from the muzzle of Bodine's gun. Flint felt the searing pain as the bullet grazed his forehead. He fired two more times, each bullet finding its mark. For several seconds the outlaw clutched his chest, then the pistol slipped out of his fingers and Bodine pitched forward.

Jumping to his feet, Flint walked over and made sure Bodine was dead. Then he hurried over to Garnet. He cut the ropes, freeing her ankles and wrists, then untied the gag on her mouth.

"Are you okay, baby?" he said gently, gathering her in his arms. He could feel her trembling as she clung to him.

"Oh, Flint. How did you know where to find me?"

He drew away and saw the bruise on her chin. "God, baby, did that bastard hurt you?"

"It doesn't matter. You've been shot! Your forehead's bleeding," she cried out in alarm.

"Just took off some skin. Let's get out of here." Grabbing her hand, they ran out of the room. He could hear men on the stairs heading up to them. "The back way." They raced down the hallway and scrambled down the rear stairs.

Once outside, Flint whistled and Sam came thundering around the side of the building. Flint lifted her onto the horse's back just as several men burst through the doorway. "Get out of here, Sam," Flint shouted. He slapped Sam on the flank and the horse took off at a gallop.

"Flint!" Garnet shouted, but Sam was already sprinting down the road.

He dove for cover behind a water trough. But he never saw the man who came up from behind and pistol-whipped him on the side of the head. Slumping to the ground, he tried to fight off the blackness that threatened to envelop him. He felt his arms being yanked behind him and his wrists being bound together. Then he was hauled to his feet and his head was dunked into the horse trough several times.

When he finally started coughing and choking, he was thrown to the ground. Opening his eyes, he found himself staring up at a man with blond hair and eyes the color of cold steel.

"It's a real pleasure to finally meet you face to face, Mr. MacKenzie." The man's southern accent was modulated and refined. "If my memory serves me right, sir, I believe you're the one called Flint."

"We met somewhere before?" Flint asked. He sat up and shook the water off his face and hair. The movement hurt like hell, but he wasn't going to give the bastard the satisfaction of knowing.

"In California, sir. Under the worst of circumstances, I'm afraid. You and your brothers were very inhospitable to me and my gang."

Shocked, Flint stared in disbelief into the man's silvery eyes. "Charlie Walden!" Instant rage consumed him. The man who had been the target of his unrelenting search for the past four years was within a few feet of him, and Flint was helpless. He began to struggle to free his hands.

"It's useless to try and free yourself, sir," Walden said with a pleasant smile. "I can assure you it's impossible." Flint knew the ruthlessness that lay behind the madman's smile. "I'm indebted to you, sir, for eliminating our mutual acquaintance. Mr. Bodine was beginning to bore me. You saved me the trouble of killing him myself. However, it would not set well with my men if I allowed the crime to go unpunished."

"Like the raid you made on our ranch during the war."

"Your bitterness has destroyed you, Mr. MacKenzie. And all because of the visit I made to your mother and sister-in-law."

"You sonofabitch!" Flint murmured between gritted teeth. He had never wanted to kill a man so badly in his life.

"Bodine killed Sarah, and my men your mother. I don't rape women, Mr. MacKenzie."

"You just lead the men who do. Did you kill the Boone brothers too?"

"Boone brothers? Oh, yes, you mean those twin boys." Walden looked genuinely surprised. "So those were your cattle, MacKenzie? I had no idea. I certainly wished I'd known that at the time. Bodine was such an idiot."

"Cut me loose, Walden. Just you and me. We'll settle what's between us once and for all. I'll let you choose the weapon," Flint challenged.

Walden threw back his head in laughter. "The weapon has already been decided upon, Mr. MacKenzie. We're going to hang you. As much as I regret cutting short this conversation, I'm afraid the young lady who rode away may return soon with help. We mustn't delay any longer. Take him away, boys."

A couple of the men yanked Flint to his feet. "There ain't no tree, boss," one of them said.

Walden shook his head and sighed. "Imbeciles. I'm surrounded by imbeciles." He shouted at the man, "Then hang him from the balcony! And get moving before help arrives."

They dragged Flint up the stairs and into one of the

second-floor rooms. He fought and kicked in an effort
to make the task as hard as possible, but Walden's men
succeeded in getting him out the window and placing
a rope around his neck. They tied the other end to the
porch railing.

Down below on the street, a group of Jayhawkers
cheered on the outlaws. Several prostitutes had also
come out to watch the hanging, their eyes gleaming
with exhilaration.

"Throw him over, boys," Walden ordered.

"If they do, I'll blow your head off."

Unnoticed in the excitement, Garnet had stepped
out through the window and now stood behind Walden, pressing a pistol against the back of his head. The
shouting ceased, and everyone stared in silence at her.

"So, you didn't ride for help after all," Walden said,
amused. "You know, if you kill me, you'll be shot
immediately."

"But that won't do you much good, will it? Don't
think I'm bluffing, Mr. Walden." The sound of the
trigger being cocked echoed in the absolute silence.

"Take the rope off him and untie his hands," Garnet
ordered calmly.

Walden's henchmen looked to their leader for instructions.

"Even if we release him, there's no way the two of
you can get out of here alive," Walden warned.

"Oh, I'm sure you'll think of a way, since you'll be
with us," Garnet said. "Tell your toadies to do as I said,
or I pull this trigger."

Charlie nodded, and one of the men removed the
rope from around Flint's neck. "Now his hands," she
ordered.

Once his wrists were free, Flint grabbed his pistol
out of the hand of the man who had claimed it.
"Thanks, Redhead," he said, moving over to Garnet
and Charlie. "Everybody just stay where you are. First
man who moves gets a bullet." He clamped his hand

on Charlie's shoulder. "Okay, Walden, we'll all back
up slowly. Garnet, you first," he ordered, pressing his
pistol to Walden's head.

Garnet had just climbed back into the room when
the sound of hoofbeats caused everyone to turn their
heads. Luke and Cleve came galloping down the road.

The outlaws drew their pistols and started firing.
Amid shouts and screams, the spectators in the street
ran for cover. Walden took advantage of these few
confused seconds. As gunfire erupted, he shoved Flint
backwards through the window into the room, then
dove for cover at the corner of the porch.

Chapter 30

"Stay down!" Flint shouted. Bullets and shattered glass flew around them as Garnet and Flint crawled across the floor. From the sound of the firing outside, he could tell that Luke and Cleve had opened up with rifles.

"Flint, look out!" Garnet yelled as one of the gunmen appeared at the window. Flint rolled onto his back and fired. The gunman fell.

"Get over in the corner and stay low," he told Garnet. "I'll be right back."

"Where are you going?"

"Sounds like some of that firing is coming from the room next door. I'm gonna take a look."

"Flint, you don't know how many men are in there."

"I'll find out soon enough," he said trying to be heard above the loud gun blasts. "We've got to get out of here. Trapped where we are, we don't know how the fight is going."

Flint cautiously opened the door and peered out the narrow crack. The hall was in darkness, but one of Walden's gang was breaking for the back stairway. Flint's shot brought him down. If he had counted right, there had been six men other than Walden. He had shot two, which left at least five. He wondered if any of the Jayhawkers had joined up with the gang. If so, Luke and Cleve had their hands full.

Flint shimmied along the wall until he reached the next room. Just as he was about to peek in the door, one of the gang came running out of the room into the hallway. After the first instant of surprise, Flint fired and the man fell. Spinning around, Flint dived through the doorway. He got off a shot at a man crouched at the window before the outlaw dived through it. Seeing the room was empty, Flint hurried back to Garnet. "Let's get out of here." He grabbed her hand and they sped down the rear stairs.

Gunfire continued from the front of the building, but all was quiet at the rear. Flint peeked out cautiously. The back of the building appeared to be deserted. "Where'd you leave Sam?" he asked.

She pointed to a building next door. "Over there, then I came in this door."

"Get over there and ride back to the hotel. This time, keep going till you reach it," Flint ordered.

"I'm not leaving now," Garnet declared.

"Dammit, Redhead, I've got to get to Luke and Cleve. I can't do it trying to keep you from getting shot. Please, just once will you do what I ask?" he said angrily.

For a long moment she looked into his eyes. "Why can't I stay and help, Flint?"

"God, baby, you've helped enough already—you kept me from being hung. I don't want you to get hurt, so will you do what I ask?"

"All right. Be careful, Flint."

As she started to leave, a rider broke from cover, firing a pistol at her. Flint dove and knocked Garnet to the ground, shielding her with his body. As he galloped away, Flint saw that it was Charlie Walden riding Sam. Flint raised his Colt for a sure shot and pulled the trigger. The gun clicked on an empty chamber.

"Goddammit!" Flint cursed. He rolled off Garnet. As

he reloaded the pistol, he whistled to Sam, but the horse was already out of hearing distance. Desperate, Flint looked around. There wasn't a horse in sight to enable him to follow Walden. He couldn't believe the bad luck. Frustrated, he muttered a mouthful of expletives. Not only had he had a sure shot at Walden, but he had lost Sam too. For a brief moment, he felt total despair. Glancing at Garnet, he saw the look in her eyes and knew she was sharing his pain.

"Guess you aren't going anywhere after all, Redhead."

She reached out and put her hand on his arm. "I'm sorry, Flint."

"Yeah, so am I." He helped her up. "I've got to go and help out my brothers."

Hearing the sound of hoofbeats, Luke turned to fire, then he recognized the rider. Wild Bill Hickok dismounted and, crouching low, came running over as bullets whizzed around him.

"Heard you fellas had a problem. Thought you could use some help," he shouted, getting off a shot.

"Much obliged, Jim," Luke said. "Cleve's across the street, and the last I saw of Flint, he was in the room on the left off that balcony. But there hasn't been any shots coming from up there in the last couple minutes, so I figure he's moved. The firing at us is coming from the barroom."

"Got any idea how many of them are left?" Hickok asked.

"No idea. Looks like those goddamned Jayhawkers joined the fight." Luke suddenly stopped talking. "Hold up, did you hear that?" Both men listened alertly. Three short whistles sounded from the trees to their right.

"That's Flint," Luke said, grinning. He returned the signal.

As Flint and Garnet came dashing across the street,

Hickok picked off one of the gunmen who unwittingly exposed himself while trying to shoot the sprinting couple.

"You two trying to get yourselves shot?" Luke grumbled when Flint and Garnet reached them.

"Charlie Walden got away—on Sam," Flint said.

"Charlie Walden! You mean he was the one who snatched Garnet?"

"No, Nathan Bodine did. He was in cahoots with Walden. I shot Bodine; that's why they were gonna hang me. If it weren't for Garnet here, Big Brother, you'd have arrived in time to see me swinging from that balcony."

"We got here as soon as McCoy told us what happened," Luke said. He grinned at Garnet. "Reckon we're beholdin' to you."

Suddenly, with guns blazing, several men broke from the saloon. They were quickly cut down by answering fire from the MacKenzies and Hickok. Then the night suddenly grew still.

"Reckon we've got them all?" Luke said after a lengthy pause.

"Yeah, all but the one we should have," Flint said bitterly.

They saw Cleve move cautiously toward the entrance of the saloon. Flint moved out to approach it from the other side. They stopped, one on either side of the entrance. They paused for a long moment, then Flint nodded to Cleve. Both men crashed in unison through the swinging doors.

Rolling to the floor, Flint raised up on a knee, Colt in hand as Cleve dived for the cover of a table. "Don't shoot, don't shoot!" the bartender shouted. He raised his hands above his head to show he was unarmed. "They're all gone."

Those who had wisely remained behind locked doors gradually started to appear, walking around looking at the slaughter. The saloon looked like a battlefield. There were three dead men in the barroom, two in the second-floor hallway, another one in a room, two on the balcony, and three on the street—besides Bodine's body on the third floor.

Garnet stood staring numbly around her, huddled in the center of the three brothers and Hickok.

"I hope this isn't more of 'em," Luke said as a dozen riders came galloping up to them.

"What in hell went on here?" one of the men asked. He appeared to be the leader of the horsemen.

Luke raised his rifle. "That's close enough, mister. Who are you?"

"Name's T.C. Henry," the man said. "I'm head of this vigilante committee."

Flint snorted. "Another committee! If it's anything like that Jayhawker committee, we might as well start shooting now."

"Maybe I can help clear up some of this, Mr. Henry," Hickok said, stepping forward. "Name's Hickok. I'm sheriff of Ellis County."

"This is Dickinson County, Sheriff. You've got no authority here. These men your deputies?"

"No," Wild Bill said.

Henry glanced at the dead men lying in the street. "Those fellas wanted in your county?"

"No. I just thought I'd step in and give these men a hand. This gang abducted one of their womenfolk—"

"Shootings! Abductions! Those are just a couple of reasons why we had to form this vigilante committee to begin with," T.C. Henry interrupted. "Since these cattle drives began, it's not been safe for our women and children to walk the streets. The good citizens of Abilene decided we've had all the lawlessness in Abilene that we intend to take."

"Sounds like your vigilante committee hasn't been too effective, Mr. Henry," Hickock said. "I suggest you get yourself a sheriff and establish some law and order in Abilene. You've been inviting this kind of trouble.

Form a council, not a vigilante committee, and set yourselves up some rules and hire yourself some lawmen to enforce them. That's the only way you'll ever make your streets safe."

"We've been planning on doing just that, Mr. Hickok. In the meantime, we're locking you fellows up. Time we start making examples of you gunslingers."

"Dammit, man, I've got to get out of here," Flint said bitterly. "Walden's gonna get away while you've got us locked in a cell."

"Who's Walden?" Henry asked.

"The gang leader. The bastard even rode off on my horse," Flint shouted.

"Walden hung two of our drovers, Mr. Henry," Cleve added calmly.

"Unless he did it in Abilene, mister, we don't care. You fellows drive up here from Texas and shoot up our streets. We don't give a damn if you kill one another, as long as it's not in Dickinson County."

"What about those goddamned Jayhawkers?" Luke asked. "We didn't start that fight."

"Mister, if any more of them start trouble, they'll be treated like any other lawbreaker," Henry said. "We've got a jail here in Abilene and we're gonna start putting it to the use it was meant for. You fellas mount up; you're going to jail."

"I ain't got no horse," Flint said angrily.

Henry cast a derogatory glance at the dead men spread out on the street. "Reckon you can find an extra mount around here. Otherwise, you can walk back."

A couple of the men came up leading horses, one of them Bodine's chestnut stallion. Grumbling, Flint hoisted Garnet up on it and climbed on behind her. He cursed all the way to jail.

Shortly after they arrived there, Honey came rushing up with Maud and Josh. "Thank God you're all okay," Honey declared. "Mr. McCoy came and told us where we could find you."

"We're fine, Jaybird," Luke said. "But we've got a problem here to work out."

"What problem?"

"They're gonna lock us up for awhile."

"Lock you up! Good Lord, what for?"

"It's a long story, but it looks like you might as well go back to the hotel." He glanced at T.C. Henry. "Before you lock us up, can we have a private word with our women?"

"Couple minutes," Henry said, disgruntled.

Garnet went over to Flint. He shook his head in frustration. "I almost had him, Redhead. He was right in my sights. At least I've seen him now, so I know what he looks like."

"You'll catch up with him again," Garnet said, trying to sound reassuring. "I imagine you'll be going after him as soon as they release you."

"You bet! There ain't nothing gonna stop me now. And this time I'll get him."

"How often have you thought that in the last four or five years, Flint?" she said despondently.

"Look, baby, until last year, we didn't even have a name. Now we've got a face to go with that name. Cleve and I will find him."

"I'm sure you will . . . one day," she said sadly.

Garnet knew that after the events of that night there would be no stopping Flint until he found Charlie Walden. He had just said so himself. She wouldn't try to stand in his way any longer. As long as he lived with this obsession, there could never be a place in his life for her—or their child.

This was their final good-bye. From the time she had met him, she had been haunted with the knowledge of this moment. Now that it had arrived, she could not say the words. Her heart swelled with an ache that she thought she couldn't bear. Her gaze lingered on his face as she felt the rise of tears. Lowering her eyes, she pretended to brush some dirt off his shirt. "Take care of yourself, Flint."

He tipped up her chin and cupped her face between his hands. She knew he could not miss seeing her tears. "Hey, Redhead, I'll be okay." He gently wiped away the tears on her cheeks with his thumbs. "How does your jaw feel?"

"It doesn't hurt."

"That's what you always say," he said gently. She felt herself flinching under the steady stare of his dark eyes. His expression grew perceptive. "What's wrong, Redhead?"

Please God, don't let him suspect. She gently caressed his cheek. "You need a shave."

"Yeah, meant to earlier."

The sight of his sheepish grin broke her restraint. She threw herself into his arms, clutching him around the waist. "Hold me, Flint. Please hold me."

His arms enfolded her, securing her in the haven of his embrace. Fighting hard against her dwindling fortitude, she drew a shuddering breath, determined to get through it somehow.

"We'll straighten this out soon, honey. You just stay out of trouble till we do." He bent his head down and grinned. "Promise?"

Her chest felt near to bursting. She couldn't answer. She nodded.

"Let's go, cowboy," one of the men said.

He gave her a quick kiss. "See you later, Redhead." Swallowing the sob that rose in her throat, she looked at him and smiled, then reached up and adjusted his hat back to its normal cocky angle.

"Good-bye, Flint," she whispered softly.

The man grasped Flint's arm and led him away. She waited until he disappeared into the other room, then she turned away and walked directly to the telegraph office.

The next morning, Honey left Josh in Maud's care and accompanied Garnet to the stagecoach office. "This is a mistake, Garnet. You shouldn't leave while Flint's locked up. At least wait so the two of you can talk it out. That's the only way to settle it."

"Honey, you know as well as I do that as soon as he's released, he'll be gone. This way it'll be easier for both of us."

"I don't believe that. It's not fair to Flint, any more than it is to you," Honey said. "You're acting too hastily, Garnet. Take time to think this out clearly."

"Oh, don't think I didn't start having second thoughts about leaving him. I lay awake all last night just thinking about it. I thought of forcing him to marry me because of the baby, but not make him give up his wandering ways. Then I'd at least have him some of the time. Poor, noble, self-sacrificing Garnet!" she scoffed.

"Then I realized something that I had never considered before. Up until now, Honey, all I've ever thought about were *my* needs. What about Flint's? That's when I realized that if I remained, I'd be doing him more harm than good."

"Why would you think that?" Honey said. "He'd have a wife and child, and still have the freedom to roam. Sounds to me like the best of both worlds."

"Honey, what was the first thing you had Luke promise when he married you?"

"Well, that he'd give up being a lawman."

"And why did you do that?"

"That's obvious," Honey said with an assured voice. "The job was too dangerous. This way there was less chance of him . . . getting killed." Her voice dropped off to a bare whisper as she grasped the point Garnet was making.

"And I don't want Flint killed either," Garnet said. "He depends on his reflexes to stay alive. He can't lose that edge. A few seconds' hesitation could mean life or death to him. As long as he's bent on this pursuit of Walden, he needs that edge. When he reaches for that Colt he wears, he can't stop to think about the wife or child back home who depend on him. The times he's hesitated because of me, he's been harmed. Now do you understand what I mean?"

Garnet's eyes misted. "I won't pretend I want to leave. And I know my leaving will hurt Flint for a while. But I'd rather hurt him than see him killed."

"But you won't forget him," Honey said. "I've come to know you, Garnet, and I don't believe you can marry someone else when you're in love with Flint."

"I do what I have to—that's why I'm a survivor, Honey. I'm going to Santa Fe to marry my cousin. I won't be the first woman who's married a man she doesn't love. At least my child won't want for anything."

"Your child is a MacKenzie. That's the name it should bear, and the family in which the child should be raised. Even if its father is off wandering somewhere," Honey added.

"I'm leaving now, lady," the stagecoach driver said. "If you're coming, climb in."

Garnet hugged and kissed Honey. "I'll miss you."

"I'll miss you, too. Isn't there anything I can say or do to make you change your mind?"

"Kiss Josh good-bye for me. I couldn't do it myself. I'm such a coward."

Honey smiled sadly. "No, you're not. You're one of the bravest people I've ever known." Her mouth curved into a loving smile. "Dumb and stubborn, but brave." Honey hugged her again. "Please write and let me know when the baby is—"

"I'll write. I promise." Before she could be tempted to change her mind, Garnet turned hastily and climbed into the coach. As the stage began to roll, she leaned out the window. "And tell Flint to be careful when he goes looking for Walden." She waved and Honey waved back.

After spending a whole night behind bars, all three of the MacKenzie brothers were ornery and argumentative. Amid their bickering, Josh's wailing, Maud's cussing, and Amigo's incessant barking, it took Hickok several hours the next day—plus a telegram from Stockton confirming Luke had once been a dedicated lawman—to convince T.C. Henry that the MacKenzies were law-abiding citizens and not the irresponsible gunslingers he accused them of being.

Following a hunch, Flint stopped to check out Bodine's stallion. The horse had the slit hoof he'd been tracking.

"Where's Garnet?" he asked upon joining the others at the hotel. Much to his surprise, he immediately encountered hostility from Honey.

"She's gone."

"What do you mean? Where'd she go?" He glanced around at the circle of faces. They all looked like they were attending a wake.

"To Santa Fe. She's going to marry her cousin."

"*She's going to what?*" He couldn't believe his ears.

"You heard me, Flint." Honey turned away in despair.

Flint had the peculiar sensation that his stomach had just dropped to his feet. "I don't believe it. She wouldn't leave without saying good-bye."

"She did that last night. You were just so consumed with thinking about getting even with Charlie Walden that you didn't notice."

Flint turned away. Recalling Garnet's actions the night before, he realized she had acted strangely—that something had remained unspoken. He had watched her walk out of his life without even recognizing it.

"What do you care, anyway?" Honey lashed out angrily. "Considering how you treated her."

He turned back to face her. "What the hell did I do?" Flint asked, throwing his hands up in frustration.

"More than likely, it's what you didn't do, Brother Flint," Cleve lamented.

"Yeah, like telling her you love her," Honey declared.

"Or promising you wouldn't ride off and leave her," Maud added.

Choking on an awareness of his own guilt, Flint glanced at Luke and saw the disapproval in his older brother's eyes. "You got anything you wanta add, Big Brother?" he snarled. Luke just lowered his gaze, which was the same as an accusation as far as Flint was concerned.

He struck out in his own defense. "I'm not the only one at fault here. She's the one who did all the name-calling. You should have heard her spewing venom like a sidewinder just 'cause I ain't like some guy she called Sir Galahad." He began pacing back and forth. "Don't know what more a man's supposed to do to please her—she's already got me shaving twice a week! Well, let her go off and marry her goddamned cousin if that's what she wants. Lord knows, once the woman sets her mind to something, there's no changing it."

"In case you're interested, she did give me a message for you," Honey interrupted.

He pivoted and looked at her hopefully. "Yeah, what is it?"

"When you go off looking for Charlie Walden, she said to be careful."

"She said that, did she?"

Honey nodded.

Flint spun on his heel and headed for the door.

"What are you going to do, Flint?" Luke asked.

"What do you think? I'm getting out of here!" He slammed the door behind him.

"Uncle Flint," Josh called out. He bolted from the bed and chased after him.

For a long moment, the other four people sat silent. Then Luke finally spoke up. "What the hell are we waiting for? We better start packing."

Josh followed Flint into his room. "Where are you going, Uncle Flint?" he asked when Flint began to jam his clothes into his saddlebags. "You going after that Charlie Walden guy?"

"Nope. Catching the stage to Santa Fe."

"How come you taking a stage 'stead of riding Sam?"

"Don't have much choice, Josh."

Josh plopped down on the bed. "Auntie Garney went to Santa Fe, too."

"I know, that's why I'm headed there," Flint said, tying the strings on one side of the bags.

"You going there to see her?"

"Nope. Going to get her and take her back to Texas."

Josh jumped down from the bed. "That's good, 'cause me and Amigo think it'd be better if Auntie Garney had the baby back home. Mama and Daddy do too. And so does Uncle Cleve."

Preoccupied with fretting over Garnet, Flint only half-listened to Josh. "Reckon they're right, Josh." He slung the saddlebags over his shoulder, and suddenly one word penetrated his troubled thoughts.

Turning, he stared at his nephew in shock.

"Baby!"

Chapter 31

G arnet picked Milton Brittles out of the crowd the
moment she saw him. A man of medium height,
he had jowls on the puffy side, although they might
have looked thinner were it not for his muttonchop
whiskers.

He appeared to be very distinguished in a gray
stovepipe hat, but looked to be every day of his fifty-
seven years. But what difference did age make, and
what did it matter if he was thick around the middle?
The black vest and long, fitted frock coat he wore did
much to disguise it, she decided. And even if he didn't
have slim hips and long, muscular legs sheathed in
buckskins, his neatly pressed pin-striped trousers, and
shiny black shoes covered with gray leather gaiters,
looked to be quite fashionable.

Garnet readjusted the flowered bonnet perched on
top of her upswept hair, fluffed up the pleated jabot at
the neckline of her blouse, gave an extra tug to the
fitted, green plaid jacket she wore, and stepped out of
the stagecoach.

Milton Brittles walked up to her. "Mrs. Scott?"

"Mr. Brittles?"

For a quick moment, they looked at each other
awkwardly, then he bowed slightly and proffered a

small nosegay. "A pleasure to meet you. My carriage is waiting."

An image of Flint MacKenzie, swinging up on his saddle with a "Let's get moving" flashed into her thoughts. She quickly shrugged it aside and put her hand on the arm Milton offered to assist her into the carriage.

"We were all greatly distressed to hear about your unfortunate experience crossing the plains," he said.

"Yes, very unfortunate," Garnet replied politely. She continued to half listen as she looked out the carriage window.

The section of Santa Fe they were riding through had tree-lined, paved streets, and the houses were stately with well-kept lawns fenced with wrought-iron grills and gates—considerably different from the small, pink adobe houses she had seen scattered around the stagecoach station upon her arrival.

Turning to admire the spires of an old Catholic church, she said, "Santa Fe is a lovely city, Mr Brittles." *A far cry from the dusty streets of Waynesburg, Comanche Wells, or even Calico,* she thought with a tug to her heart. And she hadn't glimpsed one saloon or pistol-toting, dust-encrusted cowboy since she had stepped off the stagecoach. They had to be somewhere around, but certainly not in this section of the city.

Milton stopped the carriage before a modest, two-story white house with a shaded veranda and alighted with a flourish. From the rear of the covered coach, he removed a rope with a metal weight on one end. As she waited, he attached the loose end of the rope to the bridle of one of the carriage horses, and the weighted end dropped to the street.

Once again Garnet's treacherous mind played tricks on her, conjuring up the sight of Flint dismounting and just dropping Sam's reins to the ground, or casually looping them around a hitching post. The image of him loosening the cinches of their horses when he stopped to rest them came into her mind. She closed her eyes to wipe out the vision. When she opened them again, she discovered that Milton Brittles was waiting with an extended hand to assist her out of the carriage. She put her hand in his, and instead of a warm, familiar grip, she felt clammy, chubby fingers. She looked into an impersonal, blue-eyed stare instead of warm sapphire eyes.

This man was a stranger to her. How could she ever consider marrying him?

A man and two women came out of the house and waited with expectant smiles.

"So you're Garnet," the man said, stepping forward to hug her. "I'm your Uncle George." He was a thin-faced man with a shock of thick gray hair. Stepping back, he took a longer look at her. "You're the image of your mother, Garnet. Isn't she, Jane?" he asked the woman beside him.

He was shoved aside by the short, plump woman with round blue eyes. Her tight, blond curls were capped by a crocheted square trimmed in lace and tied under one of several chins.

"My dear! My dear! Oh, what a trying experience you've had. We're so glad you've finally made it to the comfort of our bosom."

Bosom, indeed! Garnet thought as the woman hugged her to her generous breasts. "And this is your cousin, Genevieve."

"Cousin Genevieve," Garnet greeted the thin, somewhat bony, forty-year-old spinster who stepped up and hugged her. Genevieve's lusterless brown hair was parted in the middle and pulled back into an unbecoming bun on her nape. A pair of pale blue eyes met Garnet's gaze briefly before her cousin dropped her gaze in shyness. The woman was physically unattractive with one exception—she had a sweet and appealing smile.

Aunt Jane took Garnet's arm and led her into a comfortably furnished drawing room. The man seated in one of the chairs rose to his feet as soon as Garnet entered. He stood no taller than she did. His bald pate was ringed with a fringe of white hair, and his dark eyes glowed with warmth as his cherubic face split into a wide grin.

"Garnet, this is the Reverend Rheems. He will perform the wedding on Friday."

"Friday?" Garnet gasped in shock. "But that's the day after tomorrow!"

"So it is, my dear," the clergyman said. "And it's a pleasure to meet you, too."

Garnet blushed in embarrassment. "Oh, forgive me, sir. That was very rude of me."

"It certainly was, Mrs. Scott," Milton Brittles said.

She looked at him in surprise. She had felt mortified enough; his insensitive remark was unnecessary. "I haven't been myself lately," she offered in apology.

"You certainly have good cause, my dear," the reverend said kindly. "You've suffered a harrowing and tragic experience."

"Shall we sit down and have dinner?" Aunt Jane suggested, which eased the rising tension.

"An excellent suggestion," George Kincaid said. He took his wife's arm and led her to the dining room. Garnet felt Milton's touch on her arm, as the Reverend Rheems escorted Cousin Genevieve.

Throughout the meal, served by a young Mexican girl, the reverend steered the discussion away from the wedding arrangements, asking questions concerning Garnet's trip. She made no mention of Flint or the trail drive to Abilene.

She noticed that Cousin Genevieve only spoke when asked a direct question. However, several times during the meal, she observed Genevieve's adoring gaze centered on Milton Brittles.

Good Lord! The poor girl's in love with him, Garnet thought. Her uncle and aunt, as well as Milton himself, appeared impervious to Genevieve's feelings.

When Milton Brittles asked her to explain the reason for the long delay in reaching Santa Fe, Garnet hurriedly changed the subject. "Uncle George, I'm confused about the family. Is Mr. Brittles your cousin, too?"

"Only by marriage. The same as he is yours," George Kincaid said. "You see, Garnet, when your Grandfather Kincaid remarried, he already had a forty-year-old son with a twenty-three-year-old daughter, Matilda. Matilda Kincaid later married Jonathan Brittles, a widower with a son."

"And Jonathan Brittles was my father," Milton spoke up. "I was eleven years old when he married Matilda Kincaid."

"So you and my mother were the offspring of Grandfather Kincaid's second marriage," Garnet said to her uncle.

"That's right," George said. "I was born the next year, and your mother the following year."

"Is any more of the family alive today?" Garnet asked.

"Only those of us gathered at this table. Matilda Kincaid proved to be barren and never produced an offspring. And I never had a son to carry on the name. The name of Kincaid will be extinguished when I go to my grave."

"Now, now, George!" Reverend Rheems declared. "You'll depress the young lady. With her wedding so near, let's not dwell on the morbid subject of dying."

Considering that wedding Milton Brittles was good cause for depression, Garnet found the subject of dying to be very apropos.

Shortly after dinner, she excused herself under the pretense of being exhausted from the trip, and retired to her room.

Her thoughts were in turmoil. Her aunt had made the wedding arrangements as soon as she had received the wire Garnet had sent from Abilene. Two days was hardly enough time to plan how to get out of it! From below, she could hear her aunt and Milton Brittles discussing the expense of the caterer. Since she had no dowry, Milton was paying for the wedding. He sounded distraught when he heard that the wedding cake was quite costly, even though the food would consist only of tea sandwiches and punch. Her future groom made no effort to conceal his opinion that this expense was a shameful waste of money.

In other circumstances, Garnet would resent not having been consulted on the preparations of her own wedding—particularly since she had been married twice before. But since she had no intention of marrying Milton Brittles, she thought it best not to get involved in the discussion. Tomorrow she would inform them of her decision to break the engagement, and would end any further dispute on the subject.

The next day Aunt Jane had her try on the gown she had purchased for Garnet at a secondhand store. Garnet thought it to be the ideal opportunity to tell her aunt the wedding was off.

"Just think, Garnet dear, this gown can be the something old, something new, something borrowed, and something blue that every bride must wear at her wedding," Aunt Jane gushed excitedly.

"Aunt Jane, there isn't going—"

"Oh, dear! Your uncle's calling me." Before Garnet could finish, Aunt Jane hurried away to inform him where to put the furniture and rolled-up carpet from the drawing room.

Garnet surveyed herself in the mirror. It was a good thing her stomach was not yet showing any signs of the baby, because the dress was already so tight across the bust she could hardly breathe. "Let's get this tight dress and corset off before I suffocate you, sweet-heart," she cooed to her unborn child.

She shook her head as she looked at the gown. She couldn't remember ever seeing anything uglier. The blue lace gown had a high neck, with a row of tiny buttons at the back that ran from the neckline to her waist. Long, fitted lace sleeves stretched to her wrists. The skirt consisted of tiers of ruffles from waist to hem, which were decorated with tiny white satin bows. She felt she would expire in the heat before she could even get out of the hideous dress.

After trying for several minutes to release the buttons on the back, Garnet was on the verge of ripping them off when Cousin Genevieve entered and offered to help.

As the maid of honor, Genevieve was wearing a short-sleeved, yellow chintz gown. Garnet was willing not only to switch gowns with her, but places as well. In her estimation, Cousin Genevieve would make Milton Brittles a perfect wife, since the shy spinster was clearly in love with the tightfisted, pompous pharmacist.

By the time she cast aside the dress and corset, Garnet felt nauseated. She couldn't decide which made her more ill: the appearance of the gown or its tight fit. Regardless, she had another reason for excusing herself and going to bed. She'd just have to resolve the problem in the morning. She was too ill to cope with it now.

One thing she knew for certain. Even if Flint MacKenzie was cold in his grave, and God forbid she'd ever live to see that day, she would never consider Milton Brittles the proper father to raise her son—for her instinct told her that the child she carried would be a son. There could only be one rightful father for him. The fact that she had considered only Flint's needs, and not those of their child, had been reprehensible on her part.

Who was going to teach him how to rope a steer or break a bronco, read Indian signs, or tell time by the stars? And it was for certain that Milton Brittles could never show him a grin that carried to his eyes.

To hell with the wandering needs of Flint MacKenzie! To hell if he grew to hate her for denying him absolute freedom. And to hell with the quest for Charlie Walden! Obligations to the living far exceeded those to the dead.

Their child's needs had to be considered ahead of both their own.

And damn you, Flint MacKenzie, you fathered him—so the time has come for you to start acting like a father!

With that resolve, she felt as if a weight had just been lifted off her shoulders. For the first time in months, Garnet felt like her old self.

The next afternoon, as she stood beside Milton Brittles with the Reverend Rheems beginning the marriage ceremony, Garnet chastised herself for not following through on her previous night's convictions. What was she doing standing there in this hideous wedding gown? In the presence of these strangers? In the sight of God? Confident the Lord would intercede in her behalf, as He always had done in the past, she had permitted herself to go on with the charade. But good Lord! If she didn't do something quick to stop the ceremony, the minister might actually pronounce them man and wife!

God, forgive me, but You're responsible for some of this mess, too. After all, You control my destiny. Isn't it time to step in and do something?

The resonant voice of Reverend Rheems reverberated through the room. "If there be any man here present who knows why this man and woman should not be joined in the bonds of holy matrimony, let him speak now or forever hold his peace."

Not daring to lose any more time waiting on the Almighty's intervention, Garnet had no choice but to take matters into her own hands.

With a sickly smile, she haltingly raised a hand. "I do."

She heard Milton's startled gasp beside her, and the shocked exclamations of the people present. Garnet didn't know how to proceed. Should she turn to the guests and blurt out the truth, or seek the private sanctum of her uncle's study to bare her confession?

She finally got a little help from the Lord as the Reverend Rheems took command. He quickly hustled her and Cousin Milton into the study, motioning for Uncle George and Aunt Jane to accompany them.

Reverend Rheems led her to a couch in a far corner of the room and seated himself beside her. Across the room at the window, she saw her uncle and aunt consoling Milton, who was mopping his brow.

"You certainly waited long enough. For a moment I thought I would have to stop the ceremony myself," the preacher said softly, trying unsuccessfully to look stern.

"How did you know?" she whispered back.

The clergyman's eyes twinkled with amusement. "My dear, I have a direct source."

"To God?" she asked, astonished. "But I made the decision to stop the ceremony."

Further amused, he replied, "The decision was made a long time ago."

She gasped with shock. "You mean Destiny!" She was ecstatic that this holy man was confirming her belief in predestination. "Who are you?"

"A man who can easily recognize a reluctant bride."

"What gave me away?"

"I observed you were a woman in love."

"But I'm not in love with Milton Brittles," she said, confused by his remark.

"My observations exactly. Which led me to believe there was someone other than him."

"It's true, Reverend Rheems. I *am* in love with another man. I don't want to marry Milton Brittles."

"I never believed for a moment that you did," he said with a tolerant smile.

"What should I do to get out of this?"

"A little late to be asking my advice, my dear." He peered at her over the top of his glasses. "At the moment, you appear to be doing well with your own counsel. Of course, I find that more often than not being truthful helps to achieve a more expedient solution."

"Yes, I'm afraid you're right, sir." She sighed, resigned to the task ahead. "As Flint would say, I might as well bite the bullet and get it over with."

"Is Flint the baby's father?" he asked.

"You know that I'm having a baby!"

"Let's say I suspected so. The time has come for the moment of truth, my dear." He motioned to the others, and the three people in the room hurried over to them.

"Oh, you poor dear. I hope you're feeling better now." The expression on her aunt's face conveyed to Garnet that Aunt Jane had already convinced herself it was a simple case of bridal jitters. "Do you think you're well enough to proceed with the ceremony, Garnet dear? It's a pity to keep our guests waiting. And I'm afraid the ice is melting in the punch."

"I will feel much better, Aunt Jane, as soon as I get out of this dress." She drew the deepest breath the dress permitted her. "I must apologize, but I have something I should have told all of you when I arrived."

She turned her head to Milton Brittles. "You're a fine man, Cousin Milton, and I appreciate the honor of your asking me to become your wife. But I can't marry you. It wouldn't be fair to you or my baby."

"Baby? What baby?" Milton asked. "No one told me you have a baby." He directed the last remark at Uncle George.

"I don't have it at the moment, but I anticipate I will have it in about six months."

The shocking announcement left Brittles speechless. His eyes appeared to bulge out of his head as he gaped at her. Aunt Jane began to fan herself with her handkerchief.

"Well, we appear to be in a very awkward situation, Mrs. Scott," Milton blustered. "I have a position to maintain in this community, and I—"

"I don't think we have a problem at all, Mr. Brittles. If you wish, I'll make the announcement that the wedding is off."

"My dear, since you're not getting married, what are your plans?" Reverend Rheems asked kindly.

"Well, sir," Garnet said, placing a protective hand on her stomach, "this little maverick is a Texan. I think he should be raised as one. I'll go back there."

"Will the baby's father wed you?"

"He's not the marrying kind, Reverend. To him there is always another mountain to climb or river to cross."

"But an unwed mother with a baby. . . ." He shook his head. "How do you expect to support yourself and your child?"

"I can always go into partnership in the restaurant business, Reverend. And my baby will have kin in the area, too. Probably, now and again, he might even get a glimpse of his daddy. I'll make out fine. The Lord's always kind of looked out for me, sir. I think He's invested too much time in me to give up now."

Reverend Rheems smiled and nodded. "I believe you're right. You're a remarkable woman, Mrs. Scott."

"That's all well and good," Milton Brittles declared in a huff, "but what about me? I've been put in a very embarrassing position."

With a detached look, Garnet eyed the agitated

druggist. "Mr. Brittles, have you ever considered making Cousin Genevieve your wife? That sure makes more sense than marrying a woman you've just met—particularly one who's carrying another man's child."

He blanched and began to mop his brow. "Miss Genevieve, you say?" he stammered, still flustered.

"Yes. She's out in the other room right now, all prettied up for a wedding. And she's long admired you, sir. I'm sure she'd not refuse. Why not go out and ask her? All those folks came here expecting to see a wedding. I don't think you should disappoint them. Besides," Garnet remarked, her mouth curved into an impish grin, "it'd be a shameful waste of a wedding cake."

Fifteen minutes later, Reverend Rheems pronounced a relieved Milton Brittles and an ecstatic Genevieve Kincaid to be man and wife.

After kissing the bride, Garnet had just placed a kiss on the cheek of the groom when she became aware of a sudden hush in the room. Turning, she saw what had caused the silence. Flint MacKenzie stood in the doorway, looking as trail worn, dust-covered, and run-down at the heels as ever.

With the faintest of smiles, Garnet cast her eyes heavenward. *Thank you Lord, and forgive me for ever doubting You.*

Flint strode into the room, followed by Luke and Cleve. She thought she would burst into tears when they were followed by Honey and Josh. Amigo padded in behind Josh, and Maud was the last to come through the door.

Her family had arrived.

Flint walked straight up to her. "You marry him yet?"

"No." She tried to keep from throwing her arms around him.

"And you ain't gonna, either," he declared.

"Who says so?" she challenged.

"I do. You're my woman, Redhead. If you marry anyone, it's gonna be me."

"*Your woman?*" His cockiness was becoming irritating. "You dare come here, interrupt this wedding, and declare that I'm *your woman!* I think not."

"You don't figure I'm gonna let you marry Cousin Milton, do you?"

"There seems to be a misunderstanding, sir," Milton Brittles said.

Flint turned to him, his eyes sending a threatening message as he pointed a finger at him. "Mister, if you enjoy living, I don't wanta hear another word from you."

Milton drew back, trembling.

"You must be Flint," Reverend Rheems said pleasantly.

"That's right. Flint MacKenzie. You the preacher?"

"Reverend Rheems, young man."

"Well, Preacher, open that book of yours, 'cause you've got a wedding to perform. Me and Mrs. Scott are gonna get hitched."

"Well, young man, this is a rather unusual situation."

"Don't pay him any attention, Reverend Rheems," Garnet declared. "He's not going to bully me into marrying him."

So far the crowd had remained silent. Now, many of them began to mumble among themselves. When several of the men appeared to make aggressive moves in Flint's direction, he drew his Colt. "All of you stay where you're at."

"Oh my!" one of the women cried out. She slumped back in her chair, and the man next to her began to rapidly fan her.

When the grumbling intensified and the men began to look threatening, Luke drew his pistol as well. "Please. Everyone just remain calm and sit back and relax. We'll all clear out of here as soon as Flint and Garnet are married."

"But my niece doesn't wish to marry this man," George Kincaid said. "I refuse to stand by and watch her forced into a marriage at gunpoint." The outraged rumble increased among the men.

"Dammit, Flint! Will you and Luke holster those Colts, before one of them goes off," Cleve declared.

"I think everyone should calm down," Reverend Rheems advised.

"We will, Preacher, once you marry us," Flint said. He pointed with the pistol. "Get going with those words."

Garnet started to object, when suddenly she couldn't breathe. The room began spinning, and she started to sway. The last thing she remembered, as she slumped to the floor, was the startled look on Flint's face.

Flint shoved the Colt back into the holster and pulled out his bowie.

"Oh, my God! He's got a knife. He's going to kill her," one of the women cried. Clutching her chest, she fell back. Her husband sat down beside her and began to pat her hand.

Flint ignored the outburst and quickly cut off the sleeves of Garnet's gown. Then he flipped her over and ran the knife along the row of buttons. He pulled the gown off her shoulders and did the same to the corset strings.

"Oh, Good Lord! He's ripping the clothes off her!" one woman cried out, and covered her eyes with her fan.

Honey had already run over to Garnet and Flint. "Let's get this dress off her so she can breathe," Flint commanded.

"Will someone get a glass of water?" the minister called out.

"Let's give her some air," Cleve ordered.

"I'm not leaving her in the clutches of that madman," Uncle George declared.

"George, please don't argue with the man," Aunt Jane said nervously, tugging at her husband's arm.

"Come, Genevieve," Milton Brittles said.

"So much for chivalry," Cleve commented, as Brittles hurried away with Genevieve. However, the rest of the guests appeared to be too fascinated by the proceedings to budge.

By the time Garnet opened her eyes, Flint had stripped her down to her camisole and petticoat. She lay on the floor, her head in his lap. "How are you feeling, Redhead?" he said softly. He tenderly brushed tendrils of hair off her cheeks.

"What . . . what happened?"

"You fainted, my dear," Reverend Rheems said.

"You ready to read them words, Preacher?" Flint asked.

Having quickly grasped the situation, the minister glanced at Garnet. She nodded. The Very Reverend Josiah Rheems saw no reason for any further delay. "Flint MacKenzie, do you take this woman as your wedded wife?"

"I do," Flint said solemnly.

"Do you promise to love, honor, and cherish her?"

"I do that now, or I wouldn't be here."

"We're talking about the future, son."

"Put something in about shaving, Reverend Rheems," Garnet inserted.

When the startled minister looked at Flint, Flint said, "Okay. I promise to keep on loving her, honoring her, cherishing her, and I'll shave . . . at least once a week."

"Do you, Garnet Scott, take this man as your wedded husband?"

Garnet looked up into Flint's warm eyes and felt the strength in his arms holding her. She turned her head and smiled up at the minister. "I surely do."

"And do you promise to love, honor, and cherish—"

"Put something in there about never running off on me again," Flint said. "She bolts faster than a jackrabbit, Preacher."

"I think the two of you should take that vow," the minister replied, grinning.

"I do. I do," Garnet said, bursting with joy.

"Inasmuch as Flint MacKenzie and Garnet Scott have promised to love, honor, cherish, shave at least once a week, and never run off again. . . ." He paused and looked down at the pair. "Did I forget anything?"

"You got it perfect, Preacher," Flint said, with a grin that carried to his eyes.

His cherubic face glowing, the minister continued, "Then by the power invested in me by the Territory of New Mexico, I declare you to be man and wife. You may kiss the bride."

Still lying in his arms, Garnet slipped her arms around his neck as her husband lowered his head and claimed her lips.

As the assembled guests rose to leave, Reverend Rheems looked out at them. "Before I close my book, is there anyone else who wishes to be wed? If not, all those who were just married must sign a certificate of marriage."

With Cleve and Luke emitting rebel yells, the MacKenzies hurried over to the newlyweds. "I do declare!" Maud sighed, sinking down in a chair. "It's about time!"

Reverend Rheems winked at the small group gathered around them. "Shall we leave the newlyweds to themselves? I believe there's punch in the other room. Although it's been called to my attention that the ice has probably melted."

"You think the others will mind us joining them, Reverend?" Luke asked.

"Mr. MacKenzie, the way you and your brothers handle those Colts, I don't think you'll hear too many objections."

Neither Garnet nor Flint had shifted from the floor. When they were alone, Garnet smiled up at him. "I thought you were going to follow the trail of Charlie Walden."

"I had two trails to follow. I chose the one that's more important to me."

"Are you certain this is what you really want to do, Flint?"

"Yeah, Redhead, this is what I really want. What do you think of the idea of buying the Flying F from Ben Franks?"

"But you said you hate ranching, Flint."

"It's a good life. And it's a good way to raise a child." He looked at her sheepishly. "Thought maybe we'd ask Maud to come live with us. We could even find a spot for Ben Franks. He sure would be happier with us than in a city."

"For a man who liked his solitude, you've certainly had a change of heart."

"Yeah, and you're the one who changed it." He kissed her long and deeply. "I love you, Redhead." He caressed her stomach. "I hope the baby's a girl, and takes after her mother."

"So you know about the baby."

"Yep."

"Is that why you've changed your mind about ranching, Flint?"

"Nope."

"Well, what did make you change your mind?"

"Could be I fell in love with a sassy redhead."

"You don't have to do this for me, Flint. I know how you love the freedom to roam. You still can. I'll be there when you get back."

"Get back from where? I'm not going anywhere." He cupped her cheek in his hand. "Why would I ever want to be anywhere you're not? Can't think of a better place to spend a lifetime than with you."

"Oh, God, Flint, I love you." Once again he claimed her lips. When they parted, she ran a finger over his cheek. "You need a shave."

"I need a shave, a bath—and you." He covered her lips again. The kiss deepened, until they pulled apart at the sound of a knock.

Honey poked her head in the door. "May I come in?"

"Yeah," Flint said. He stood up and pulled Garnet to her feet.

"I brought you something to wear. Your aunt got them from your room. Haven't heard of too many women getting married in a camisole and petticoat."

Garnet quickly put on the bodice and skirt Honey handed her as Flint picked up the remnants of the wedding gown. "Tell me, Redhead, would you have married Cousin Milton?"

"Of course not. Why would I? My son's a MacKenzie," she said proudly.

She glanced around at the rest of the family who had come back into the room. "By the way, that was a secret. Who told you I was having a baby?" she asked.

Garnet frowned suspiciously at Honey.

Her green eyes flashing angrily, Honey turned to her husband.

Grimacing, Luke looked accusingly at Cleve.

Shrugging with wide-eyed innocence, Cleve glanced at his nephew.

After a shameful sidelong peek at Amigo, Joshua hung his head.

And with a muffled whimper, Amigo stretched out with his head on his front paws, and closed his eyes.

Later that night, freshly shaved, bathed, and barefoot, Flint left the bathroom and hurried down the hall of the hotel to the room where Garnet waited. After locking the door, he turned to his wife and pulled her into his arms. His mouth met hers, devouring its softness in a kiss that left them both aroused and aching for more.

When they drew apart, she looped her arms around his neck, her emerald gaze sparkling as it locked with the warm sapphire of his. "I warned you this would happen, Flint. I knew you wouldn't be able to resist falling hopelessly in love with me."

"That you did, Redhead. And I intend to show you just how right you were. But at the moment. . . ." Between each word, he teased the tip of her nose, her eyes, and her lips with a series of light, feathery kisses, "I'm feeling a serious need for some distraction."

Smiling seductively, she stepped away and began to remove her gown. "How much of a distraction do you need?"

He grinned. "Oh, I need a powerful big one, lady."

When she stood naked before him, the desire in his hungry eyes heated her blood to a sensual warmth that carried to every nerve in her body. She trembled with an exquisite shiver of excitement when he began to shed his own clothes.

Boldly, she stared at the magnificence of his naked male physique: broad, sinewy shoulders that sloped into his muscular arms and chest; a flat, lean stomach that curved into narrow hips; his strong thighs and long, sturdy legs covered with silky black hair.

She shook her head in amazement. "How could I ever believe for a moment that I could give you up?"

Flint's amused gaze remained fixed on her face. "Can't figure that out myself. Ah, tell me, Redhead," he asked, as he toyed with the locket that hung between her breasts, "when your ma told you how to distract a man, did she ever mention how distracting a naked man might be to a modest lady like yourself?"

"Are you making fun of me?"

"Just asking," he said innocently.

"Well, to be truthful, Mama didn't. And I must confess, maybe she should have. . . ." Irresistibly drawn, she returned her gaze to his hardened shaft, thrusting boldly out of its nest of dark hair. "Especially considering how *big* a distraction it is," she declared with awe. Devilment gleamed in her eyes as she arched a delicate brow. "And it appears to be getting bigger by the second."

Groaning, he shook his head. "Oh Lord, Redhead, you're shameless! It's no wonder I love you."

Grinning, he pulled her into his arms.

Author's Note

Dear Reader:

I hope you enjoyed Flint and Garnet's story enough to look forward to reading Cleve and Raven's when *The MacKenzies: Cleve* is released in June 1997. I've really enjoyed writing this series and I'm going to miss all of those MacKenzies.

Regarding the scene in the novel in which Garnet becomes intoxicated while she is pregnant, in no way do I wish to give the impression that I condone or encourage the consumption of alcohol during pregnancy. Poor Garnet doesn't have the knowledge that you women of the '90s have today.

Always follow your doctor's advice about what's best for your health and the health of your unborn child. The only additional medical advice this author is qualified to offer is that a commitment to love can be pretty good for your health, too!

My warmest regards and heartfelt wishes for love, happiness, and good health to all of you and those you love.

Sincerely,

Ana Leigh